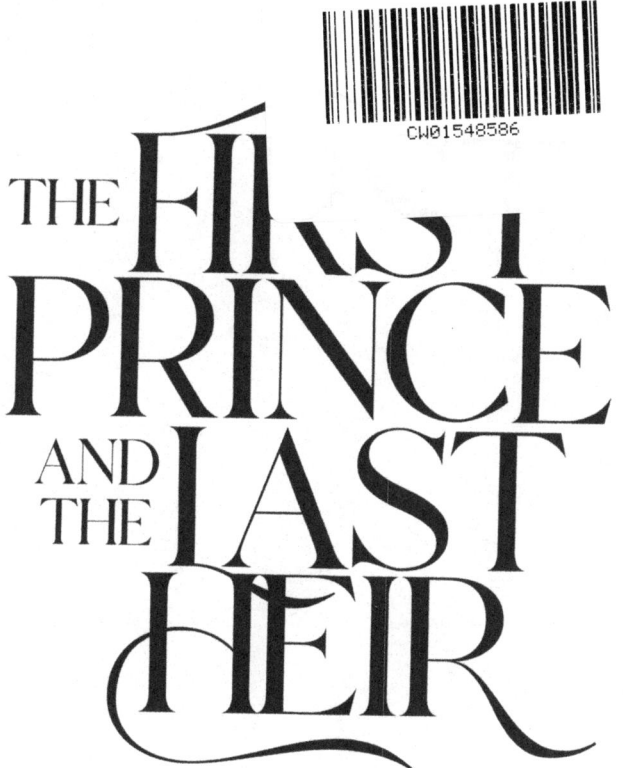

THE FIRST PRINCE AND THE LAST HEIR

HOPE ABROM
AMANDA ABROM

Copyright © 2024 by Hope Abrom and Amanda Abrom
Cover design by Seventhstar art.
All rights reserved.
No part of this book may be reproduced in any form or by any electronic or mechanical means, including information storage and retrieval systems, without written permission from the author, except for the use of brief quotations in a book review.

To the friends who join us as we take on life's trials
To those who love us despite our flaws
And to the siblings who we need more than we realize

Spirit Guardian
Guardians that command with air and flight

Mind Guardian
Guardians that project dreams or nightmares

King Claude Mirage

Soul Guardian
Guardians that manipulate plants and rock

Princess Kiran Dhara

Life Guardian
Guardians that mend injuries and bend water

Void Guardian
Unknown guardian branch, terminated years ago

In lands of myth where magic reigns,
Four realms entwined, the last contained

The first, where guardians rule the air,
Banishing darkness and despair

The second, beneath the starry veil,
In silver light, phantoms prevail

The third, where ancient treasures flow,
Trails of leaves and soil grow

The fourth, the songs of waves and tide,
Harmony in currents where secrets hide

Four locks unseen, to trap a foe,
A final crown will be bestowed

Claude
PROLOGUE

Celestaire had come to invade. The alarm blared through the Ilusaurian castle, alerting everyone to the incoming danger. Another guardian was dead—and Celestaire blamed King Claude. He hadn't killed anyone, but no one believed the Mad King.

By the time Claude reached the battlefield, it was already tainted with dead bodies. His own guards, dressed in black and silver, were like shadows against the Celesta soldiers.

The rain was slick against Claude's armor. Pierre and Sacha, his two personal guards, flanked him on either side. Pierre was small, wielding his bow and arrows, while Sacha was nearly a giant, crushing everything in his wake.

It was mass chaos on the field, with no order or structure to the Ilusaurian lines. They didn't even appear to have a front line. The archers and ballistas were holding back a majority of the Celesta forces, but it wasn't enough.

There was no time to regroup the Ilusaurian troops. Claude strode into the battle, unsheathing his sword, and kept one hand free to channel his power.

Magic erupted from deep inside his chest. On the eastern side of the battle, he caused a crack in the ground, projecting the rift he had seen take over many of his towns. Celesta soldiers skidded to a halt, their attack temporarily blocked. However, it wouldn't be long before they discerned the crack in the earth was no more than a mirage.

"So what part was real?"

"It doesn't matter anymore."

He remembered the tears in Magdalena's eyes, as if she hadn't been the one to stab him in the back. Moments earlier, she had thrown a vial of smierc at him and accused him of murdering King Bogdan and Aleksy.

No. It wasn't Princess Magdalena.

That woman...Dagmara...the traitor and imposter. The false princess who entrapped him in a fraud marriage.

The woman who undoubtedly stole his heart.

From the moment he gazed into her emerald eyes, as bright as the molten sun, she had ensnared him in her trap. It had all been a lie, despite how certain Claude had been that she was falling for him too. She had been compassionate, she had treated him as an equal, she—

Pain threatened to drown Claude. It coursed through his veins, denial and anger warring inside, as he threw himself into the throngs of battle. He projected thousands of silver snakes, slimy and glistening with rain as they slithered through the mud. It was a tactic he used often to expel the Celesta soldiers from their horses. He summoned silver fire—false arrows—anything he could use to distract the soldiers long enough for his own guards to slay them.

The screaming was like a song, propelled by the rhythm of the pounding rain. Explosions rang through the air, debris pelting those fighting on both sides. The scene before Claude was like a painting. Red and black hues attacked one another, surrounded by silver wisps of magic, all muted from the rain like a watercolor landscape. He was half blind, unable to see out his eye that was scarred by the assassin who had killed his parents, and the rain made his vision even more impaired.

But he would not falter.

Lightning cracked above, brightening the midnight battle for a brief moment. The thunder that followed pummeled Claude's senses, exacerbating the headache that thumped against his skull. He was using too much magic, but he didn't care.

He had no reason to care anymore. Not after what Dagmara had done.

Claude decapitated the nearest Celesta soldier. His emotions drove him to slice, and thrust, and kill.

Kill.

He was a monster after all. That's all the Mad King was.

He barely noticed the blackbird swooping down from the sky before it was too late. Talons reached for his face, igniting an excruciating pain as the claw shredded his skin. He stumbled back, reminded too well of the night he had lost his vision in his left eye.

Claws raked across his back, the bird's talons ripping into him. Claude let out an excruciating scream before whirling on his heel and swinging his sword.

But he couldn't see anything. He reached for his face, but the blood wasn't his. The bird hadn't left a mark, even though the torment felt too real.

Just like the torment that had ripped him apart when Magda—no, *not* Magdalena—*Dagmara* blamed him for killing her family.

Once again, talons raked against Claude's chest, the pain passing through his breastplate and ripping his flesh. Claude screamed, collapsing onto his hands and knees.

The slosh of the mud under his palms returned him to reality. He gasped for breath, trying to catch his bearings. His people needed him. They were getting slaughtered. The sheer number of Celesta soldiers was increasing by the second.

Dagmara had saved him from the bird's torment once. She was the only one who had. By the guardians, even the thought of her tore him apart.

And somehow, merely the thought of her, surged adrenaline through his body. His kingdom needed him.

Claude broke from the darkness, leaping to his feet as he lunged forward, throwing himself back into the battlefield. He projected every danger that came to mind. More Ilusaurian guards, hounds, flying spears. Anything and everything to hold back the line. He no longer noticed the blackbird, swooping around the field, invisible to everyone else but him.

Exhausted, Claude peered out at the expanse beyond. Across the battlefield, red uniforms stained the dead plains like blood. Nearly a thousand bodies littered the hillside.

There were more soldiers on the way. Placed at the head of the new recruits was a trio of soldiers on black stallions. One of them carried a red banner with a golden owl, as if they had to announce the attack was from Celestaire. The rain impaired Claude's vision, but he knew the lead of the trio was Reon. Their entire friendship had been thrown away, discarded like waste. Friendships didn't matter when they had to be loyal to their kingdoms.

And what loyalty was there? Claude had done nothing wrong. He hadn't killed Guardian Sora.

Claude would put Ilusauri first, as he always had. There was nothing he wouldn't do for his people. Every deal he took, every move he made, every difficult decision was for the betterment of his kingdom.

And the safety of our people.

Dagmara's voice slithered through his head, sending a chill through his body. Pain surged through his chest, having nothing to do with his injuries. Her betrayal ricocheted through him again and again.

Claude had lost her love. And now, Ilusauri was losing the war.

If Claude lost Ilusauri, he would have nothing.

He proceeded forward into the thick of battle, knowing he only had one choice left. He heard Pierre call his name, but he ignored his guard and strode further into danger. As Claude anticipated, a Celesta soldier charged toward him, sword in hand. Claude met his gaze and said, "*Join me.*"

The soldier froze, then pivoted, and attacked one of his comrades.

Claude looked to the next soldier, saying, "*Fight with me.*" And he obeyed.

Again and again, Claude commanded the Celesta soldiers to switch sides. A headache burned at his temples, but he ignored it. That pain was nothing compared to the betrayal he still felt.

"*Turn against your friends,*" he said, "*attack the Celesta.*" He continued until he had a sizable force of Celesta on his side, and fellow companions were backing away, stunned.

Finding the trio on the hill in the distance again, Claude raised his sword, pointing it directly at Reon. It was both a challenge and a warning.

Seeing the chaos amongst his own ranks and the Celesta fighting one another, Reon lifted his hand into the air. A horn blared through the pounding of the rain, signaling their retreat. Reon fled, and the Celesta soldiers followed, their transformed companions in pursuit. The soldiers Claude had compelled would fight until exhaustion killed them, or they were met by a friend's sword. Whatever came first. He had compelled them all to death.

A long time ago, he had promised himself to use compulsion sparingly. Yet, here he was, watching the men he had transformed chase the Celesta out of his kingdom.

When cheers and hollering rang out amongst the Ilusauri, Claude felt no guilt. Only the remnants of betrayal, simmering in his heart.

"She's gone," Martine stated in the threshold of the royal study.

"What do you mean, she's gone?" Claude demanded. He had avoided facing the casualties of war, so he found recluse in his study.

Aside from a healer, Madame Annette and Pierre were also in the room.

Claude yanked out of the healer's grasp.

"Your Majesty—" the healer began to object, in the middle of stitching a gash in Claude's bicep.

The stitches tore as Claude rose to his feet, but he didn't care. The pain in his heart was more mind numbing than his physical injuries.

"Get out!"

The healer scampered from the room without even grabbing their bag.

To Martine's credit, she held Claude's gaze. However, Claude noted Pierre shifting closer, prepared to intervene.

"Where is Dagmara?" Claude asked, his voice ice cold.

"I don't know," Martine replied. She cleared her throat. "The door was locked to your bedroom, but she wasn't inside."

There was only one other way out of Claude's bedroom, in the event of an emergency. He roared, "You're telling me she knew where the passageway was? Who told her how to access it?"

"I told you this girl was trouble from the beginning," Annette scoffed, folding her arms.

Claude snapped his attention to his advisor. "I swear by the founding guardians I will exile you if you say one more negative thing about her."

Annette clamped her mouth shut.

"I found someone you may want to speak to," Martine said before calling, "Sacha, bring her in."

Bernadette, the Queen of Azurem, entered the room, trailed closely by Sacha. The burly guard didn't have to touch the queen. She entered the study voluntarily, her chin held high in the air.

"We caught the queen trying to escape by carriage," Martine explained.

A new anger surged through Claude's body. He stormed forward, disregarding the blood dripping from his wounds.

"You wanted to make me look like a fool, didn't you?" Claude yelled. "After all the medicines I started sending to your kingdom, after the alliance I offered, you and *that woman* were using me the whole time!"

Bernadette folded her hands in front of her dress, wet from the rain. She replied with a voice both calm and lethal: "I don't know what you're talking about."

"Don't offend my intelligence," Claude said. "I caught your pawn, Dagmara, and you were trying to escape. Why did you and the real Princess Magdalena—your daughter—deceive me? And where is Dagmara now?"

Queen Bernadette's expression flinched ever so slightly. "I have nothing to do with this. I was trying to escape the Celesta attack," she responded. "I don't want to be caught up in your war, and my kingdom needs me alive. Your troops were getting destroyed."

"They don't usually get destroyed," Claude snapped.

"Sabien was absent," Pierre jumped into the conversation. "No one was giving us orders so it was a free-for-all."

"What? Where is he?"

Pierre shrugged.

"Martine, go find him," Claude ordered.

The female guard nodded before exiting the room.

"As for the switch," the Queen of Azurem continued, "now that you know the truth, there is no point in hiding anything from you. My daughter, the real Princess Magdalena, kept me in the dark about it. I thought she was here. I was as surprised as you to find out that Dagmara took her place. I recently learned that Magdalena is with Queen Sanyal in Flaustra. I don't know where Dagmara is, but I know for a fact that she would not have run from you."

"Queen Sanyal is dead," Annette announced. "Their head of correspondence sent a Scribestone. It was an assassination."

Bernadette's face paled. "Is Magda safe?"

"The message didn't mention Princess Magdalena or Queen Sanyal's daughter, Princess Kiran," Annette replied.

Bernadette gasped. "Your Majesty, you have to go save my daughter. Our kingdoms made an alliance. It is your duty to protect her."

"No," Claude said bitterly. He felt the ring on his hand—the wedding ring with Dagmara's blood concealed inside it. He had refused to take it off yet. "I didn't make a vow to protect your daughter. I made it to a false queen."

"Then do it for Dagmara," Bernadette pleaded. "Dagmara came here to protect Magda. It is what she would want."

Claude opened his mouth to object, but Martine appeared in the threshold. "Sabien is nowhere to be found. The last person who saw him was a guard on duty outside your chamber. He said Sabien took over his post moments after you dropped…Dagmara…off at your bedroom."

Confusion coursed through Claude's mind. "I was wondering why there weren't guards outside when I arrived to check on her. So, Sabien was inside my bedroom when Dagmara and I fought…" Claude couldn't finish his sentence. It wasn't possible. It didn't make sense.

Sabien and Dagmara had disappeared together.

"I have a bad feeling, Your Majesty," Martine spoke up. "Dagmara mentioned Sabien was making her uncomfortable. I witnessed many uneasy moments between them. What if she's in trouble? What if she's with him against her will?"

A brief moment of fear surged through Claude, but he immediately shoved it down. His feelings for this woman were acting up again. They couldn't. She had betrayed him.

The words tasted like acid in his mouth as he said, "Maybe they're working together. He went to Magdalena's coronation, maybe that's when their alliance started."

"No. Dagmara would not have killed my son," Bernadette

objected, "And we didn't allow Ilusaurians inside. However, the assassins were from Ilusauri—and one escaped."

"What are you saying then? That my captain was the assassin that killed your family?"

"It's possible," Bernadette said, her voice steady.

Claude's brow furrowed. He protested, "But Sabien doesn't have magic. He couldn't have been the assassin that killed the guardians. Dagmara is the one with Life magic."

Bernadette scoffed. "Dagmara doesn't have magic."

"What would you call that display at the wedding then?" Claude countered.

"Anyone in the room could have done that," said Bernadette.

"Her Majesty is right. Dagmara doesn't have magic," Martine concurred. "Back in Nouchenne, the hounds didn't stir when she went up to them. We were there for a long time. They only woke up when you arrived."

"But she healed me in Sailonne," said Claude. "She has magic."

"Actually…" Pierre muttered.

All eyes whipped to him.

"She said she couldn't. She was crying, afraid she couldn't save you. Then…Sabien forced her to heal you."

Sabien? Was it possible he had Life magic? He had been acting weird recently…disappearing for long periods of time and ignoring responsibilities. But why would he join the First Prince? The First Prince wouldn't have been able to reach Sabien unless—

Concern flooded Claude's body. His mind flashed back to a year ago when Sabien's fiancée—the previous captain of the guard who had sponsored Sabien to join—randomly died. Sabien was both beside himself and kept saying, 'it was meant to be'. It was when his and Claude's disagreements with one another began, and when everyday conversations between them teetered on the edge of arguments. They had been friends since childhood, but ever since Sabien took his fiancée's position as captain, he had changed. The First

Prince would have been able to reach Sabien if he fell too deep in his grief.

Claude's mind ran rampant as the conversation continued around him.

"Say this is true, why would Sabien bother kidnapping Dagmara?" Annette asked.

"Dagmara is my daughter's best friend," Bernadette replied. "Sabien will use Dagmara as bait to get to her. I'm telling you, Magda is the one in danger."

"Our kingdom won't waste our resources on your daughter after this scandal," said Annette.

"Our kingdoms are in an alliance. The world doesn't know about this scandal, and we can keep it that way to preserve the legitimacy of the crown."

"And have Claude marry an imposter?"

"They're already married," Bernadette said.

"We're fighting a war, we don't have time for this," Annette replied.

"I will send Azuremi troops to aid Ilusauri against Celestaire if that's what you want," Bernadette stated. "Someone out there is killing the guardians. This is bigger than all of us. Saving Magda is the priority, not only because she is my daughter."

Claude couldn't focus. His mind replayed the conversation with Dagmara again. Thoughts and emotions tumbled through him as the pain continued to radiate in his chest. He didn't know what was real.

He couldn't believe Sabien would manipulate or hurt Dagmara, but at the same time, he *wanted* to. Because that meant that Dagmara still loved Claude.

His mind flashed to the servant who poisoned them on the terrace —it had been one of the first days that Dagmara was at the Ilusaurian castle. The coroner had said the servant had drowned in prison, which at the time, seemed impossible. Only one person had led the servant to the prison, and that was Sabien Renaud. If Sabien had Life Magic, he could have ordered the servant to poison Dagmara and then killed the servant before he could reveal the truth.

It all clicked in Claude's head. He knew his words carried weight, and even so, he said, "It seems Sabien is the one with magic. He must be working with the First Prince. He must have killed Bogdan and Aleksy, and now, he's taken Dagmara."

Her blood was in Claude's ring, and his in hers. He had made a vow, and he was a man of his word. She was in danger...or worse.

Dead.

Claude stormed to his desk and picked up his sword.

"And where do you think you're going?" called Annette.

"Get Azuremi troops to reinforce us while I'm gone." He proceeded to the exit, fire burning in his veins.

"You can't leave at a time like this! What will people think?"

He didn't care what anyone thought.

He was the Mad King.

And Dagmara was his queen.

"Claude!" Annette yelled. "Where are you going?"

Claude didn't hesitate.

"I'm going to save my wife."

PART ONE

The Escape

CHAPTER 1
Magdalena

Magda could barely catch her breath. She was still underneath Vex's hideout in the tunnel where she had killed an assassin sent by the First Prince. The fight was gruesome, and Magda had almost succumbed to her injuries, but luckily, she had survived unharmed. She clutched her side, catching her breath, as she stared at the wall, sitting in the secret room underneath the trapdoor.

Odie and Ishani were next to her, and Ishani still remained unconscious.

The trapdoor was above, but Magda couldn't move. She couldn't breathe. It would be easier to submit to exhaustion, slipping into darkness in the basement of Vex's headquarters, and no one would find their bodies in the maze of the Marauder's gambling house.

Vex's gambling house was hidden on the docks in Eloquas, now completely deserted, after the notorious guild leader had been killed in a scuffle. Killed by the young musician that had pulled Magda into the beauty of the city, Ravi Kalal.

A few hours earlier, she and Ravi had snuck into Princess Kiran Dhara's birthday ball, disguising themselves as members of the guild using a stolen invitation. Vex's invitation. It hadn't been long until the party turned unexpected, with Ravi sneaking away to visit his imprisoned sister, and an assassin breaking in to murder the queen. Queen Sanyal, the guardian and leader of Flaustra, had been killed in front of both her daughters.

Another guardian was dead. The thought made a chill snake through Magda's spine. She didn't wish losing a parent on her worst enemies, let alone the two young princesses of Flaustra.

She pushed herself to shaky knees, grabbing onto Ishani. In the same night, Magda had also realized that Ishani was not only a Guild Captain, but the elder princess and heir to the Flaustran throne. If anything happened to Ishani, Flaustra would lose more than one of the members of the royal family tonight, and Magda would not let that happen. Ishani was still unconscious, having been knocked out by the assassin, and a trickle of blood ran along her forehead.

Magda attempted to yank Ishani up the ladder, but to no avail. Odie did the same, latching onto Ishani's jacket, and pulled alongside Magda, although there was no way to make the climb with Ishani in their arms.

But Magda wouldn't let another person die.

The thought brought back memories of her deadly coronation, where her father and brother were killed by a group of assassins. Prince Aleksy, King Bogdan, and Queen Sanyal were all casualties of the assassins' war against the royals. Afterwards, Magda had run to Flaustra, taking passage across the sea on Ishani's ship, the Starway. She had wanted to find out why she exhibited Soul magic, completely different from the rest of her family, who wielded the power of Life. But the journey had only proved to reveal more questions than answers.

Ravi had run to get help when the tunnel had caved in, and she had hoped he would return in time. However, Magda had successfully been able to blast through the rocks on her own, harnessing the power of the water.

She had no idea how she had been able to harness the power of

Life. She had thought, all this time, that she was a Soul Guardian, channeling the powers of the earth. Now, it appeared Magda had two forms of magic, both Life and Soul, but it didn't make any sense. All she knew was that the water had seeped across her own gushing wounds, healing her while the cerulean magic invigorated her veins.

If it was true, she controlled the power of Life.

Magda knelt down next to Ishani, touching her palm to her forehead.

Odie whimpered at Magda's side, putting his head on her lap.

"I'm fine, don't worry," Magda reassured her pet. She ran her hands over her stomach, indicating where her wound had just been and attempting to explain to her dog that she had, in fact, miraculously healed herself.

Odie tilted his head in confusion.

Magda touched Ishani's forehead, and the trickle of blood stained her fingertips red. Then she placed her hand over Ishani's soaked clothing, feeling the magic once more between her fingertips. Suddenly, an ice-blue glow circled over her fingers, and the water from Ishani's clothing trickled over the gash on her forehead. In seconds, the cut had sealed, and Ishani's clothes were completely dry.

Jerking back, Magda's eyes shot open. She undeniably had Life magic.

Ishani was still unconscious, and she didn't open her eyes.

A thundering of footsteps pounded on the floor above.

Odie placed his head on Ishani's thigh, looking up at Magda as though he understood the intensity of the magic that had been discovered.

"That's right," she said to her pet, "Watch over her for me."

Magda stood up, glancing up the ladder that led to the main area of Vex's tent. She climbed up, peeking her head through the trapdoor and into Vex's gambling house.

"Magda?! I'm coming!" Ravi shouted.

"Here!" Magda called, pushing open the trap door.

She jumped up, running toward Ravi and leaping into his arms. He barely kept his balance as he caught her around the waist, holding her inches off the ground.

"You're alive!" He set her down, examining every inch of her face.

"Yes," Magda said before kissing him on the lips.

"I was so scared," Ravi admitted, kissing her over and over. "I didn't think I would make it back in time. I thought you were going to drown. How? How did you get past the rocks?"

Suddenly she was aware of the officers standing around, watching them. She pulled away from Ravi before addressing the officers, "Princess Ishani is down there, and the water is still rising. Get her back to the palace at once!"

The officers nodded and frantically rushed to the trapdoor. When they had completely descended, Ravi took a good look at her, seeing the blood all over her ripped clothes. "You're hurt!" he exclaimed frantically.

"No, not anymore."

"What do you mean? I thought for sure—there was so much blood." He touched her stomach and waist before checking other parts of her body.

"Ravi," Magda stopped him, taking his hands in hers as she removed them. "I healed myself."

He stilled, staring blankly back at her.

She continued, "I have Life magic. The gift of healing and water."

"Like the Azuremi guardians and the rest of your family?"

"Exactly."

"I thought you had Soul magic?"

"I do," said Magda.

"How is that possible? There has never been a guardian that can wield multiple forms of magic."

"There has...," said Magda, "The only person in recorded history that controlled all branches of magic was the First Prince."

"The First Prince? I barely know anything about the old legend," said Ravi. "His line of magic was extinguished one thousand years ago, right? So he wouldn't have any descendants."

"That's what the stories say," said Magda, "but I don't know what the truth is."

Ravi went to respond, but the officers had returned from the basement, carrying Ishani between them. "We need to get back in the carriages, it's not safe here," an officer retorted, pointing to the exit.

Ravi nodded.

Before Magda could say anything else, Odie bounded up from the basement, but instead of going for her, the dog went right for Ravi. He leapt up onto Ravi's chest, licking Ravi's face ferociously with a slobbery tongue.

"Yes, good boy, you found the assassin and you saved Magda!" Ravi laughed. "Yes, I know you're hungry. Let's go home, you deserve a treat!"

Magda couldn't help but smile. She began following the officers, heading to the carriages. "Odie, come!" she called.

But before Ravi followed, he ran over to one of Vex's overturned chests, grabbing a few glass vials in his hands and shoving them in his pockets. "Let's take some while we still can," said Ravi, "Remember how I told you Vex hoarded medicine from all his trades around the kingdoms? Specifically Ilusauri."

"Yes," Magda remembered, crossing over to him. "You stole herbs and vials for your sister Prisha, right?"

"Vex always had interesting concoctions," he mused, "and unless you're personal friends with a guild leader, you never know when you might need them." Ravi stood up, handing Magda a few more vials, before saying. "Alright, that should be enough. Let's go."

When they reached the Flaustran palace, the carriages rolled directly into the courtyard garden. It was almost daybreak, as they had been out all night hunting down the Soul assassin. The partygoers had gone, but the garden remained scattered with streamers and lanterns, signaling the end of the celebration. Kiran, the younger heiress to the Flaustran throne who had celebrated her birthday ball that evening, burst out the front doors. She sprinted across the gardens, her dark, curly hair bouncing in the wind, her eyes alight with lingering specks of Soul magic that signified her status as a royal and a guardian.

Kiran ran immediately to her older sister Ishani, who was being carried on a stretcher by the officers. She let out an ear-piercing scream as she watched the officers carry her sister inside the palace. She turned to Magda and Ravi. "What happened? Is she alive?!"

"Yes," Magda said, "but she needs to rest."

"Did you kill the assassin?" Kiran asked. "Are we safe?"

"Magda killed them," Ravi announced, "and saved Ishani's life."

"I...have Life magic," Magda admitted.

Kiran's eyes widened. "Are you serious? You have Life *and* Soul magic?" She let the words sink in. "I don't know what that means but thank you for saving my sister. I'm sure my mother would thank you too. I can't believe that the assassin killed her. I can't believe she's dead...," Kiran's voice cracked.

Magda pulled Kiran into a strong hug. "I'm so sorry. I'm sorry that this is happening, and I'm sorry you lost a parent. It's not easy, but I'm here, and I'll be here as long as you need."

"Thank you. Thank you for being such a good friend." Kiran sobbed into Magda's shoulder. "And thank you for helping Ishani. I don't know what I would do if something happened to my sister."

Magda's heart clenched. She thought of her family, and the funeral that followed when they had buried her brother and father.

Ravi embraced the girls, holding them both close.

"Let's go inside," Kiran said, defeated. "You both need to rest."

Ravi turned to Magda, squeezing her hand. "Goodnight, Magda," he shifted in his stance, unsure of the words.

"Please stay at the palace with us," Magda said. "It's late."

"I don't mind heading back to town if you'd like to spend time with your friends," Ravi assured her with a smile. "The night is young and the stars are bright."

"No," Kiran said, leaping up and giving Ravi a hug. "You saved my sister too. You can stay at the palace as long as you need. You're one of us now."

"I...," Ravi looked at them both, seeming overwhelmed at the offer. "Alright, thank you, Your Highness."

Then they all began walking inside. When Magda reached the doorway, exhaustion consumed her. Her head clouded, and she had to use all the strength in her body to prevent herself from passing out in blackness.

Odie could sense the shift, and he nudged his nose against Magda's thigh.

Do you still want answers? I'm the only one that can provide them.

Magda shuddered, attempting to wrench herself from the darkness. The voice that she had been hearing for the past few weeks was back. For weeks, ever since she had left Azurem, a strange voice had been penetrating her thoughts, leaving her with more questions than answers. Its identity and motives remained a mystery to Magda.

Why should I trust you? asked Magda.

The voice laughed. *You don't have a choice. There is no one else.*

A slew of barks beside her brought her to her senses. In another instant, she was back in the gardens. Odie was at her side, jumping against her legs.

"Shhh, Odie," Magda whispered.

Magda followed Ravi and Kiran into the palace. She wasn't ready to tell her friends about the secret voice in her head, even if the voice promised to provide her answers. But one question lingered on her mind:

Who were they?

CHAPTER 2
Dagmara

The darkness was familiar, enveloping Dagmara like a thick blanket. On a normal day, stars clouded her vision, making her momentarily blind, and this darkness was no different.

Wincing from the pain that radiated through her shoulders, Dagmara opened her eyes. Her eyelids were heavy and her body was stiff, signaling she had been in one position for far too long. A migraine pierced her temples, but she disregarded it as she focused on her surroundings.

Red. The color red surrounded her on every side, highlighted by golden strips and tassels. The entire wall on her left was covered with tinted glass windows from floor to ceiling. It was dark, but not pitch black yet. She could make out a rocky cliffside, and a dozen white-oak trees separated her from the stone. The landscape provided no indication of where she might be. The frosted glass hinted at a colder climate, and she could only assume she was in the mountains. But which mountains? How did she get here?

She was lying flat on a soft mattress, and a thick blanket covered her. Another indication that she was in a colder area. Hastily, she glimpsed underneath the sheet, seeing she was dressed in a long, fleece nightgown. It was unflattering at best. However, it was the only thing keeping her warm in this frigid room.

Gazing at the space before her, she saw a circular table at the center, surrounded by three padded stools. She could see a few items scattered across the table, but couldn't make out what they were. Across the room, a fireplace was unlit and empty. A crimson bench was against the furthest wall, right beside a wardrobe. A single dress hung on an iron wire, latched against the wardrobe door.

Her heart plummeted in her chest. She jolted upright, throwing the heavy blanket off her as she scrambled to the edge of the bed. Her stomach somersaulted, sending a wave of dizziness and nausea through her, and she gripped the mattress for balance. Stark horror coursed through her as she stared at the bloody dress.

Her wedding dress.

It was ripped down the sleeves, stained with blood, and thick mud clung to the bottom. The entire hue was an eerie gray, as if the rainwater had drained the white color out of it. Flashes from her wedding night came to the forefront of her mind.

After finding insurmountable proof linking the Mad King to the murders of Bogdan and Aleksy, she had accused him in his bedchamber. But she had been wrong. It wasn't the Mad King who was behind the murders—it was Sabien. He had told her as much, right before he stabbed an iceblade through her stomach. Twice. Then she fell unconscious and ended up here—wherever *here* even was.

Sabien Renaud.

He was a Life Guardian, granted magic by the First Prince himself.

The First Prince will rise.

The eerie sentence she had seen once on a cavern wall with Martine sent a chill through her spine—the same cavern with vicious, magical hounds. The First Prince was real, and he was giving magic to specific assassins and sending them to kill the true guardians. An assassin had succeeded in killing Claude's parents, supposedly Guardian Sora in Celestaire was dead, and Sabien had succeeded in killing Bogdan and Aleksy.

A newfound anger surged through Dagmara's body. The whole reason she had swapped places with Magda was to avenge both Bogdan and Aleksy's deaths. Now, Sabien had taken her here, planning to use her to aid him in killing Magda. He thought Magda was the last Life Guardian, and since he was responsible for taking out the Life Guardians, Magda was his target. If only he knew Magda had Soul magic—would he still hunt Magda down? Dagmara wasn't willing to find out. She simply had to kill Sabien first.

It would be no more difficult to kill him than any of the other men she had assassinated. Yet, she didn't know where she was, and she had no weapons or potions on her. After she devised a plan, she had to get out of here. She had to get back to the Ilusaurian castle and find Claude—

Her breath hitched.

King Claude Mirage.

She could almost see his face now as he experienced her betrayal. He had done nothing to deserve what she did to him, and she hated herself for letting her emotions spiral her into the accusation. She could feel her heart breaking once again as memories of him flashed in her mind. How he pleaded with her in the greenhouse to save his people, how he saved her from the hounds in Nouchenne, how he played Soulaye with her and danced with her and carried her to his chamber—

Shaking her head, she forced the memories to halt lest she start crying. Swallowing the pain and burying her grief as she was so used to doing, she pulled herself from the bed.

The ground was cold against her bare feet, and she stopped at the wardrobe to check for shoes, but it was empty. She had to escape before Sabien returned. She headed for the door and reached for the latch, but it was locked. She realized that it didn't open outward, but slid to the side, so she yanked at it, using her full weight, but it wouldn't budge. Her heartbeat quickened as fear settled in, and she channeled it toward her mission.

Racing toward the windows, she tested each one, but there was no way to open them. As she scanned the room for another exit, she saw the items laid out on the center table.

Her jewelry.

She recognized the necklace and earrings from her wedding night, but she only had eyes for the ring. Picking it up, she remembered the ceremony vividly. Claude had pricked his finger and dropped an ounce of blood inside the ring before putting it on her hand. A piece of him was in the ring.

Dagmara slid the jewelry on her middle finger. It was heavier than she remembered, matching the weight of the guilt in her chest. However, it brought her some semblance of comfort.

Then she heard a noise on the other side of the door.

Sabien.

She had nothing to defend herself.

Her eyes flicked to the iron hanger her wedding dress was dangling from. Without hesitation, she ripped the gown off the hanger. It was a sad excuse for a weapon, but if she hooked him at the right angle—in the right location—she could make her escape. She raced to the other side of the wardrobe, barely concealing herself on the opposite side of the furniture, just as the door swung open.

Holding her breath, Dagmara waited in the stark silence that followed.

There was a faint creek on the floorboard.

Then a voice: "You better not make me spill these drinks."

Dagmara's body went rigid. It was a woman's voice, and although she spoke in Ilusaurian, she had a thick accent that reminded her of Reon's. Was the woman Celesta?

"I'm the one that helped you out of that muddy dress, you know."

There was a shadow on the floor as the woman moved into the room. Dagmara couldn't bring herself to attack, having no idea if this woman was innocent.

The woman rounded the side of the wardrobe, coming into view. She set a silver tray down on the center of the table before turning to face Dagmara. She was gorgeous, with silky, blemish-free skin and a round face. She was at least a few inches shorter than Dagmara, with a petite frame to match. Her jet black hair was perfectly straight, cascading halfway down her back. She wore tight fitted pants and a bright red top that left little to the imagination.

"A hanger?" she laughed. "You'll have to do better than that."

"Who are you?" asked Dagmara, surprised by how hoarse her voice was. She was so disoriented, finding the correct words in Ilusaurian was harder than she remembered.

She pursed her lips, considering whether or not to answer. "Guess."

"You want me to guess your name?"

The woman's brow furrowed. "You're not as fun as he said you were." She whirled on her heel and took a seat at the center table, crossing her legs. "Guardians, it's cold in here," she said under her breath before picking up a steaming mug from the tray. There was a second mug on the platter. Next to it was the single gray key she had used to open the sliding door.

The woman shifted the tray toward Dagmara. "You must be parched. Drink. And drop the hanger."

Dagmara eyed the steaming mug, knowing how easy it was to slip a potion inside. She couldn't make herself more vulnerable than she already was.

The woman took a dainty sip out of the mug she was holding, closing her eyes. Dagmara's gaze shot toward the door that the woman had left open. Then she fixated on the key on the tray.

Pretending to obey her order, Dagmara let the hanger drop to the ground before she uneasily approached, inching her way toward the table and the key. "You said 'he' earlier—do you know Sabien?"

A smirk began to crease on the woman's face. "I would say he and I are...quite familiar with each other." Her full lips creased into a grin.

Dagmara picked up the mug meant for her and slowly brought it toward her chest. Her throat was dry, begging for any liquid, but this was not the time to accept free beverages. She could still see the key in her peripheral vision.

"You have a nice home here in Celestaire."

"Thank you, I just—" the woman stopped short.

The woman had confirmed Dagmara's suspicions, almost too easily, that they were somewhere in Celestaire. Then the woman's smile fell as she realized her mistake, and she snapped, "I'm not into your prying. You just woke up after days of being out. I want to know about you. More importantly...why Sabien kept you alive."

"I guess he has a thing for me."

The woman gripped her mug tighter, her knuckles turning white, and Dagmara took her chance.

She chucked her mug at the woman, ensuring the hot beverage would splash directly in her face. The woman attempted to block, but was not fast enough, and screamed as the liquid singed her skin.

Lunging forward, Dagmara grabbed the key and raced out the door. She didn't think twice. She slid the door closed, shoved the key in the lock, and locked the woman inside.

She barely had time to survey her surroundings. She was on the second story balcony of a large foyer. Wooden columns adorned with red ribbons were spaced throughout the room, and the dark wood of the walls would have made it feel cozy inside—if this place wasn't her current prison. There was no one else in the room, and there wasn't even a piece of furniture. Another sliding door coated in frosted glass was her passage to freedom.

If anyone else was in the building, they would've heard the

woman scream. Dagmara didn't have time. She saw the stairs and took off toward them, descending as fast as she could. The ugly fleece dress limited her movement, but she wouldn't spare another moment as she raced to the door. Sliding it open, she was met by a courtyard.

The courtyard in front of her wasn't large. A giant white tree sprouted in the center of the space, surrounded by an oversized pond, its edges turning to ice. Stepping stones traced a path across the courtyard and over the pond, but they were slick with frost.

There had to be another way out.

Turning over her shoulder, Dagmara saw another door hidden beneath the balcony she was previously on. It was a giant oak door framed by windows. She was about to run toward it when a loud bang reverberated through the room.

The door upstairs that Dagmara had exited—and locked behind her—flew off its track. Wood went flying as the door burst out of the frame and came careening off the side of the balcony, shattering the railing to pieces. The door landed with a hard thud directly between Dagmara and the exit.

Stumbling back from the debris, Dagmara gripped her chest to quell her frantic heart.

The woman emerged from the broken door frame, half her face bright red from the hot liquid. Her expression was filled with malice as she sauntered forward, strode through the broken railing, and stepped off the balcony.

The woman didn't fall. She gracefully floated down to the first floor, a gentle breeze rustling her hair. She landed on the remains of the door, her menacing gaze set directly on Dagmara.

A gaze that contained vibrant red irises.

Fear flooded through Dagmara. This was magic she had never seen before. There was only one guardian type left that Dagmara hadn't encountered in her life.

A Spirit Guardian.

"You'll pay for that," the Spirit Guardian said before thrusting her hand forward.

The air stirred, and a sudden wind pummeled into Dagmara's side. She was knocked off her feet, thrown through the courtyard doors, and splashed into the pond. Pain rippled through Dagmara's shoulder upon impact, and she struggled to pull herself to her feet. She needed to escape. But she wasn't fast enough.

The air began to swirl around her, beating against her face. Her hair flew in haphazard directions, and she tried to cover her eyes with her forearm. She could feel the water slipping away, her body rising into the eye of the storm. It was as if she had no control over her limbs as her entire body began to levitate, strangled by the wind that spun around her. She could no longer keep her eyes open against the pressure. The air was swirling faster. Choking her—suffocating her. She didn't know which way was up any longer until—

"Junne!"

The air relinquished her, and she slammed to the ground once more. She gasped, choking against the foul pond water and struggling to her hands and knees. The frigid water caused her muscles to tense, and every ounce of her body screamed in pain as she sucked in a breath. She heard voices shouting at one another, but she couldn't make out the words. Her head was spinning and darkness danced in her vision, taunting her into oblivion. With her fleece dress now sopping wet, it tried to drag her down into the pond. The entire side of her body was throbbing from the fall.

Then the water receded. It withdrew from her body, leaving her in a small circle of mud and algae. Dazed, Dagmara stared in awe as the water danced around her, as if she was enclosed in a glass, circular fence—and the water could not pass the invisible barrier.

Footsteps sloshed on the soggy ground. Beside her, she sensed someone approaching. She didn't have to look up. She knew who it was as he crouched beside her and spoke, "Glad to see you're finally awake. I thought I accidentally killed you."

His melodic voice ended in a low chuckle. Then his fingers grazed the bottom of her chin, lifting her head up to meet his piercing gaze. His irises were icy blue, reacting to the magic he had used to create a dry landing for his shoes in the center of the pond.

Then the Captain of the Ilusaurian guard smirked. "Did you miss me, Dagger?"

CHAPTER 3
Magdalena

Magda raced to the Flaustran Scribestone, Odie at her heels. She needed to find out what had happened in Ilusauri. She didn't know if her mother and Dagmara had gone through with the wedding to Claude, and what had transpired after that. Was Dagmara, and technically Magda, married to Claude? Had they called off the wedding?

The Scribestone was located in the Flaustran library, nestled in between plants and vines that snaked up its foundation. The library was not only full of bound books, but also scrolls, older than the texts found in Azurem.

Odie dashed forward first, letting out a forceful bark as if he had been the one to discover the mysterious object for the princess.

"Good boy, Odie," Magda said. She embraced the stone, putting her hands on either side, and a series of words emerged, glowing in sparkling ink.

One message from Queen Bernadette Krol, Ilusauri

Dear Magda,
    I am beyond infuriated with this ridiculous plan! I cannot believe

you are in Flaustra and that you would keep a secret from your mother like this.

Celestaire invaded Ilusauri. Dagmara went missing in the chaos, and Claude is going after her. Claude knows it's not you, and that Dagmara works for the crown. She was kidnapped by Claude's captain, Sabien Renaud, who has also been charged with murdering your father and brother. He is an assassin working for the First Prince. They picked up a trail leading South, but lost it in the storm, so no one knows where Dagmara has been taken.

Magda stopped reading the letter. Dagmara had succeeded in solving the mystery and confirmed that Claude wasn't behind the attacks. Now, Dagmara had been taken by her family's murderer, all because Magda had switched places with her. The news filled Magda with a wave of grief. She would never forgive herself if something happened to Dagmara.

"Dagmara is missing!" Magda looked down at her dog. At the sound of Dagmara's name, Odie's ears perked up, but he didn't make a sound.

Magda continued reading:

I am about to make haste back to Azurem. Things are deteriorating quicker than you could imagine. The sickness has spread, and I have set up camps and ordered more doctors to attend to the needy. There is not enough medicine coming from Ilusauri because Claude's land is dying, struggling with drought. In addition, more refugees are coming from the Azuremi mountains in the north, telling us that their homes have been destroyed by avalanches. Azuremi villagers come to the fortress with tales of chasms spurting from the earth and dark magic.

Dagmara told me that you do not have Life magic. This must all be connected. With no guardians anymore in Azurem, Claude says our kingdom could die. Magda, I do not know what this means, but I need you home.

Love,
Mom

Magda stepped back. Somehow, Azurem was deteriorating. It didn't make any sense, for Magda had not seen any elements of dark magic on her journey throughout the countryside to come to Flaustra. Had things changed that much in the past few weeks?

Odie nuzzled against her legs, as if indicating it was time to go. She quickly penned a reply to her mother.

Mom,

I'm sorry for putting you through this. There are no words to apologize. I understand how serious this is and I will come home to Azurem, but first I must find Dagmara. If what you're saying is true, and dad and Aleksy's killer has kidnapped her, I need to rescue her.

If they're going South, they must be heading to Celestaire. If Celestaire and Ilusauri are really at war, Sabien might think Claude won't be able to follow them there.

I can't lose anyone else, and it's my fault she was in that position.
I love you, and I'll be home soon.
Magda

The words disappeared as quickly as she had written them. She needed to get to Celestaire immediately.

When Magda and Odie exited the library, they emerged into the inner palace gardens. Up ahead, Magda heard shouting coming from the center of the courtyard.

Odie let out a sharp bark, before sprinting ahead of Magda as fast as lighting. His barking intensified, becoming louder even as the distance between them increased.

She quickened her pace, traversing through the flower beds, before reaching the gazebo. Suddenly, an ear-piercing scream echoed through the courtyard.

She spotted Ishani next to the front gate of the palace. The captain was engaged in a fierce battle against three figures dressed in palace uniforms.

"Ishani!" Magda yelled, sprinting across the garden in Ishani's direction.

Ahead, Ishani twirled, raking her double axes down the side of one man's frame, before kicking another man in the chest who was charging at her. Ishani fought relentlessly, as expected by any captain of a Flaustran guild. But in this case, Ishani had also been a guardian before her sister Kiran had won the trials, making her all the more skilled at combat.

The second man was thrust onto his back, giving Ishani enough time to launch an axe across the space and into the third man's chest. The first man still stumbled, and she spun once more, using the axe to kill him from behind. Finally, she placed her boot on the neck of the palace officer who had fallen.

Ishani held her remaining axe in his direction saying, "Who sent you? Who are you working for?"

"I'll never tell," he grumbled.

"Tell me if you want to live."

"You'll kill me anyways. Long live the First Prince."

Ishani lowered the axe.

Then Ishani snapped up to see Magda at her side. However, she didn't address her. Instead, she addressed the gate officers who were also frozen in their shoes. "You all just stood there! No one thought to intervene?" she snapped at the officers.

"We're sorry, Your Highness," they said.

"I told you not to call me that," Ishani grumbled. "Get these bodies out of here."

Odie had padded over to the axe that Ishani had thrown, picking it up between his teeth and handing it back to the princess.

Finally, Magda found her voice again. "Are you alright?" she asked. She had to admit, the thought of rushing into one-on-one combat was terrifying.

"Ishani, where are you?!" yelled Kiran, running out from the palace doors, with Ravi directly behind her. Then Kiran leapt up and hugged her sister. "I heard you scream!"

"I'm fine. That was nothing." Ishani wriggled out of her sister's embrace, pulling away.

Ravi approached the three. "Who were these people?" he asked. As he did so, he reached down and acknowledged Odie, who was already slobbering his tongue all over the young man.

"More assassins. They thought I was Kiran," Ishani guessed. Then she referenced her hair, which was pulled back in a bun with a sparkling headband. Other than the fact that Kiran's hair was curly, the sisters would have looked similar from afar.

Ishani turned to Kiran. "It's not safe for you here. We need to find somewhere to go into hiding temporarily, where you can still rule."

"Why is this happening?" asked Kiran, surveying the dead bodies.

"Why do you think? Remember what mom always said?" Ishani asked.

Kiran remembered the story, "The original guardians locked away the First Prince in a tomb, sealed with four magical blood locks, and the locks are rumored to be held in check by the lives of the guardians today. But we never believed it was possible."

"I think the assassins are killing guardians because they want to break those locks," Magda deduced.

"They want the First Prince to be released," Ravi said breathlessly, almost to himself.

"Whatever is true, I'm not losing my sister," said Ishani. "We're leaving Flaustra."

"Where would we go?" asked Kiran.

"I have a contact in Celestaire who can hide us," explained Ishani.

Celestaire. It was South of Ilusauri and where Dagmara had likely been taken. Magda had to save her friend. Sooner or later, she would have to face the Mad King and discuss their alliance—and marriage—but saving Dagmara was the priority.

Magda blurted out, "I have to get to Celestaire as soon as possible. I received a Scribestone from my mother. Ilusauri and Celestaire are at war. And—"

"At war?" Ravi interrupted.

Ishani answered, "Kiran's advisors told her. This must have something to do with Claude's letters."

Magda remembered the letters she had found on Ishani's ship from the Mad King. Ever since Queen Sanyal had died and they had gone after the assassin, Magda had forgotten all about them. She never had time to ask Ishani why she was in communication with the Mad King.

"Why do you say that?" asked Magda.

"Claude was searching for something across the kingdoms, and my mom and I thought it was the First Prince's tomb," said Ishani. "He must've been searching in Celestaire too, maybe that provoked the war."

"No," Kiran began under her breath. She fiddled with the extra fabric of her skirt. "My advisors say the war was initiated because Guardian Sora is dead, and Claude killed her."

"What?!" Magda and Ravi gasped simultaneously.

"If he killed Sora, who's to say he didn't send the assassins who killed our mom too?" Kiran questioned. "Or Magda's family?"

"No. Claude isn't responsible," Magda muttered.

And like that, Magda poured out the entire story to the two princesses. She told them about how she suspected that Claude killed her brother and father. She told him about how Claude had asked for her hand in marriage, the switch between her and Dagmara, and that

Claude was innocent. The real assassins were under the command of someone named Sabien.

"Now you understand why I need to get to Celestaire," Magda said, grabbing Kiran's hand. "I need to save my best friend."

"You want to run into a war?" Ravi's voice was laced with concern.

Kiran's doe-like eyes widened. "Celestaire is massive, and you have no idea where Dagmara is! This could be extremely dangerous."

At the sound of Dagmara's name, Odie let out two barks this time. He pulled away from Ravi, turning his attention to Magda.

"I have to save Dagmara," said Magda, "I'm the reason she was in Ilusauri in the first place, and I would never forgive myself if something happened to her. She's like a sister to me."

Something flashed behind Kiran and Ishani's eyes as they looked at each other in understanding.

Ishani spoke first, "We want to help you find Dagmara, but the guardians are still being targeted, and I'm getting my sister to safety."

"Then let me help," said Magda.

"You think you can fight off assassins?" Ishani chuckled.

"I killed one, and I saved your life."

"We got lucky," said Ishani.

"Then you can train me in combat on the journey."

"Another princess means another target," Ishani said, "and your boyfriend and dog will be deadweight."

Ravi opened his mouth to object, but Kiran cut him off.

"I want her to come, Ishani. She's one of the only other guardians, and we can help each other. Please."

Ishani considered her sister's words, before reluctantly agreeing, "Fine. We'll take my ship to Celestaire." Ishani turned to Kiran. "You can bring your elite officers, and I'll enlist my most trusted men."

"And you're certain you trust your contact in Celestaire? And your officers?" Kiran asked again.

Ishani nodded.

"Alright," Kiran agreed with her sister. "We leave at midnight tonight."

Magda agreed, but then her heart sank. She looked at Ravi, who had been watching the conversation silently. She knew he wasn't a royal, or a guardian, and he had a life and family in Flaustra. She didn't want to force him to come with her, but at the same time, she didn't want to say goodbye.

"Will you come with us?" Magda asked.

Ishani let out a large sigh. "He might not have a choice."

"What do you mean?" Ravi asked.

Ishani shrugged, before unfurling a piece of paper, "I was going to tell you, but figured we have bigger problems. One of my officers brought this to me. This has been posted all over the city and specifically sent to Guild Leaders to keep a lookout."

She held out a large poster with Ravi's face plastered on it, and underneath, it read:

> *Ravi Kalal, wanted for the murder of*
> *Vex, Captain of the Marauders Guild.*
> *5,000 coins for location*
> *50,000 coins for delivery to Dreadmarrow*

Magda remembered the treacherous guild leader who had kidnapped Odie a few weeks ago. Ravi had helped her rescue Odie, but it resulted in a struggle. Ravi had killed Vex, the Captain of the Marauders Guild.

Ravi held his hand to his forehead. "Everyone is going to be searching for me now. Dreadmarrow is a death sentence."

"This doesn't mean anything," said Magda, reaching out to grab the paper and crumbling it in her hands. "Can we pardon Ravi just as we pardoned his sister? He saved my life—the life of a guardian."

"It doesn't change the bounty that's already been put on his head," said Ishani. "Anyone can still claim the reward at Dreadmarrow."

Reaching out, Magda laced her fingers with Ravi's. She didn't want Ravi to be sent off to Dreadmarrow, where she would likely never see him again—where no one would ever see him again. The prison was located on a deserted island in the middle of the sea, and it was rumored that once you arrived you only left in death. Even though she was a guardian and a royal, it would be nearly impossible to get Ravi out of that place. Guardians had limited jurisdiction on the island's no-man's land, and usually by the time the paperwork was in place, prisoners had already died or been killed.

"You're not going to Dreadmarrow. Escape the city with us," suggested Magda.

"If he leaves, he'll never make it back through the city's immigration gate," said Ishani. "He'd be leaving Flaustra forever."

"Forever?" he echoed.

He met Magda's gaze, the expression in his eyes causing her heart to break. Then he said, "Alright."

"Don't miss the ship," Ishani instructed. "We leave at midnight."

Ravi nodded, his voice solemn, as he reached down to pet Odie once more. Then he turned to Magda. "Before we set sail, there's something important I need from my mom's shop."

"What's that?" asked Magda.

Ravi cleared his throat, "Something I think that could help your kingdom."

CHAPTER 4
Dagmara

The hard ground sent a ripple of pain through Dagmara's shoulder. Sabien had dragged her back inside, throwing her on the floor in the center of the room. The fleece dress weighed her down, and icy water formed a puddle around her. Her hair was soaked, plastered to the sides of her face, and she shuddered from the cold.

"Let's get two things straight ladies," Sabien said. "No killing, and no escaping. Understood?"

"She threw boiling water at my face." Junne stepped up to Sabien, gesturing to her cheek.

"I hope it blisters," Dagmara said under her breath.

Junne lunged forward, but Sabien had already caught her by the wrist, holding her back. "No killing," he repeated. "I need her alive."

Junne's eyes were filled with anger. She whirled to the captain. "At least heal it."

"I've never healed a burn before."

"Sad excuse for a Life Guardian then, aren't you?" said Dagmara.

This time, Sabien was the one to shift forward. The back of his hand collided with Dagmara's cheek. The force knocked her off her knees, and she barely caught herself before her face slammed into the ground.

"Don't test me," Sabien growled. "I told you already, I'm not afraid to take you to the brink of death and heal you, simply to do it all over again."

Dagmara's cheek was still tingling from the blow. Pain radiated through her temple, and she could hardly focus. The wet fleece clung to every inch of her body. The ice water was seeping through her skin, freezing her bones. Her teeth rattled, and she tried to prevent her entire body from shaking.

"Remind me again why we're going through the trouble of keeping her alive?" Junne asked.

"I'm using her as bait to kill the last Life Guardian."

Junne laughed. "Right, because you couldn't kill Princess Magdalena the first time."

"You killed an old lady on her deathbed. I killed a guardian preparing for the trials. We are not the same."

Instead of being offended, Junne smiled, shifting closer. She trailed a single finger down the center of his chest. "That's what you think."

Putting the pieces together in her scrambled head, Dagmara's chest tightened. Junne was the one who had killed Guardian Sora. It was the event that started the war between Ilusauri and Celestaire, all because they blamed Claude—just as Dagmara had blamed Claude for Bogdan and Aleksy's deaths.

But it was Sabien who sent a knife through Aleksy's heart.

Rage burned through Dagmara, but her jaw was chattering from the cold, and her hair was like ice against her cheek. "A-Aleksy didn't deserve what you did to him," her voice was no more than a whisper.

Sabien crouched in front of Dagmara, right where she wanted him. "I felt powerful when I killed your prince. And I enjoyed it."

Dagmara lunged, swinging her fist toward Sabien's face. He was too fast, easily dodging the blow. Or maybe she was too weak.

Then she heard a crack as his knuckles collided with her jaw. She careened sideways, her shoulder slamming against the floor moments before her temple did. A faint ringing dancing in the back of her mind, and her vision blurred. The side of her face was on fire. All she wanted was to close her eyes and succumb to the agony.

"And where is Princess Magdalena?" Junne asked.

"Flaustra," Sabien replied, rubbing the back of his knuckles. "She told me when I had a dagger in her abdomen."

Dagmara remembered that night vividly. She should have never admitted where Magda was—but she wasn't ready to die.

Now she was at the mercy of two murderers that possessed the magic of the guardians. It would take everything she had to find a way out of this alive. She had to think of a way out of here. She had to think of a plan. Somehow, she needed to get Sabien to trust her again—if he ever did. She could lure him into her trap.

"I can't help you if I freeze to death," Dagmara stammered. "I'll take that hot beverage now, Junne." She flashed the Spirit Guardian a closed-mouth smile before slowly bringing herself to an upright position. She winced, pain radiating through her face, her entire body exhausted and dizzy.

"I don't take orders from you," Junne retorted, crossing her arms in front of her petite frame.

Sabien shook out his hand from the blow, rising to his feet. "Find her something else to wear so she doesn't freeze to death and bring her that beverage. We leave for Flaustra in the morning."

"What?" Junne snapped. "You're certain she's not lying? What if Magdalena isn't even in Flaustra?"

Sabien hesitated for all of a moment. "Dagger and I are working together now, aren't we?"

"Of course." Dagmara returned his smile, though it made her sick. Maybe getting Sabien to trust her was her way out. If she could get him on her side, she could sneak out, ideally gutting him on the way.

"Let's be certain then." Junne crossed to a panel on the wall.

Pressing against the wooden plank, it popped open, revealing a hidden compartment.

Lifting her head, Dagmara tried to see what was concealed inside. She committed the location of the compartment to memory. She barely made out the glint of a sword before Junne had slammed the compartment shut, carrying a vial filled with purple, iridescent liquid.

However, if there was one thing Dagmara knew, it was potions. She would have recognized truth serum in her sleep.

Horror crashed down on her. She would *not* be subject to torture by truth serum.

She attempted to scramble to her feet, but Sabien planted his boot on her chest and thrust her back to the ground. Her breath escaped her, and she choked as she struggled for air under the pressure of his shoe.

Meanwhile, Junne sauntered to Dagmara's side, squatting on the ground and gripping her chin.

"Open wide," she said in a sing-song voice.

The vial was shoved into Dagmara's mouth. She gagged, nearly choking on the potion. The moment it touched her tongue, she felt it like fire. The potion was acidic, burning her throat as it entered her body. She tried not to swallow, but she was choking on the substance. She felt a jolt through her chest as the potion coursed through her veins.

Junne withdrew, rising to her feet with the vial still in her hand.

Sabien released the pressure from Dagmara's chest, and she rolled onto her side, coughing violently.

"Are you simply saying you'll work with Sabien so you can stab him in the back later?" Junne asked immediately.

"Yes."

The word slipped from Dagmara's lips before she had a chance to process the question. How was that possible?

"Hmm," Junne mused, unfazed. "And have you been completely honest about the princess?" Junne asked.

"No."

Once again it was out before Dagmara finished comprehending the question. Her eyes went wide as she stared up at her captors.

However, Junne and Sabien were busy exchanging a glance with one another. Sabien returned his gaze to Dagmara, his eyes curious. "I don't take kindly to lying, Dagger."

"I thought you could tell when I was lying," Dagmara replied, struggling against the truth serum. If she was using more words, maybe she could work around the questions they were asking. "I guess you've lost your touch."

"Don't think too much about my touch, it may keep you up at night."

"Doubtful."

"Enough," Junne cut into the conversation once more. "Do you know where Magdalena is?"

"Yes."

Startled, Dagmara shut her mouth tightly. The truth serum was strong.

She had to be stronger.

"Where is Magdalena?" Sabien pried.

Instinctively, her body tried to respond right away. She bit the inside of her cheek, clamping her mouth shut, but every inch of her began to burn. There was no antidote for truth serum, she would have to let it run through her system. But she could fight this. She was smarter than this. She didn't know Magda's exact location in Flaustra.

"I don't know exactly," Dagmara blurted out before slamming her mouth closed immediately. The answer seemed to work, settling her pulse and the excruciating pain lacing through her veins.

He crossed his arms. "Is she in Flaustra?"

The fire returned, beginning in the pit of her stomach and extending through the rest of her body. If there was a way she could buy Magda time—if she could prevent Sabien from going to Flaustra

—she would do whatever she could. She had to protect her friend or die trying.

She bit her tongue so hard she drew blood, but the truth serum was overpowering, urging her to answer. Pain seared through her temples, and although she was shivering, sweat began to bead along her forehead.

"As much as I love seeing you struggle, this battle is futile," Sabien coaxed. "Even those trained in potions aren't strong enough to withstand truth serum."

"Maybe you can't," Dagmara said through gritted teeth, "but I'm stronger than you."

A low chuckle escaped Sabien's lips. "Is that so?"

"Yes."

"One of us is standing, and the other is on her knees. I think that is demonstration enough that you are inferior. Yet I must admit, this is not how I expected we'd get into these positions."

"It's sad you have to force women to their knees."

A frown creased Sabien's face. "Answer me, is Magdalena in Flaustra?"

The pain was unbearable, resurfacing with the question that lingered in the air. But Dagmara was strong. She had to be. She had no other choice.

"I hope not," Dagmara said. Suddenly the tension lifted, and the discomfort eased. Letting out a sharp exhale, she raised an eyebrow at Sabien invitingly.

Sabien narrowed his eyes. "What kind of answer is that?"

"The truth." Those words slipped out before Dagmara could fight the pain.

"Tell us where she is," Junne ordered.

"That's not a question," Sabien snapped, silencing her. Then he knelt in front of Dagmara, meeting her at eye level. "Dagger, let's not make this more difficult than it needs to be," he said, stroking a single finger down her cheek. She wanted to jerk away, but held firm, refusing to break eye contact and let him win. "We're on the same side, you and I—assassins simply completing tasks assigned to them. This argument was fun at first, but now I'm done with you."

"You didn't last very long," Dagmara sneered. "How disappointing."

He gripped her chin, his fingers digging into her flesh. "I'm tempted to rip your tongue from your mouth."

"I'm afraid that defeats the purpose of getting me to talk."

He leaned in closer, his breath beating against her face. "True. And I would miss the way my name sounds on your lips, among other words I can't wait to hear you say."

"I guess we're at an impasse."

"Not yet. Is Princess Magdalena in Azurem?"

Her mouth parted, and the word 'no' nearly slipped from her lips immediately, but she bit back the reply. This time, the pain was overwhelming. She could smell blood. The room was blurred as darkness danced in her peripheral vision. Sabien's face morphed into two, dizziness overcoming her as her entire body fought the truth serum.

This is what the guardians ordained for us. Be brave. Be selfless. Be loyal.

Her mother's words flooded to the forefront of her mind, shocking her. It was what her mother had always said when she had trained Dagmara. And Dagmara had shoved the motto away, forgetting about it after her mother was pronounced dead. But somehow, in this moment of agony, she clung to those words as her lifeline.

For all Dagmara knew, Magdalena could have returned to Azurem. In truth, she had no idea where exactly Magda was, even though she hoped she was safe in Flaustra with Queen Sanyal.

"She *could* be in Azurem," Dagmara managed.

Sabien released her face, shoving her away in the process. He glared up at Junne. "You gave her truth serum?"

Junne scoffed. "Yes. Maybe it wore off in the time you wasted bickering."

"Maybe you didn't give her enough."

Dagmara leaned closer, whispering. "Maybe you suck at asking questions."

She anticipated his backhanded slap before it met her cheek. At least it would even out the pain from his punch earlier. Before she hit the ground, he grabbed her by her bicep and yanked her to her feet. She stumbled to keep up, the world spinning around her as she was dragged to a door at the end of a narrow hallway.

"Where are you taking me?" Dagmara asked.

"A new holding room while we fix the door on the last one," Sabien growled.

He yanked open the door and threw Dagmara into the darkness.

She was falling before she registered what was happening, tumbling down the flight of stairs. Agony laced through her hips and shoulders as they made contact with each stair, and both wrists jolted in searing pain as she tried to catch herself. She failed to slow her momentum, finally hitting the solid ground in a petrifying thud.

"I'll return when you're ready to cooperate," Sabien called before slamming the door, extinguishing the only source of light.

There was too much pain to move. Instead, she laid in a crumpled heap at the bottom of the stairs, her frozen dress sticking to every inch of her body. She wondered if Sabien and Junne had other plans for her—besides getting to Magdalena. How many methods of torture were there to withdraw information? She wondered how many days her mom had survived. There was no doubt her mother was put through the most agonizing form of torture, whatever that may be.

As Dagmara lay in the darkness, she continued to dream of her mother, tortured to death by a Life Guardian. Was the same fate in store for her own life?

CHAPTER 5
Magdalena

That night, the four left the palace at midnight. They moved quickly out of the interior courtyard and got into a central carriage. Next to them, two other carriages would be used as decoys, going to other parts of the city with their own set of officers. Their carriages reached the central district of Eloquas, passing the statue of Queen Sanyal and heading to the town circle near Ravi's apartment and his family store.

The carriage pulled onto a side street. "Get out here," said Ishani, opening the door for Magda and Ravi. "We'll meet you at the docks. I can't have Kiran's carriage rolling up next to a fugitive's house."

"Ravi's not a fugitive," Magda retorted, although she agreed with Ishani's logic. Then she turned to Ravi. "Let's hurry up and get what you need."

Ravi and Magda jumped out of the carriage and dashed through the streets of the Flaustran capital, careful to stay off the main roads. They circled around the small alleyways and side-streets. Luckily, it was late, and the unbearable heat had subsided, leaving only a pathway of clear stars above.

"We're almost there," said Ravi.

Soon they came to his mother's shop, the *Gilded Silks*. After a quick tap on the door, Ravi pushed it open and led the two inside.

"Laila? Mom? Prisha?" he called out.

Laila, Ravi's older sister who had been let out of jail, sprinted out from the kitchen into the main room. All around were shredded fabrics and overturned sewing kits. Dresses sprawled on the floor, and beads and jewelry were scattered in all directions.

"Ravi!" she exclaimed.

"Where are they!?" Ravi asked, tearing into the room before heading into the rest of the house.

Laila chased him into the kitchen. "Mom sent a note that people came to question her about your whereabouts and take you to Dreadmarrow. She and Prisha left for the countryside."

"I can't believe this is happening...right when you're free," Ravi said.

"I'm only free thanks to your girl," Laila said, eyeing Magda, "but I saw your wanted posters all over the city. You have to leave now."

"I already have plans to leave tonight, but I need the journal. I think it can help Azurem."

Laila let his words sink in before dashing to one of the floorboards, lifting it up before pulling out a leather bound notebook. Then she handed it to Magda. "If you're helping Ravi get out of here, it's the least I can do. This is all of the research I compiled on how we saved Prisha from her illness. I gathered a list of concoctions, illnesses, and stole medicines and potions from every guild, who have logs and herbs from every kingdom. We had planned to publish this as the first of its kind medical book, but...," her voice broke "...things went bad, and I ended up in jail."

Magda graciously accepted the journal. "Thank you."

Laila reached to give Magda a hug. "Take care of my brother," she said.

Magda hugged her back.

Ravi turned to Laila. "I don't want to leave you here to deal with this on your own."

"I'll be fine," said Laila, turning to Magda, "Promise me you'll make him leave."

"I promise," Magda said, "but we need to go. The longer we stay the more chances we have to lead someone to Kiran."

"Let's go out the back way," Ravi agreed, beckoning Magda through the kitchen.

Then the two disappeared into the night, heading for the docks.

On the docks, Ishani's gorgeous ship, the Starway, was ready to depart. Its sails were raised high, featuring the glittering symbol of a peacock feather—the symbol of the Fowler's Guild—fluttering in the midnight wind. The Flaustran princesses and their elite officers were already on board. The dock was crowded, with endless shipping containers and crates scattered across the wood.

Ravi and Magda circled toward the ship, passing through the shadows. When they were halfway to the gangplank, Magda stopped him and touched her hand to his shoulder, "Are you alright? That can't have been easy."

"As much as it hurts me to leave my family, you saw what happened at the shop. I have no choice but to leave," he paused, looking back at the city as his voice broke, "even if it means I will never be let back into this kingdom."

A pang of guilt fluttered through Magda. She knew how much his family meant to him, and if it wasn't for her, Ravi wouldn't have killed Vex. It was Magda's fault Ravi was in this situation, with no choice left but to desert his home and family.

"I've messed up everything for you," said Magda.

"No," Ravi shook his head. "If I didn't meet you, and you didn't obtain a royal pardon from Kiran, Laila would still be in jail. And Vex would still be out there, pressuring me and blackmailing me for information and secrets that I picked up as a musician on the streets. I would be a slave to the guilds for the rest of my life. I think...," he paused for a long moment. "I think things were meant to happen the way they did."

"So you don't regret meeting me?" asked Magda.

"What?" Ravi asked, taken aback. "Don't be ridiculous. I told you that your battles are mine, no matter the cost. Where is this coming from?"

"Sorry," Magda admitted, thinking back to Dagmara. "I have a lot going through my mind right now. But, we'll be together, and that gives me hope."

"It's the one thing that gives me comfort, knowing you'll be at my side," Ravi smiled. Then he stiffened, alert to their surroundings, "Someone's coming."

A figure appeared from the darkness. Odie bounded forward, greeting Ravi with a playful jump, before circling around the pair twice. Then another shadow crossed the moonlight, and Ishani appeared over Magda's shoulder. Her voice was a hushed whisper, "We have to leave now. There are eyes on us."

"Where?" Magda scanned the docks, but she couldn't see anything past the dimly lit barrels and crates.

"Don't look—"

Ishani stopped mid-sentence as the shadow moved.

Odie's stance shifted, and the fur on his back raised.

Suddenly, a clamor of boots and scraping metal sounded behind them. Emerging out of the blackness was a group of officers holding knives and wearing the insignia of the beast on their chest. They stood at the edge of the alley, blocking the pathway back into the city.

"Not so fast," said a voice, booming loud over the lapping waves hitting the pier. A man stepped out in front of the group, coming face to face with Ravi. Odie remained near Ravi, his teeth bared as a growl escaped from his chest.

Ishani put her hand in front of Magda to stop her from moving forward.

"Warren. You're on my dock," Ishani snapped.

Warren wore a purple top hat and matching coat, and a scruffy beard framed his face. "Captain Dhara. There's no need to make this messier than it needs to be. That boy should be ours. Vex was our captain, and we deserve to take out our revenge on Vex's murderer."

Ishani laughed, and her hand grazed the axe on her hip. "Oh, please, I know you're only in it for the money, not revenge."

"Then why don't we both take him to Dreadmarrow and split the earnings?"

"Too bad I don't like sharing," Ishani replied.

"Neither do I."

Then Warren and his men moved forward to grab Ravi.

CHAPTER 6
Magdalena

Arrows began whizzing through the air as Ishani's officers on the ship took out Warren's men. Warren lunged for Ishani, but she was too quick. She took one axe and sliced it against Warren, before turning around, grabbing Magda's hand and running toward the ship. "Come on!" she yelled.

Magda, Ishani, Ravi, and Odie took off for the ship, heading across the dock. Odie dashed between them, bounding ahead and boarding the ship first. The dog leapt up next to Kiran, who stood watching from onboard, and the younger princess pulled Magda's pet behind the ship's railing for cover.

Ravi knocked over one of the barrels, sending it crashing in the men's direction, before another officer lunged toward him. Ravi stopped and grabbed the attacker's wrist, before punching him across the face and pushing him off the dock into the water.

Ishani reached the gangway, and as she boarded the ship, she took her axe and swung it cleanly through the ropes that were tying the large vessel to the dock. The ropes swung out to the boat, hanging down from the sails like snakes in the wind, and the ship began moving to the rhythm of the water, heading out to sea.

"What are you waiting for?!" she called back to Magda and Ravi.

Magda and Ravi darted forward, racing up the gangway and darting across the make-shift bridge to reach the Starway. In the corner of her eye, Magda spotted the gleam of a sword, coming right from Warren. "Look out!" Magda yelled.

Ravi slipped on the slick wood, screaming, and he reached up to one of the hanging ropes for support. He latched onto a rope to catch his balance, swinging outward over the sea.

Magda turned to Warren and thrust her hand out, finding the power of water. Cerulean magic swirled in her palm, and she envisioned a maneuver she had seen her brother Aleksy execute many times before. In an instant, she channeled the magic, seeming to grasp the water in her fingertips. The water flew toward Warren, solidifying as it did so, until a ricochet of ice daggers ripped through Warren's body, finding purchase deep in his chest.

Ravi swung back in their direction, using his legs to push Warren off the gangplank. Warren's dead body, full of ice spikes, landed into the dark water with a splash.

How was this happening? Magda hadn't done any experimenting or training. Why did she already have full control of the water, manipulating it with barely anything but an idea in her mind?

"Run!" Magda yelled, grabbing Ravi's arm and pulling him onto the ship. He stumbled, feeling heavy as he grabbed onto her shoulders for support. They boarded the ship, but as soon as Magda went to embrace Ravi, she gasped in horror.

Blood seeped from a wound in Ravi's side, coating his clothing crimson. She thought they had escaped Warren's attack, but his blade had made contact, leaving a horrifying gash in Ravi's skin.

Ravi's lips shuddered, and he looked down at the blood. "Magda...," he attempted to say, as he crumpled to his knees.

Magda screamed in agony. She tried to pick up Ravi, but he moaned in pain as she moved his body. Around her, she scanned for help, but the ship was in chaos. Ishani was screaming more orders at her men, who had finished readying the sails. Kiran's officers had joined Ishani, pointing their weapons down at the remaining members of the attacking guild.

Kiran was at the helm of the boat, channeling the power of the Soul. She stared out at the pier, magic jolting through her body, as the earth surged through her veins. Kiran's hand thrust forward, finding the stone pires that held up the dock in her mind and crushed them with her senses.

One by one, the pires holding up the pier next to the street began to crumble in a domino effect. The men blocking the entrance to the city tumbled into the water, getting swallowed by the black sea.

"Kiran!" Magda screamed over the commotion. Her heart was beating frantically in her chest, and all she could think about was keeping Ravi alive. She would never forgive herself if Ravi died tonight.

Upon hearing Magda's call, Kiran raced to her aid. They hoisted Ravi between them, struggling under his weight. A minute later, they had managed to drag Ravi into Ishani's office, followed by Odie, who was watching as they laid Ravi down in the center of the room. "Quick, find water!" Magda yelled to Kiran.

Kiran raced to a cabinet, opening it frantically to search for a bottle. "What about the ocean?" she asked.

Then Odie let out a whimper, nuzzling a pitcher on a side table. Instantly, Magda rushed to the pitcher, and thanked the guardians that it was full of water, before dashing back to Ravi's side.

"Nothing's going to happen to you," said Magda, putting pressure onto Ravi's wound, which was already gushing profusely.

Ravi let out a scream of pain.

Quickly, Magda poured the water over him, letting it slip between her fingers. She hoped it would be enough. In an instant, she felt the sparks of magic electrifying her body. One by one, her fingers felt the sensation of magic pass through, and she knew her eyes were turning blue. The water continued passing over Ravi's body, and when the pitcher was empty, the water retreated from

Ravi's clothes, sucking into Magda's hands once more before spreading out over the wound.

When Magda removed her hand, Ravi's shirt was completely dry. Even though the magic had appeared to work, anxiety flushed through her body. She hoped that she had done enough and that he would wake up again.

All of the sudden the ship lurched to the side. She heard Odie let out a whimper, and Kiran screamed as they all were flung to the left. Magda toppled over and slid on the slick wood as the pitcher spun out and away from her. Blackness consumed her entire body, but this time, it was clear it wasn't from exhaustion. The world shifted, and the colors drained from her surroundings.

Let's play a game. The voice was back.

Magda found herself in a pitch-black space, and the Void sucked all sensation from her body, paralyzing her in one spot on the ground in the center of the emptiness. All she could do was turn her head, scanning the vastness for any sign of the mysterious sound.

What? He continued. *You don't want to play, Princess?*

Magda struggled to stand up, but she was weak from using so much magic. *Who are you?* She demanded. Magda tried to spot the source of the voice. It was the same voice she had heard all throughout her journey in Flaustra. She was alone, in a black hole of nothing, with only the voice at her side.

The game is...let's see who gets their powers first. It seems you have already found the Soul and Life magic, but what about the others?

Magda was startled that this voice knew she had used the water magic. How was he reading her mind? Did he know she was planning to escape to Celestaire to save Dagmara? Did he know she was on this ship right now? Quickly, she tried to stop thinking of any of her friends or plans. Instead she responded:

Alright. It seems you already know I have two branches of magic. What about you?

I have Soul magic. And Void magic. So it seems we are even.

Void magic? Magda was confused. *There is no Void magic anymore.*

Are you sure, Princess? He retorted.

Magda's thoughts were spinning, for she had no idea how to make sense of the voice or the strange space she found herself in. How did this voice have two branches of magic like her?

She heaved herself to her feet, struggling on unsteady legs. *Before, you said you had answers. What did you mean?* She asked.

A whooshing noise sounded behind Magda, but she was still frozen in her shoes and couldn't move a muscle. Suddenly, she was aware of the warmth of someone's body standing behind her. Her entire body tingled, as if they were barely brushing themselves against her.

I've never felt you here before. Magda said.

The man let out a laugh, before leaning closer, his breath dancing against her ear. *I'm growing stronger. Aren't you curious if it's really me standing behind you? Or am I an illusion?*

I think it's you. Magda responded, curiosity encouraging her to turn around and face him, but fear holding her in place.

It is a form of me.

So an illusion or not?

A projection. Not with Mind magic, but with the Void.

Stop being cryptic. You promised me answers. Magda persisted.

Patience, Princess... His voice sent a shiver up her spine.

But she wasn't patient anymore. Magda whirled around to face him, afraid he would disappear, laying her eyes on the mysterious figure for the first time.

Standing in front of her was a young man, only a few years older than herself. His porcelain skin seemed to glow against the dark, as though he was illuminated against the black magic that imprisoned him. He had light blonde hair and stark features, sharp enough to cut glass. Spiked gold and navy armor decorated his neck to his hands, and wisps of violet magic flickered in his light-blue irises. He held himself upright, his stature god-like.

Her breath caught in her throat as she laid eyes on his golden crown, resting on his blonde hair like a halo. He was not just any man, he was royalty.

She was expecting to feel a pang of fear, but instead her body urged with intrigue. She forced the next thought through her mind.

I know who you are.

Say it. He demanded, his voice slithering into her mind.

The First Prince.

There was a long, drawn out pause. He inclined his head as a closed-lip smile creased on his face.

Yes. I am.

Magda had to stop herself from trembling. The First Prince was the young man from the legends, who was rumored to encompass a furious evil. Every guardian swore an oath that never again the First Prince would rise, and they were taught the story of how he killed his brothers at a young age. Every school child knew the legend of the First Prince.

According to her mother's Scribestone, this man had sent assassins to kill her family and the other guardians. He had condemned her to death as well, for his assassins were also supposed to murder her at her coronation. However, she had gotten away unscathed. Now, she was standing before the murderer face to face.

Her body filled with dread, and Magda's heart beat faster. A sickening knot twisted in her stomach as she realized this man had been searching her thoughts for the past few weeks. This man had ordered her family's deaths. Why had he entered her mind, if not to get close to her and finish what he had started?

You are the one sending assassins to kill the guardians. She needed to hear him say it.

Yes. The answer sent a chill up her spine. If he was killing guardians, it meant he also wanted to kill Magda.

Don't worry, Princess. He said calmly. *You're different from the rest. Your blood is not tied to a lock. We're special, you and I.*

Because we have multiple gifts. Magda answered the question that had been swirling through her mind. *So are we the same?*

Not exactly. You come from the Life lineage and I came from the Void lineage. The same powers, different families.

All of her thoughts were spinning out of control. She questioned him, *If we're not related, how do we have the same powers? Multiple powers? And how do you only have two? I thought from the legend you had all five. Does that mean I have all five too?*

Ah, such a curious mind... His voice was hypnotizing.

Her eyes drifted to the only light in the space, glowing from the crown on his head. While it was certainly made of gold, a violet hue illuminated it, mirroring his eyes. Violet. She had never known that color of magic before.

Her thoughts roiled inside her head, and suddenly a vice grip locked around her wrist. She screamed, yanking her hand back, but it was as if the shadows themselves had grabbed her. The light illuminating from The First Prince vanished, and he disappeared. But the darkness wouldn't let go. It latched around her waist, suffocating her, yanking her hard. She screamed against it, fighting until her elbow met something solid.

"Magda, stop!"

She recognized that voice. The darkness vanished, and her surroundings reignited. She was back on the ship in the cabin, and Ravi was holding her around the waist to stop her from thrashing.

"Stop, it's just us!" Kiran shouted.

Magda calmed down slightly in their arms, but her heart was about to beat out of its chest. Ravi and Kiran held her, dragging her over to Ishani's bed and hoisting her up onto it. They both sat next to Magda on the bed, while Ravi wrapped his arms around Magda. Odie padded on the other side of the room, sniffing around the blood and water that remained spewed on the floor.

"You're alive!" Magda shrieked, giving him a strong hug. She placed her hands all over his body, looking for the wound.

"I'm perfectly healed," said Ravi, "you saved my life."

"You saved mine," Magda said.

"Are you alright?" Kiran asked Magda. "You were in a trance."

"I was in something called the Void, I think. I can't explain it right now," said Magda. She remembered her encounter with the First Prince, his striking features, the golden crown, and his violet-tinted eyes.

Kiran reached out to take Magda's hand in hers. She spoke sweetly, "You're safe now."

Magda nodded. Deep down, she couldn't help but think that she had somehow cheated death by saving Ravi's life. Just the thought of that much power was unnerving.

Then Odie charged between them all, jumping up onto the bed beside the trio and trying to push his way into Magda's lap. They laughed, embracing Magda's pet, who let out playful barks as he jumped around the bed, finally finding a spot to lay down next to them.

Magda turned to see Ishani in the doorway, staring right at her. She had no idea how long the elder princess had been watching the scene. Ishani scoffed:

"So much for a low profile escape."

CHAPTER 7
Dagmara

There was no way to keep track of time in the darkness. Someone had thrown down a change of clothes, a stale piece of bread, and a canteen. Whether it was Junne or Sabien, she didn't know. Somehow she managed to change out of the freezing fleece nightgown and into something dry. Stumbling through the darkness, she found the wall eventually and slid down to a seated position. She curled her knees to her chest, wrapping her arms around her to keep warm.

Everything in her body ached from her shoulders to her tingling fingertips. Nausea roiled inside, until the weight of simply holding her head up was too much. She tilted to the side, resting her cheek on the hard floor. Although the pain of Sabien's blows lingered, she knew this was her health condition flaring. She had no salt to ease her dizziness and no potions for her pain. How was she supposed to fight Sabien? Any normal person would struggle fighting off two guardians, and she wasn't normal.

Her mother's voice echoed in her ears.

This is what the guardians ordained for us.

Be brave. Be selfless. Be loyal.

This was for the safety of the people she loved.

The safety of our people—the betterment of our kingdoms—

She shut her eyes, refusing to think about Claude and the two sentences they had shared with one another time and time again. He wouldn't come for her. No one was coming for her. She had to save herself, as she always had before.

She heaved herself from the ground. It was pitch black in the basement, but she was going to find something. There had to be something here she could use as a weapon. She would not give up hope. Not yet. Even if she couldn't fight her way out—she could manipulate Sabien.

Her shaking hands caressed the walls, feeling for a loose nail. As she searched, she heard a noise. A gentle flutter sounded in the basement, followed by a faint caw. There was something else down there with her, though she wasn't sure what. Or maybe, it was a trick of her imagination.

She kept searching for a weapon.

Sabien dragged her up the staircase and into the main foyer. The guardians weren't kind when they flattened her to the ground and shoved the vial of truth serum down her throat.

"When was the last time you had correspondence with Magdalena?" Sabien asked. At least he was speaking Azuremi so her brain could comprehend his sentence. However, the way Junne sulked behind him hinted that the Spirit Guardian couldn't speak Dagmara's native language.

"In Azu—" Dagmara's body jerked forward. Her veins were on fire, and every muscle in her body clenched. The truth serum caught her lie, even though it wasn't her intention, and was punishing her for it. There was so much pain, she could hardly open her mouth to say the truth: "I sent her a Scribestone in Ilusauri."

Gasping, Dagmara stabilized herself on her hands and knees.

"What did you tell her in that correspondence?"

Ringing started in her left ear. Her vision became hazy. She had to fight.

"I wrote about you actually," Dagmara said through gritted teeth. Truth.

Sabien cocked his head, a bemused smile creasing his lips. "What did you say about me in the Scribestone?"

Nausea roiled in her stomach. Technically, she didn't *say* anything. She *wrote* it. Maybe she could coax the truth serum into agreeing with her. Her mind fixated on his word choice as she formed her response.

"I told her that you were alive." *Truth. No pain.* She followed up with another truth. "But I wish you had died when I stabbed you in the chest and shoved you into the ravine."

His expression darkened. He reached forward and grabbed her by the chin, forcing her to look up at him. "But if you had killed me then, we would have missed out on so much fun," he said. He ran his thumb across her bottom lip. "The kiss in the library...the games... taking the life of your precious king and prince."

Aleksy.

Dagmara shifted forward and bit down on his thumb, as hard as she could.

He reeled back, letting out a violent curse word in Ilusaurian. Dagmara tasted blood. Her victory didn't last long. His boot met her face, and she fell into darkness once more.

Moments before her vision went black, she heard Junne's voice: "Why don't we take her to Viette?"

Sabien replied, "That will be our last resort."

She wasn't sure how many times the cycle had continued. She didn't know what day it was. At first she tried to count the loaves of bread and water they tossed down, but lost track in her delirium. Were they feeding her twice a day? Once a day? She didn't know.

Her fingers bled, carving out a nail in the wall. She would use it. She would get out of here.

Another wave of dizziness pounded her body, and she let her forehead fall against the wall. She needed salt. Her body was fighting her, unable to heal the bruises inflicted by her captors. This was the real Sabien—the assassin working for the First Prince. Not the captain from Ilusauri.

A sudden breeze blew through the room, and a flap of wings caused Dagmara to jerk back. Something flew by her, disappearing into the pitch darkness.

"Hello?" Dagmara tried, but her voice was hoarse. If there was a bird down here—maybe there was an exit. Maybe there was—

Her heart stopped. It was the blackbird. It had to be. The figment of her imagination that only she and Claude could see. She had witnessed it the first day she had met the king, and it had been haunting the king since his parents had died. Was he close to her location now?

No...Claude no doubt despised her. She didn't blame him. He wasn't coming to save her.

Either it was a normal bird who got trapped down here with her... or she was officially mad.

CHAPTER 8
Magdalena

*P*rincess. The First Prince's voice was back.

Magda let herself fully manifest in the space. She was back in the Void. This time, more elements surrounded her. Above, a faint outline glowed, as if a translucent ceiling masked the vast darkness. The violet magic was intoxicating, creating an illusion as if glowing gemstones lined the curved walls of a cavern. In the far distance, walls entrapped her, although they were barely visible in the blackness.

Suddenly there was a large whooshing noise, and the First Prince stood before her. He was still dressed in his navy armor that snaked down his arms and muscular chest. His blonde hair flipped around his crown, and he stepped towards her with broad strides. The violet twinkle in his eye was like a trance, and his porcelain skin and golden crown illuminated the dark space. He didn't stop until he was inches from her.

Her breath hitched, and she could feel her heart pound against her chest.

It has been so long since someone else has been inside the Void. Since someone else has seen the real me. He said. Then he began to lift his hand, reaching for her cheek. *Far too long since I have been able to...*

His voice drifted away, lingering in her mind and caressing her thoughts. He raised his hand toward her, his fingers inches from touching her cheek, but he froze moments before his touch reached her face.

She shuddered, letting out an unsteady exhale. She didn't know if they could touch each other in this space...but something inside her wanted to find out. She stared up at his eyes and his chiseled face, wondering if he could read her desire in that moment.

Since you've been able to...? She prompted, leaning closer.

He inclined his head, a flicker of curiosity dancing in his eyes—of a yearning that Magda knew matched her own. But he didn't follow through. Instead, he withdrew his hand, drawing it behind his back as though to extinguish a flame.

Princess, we are not supposed to be friends. We are supposed to be mortal enemies.

Then I should at least know my enemy's name. Your real name.

A subtle laugh rumbled deep in the space. *I was waiting for you to ask.*

Tell me. She urged.

My name is Eligor Blaide.

Magda shot upright in the bed. She turned her head to see Ravi sleeping beside her, and Odie curled at her feet. Each time she was sucked into the Void, the space further revealed itself.

Finally knowing the First Prince's name made his looming presence feel all the more real, unnerving her to the core. What did the First Prince want and why was he in her head? Why was he considered to be evil and feared by all? Everyone knew the legend that he killed his brothers, but was that the entire truth?

She stole a glance at Ravi, who was sleeping peacefully, and hadn't stirred. She wanted to let him rest. Ishani had made everyone work on their fighting skills on board. Ravi was included in the training with the other crew members. Meanwhile, Ishani had more private lessons with both Magda and Kiran.

Magda threw back the blankets and jumped down from the bed before reaching the door. There was no way she could sleep any longer tonight. They had been sailing for a few days, and she was getting antsy. She wanted to get to Celestaire now.

Odie had already perked his head up, but Magda cautioned him. "Odie, stay. I'll be back."

Hesitantly, Odie rested his head on his paws.

Magda tiptoed her way through the ship, attempting to steady herself as the vessel bobbed beneath her shoes. Then she raced up to the main deck before crossing to the front of the helm. She opened the door and descended to the Captain's Quarters. There was only one person on this ship who had been a guardian for five years, and maybe they could finally answer Magda's questions.

"Ishani?" Magda whispered, before peeking her head inside.

She spotted the young captain sleeping at her desk, with her head down on the map.

"Ishani," Magda attempted to wake her, stepping further into the cabin. Upon doing so, she noted that Kiran was asleep in the bed in the corner of the room. When she heard Magda's call, she rolled over and her head perked up. "What's going on?" she asked.

"I have to talk to you both," said Magda. Magda crossed over to the desk and placed a gentle hand on Ishani's shoulder. "Wake up," Magda whispered.

Ishani perked up. "What is it?" she groaned.

Kiran rubbed her eyes as she approached the other two, before sitting back on one of the nearby tables, letting her feet swing underneath her. "Tell us," Kiran urged, her voice unusually peppy for this hour.

"I saw the First Prince," said Magda.

Ishani's brow furrowed. "In a dream?" she asked.

"No," said Magda, circling the table and sitting opposite Ishani. "I can't explain it. It's a new space entirely."

Ishani wore a confused expression. She rose from her chair, before heading to a side table that held a glass bottle. She poured glasses of water, before returning to Magda and Kiran and handing them each one.

Kiran took a sip of her drink, saying, "It sounds like the Void magic."

"But the Void magic was locked away when the First Prince was enclosed in his tomb," Ishani mused, plopping down into the chair across from Magda.

Magda continued, "Well, the First Prince told me he has the Void magic and the Soul magic."

"That can't be right. If it really is the First Prince, he was said to have all five branches of magic," Ishani corrected her.

"Then why would he tell me he only has two?" asked Magda. She stared at the water in her glass as she spoke, turning it to ice, and back to water.

"Maybe he's slowly regaining his magic as the guardians are killed," Kiran's eyes widened as her voice shook.

"No. Weren't you listening?" Ishani asked. "He has Soul and so do you, so it doesn't make any sense."

Kiran searched for another explanation. "Maybe, the magic he can wield has nothing to do with the current living guardians and has to do with something else."

"I don't know," Magda shuddered. "He seems extremely powerful."

"Well, magic grows exponentially stronger the longer you have it," explained Kiran, the yellow sparkling against her irises. "I've only had my gift for one year, while Ishani had hers for five…before the trials." Her voice grew solemn as she said, "My mom was the strongest."

"Does that mean Eligor is one thousand times more powerful than the current guardians?" Magda feared.

Ishani shrugged, "If the First Prince really is rising, I'm not sure he is technically alive while in his tomb."

"Maybe those years don't count while he's locked away," Kiran offered.

"Let's hope," said Magda, "but there's still something we're missing."

"There's a lot we're missing," Ishani scoffed. "Even the Mad King himself, with all the resources at his disposal, hasn't been able to solve this for nearly a decade." Then Ishani pointed to the map on the table. "These are all the locations that guilds searched on Claude's behalf. I guessed he was interested in the tomb. We were instructed to specifically look for rifts, animals, and the presence of magic, and leaders sent logbooks to Claude in exchange for checks."

"Mom knew you were willingly giving information to a foreign king?" Kiran piped up.

"Originally I didn't want to get involved, but she asked me to be a double agent for Flaustra," Ishani said. "I made sure to be the main point of contact and find out the truth on all the locations that had been searched by fellow captains, as technically I'm the only captain that has any experience with magic. There is no source of magic in any of these places, meaning the First Prince's tomb is not there." She pointed to the markings on the map.

Magda eyed the table once more. Xs were spread out all over the intricate map, marking locations where Claude had commissioned guild leaders to search across the continent.

"And you gave all of the logbooks describing these places to Claude?" Magda questioned.

"Not before I made copies." Ishani tilted her chin to a bookshelf, and Magda grinned.

Magda promptly darted over to the starboard side of the ship, before scanning a series of leather-bound journals, and she chose one before flipping through the pages. Sure enough, it was a series of coordinates and charts written hastily in Flaustran cursive.

Kiran asked, "But why would Claude want to find the tomb? Magda's mom says he's innocent and not related to the assassins."

"Revenge?" Ishani shrugged her shoulders. "I think we all would like to kill the people that murdered our parents. Even if our mom wasn't the best mother."

Magda nodded, curious what Ishani meant by her last statement, and crossed back over to the desk. At least, wanting to avenge a parent was something she and the Mad King had in common—or, she and her husband had in common. The thought slipped her mind daily that technically they were married.

She picked up her glass again, dipping her finger over the lip to practice turning the water into ice and back again, this time much faster. "I'm sorry about your mom," Magda said to them both.

"She...," Ishani's eyes darted to Kiran's, "wasn't the most loving parent to either of us."

"What do you mean?" asked Magda.

Kiran explained matter-of-factly, "She always played favorites and never took our insights into what we thought was good for the kingdom. We also never really bought into all the legends and traditions. We didn't think that guardians should have magic and also rule."

"Then she was even more livid that I threw the trials and let Kiran win," said Ishani.

"But just because she wasn't the best mom, it doesn't make it any easier to lose her," Kiran paused, beaming as she looked at Ishani. "But we have each other."

Ishani gave Kiran a soft smile in return.

"Why didn't you want to be a guardian?" Magda asked Ishani.

Ishani shook her head. "I knew my mom would always be reigning over my shoulder, so I chose a life out at sea like our dad. Besides, having the magic for five years was enough."

Magda nodded. The glass had completely hardened now, full of ice. "Sometimes I wonder what would have happened between Aleksy and me, if we were forced to fight together in the trials. Would he have gone easy on me, letting me win, or would he have just taken the powers and the throne? Would we actually both have tried our genuine best to beat the other?"

"It makes the story about the First Prince even stranger, doesn't it?" asked Kiran. "If he was more powerful than his other brothers, why kill them if he could have just beaten them in the trials?"

"I don't know," said Magda once more. "I need to figure out more about the Void lineage and its power."

"Beats me," Ishani laughed, "The Void was never something I learned about during guardian lessons. I'm afraid the only other person who can tell you about the Void is..."

"...the First Prince," Magda finished her sentence. "He's the only living..." she paused, wondering if he was actually alive or not. So she said, "He's the only remaining person that has ever experienced or will have experienced the Void magic, considering his family line was extinguished."

"But he's locked away, and so is the Void, so does it really matter?" asked Ishani.

"Not if he escapes," said Magda, "and he will if he kills all the remaining blood-line guardians."

"Right," Kiran agreed. "That includes me and you since Claude didn't have magic when his parents died, thus Ilusauri had no reigning guardian for years, so that lock would have been broken."

"The prince said I'm different," said Magda, "Maybe, since I have multiple powers, I'm not connected to the original bloodlines."

Ishani's eyes widened, "Meaning Kiran is the only one left."

CHAPTER 9
Dagmara

Had it been weeks? Days? Only hours? Dagmara had no semblance of time anymore, trapped in the darkness.

No words were passed between one another as Sabien came to collect Dagmara in the basement. She had dug at a nail in the wall until her fingers bled. She was so close—she almost had it out. The next time he came to greet her, she would surprise him with her own greeting. But this time, she had to manipulate him with her words.

They reached the foyer momentarily. Fire was lit in the hearth, warming the room from the frigid air outdoors. The light was blinding as it poured in through the glass windows to the courtyard. Dagmara covered her eyes with the back of her palm. The sun was setting, casting an orange glow into the room. She wasn't used to being up here in the light. Something was different today.

"Come," Sabien beckoned, traveling up the staircase.

She hesitated, if only to catch her breath. "Where?"

He glared over his shoulder. "You lost your opportunity to join me in my chamber the moment you started lying. We could have worked together from the beginning."

"I'm not lying anymore," Dagmara insisted. "Magda could be dead for all I know."

"She's not dead. I'm about to find out what you're hiding." He gestured up the staircase, his eyes narrowing.

Her heart hammered in her chest, but she forced her legs to stop shaking long enough to climb the steep stairs. The darkness threatened to render her unconscious. She reached for the support of the banister, using it to hoist herself upward, praying she wouldn't collapse unconscious and fall backward down the staircase. Reaching the top, she acknowledged that the door Junne had blasted open the first day here had still not been repaired. Instead, Sabien led her into a large bathing chamber.

It was ornate, with a plush couch and vanity next to the door. A black suit was folded on the seat, no doubt belonging to Sabien. A large divider separated the entrance of the room from the bath. Hanging from the divider was a long red dress and a mask.

"Bathe and get dressed," Sabien said. "We're going to a masquerade."

Dagmara parted her lips to object, the absurdity of the statement knocking her off guard, but then she thought better of it. He was taking her to a masquerade—with other people? Outside of this manor?

"Where is this masquerade?" Dagmara asked.

"Do you have to push back on everything?"

"Unable to answer a single question of mine?"

Sabien exhaled sharply. "You'll find out when we get there."

This could be her escape. She had no energy left, and every muscle ached, but if this was her only chance, she would find a way.

"Some privacy, maybe?" she asked.

An eyebrow raised on his head. "There's a divider."

"You're joking."

"I'm not leaving you alone."

"Then have Junne come in."

"She left to get there early."

Dagmara was silent, waiting for him to exit.

He wouldn't budge, placing his hands on his hips. "I can remove the divider entirely if you like."

"No," Dagmara blurted out. She began to step behind it, but Sabien blocked her, forcing her to crash against his chest.

"If you need help, remember I'm only a few paces away." He smirked.

"You? Help?" Dagmara sputtered.

"I am very experienced at undressing—"

She shoved her hands against his chest, knocking him away. "Stay on this side of the divider."

A low laugh slipped from Sabien's lips. "We will see."

She didn't know what trap this was, but if there was any chance for her to attend this masquerade and disappear into the crowd, she had to try.

Yanking the dress from its hook, she disappeared behind the divider. She tentatively removed her clothing, all too aware of the light pouring in from the window and how her silhouette must have looked from the opposite side of the paper-thin divider. She heard Sabien as he removed his clothing and changed only a few feet away.

She didn't mind how cold the water was, for she was merely relieved to feel clean again. She took her fill, her throat parched as she drank the water without restraint before using it to wash herself. She had lost count of the days. How long had she been in the basement? She washed the blood from her fingernails, removing any evidence of her trying to get the nail out.

But he was finally giving her a chance. Maybe she didn't need to dig out the nail in the basement. Maybe all she had to do was to slip out unnoticed during this masquerade.

She went to put on the dress and realized how tiny it was. It would barely cover her chest. Were they attending a masquerade or going to a brothel?

"I'm not wearing this," Dagmara called.

Sabien answered, "You don't have a choice."

"This is not going to fit."

"Don't worry, it's bigger than it looks."

Dagmara scoffed, yanking the dress over her head. "I'm sure you tell that to every woman, don't you?"

There was a pause, and for once Sabien was silenced at her rebuttal. Then a low laugh escaped Sabien's lips. "I don't have to."

The dress hugged every inch of her body. However long she had been trapped, it had been long enough to lose weight. Her face was still swollen and covered in bruises, and she slipped on the mask. Nothing could hide her exhaustion, and the headache pulsing at the back of her eyes. Freedom was so close.

She stepped out from behind the divider.

Sabien was lounging on the chair, his feet propped up on the vanity. He held a large red cloak, lined with golden fur. He was now dressed in regal black attire, similar to his Ilusaurian uniform. The leather pants and matching jacket clung tightly to his rippled muscles, and his shirt dipped in a low-v, exposing his smooth and tan chest.

Scanning her entire appearance, Sabien let out a whistle. "Not bad now that the mask is covering your hideous bruises."

"If only I could thank the man who gave me those bruises."

"You can show your appreciation for me at any moment, Dagger."

"Do you have a mask to hide your hideous face?"

He smirked. "My face is anything but hideous, and I know you secretly agree." Then he withdrew a white mask, placing it over his entire face and concealing all his features. There was a painted black symbol on the forehead.

A shudder raced down Dagmara's spine. It was the symbol of the First Prince. It was the mask Sabien wore when he killed Aleksy. Her body turned to frost as her fear resurfaced. Her nausea intensified, and she caught herself against the wall before she could pass out.

"Your mask may hide your injuries, but your body is too easy for me to read." Sabien planted his boots on the ground and rose. "Take this," he said, tossing the red cloak to her. "To cover the rest of your failing body."

She barely caught the cloak before it hit the ground. Then she did as she was told.

She stayed alert at every moment, taking in her surroundings as they descended a steep hill. She was careful not to lose her footing and tumble down the mountainside. The air was frigid, and a light dusting of snow coated the earth. White trees rose from the ground on all sides. She wouldn't be able to outrun Sabien, not through a forest, and not while she had no energy left. Who was she kidding, she wouldn't be able to outrun a guardian even if she was perfectly healthy. But she could find a weapon. Or maybe there was a house in the distance.

Yet there was neither. It was better to wait and find help at the masquerade.

They rounded the cliffside, and the dirt under their shoes turned to sand. A large body of water came into view, disappearing into the fog as far as the eye could see. The pond's reflection was crystal clear, as if it was a perfect mirror for the clouds and pines that surrounded it. It wasn't completely frozen over, but was certainly close. A small boat waited for them.

She didn't smell salt, and the water was still. Her mind raced with all the information she had gathered so far—Junne was Celesta, they were near a fresh-water lake, and they were hidden in a mountainside.

It hit her like a stone to the chest. They were at Mirror's Edge, and they had to be close to the Sapphire Pass. Somewhere through the mountains, Ilusauri was on the other side.

"In," Sabien ordered, gesturing to the boat.

She fired him a glare before obeying, but stopped short. Through the treeline, she could barely make out a faint violet glow. Her eyes narrowed, watching in anticipation.

A massive paw with talons breached the shadows, stepping onto the sand. Iridescent scales slithered up the creature's leg, transforming to fur in order to cover its gaunt features. Drool dripped from oversized fangs.

The hound. It was the same dark hound she had seen in Nouchenne—one that wakes to guardian magic.

The hound met Dagmara's gaze, sending a chill through her entire body. It didn't feel like it was looking at her, but rather *through* her. Her chest tightened in response, but her curiosity about this creature washed away the initial fear.

Then the hound snapped its head to Sabien. Its ears flattened before it let out a loud howl.

"In!" Sabien yelled, grabbing Dagmara by the shoulder and throwing her down into the boat. It tipped with her weight against the sand.

The Ilusaurian Captain grabbed the edge of the boat and shoved it off the bank, his muscles pulling at the seams of his suit.

The hound started charging across the clearing, and more hounds began to pile out from the trees. What dark magic controlled them?

Sabien swung his legs over the side at the last minute, landing gracefully in front of Dagmara. He didn't sit, however. He remained standing, perfectly balanced. His eyes began to glisten, an icy blue hue dancing at the edge of his pupils. The water obeyed his command, bending to his will until the boat lurched forward and sailed across the lake moments before the hounds reached them.

Dagmara caught herself before falling, the boat tearing across the water and entering the mist.

"You were just going to stand there until they ate you?" Sabien snapped.

"I...don't know," Dagmara muttered. "Do you know what they are?"

"They belong to the First Prince."

Her eyes widened. The locks breaking...the rifts opening and spilling out creatures from their depths...the First Prince *was* rising.

"But they only wake when they sense magic?" Dagmara clarified.

"They are a part of the fifth branch of magic that is locked away with the First Prince. I'm assuming they're dormant without that magic released, but the little magic they absorb from nearby guardians awakens them."

"The fifth branch is the Void magic," Dagmara muttered. "What all does it do?"

Sabien laughed. "Oh no, I'm not here to answer all your questions. I've entertained them long enough."

As the boat raced through the frigid air, the cold wind seeped through her cloak, chilling her to the bone. Her nose began to run behind her mask, and she buried her hands in her pockets. She didn't utter a word, her mind racing. She was free. She was outside the manor—and yet she was trapped on a small boat with a guardian who commanded the water. There was nowhere for her to go.

Just when the sun disappeared behind the mountains, an island came into view. It appeared deserted, nothing but bare trees and a single snow-capped mountain. And the boat was heading straight toward it.

The original plan of escaping was becoming a more distant dream. She couldn't outrun a guardian, and she certainly couldn't out-swim a Life Guardian through a near-frozen lake. Was he planning on leaving her here on the island? Perhaps exile was better than death by his hand.

When the boat ran ashore, Dagmara was certain her limbs were frozen. She wanted to curl up in a warm bed and fall asleep forever.

Sabien seemed unaffected. He jumped out of the boat, landing on the sand, before yanking her out. Her head spun with a wave of dizziness at the quick change in position, but he didn't give her time to refocus. She was halfway up the beach when the blackness in her vision cleared, his grip on her hand as strong as steel. She was about to open her mouth to ask what they were doing, when he pulled her off the sand and onto sturdy ground.

As though they had crossed an invisible threshold, the world before her shifted. The snow-capped mountain transformed into a dazzling villa.

Made out of jet-black rocks, a villa protruded from the mountain side. It scaled two cliff ledges, and a single, glass balcony splayed dangerously over the lake. A series of gothic spires blended into the trees, as if they were part of the prickly pines. On top of the largest tower was a purple flag with an emblem that Dagmara had never seen before. Even without the illusion magic blocking it from sight, the formidable structure could have camouflaged perfectly into the stones.

"Well, Dagger, welcome to Viette's playground."

"Who's Viette?"

The grin on Sabien's face was sinister. "You're about to meet her."

CHAPTER 10
Magdalena

Magda was in her cabin, sitting on the edge of the bed. Strewn across the floor were the logbooks she had received from Ishani. Odie was helping her sort through the books, bringing her a new one from the floor each time she finished decoding the former. They were set to arrive in Celestaire by dawn, maybe earlier. They were close. She had to take this time to read as many logbooks as she could.

She had been pouring over each one, reading page after page in Azuremi, Ilusaurian, Flaustran, and Celesta. Ishani had gathered information from each one of the guild captains, who had also paid for information from other captains and traders they had met at sea. It seemed as if all corners of the earth had been searched for sources of magic, or whatever King Claude was looking for. There was not one inch of the kingdoms that hadn't been chartered or logged.

It didn't make any sense. Was there another place in their world that hadn't been explored?

Looking for my tomb? The voice was back.

The sudden words surprised Magda, and she attempted to swallow her fear. She had to understand more about The First Prince's magic and his assassins, and maybe, it would be useful in saving Dagmara. Maybe, it would be useful in understanding her own powers. She couldn't shut him out.

Maybe I am. Magda retorted.

It would be nice to see you in person. The First Prince said, his luscious voice hypnotizing her mind and intoxicating her being. The darkness threatened to consume her and yank her into the shadowy depths of the Void.

All of the sudden, Odie leapt up onto her body, barking furiously. He made her stumble, back onto the bed, before Odie jumped on top of her once more, circling her and licking her face.

"Odie, calm down!" she smiled, watching Odie leap off the bed and grab another journal between his teeth, before returning it and handing it to Magda.

Curiously, Magda took the item from Odie, opening the thickly bound journal. She realized that it was the journal that Laila, Ravi's sister, had gifted them, filled with hundreds of pages of notes describing rare diseases, concoctions, poisons, medicines, and antidotes. The amount and depth of the information contained was remarkable, as if Laila had researched every type of affliction from across the kingdoms. Somehow, she had pooled the most relevant information from every guild, from every trade route, even as far as the Mystic South. Only certain guilds dared to wander into the no-man's land, searching for artifacts among its ruins. How was it possible Laila had been willing to part with this wealth of information?

The Flaustran cursive was difficult to read, and when Magda stumbled upon an illness that reminded her of zowach, her heart lurched in her chest. Quickly, she sat up, running for the door with the journal in hand. "Stay," she told her pet, before she walked up to the deck.

Odie whimpered, pouting at the door and attempting to nuzzle his snout between the frame as she tried to close it.

"Stay," Magda repeated. "I'll be back soon."

It was dark outside on the deck, and stunning stars filled the black sky. They were far away from Flaustra and the lights of the city that polluted the sky. The cool breeze and lapping waves of the ocean calmed her senses, and somewhere, the soft sound of a violin rang from the upper deck.

Magda darted along, following the music, which matched the rhythm of the dark waves brushing calmly against the ship. Everything under the ocean was a complete mystery to her, but somehow deep down, she had the power to channel it all. Water could carve mountains, bring life, and sustain agriculture. Being a guardian was powerful enough, and suddenly she had more than one gift. She suspected she had all five, just like the First Prince. What did she do to deserve all that power? And how could she ensure she wouldn't abuse it?

Magda turned the corner, seeing Ravi on the upper deck, playing on a violin that he no doubt had found among the ship's many treasures. The light slurs of the waltz rang out as the bow slid across multiple strings at once, letting the harmonious chords echo in the air. His wondrous fingers spanned across the neck of the violin until they slid up toward the bridge, ending in one melancholy note.

Ravi turned, seeing Magda standing before him.

"That was beautiful," she beamed.

"Just trying to take in the peace out here while we can," said Ravi, referencing the stars above.

Magda looked up, remembering his small apartment in Flaustra and the skylight that opened to the heavens. Even though at that point her adventure had already begun, for some reason everything felt simpler then. She longed to go back to those moments, lying in Ravi's arms. She longed to feel his warmth against her as they held each other in the comfort of his home, free from constant attacks and the weight of the world on their shoulders.

Magda started, "The first night we met, you showed me the stars and told me that my brother and father were looking down on me. Maybe, in some way, your family is too."

"Yes." A twinge of sadness was placed in Ravi's voice. "But Flaustrans believe that the stars are reserved for the dead. So, for me, only my father is up there."

"You've never told me about him before," said Magda.

Ravi took a deep breath. "He died when I was twelve."

Magda waited to see if he would tell her more, and after a brief pause, Ravi continued, "He was also a musician. One day, there was a street fight over the money that was made after the show, and he was killed in the scuffle."

Magda reached her hand out, interlacing it with Ravi's. "That's horrible. I'm so sorry."

"It was a long time ago, and I have him to thank, for that's why I became a musician." Ravi gave her a warm smile. "Laila says I was the only sibling with any musical talent," he laughed, as his eyes drifted out to sea. "So I took my dad's violin to make money for the family. I guess I could have sold the instrument for coin, but I just couldn't part with it."

His demeanor shifted, and Magda moved closer to him. She said, "Your family will be safe. You have to believe that."

"I know."

"And I think your sister is a genius," Magda grinned, pulling out the journal for Ravi to see in her hands. "This is incredible. Do you think you could translate some of the technical medical terminology for me, so I can understand better? I'm so excited to get this back to our doctors and our advisors. Maybe, this could really help people. Maybe, we could actually have a chance at beating zowach. Maybe, my mother..."

Magda stopped, thinking of her mom. Her throat clenched as she was pummeled with an overcoming feeling of emptiness. She had deserted her mom when her mother was at her lowest point, grieving her husband and son. She had left her kingdom when they had needed her the most.

Ravi reached up to stroke her hair and read the expression behind her eyes. "You miss Azurem, don't you?"

Magda nodded. "It's so hard without my mom, Dagmara, and Teos. They mean everything to me, and so do you. I...I want you to meet them."

"I would love that," Ravi said sweetly.

"You'll see an entirely different side to me. There, I'm a princess, a guardian, and an heir to a throne. Sometimes, it's terrifying to think about," Magda admitted, not wanting to meet Ravi's gaze. "I don't know if I can live up to the expectations everyone has for me, but it's who I am, and at the end of the day, I have to accept it."

"I've already accepted it. Although the events over the past week seem so surreal. I can't believe suddenly you are a guardian, and now I'm traveling across the kingdom with three princesses!" He grinned. "It's not what I pictured exactly, but now that this is all happening, I couldn't envision anything different."

"What did you envision?" Magda prompted.

"I always saw myself as a musician, but those dreams were never specific to Flaustra. If Azurem is our best option, I am content with that."

Something struck Magda when listening to Ravi's words. It was one singular word. *Our.*

She set the journal down on the crate next to his violin, stepping closer. She asked, intentionally, "Tell me, is this because you have to leave Flaustra, or because you want to?" Magda asked, thinking back to his impending prison sentence once more.

"Because I want to," said Ravi. He placed his hand on her cheek, intertwining his fingers in the wisps of her silver hair. "And because I have hope in a future for us."

"Even if I might be married to someone else?"

"Well, I'm not really looking forward to punching the Mad King in the face," Ravi laughed, "but if you want me to, I'll do anything necessary in order to win your heart."

"You already have that," Magda smiled. It was the truth, but even so, her confidence wavered that it would ever be possible to make her own decision about who to marry.

Ravi leaned in, kissing her tenderly. She let the kiss consume her, allowing herself to feel safe for one moment. He continued pressing his lips to hers, while his one hand reached around to the back of her neck and the other slid along her lower back.

Magda let her hands drift up his chest, linking her arms around his neck as she pulled him fiercely against her. He responded to her movement and turned her against one of the masts, pushing his hips tightly into hers as he grabbed her face in his hands. She let his weight press against her, his warmth flooding through her body. He kissed her intensely, holding her firmly in place as his tongue tasted every inch of her mouth and her lips, ravenous for every part of her.

Magda hoisted one leg up around his hips, gripping onto him and pulling him even further into her chest. She wanted him closer, so that there was nothing between them and nothing stopping him from taking all of her.

His one hand moved down her neck and the front of her body, caressing around her figure. Then his hand looped around her thigh, yanking her in closer, and his fingers lingered underneath her, causing heat to rise in Magda's stomach. She wanted him to fill every ounce of her with desire, taunting her with each of his movements before allowing all of it to come crashing down in a passionate release. She didn't care that they were out on the deck. She wanted all of him here and now.

Her fingers swirled down to the bottom of his shirt and brushed against his belt, finding the soft touch of his skin underneath the fabric. His right hand mirrored hers, gripping the fabric at her waist.

Magda relaxed into his touch and threw her head back as his other hand gripped around the back of her neck. She allowed him to kiss every part of her sternum, pressing her deeper into the mast, so she could feel every inch of him taught against her.

Suddenly a distant shriek sounded from above. From her position, Magda opened her eyes and looked up, squinting in the darkness to make out figures moving in the crows nest.

"What's that?" she asked, referencing the movement.

Ravi looked up, but didn't stop touching her. "It looks like—"

The object was flying toward them. The two shrieked as a body fell from the sky. With a loud snap, one of Ishani's crew landed on the deck. The wooden boards snapped under his weight, the sound ringing through the dead of night.

Magda pulled away from Ravi. A gasp escaped her lips, and she covered her mouth, staring at the dead sailor. "He fell—"

"No," a female voice called from above. A figure was perched on the railing of the crow's nest. The silhouette jumped from the sky, landing on one of the yardarms, as effortless as a cat. "I pushed him."

A gust of wind blasted into the sails, overpowering the ship and causing it to accelerate. Suddenly, the previously still air was whipping at their bodies, and the mast wrenched to the side as the current forced the Starway to change course.

Ravi and Magda were thrown forward, ramming themselves into a heavy crate. Magda slipped from the sudden force, sliding across the deck on her stomach, but Ravi caught her forearm. The wind around them began to accelerate, beating against Magda's face. The ship was flying through the night, the sails flapping against the harsh wind.

Looking up, Magda saw the woman perched on the yardarm, unaffected by the wind. Even in the darkness, her bright red eyes were aglow.

Red. Magic.

This was a Spirit Guardian.

And if Guardian Sora was dead—this was an assassin from the First Prince.

CHAPTER 11
Dagmara

Dagmara and Sabien had arrived at the masquerade.

The entrance to Viette's villa was protected by a dozen guards. None of them moved to intercept Sabien and Dagmara. They glanced at the mask Sabien wore, then their interconnected hands, before returning as still as statues.

The large doors were propped open, inviting new guests to enter. The villa towered high in the air, making Dagmara feel small. Even the bridge to reach the front gate was longer than she had anticipated, and all her energy was drained by the time they crossed the threshold into Viette's fantasy.

The music was eloquent and hypnotic, casting an ethereal ambiance through the glistening room. The heavy air smelled of sweet incense and smoke. On the walls were neon murals, depicting sensual acts between abstract effigies. Depending on the angle from which you viewed them, the murals changed positions. Above, purple and red lights cast a puzzle of shapes on the floor.

There were at least a thousand people in the large space, plastered together. Dagmara could almost taste the sticky sweat in the air that lingered around the mass of bodies swaying mechanically to the music. It wasn't choreographed, and many lazily leaned on each other as though they were drunk. Everyone wore masks, their faces invisible to Dagmara. She had no idea who any of these people were, and she would never know if someone was hidden among the crowd.

"There's more than dancing," Sabien said, tightening his grip on her hand and pulling her into the mass. He led the way through the dancers. Some were dancing in couples, others were swaying to their own beat individually. They moved out of his way as he brushed past them, easily making space for him to lead Dagmara through. Despite there being so many people, they were all quiet, enjoying the music. It was unnerving to not hear a single whisper through the crowd. She had to be mistaken. Maybe the music was too loud, and she couldn't see them whispering behind their masks?

They broke through the border of the dancers and arrived at a large pit, barred by a waist-high barrier. Dagmara and Sabien peered down into the giant arena, alongside hundreds of others watching with intensity. Far below were warriors fighting off against a giant white beast. Dagmara vaguely recognized the beast from her children's books, some combination of a bear and a wolf native to Celestaire. Its fangs snapped wildly, decapitating one warrior instantly and throwing his body onto a pile of other human remains.

Large doors surrounded the arena, no doubt hosting more beasts. Who were these warriors? And what was the prize for winning this tournament?

Wincing, Dagmara shut her eyes, thankful that the mask covered her reaction. The rest of the crowd cheered. A thunderous roar rang through the grand space, cutting through the elegant music like a knife.

Sabien leaned closer. "Riveting, isn't it?"

"I prefer the dancing."

"Then let's dance. I'm sure Junne will find us on her own." Sabien grabbed Dagmara's hand once more, pulling her away from the edge of the barrier and back into the heat of the dancing bodies. He slid one hand around her lower back, yanking her toward him until her chest crashed against his.

Her breath hitched at his proximity. She could feel her stomach roil with unease, threatening to make her nauseous. He towered over her, and she glared up at him.

She wanted to rip the mask from Sabien's face. She wanted to find a sword and plunge it through Sabien's heart. He was the one who had killed Aleksy. He was behind everything, and yet he framed Claude, a man who was supposedly his friend. He wouldn't stop until he killed Magda. She could still feel the weight of his fists, the pain of his grip, and the terror of the truth serum. Who knew if he would make Magda's death swift.

The only way to stop Sabien was to kill him.

"Fantasizing about me?" Sabien asked, his baritone voice melodic.

"I'm fantasizing about killing you."

He leaned in closer. "I've never been more turned on."

Dagmara jerked back, but his grip on her was like steel, and he pressed her closer. Even through the thick fabric of the cloak she wore, she could feel his muscles against hers.

"What happened to the woman in the tavern? The seductive assassin?" he asked. "I miss her."

"You don't deserve her."

Staring into his mask made every inch of her body tense. Memories flashed through her thoughts, and she desperately fought to quell her fear.

"What about the woman in the library? If I remember correctly, you made the move on me."

The memory of her kiss with Sabien tasted like acid. "I did what I had to for my mission—a mission to protect the people I love." Keeping her voice even was harder than she wanted it to be. She prayed he couldn't feel her whole body begin to shake.

"The boy from the letters—Teos? Or Magdalena? I don't see any of the people you claim to protect coming to rescue you."

"Magda is smart to stay far away. I don't want her near you."

"You're so loyal, and to what end?"

"Says the man who backstabbed his own best friend with no hesitation."

"I never backstabbed Claude," said Sabien. "He was a good friend, offering me a role as the captain, being there when I needed him. But then the First Prince was able to offer me even more. That is all there is to it."

"What happens when you break all the locks and the First Prince is free?" Dagmara ventured.

"The world will change for the better," Sabien said. "The First Prince is the true Master Guardian. He is more powerful than us all." His eyes glistened through the slits in his mask. "He will place us on the thrones beside him and create new guardian lineages for the next millennia. My blood will be bound to the land, and for centuries to come, my sons will be Life Guardians, thanks to the First Prince. And the majestic world that was locked away with him will finally resurface."

"The Void," Dagmara echoed.

"The barrier between worlds is already cracking. The Void world is becoming stronger with each lock that is broken."

Cracking...the rifts...where the hounds were escaping.

"If he can make other guardians, who's to say he can't make another Life Guardian and replace you?"

"He can only make one guardian per branch. Unless I'm dead, he can't make another Life Guardian."

She knew Sabien was spilling more information than he should.

"But there were other assassins at the coronation."

"I enlisted them myself. They didn't have magic and weren't from the First Prince. They wouldn't be dead if they were guardians."

"If only you were the assassin I killed," Dagmara muttered.

He leaned in closer, pulling her tighter against his chest. His mask brushed the top of her ear, his voice a whisper. "Hear the bloodlust in your voice? You would be a perfect asset to the First Prince. Magdalena's no friend of yours. She threw you to the wolves, so let's go take her down together. I love seeing you wield a blade."

A chill raced down her spine. She raised herself on her toes, returning the whisper to his ear. "The next blade I wield will be driven through your heart."

"You tried that already." He shifted his lips from her ear, his face moving in front of hers. He was inches away, and the only thing separating them were the two masks. His hand laced tighter around her lower back, his fingers digging into her. "If you're going to try to kill me, you'll have to be more clever. I don't easily let my guard down."

"You did once."

"In the library? No, I knew you were stealing the keys the whole time," he replied. Then he shifted his hands to her face, removing her mask. The cool air flushed her cheeks. "But feel free to try and distract me with your lips again." He leaned in closer, the mask hiding his face. The symbol of the First Prince was still painted on the front, a clear indicator of his allegiance.

Shifting toward him, Dagmara lifted her hands to his face. She gripped his mask under her trembling fingers before raising it off his face. His features came into view, his eyes fixated on her, and his lips slightly parted. She waited for him to lean in, closing the remaining distance between them before she whispered, "I'd rather die."

Sabien shoved her back, and she slammed against the nearest dancing couple. He chucked her mask to the side, recorrecting his own on his face.

"Stay here," Sabien ordered. "I'll go find Viette."

"I would start looking by the gaudy dais," Dagmara snapped.

Sabien scoffed before disappearing into the thick of the crowd.

Now that her mask was off, it was no doubt everyone in the room could see her ruined face. Reaching to the nearest woman, she gripped the stranger's hand tightly. "Please, you must help me," she whispered under her breath.

The woman continued to sway, unfazed by Dagmara's grip on her wrist. In fact, her head didn't even turn in Dagmara's direction.

Reaching out, Dagmara gripped the edge of the woman's mask and yanked it free. The ribbon tie easily came undone, and the mask slipped from the woman's face.

The woman's eyes were silver, and a haze covered her expression as though she wasn't present at all. The silver in her eyes—the distant stare...

She was under compulsion.

The masquerade suddenly made sense. They all wore masks to hide the fact that they had been compelled. They were doomed to complete the task assigned to them when they had first been compelled—or else they would never be free.

No one here would help her.

Stumbling back, Dagmara tried to retreat. She had to escape. She shoved her way through the crowd, elbowing dancers on either side. The exit was in sight. It was so close.

Breaking out of the turmoil, she raced for the doors. The guards may be compelled, but maybe they would let her through. They hadn't stopped her when she had arrived.

She nearly reached the exit when she slammed into a large chest. It was muscular and strong as stone.

"Going somewhere?" Sabien asked, smirking down at her. "You failed my test. I told you to stay put."

Without hesitation, Dagmara retraced her steps, disappearing into the dancers once more. She jostled through the bodies, tripping over people's feet as she desperately tried to find another way out. A window? Maybe the doorways in the fighting ring? She couldn't risk jumping down there into the brawl.

Before her thoughts scrambled into a plan, the hypnotic music screeched to a halt. Everyone in the room froze.

Panting, Dagmara skidded to a stop as well, trying to blend in. She could hear the rapid beating and the pounding of her heart. For holding so many people, it was astonishing how *quiet* the enormous room had become.

Then, as though all of them were instructed by a single command, unheard by Dagmara, every person in the room shifted their attention to her. Their gazes were chilling, as though a thousand ghosts were peering into her soul.

Frozen fingers laced around her wrist.

Jerking back, Dagmara screamed. Instantaneously, all of the guests started reaching for her, grabbing the fur of her cloak or tracing their fingers through her hair. She fought back, staggering away from their outstretched hands and knocking against others who stood completely still. It was as if they were guiding her—pushing and prodding her toward—

The bodies against Dagmara's back stepped aside, and she fell into empty space. Her tailbone slammed onto the marble, and she scrambled back on the ground, separating herself from the crowd, still feeling their frozen fingers against every inch of her body. Yet the compelled people remained where they were, as though they were standing before a barrier that was invisible to Dagmara's eyes.

"That's her." Dagmara would recognize Sabien's suave voice blind.

"Yes, I'm aware the only uncompelled girl in this room is *her*, Sabien, but thank you for your immaculate introduction."

Dagmara's eyes widened. Whirling around, she faced the voice.

Sabien was standing directly before Dagmara, hovering over her position on the ground. Beyond Sabien, was a throne, gilded in gold. Five scepters each holding a colored gemstone protruded from the back of the throne, and the lights created a prism effect that shone on the individual sitting in the regal chair.

Sitting on top of the throne was the most beautiful woman Dagmara had seen in her life. Her age was indiscernible, her skin was nearly glowing, and her red hair was twisted up into a golden crown. She held a golden goblet, filled to the brim with red wine, and she peered down at Dagmara as though she were an insect—merely an inconvenience.

The woman swirled her wine, not even bothering to make eye contact. "Welcome," she said, her voice laced with boredom. Then her gaze met Dagmara's, and the silver in her irises was unmistakable.

This was Viette.

And there was no doubt that Viette was a Mind Guardian.

CHAPTER 12
Magdalena

Ravi and Magda stood face to face with the assassin—a Spirit Guardian.

The door on the lower deck burst open, Ishani and Kiran flooding out into the night air in response to the commotion.

The assassin in the sky saw the threat, whipping her head in their direction.

"Get down!" Magda screamed over the billowing wind.

The ship was once again thrust in another direction, and Magda slammed against Ravi's chest. The ship erupted into chaos, sailors running from the magic, while others raced to lower the sails.

Below, both princesses struggled against the shifting air currents, reaching out for anything to steady them. Then Ishani withdrew her axes, bracing herself for the enemy.

Magda needed a weapon, and she needed it fast.

There was a soft thud, a brush of wind. Magda steadied herself against Ravi, regaining her own footing as she saw the assassin land directly in front of them.

"A Flaustran ship with an Azuremi girl," the assassin spoke, and her voice carried above the air. "What are the odds I caught sight of your flag? It must be fate." She was speaking Ilusaurian, but had a bright Celesta accent. She wore a beautiful red cloak, her black hair fluttering in the wind behind her. She also wore a polished white mask, painted with the symbol of the First Prince.

The same mask of the assassins that killed Magda's father and brother.

The woman continued, "You look just like he described. What are the chances you came to us?"

"Who are you?" Magda demanded, hearing her voice shake.

"Guess."

"Answer me," said Magda.

She let out an exasperated sigh. "My name is Junne. Not that it matters."

A weapon. Magda needed a weapon. She could hear her heart pounding against her chest as her mind raced with what she could control with her magic.

Suddenly, footsteps pounded behind them, and Ishani and Kiran ran up behind Ravi and Magda.

"Get off our ship," Ishani said forcefully.

Junne slowly tilted her head at Ishani's words, unable to understand Flaustran. "Let's just say...I'm friends with Dagmara."

The world tilted on its axis. Magda stepped closer. "Where is she?!"

The woman laughed. "I can't wait to tell him that I'm the one who killed you."

Magda's blood turned to ice. The woman raised her hand forward toward Magda.

"Move!" Kiran yelled, shoving Magda to the side.

The blow that was intended for Magda hit Kiran. A huge gust of wind collided against her chest, and she went flying backward, her feet off the ground. The wind propelled her into the rail, and she flew over the edge into the darkness.

"No!" Ishani screamed.

An axe flew through the air, the glint of silver catching both

Magda and Junne's eye at the same time. Moments before it struck Junne, a slight shift of the air around her caused it to go off course. Ravi leapt out of the way, spinning behind one of the crates and scrambling to pick up Ishani's axe.

Ishani and her men would fight Junne. Magda needed to save Kiran.

Racing to the edge of the boat, Magda peered down to the sea below, but could only see darkness. The ocean was churning in the wind, beating against the ship hull in ferocious waves. Kiran would never survive.

But Magda controlled the water.

There was a small movement, beyond the ship, already waves away. If the ship continued in this violent wind, it would only be a few more moments until Kiran disappeared into the darkness and would never be found.

Tearing off her jacket, Magda hoisted herself up on the rail, fighting the beating wind, and launched herself into the ocean. The air pounded against her as she descended, falling to meet the sea below.

The weight of the water pummeled against her, nearly knocking the wind from her as she landed with a loud splash. The current was strong, threatening to pull her under the ship hull, and she thrashed her arms and legs out, fighting.

The surface. She had to find the surface.

As if the water could hear her thoughts, it guided her in the correct direction. Her head burst from the water, and she gasped for air. The salt clouded her senses, burning her eyes. The dot she once saw had already disappeared.

"Kiran!" she screamed, choking as salt water flooded her mouth. "Kiran!"

She couldn't lose her, not when the fate of the world depended on Kiran staying alive. She had taken the blow for Magda without a second thought, protecting her without thinking of the consequences.

The current shifted direction, Magda's fight against the water easing. She was drawn out further into the darkness, until a small thrashing figure came into view, barely visible in the darkness.

"Kiran!" she screamed once more, her breath nearly leaving her.

The water answered her, shifting and bending to her will. It drew Kiran back toward the ship, back toward her.

Kiran slammed into her, gasping, "Magda!"

She grabbed her tightly, barely able to make out her face, her legs kicking forcefully to stay afloat. "I have you!"

Kiran struggled to stay above water, the salt colliding against her face. She choked for air, the energy draining from her body as she fought to tread against the ocean waves. "But the ship!"

Looking over her shoulder, Magda understood her fear. The ship was flying away, farther than Magda imagined. The glistening lights along the ship were like a beacon, urging Magda to return.

"Hold onto me," Magda ordered. "Don't let go."

Kiran obeyed, but her thrashing legs underwater collided with her own.

Bring me back. She commanded, praying the founding guardians would guide her.

Praying Aleksy would guide her.

She didn't know what she was doing. She didn't know how to command the entire sea. But maybe as a Life Guardian, the ocean could detect her desires. It wouldn't kill her.

It would obey her.

A wave collided against her back, rising her and Kiran into the current. The ocean swept her in the direction of the ship, and she gasped, her thoughts urging it forward.

Bring me back. Bring me back.

She held fiercely to Kiran, her arms around the younger princess, and gripped her shirt as though she would slip from her hands once more. Kiran clung as firmly to her.

The ship grew as they advanced forward, the light brightening. The wave began to crescendo, raising higher and higher into the air. It was bringing them to the deck, the sea churning as the wave reached ten feet tall—twenty feet tall—

It would capsize the ship.

Enough, enough!

The wave collided with the Starway, careening it to the side. A joint scream rang from the sailors. Magda's shoes caught the rail, and she tumbled forward, losing Kiran in the impact. Her body slammed against the deck, pain ricocheting through her shoulder. A crate snapped beside her, and Kiran's body thrust into the wood. She heard Kiran gasp for breath, coughing—which meant she was alive.

The ship rocked back in the other direction, leveling out. Scrambling to her feet, Magda searched the deck. Ravi was grasping onto the mainsail, with a death grip on the wood. Ishani was sliding across the surface, gripping a thick rope, and red blood was dripping from her face. The ocean wave had drenched everyone on board.

A few feet away was the red cloak. Junne was sprawled on the ground, coughing as she pulled herself to her knees. She ripped the mask from her own face, gasping and choking on sea water.

Reaching out to the water that coated the deck, Magda summoned it to her.

The water congealed into an ice shard, a pointed blade at one end. Magda gripped it in her palm, starting for Junne in long strides.

"How do you know Dagmara?" Magda yelled. The wind and the waves were now fighting against one another.

Junne looked up, her eyes wide, glistening with red.

Thrusting the ice shard forward, Magda aimed for a nonlethal blow.

But the wind knocked into Magda's hand, the force enough to teeter her off balance.

In the same moment, Junne scrambled to her feet, the wind whipping around her in a small tornado. She tried to take flight but fumbled. Her winter cloak was soaked, weighing her to the ground. Junne glanced over her shoulder at Magda as she ripped her coat off, freeing herself from the additional burden. Then Junne utilized a crate to launch herself in the air. Magda watched as she flew into the dark sky, until she disappeared into the night.

Kiran raced up beside Magda, staring up into the night. "A Spirit assassin. Are they all teaming up to come after us now?"

"I don't know," Magda admitted, "but she mentioned Dagmara."

Whirling over her shoulder, Magda searched for Ishani and Ravi. Ishani was barking orders to the sailors, encouraging them that the danger had passed. Ravi limped over to the two, holding his ribcage in pain.

"Are you alright?" Magda yelled, rushing to his side. There was blood racing down his temple. She reached up to touch his face, but he caught her hand.

"I'm fine," he assured her. Placing her hand in his, he yanked her toward him. She collided with his chest, drenched from the ocean water and smelling of salt. He pressed a kiss to her forehead before tightening his grip around her body.

Softening into his embrace, Magda let out a deep breath. She closed her eyes, burying her face against his chest and holding him close.

"Magda, you saved my life," Kiran chimed. "Thank you."

Magda rushed the younger princess and embraced her in a hug.

Another body collided with theirs, and Ishani smashed into the hug, gripping the two girls in her arms. Her hair was plastered to the side of her face, water dripping from her clothes. She held one axe, blood dripping from a wound on her cheek.

"Don't do that to me again!" Ishani yelled. "Don't run into danger."

Kiran pulled away. "You can't keep me in a bubble forever. I'm one of the last guardians with magic. I'm one of the only people that can fight off these assassins."

"Then work on your magic," said Ishani. "Both of you," Ishani snapped at Magda and Kiran. "It was two against one, and both powers together should have trumped that of a Spirit Guardian."

The words were biting, but Magda knew Ishani was right. Both she and Kiran had almost died. And, Magda had nearly capsized the ship with her Life magic. She had to be careful—but at the same time, she hadn't felt more alive. The water rejuvenated her, ignited all her senses. For the first time with her magic, it hadn't drained her, but made her feel more powerful. After all this time learning the Soul magic, it was the Life magic that came more naturally. This was what she was supposed to be—just like her brother and father.

"I will work on it," Magda promised.

"Me too," said Kiran bashfully.

"That girl was sent by the First Prince," Ravi announced. He held the red cape over his forearm and the mask that Junne had discarded.

"A Spirit assassin..." Ishani muttered.

"And she knew Dagmara," Magda echoed. "Which means she might be able to lead us to her."

Kiran ran her hands along the edge of the fabric, picking a thorny bramble out of the thick cloth. "This plant...," she mused.

"It's native to Celestaire," Ishani finished her sentence.

"Not just anywhere. It thrives in a cold, mountainous climate, but it also needs ample water," said Kiran.

"You know all of this from a plant?" Ravi asked, skeptical.

Kiran giggled as she said, "Are you forgetting we're all Guardians of the Soul? I know a thing or two about botany."

Ravi nodded sheepishly. "Good point."

"My best guess is the Sapphire Pass," Kiran announced. "It's close enough to Mirror's Edge for water but would be the coldest region in Celestaire at this time."

"Maybe she traveled through that area," said Ishani. "One piece of a plant means nothing."

"She can fly," Magda said. "She wouldn't have been trekking through the mountains unless she had a specific reason to be on the ground."

"Alright," Ishani announced. "Then Kiran and I will do our best to avoid the mountains on our way to the safe house."

"And I will go straight there," Magda nodded. "Ravi—are you going to the safe house with them?"

A soft smile creased Ravi's face. "You should know by now I'm going wherever you go."

Her heart skipped a beat, and Magda tried to suppress her own butterflies, but knew her face was turning bright red.

Then Kiran piped up. "We can't be too far from land, right? I'm not familiar with Spirit magic, but Junne probably can't fly too far into the ocean."

"We're closer than you think," Ishani replied. Then she nodded off to the horizon.

Following her gaze, Magda peered into the dark distance. A small flicker of light lit up the expanse, growing closer with each passing moment. A town was glimmering in the distance on the horizon.

Celestaire was in sight.

"Hold on, Dagmara," Magda said under her breath. "I'm coming."

You will be too late to save your friend, Dear Princess. Eligor was back in her head.

His voice startled her, and suddenly she boiled over in anger. If Eligor was in control of his assassins, including Sabien, it was likely he knew where Dagmara was being held.

What do you know about my friend?! Magda yelled. *Where is she?*

A low, chilling laugh filled the Void. *If you want to save her before her time runs out, then you will need to listen to my directions carefully.*

Why should I trust that you will lead me to her? asked Magda.

Have I lied to you before?

Magda shuddered, knowing that Eligor's assassins wanted to kill guardians like herself. But she had no choice. While she had guessed Dagmara was in the Sapphire Pass, they had no other leads. She could refuse Eligor's help and instructions and not make it to Dagmara in time. Or, she could accept Eligor's help, gambling her own life, but maybe she would have a better chance to find Dagmara, and then they could all escape together.

Dagmara had risked her life for Magda, and it was time Magda returned the favor.

Interested in my offer? Eligor asked.

Magda took a deep breath. *Lead me to her.*

CHAPTER 13
Dagmara

The sheer terror of meeting a Mind Guardian's gaze had been long forgotten until that very moment.

Immediately Dagmara squeezed her eyes shut and lowered her head, making certain this woman couldn't weasel her way inside her brain.

Viette exhaled, staring at Dagmara in silence, but Dagmara refused to move. She wouldn't look up.

Then Viette cleared her throat abruptly, pitching her voice lower. "Why is she here, Sabien?"

"She's here because she's hiding something."

"I see by her face you couldn't get it out of her," Viette muttered. "Did you try truth serum?"

"She fought it."

"Interesting." The Mind Guardian hesitated, no doubt examining every inch of Dagmara. "Take off that ridiculous mask, Sabien, I can't stand the sight of them. Where's the other one of you?"

"Don't act like you don't know her name," said Sabien. By the sound of it, he was removing his mask, but Dagmara fixed her attention on the ground in front of her, not taking any chances by looking up. "Junne was supposed to meet me here," Sabien finished.

"Hmm, no...no Spirit Guardian in skimpy attire has been seen here. Now, who is this woman and why should I care?" asked Viette.

"She swapped places with Princess Magdalena in a marriage to King Claude. Magdalena is the last Life Guardian alive and Dagmara," he paused to point at her, "is hiding where she is located."

"King Claude," Viette mused. She took a leisure sip of her wine. "How is the other Mind Guardian? Still half blind?"

Dagmara's heart nearly stopped.

"He was so brave for a young boy," she continued.

"It was you!" Dagmara snapped her head up.

"Stay on the ground. Eyes on me."

Viette's voice was barely audible, but her eyes twinkled with iridescent silver. Her words sifted through the air, meeting Dagmara's ears and flooding her senses. Her thoughts paused—every urge, every hesitation—vanished for a brief moment.

Then it returned with an onslaught, all of Dagmara's emotions slamming against her mind in one blow.

Shuddering, Dagmara blinked, clearing the thoughts before meeting Viette's silver gaze once more.

Viette cocked her head, peering at Dagmara. Then she crossed her legs leisurely, leaning back on the throne and swirling her wine. "I can take away your pain, girl." Her eyes sparkled with silver. "It only takes a few words."

"No," Dagmara said.

"Who do you think the rest of these people are?" Viette used her wine goblet to gesture at the crowd. "They asked me to relieve them of their pain, so I did."

"They're not even people anymore," Dagmara argued. "They're shells of human beings. Let them go."

"I have no intention of letting them go. They chose this knowing the consequences—well, most of them," Viette replied. "Besides, I'm bored, and they're my source of entertainment."

"We don't have time for this," Sabien growled.

"And they are in no pain," Viette replied to Dagmara as though Sabien hadn't spoken. "I could do the same for you. I could relieve your pain, strip your worst memories. I could make you forget the Mad King entirely."

"No!" Dagmara blurted out, dropping her gaze to the ground to hide her eyes from Viette. She couldn't let Viette take her memories of Claude.

"Can you stop playing with her and ask what she's hiding about Magdalena?" Sabien growled.

"Sabien, your voice hurts my ears," Viette said, unenthused, "so shut up before I make you leave."

"How unfortunate you can't compel another guardian," he said, sarcasm in every word.

"I don't need to," she countered. "By the time you can summon an ounce of water from Mirror's Edge, I will have you on your ass. Someone get me more wine!" Viette announced, holding her goblet out. A masked soldier approached, taking the wine glass from Viette before disappearing once more. "You, imbecile, brought her to me, so she's mine now," Viette stated.

Sabien stepped forward. "This isn't ludicrous. She has information. Now get it out of her. Or are you not as helpful as I thought you would be?" He crossed his arms, raising an eyebrow at her.

Viette rose from the throne in one fluid motion. Her dress fluttered around her stunning figure, hugging every curve. "You're the one that hasn't done your job," she snapped. "I broke the Mind lock eight years ago. Every other assassin has been a disgrace, including you. Eligor and I are not pleased."

Eligor...was he the First Prince? This Mind Guardian knew him by name?

"But what I don't understand is why you still care about Princess Magdalena," Viette said. She glowered at Sabien. "Because the Life lock is already broken."

"That's impossible." Sabien scoffed. "Magdalena is a Life

Guardian. I saw her coronation."

Viette brushed her hair behind her shoulder. "I'm simply stating facts. Only the Soul lock remains."

"So..." Sabien mused. "Magdalena is already dead, and I didn't even get to do it?"

A sickening feeling crept through Dagmara's stomach, and her heart began to pound against her ribcage. Magda wasn't dead, she knew that deep in her soul. However, she also knew that Magda didn't have Life magic. She had Soul magic. It was the secret she had been dying to keep hidden. But, if Magda had Soul magic, it would make sense that the Life lock broke when Bogdan and Aleksy died.

"I don't know, and frankly, I don't care," Viette said, her words crisp. "All that matters is the remaining Soul Guardian, and then Eligor is free."

"I don't believe it," Sabien objected. "Can you do what I came here for and ask Dagmara what she knows?"

Viette jolted her attention back to Dagmara. Then she stepped down from the throne, standing directly in front of Dagmara. "Look at me, girl."

Eyes on me.

She was supposed to be watching Viette. Dagmara looked up and met Viette's gaze.

"Dagmara," Viette began, her eyes shimmering. She kneeled before Dagmara, meeting her at eye level. Reaching out a hand, she touched the bruise on Dagmara's cheek tenderly. Her fingers were soft, but Dagmara jerked back regardless.

Frowning, Viette withdrew her hand and rose once more. Her gaze was mesmerizing, captivating, and all-consuming. *"Tell me, and spare no detail, what secret about Princess Magdalena are you keeping from Sabien?"*

The compulsion washed over Dagmara like a wave, stripping her of emotions for a brief moment before her emotions returned in full. She thought compulsion would be like truth serum, forcing the words out of her before she had time to think, but it was as though she had all the time in the world. She had been warned by her mother that if you were compelled, you had to complete the task to be set free.

She had to think of something. Maybe it was time to finally tell the truth—seeing as Sabien now knew that the Life lock was unlocked. She could either run with the idea that Magdalena was dead, but then they would kill her here and now, not needing her for bait. She would have a better chance at survival if she told them the truth. Maybe then they would still need her for more information at least. She didn't know how compulsion worked, and maybe the truth would set her free.

"Magda isn't a Life Guardian. She has Soul magic," Dagmara announced. "Prince Aleksy harnessed the magic behind her coronation ceremony. It was all a facade."

Silence followed. The thousands of people in the room ceased to exist. The two guardians and Dagmara were the only people who mattered—all of them waiting for Dagmara to say more, but she refrained.

Viette's wrinkle-free face creased as her brows raised. Her eyes widened a fraction of an inch before she grinned, like a predator who had caught their prey. "Well this is the most interesting information I've had the privilege of receiving in years."

"That's impossible," Sabien argued. "Ask her again."

"Careful, boy," Viette warned, "it almost sounds like you're doubting my magic."

"How can she have Soul magic?" Sabien raked his hand through his hair. "And how do you know the Life lock is broken? The First Prince wouldn't tell you and not me. Maybe you're the only one lying."

"Don't turn this on me," Viette scolded. "It is clear by the Void slipping out of the tomb. There are rifts in Ilusauri, Azurem, and Celestaire. You've just been too hyper fixated on this princess to observe the facts."

"But how can an Azuremi princess have Flaustran magic?" Sabien insisted.

"It doesn't matter. We shouldn't waste our time with that kingdom or its Azuremi princess longer than we have to. Remember what happened when the previous Life Guardian wasted his time taking out their last assassin?" Viette stated.

Assassin? Did she mean—

Dagmara scrambled to her feet. "What do you know about the last Azuremi assassin?" Viette knew the Life Guardian that was sent to torture and kill her mother. It had to be.

Viette held up her hand. "*Quiet*." She ordered, her eyes shimmering silver. They narrowed slightly, scanning Dagmara down to her feet, then back up to her face. Her lips thinned as she inclined her head, watching.

Dagmara silenced herself, but she wasn't finished. Viette knew more.

"Even if this is true...Princess Magdalena has Soul magic...then I'm not giving up on finding and killing her," Sabien confirmed. "Wouldn't she need to die for the Soul lock to break?"

"How should I know?"

Sabien shook his head. "This feels wrong."

Dagmara wanted to interject into the conversation. She wanted to know more about the Life Guardian that killed her own mom, but remembered Viette's instruction to be quiet. She didn't feel obligated to remain silent, but didn't know how the compulsion worked, and wanted to avoid any pain similar to the truth serum.

Viette was backing away, returning to her throne. Her attention drifted away, her silver eyes scanning her surroundings. Then she announced, "Incoming."

As she had predicted, a new guest entered the building. The wind swirled as Junne flew inside. She hurled herself toward the platform at the dais before landing in an uncoordinated roll. She remained on one knee, panting and gasping for air. Her entire body was drenched, her hair plastered to her cheeks as though it had frozen on her flight here.

"Where have you been?" Sabien scoffed.

"Clearly she stopped for a swim in Mirror's Edge." Viette rolled her eyes before plopping back on the throne. "Where is my wine!"

"No—" Junne gasped, then choked, before catching her breath. "I made a detour and saw a Flaustran ship on the horizon. I went over to investigate, and you'll never believe what I discovered."

"What?" Sabien prodded.

"Guess."

"I don't have time for games," Viette interjected. "So tell us or leave."

"There was a girl with Life magic," Junne announced.

Shock rattled through Dagmara's body. Another assassin?

Sabien shifting closer. "Are you sure?"

"Am I sure a magical wave and ice shards almost killed me? Yes, Sabien, I am, thank you." Having caught her breath, Junne rose, straightening her posture. "And the woman that controlled the magic was an Azuremi girl with *silver* hair."

The air chilled, and a pit formed in Dagmara's stomach.

Magda?

She was on her way here? Her blood pulsed with hope before it met a tragic end.

But no—it couldn't be. Magda didn't have Life magic. Silver hair was rare, yes, but it wasn't impossible that there was another Azuremi girl out there that looked similar to Magda.

"Did you hear me?" Junne blurted out. "Princess Magdalena is coming for this stupid girl. She's walking right into our trap!"

Sabien's eyes narrowed. He fired a glance at Viette.

"Your compulsion didn't work."

"It did," Viette bit back.

"What compulsion?" Junne asked.

"Dagmara said Magda has Soul magic," Sabien replied before

glowering at Dagmara. "Did you lie about Magda's magic?"

"No!" Dagmara blurted out. "I told you I—"

Viette slammed her palm on the arm of her throne. "Quiet!"

The room went still.

The Mind Guardian's eyes twisted in color, a vibrant shade of silver filling her irises. "*I told you to be quiet,*" she said, her focus directed at Dagmara.

Once more, Dagmara felt the words brand against her mind. The compulsion stripped away her ability to speak for a brief moment before releasing her. Dagmara kept her mouth shut.

"The Life lock is broken," Sabien filled the silence. "It couldn't have been…"

"I'm telling you what I saw," Junne retorted.

"If it isn't Magdalena, I want whoever it is dead anyway," said Sabien. "I have to be the only Life Guardian left standing when the First Prince rises."

"I'm sure he will know who she is—at least he can tell us if he gifted magic to another assassin," Junne stated. "We should speak with him."

"You can't summon him," Sabien argued. "He finds you."

"Then I'll go to him," said Junne.

Sabien laughed.

Go to him? Dagmara's mind whirled. Meaning where he was locked away? Was it a physical location?

"I can fly there," Junne announced.

"Then what?" Sabien asked. "If anyone is going to him, I will. The water will obey me."

"No," Viette blurted out, intervening in the conversation once more. "No one is going to him. You two may be able to get there, but only I can get out," she said. Her fingernails dug into the arms of her throne. "I will speak with him," she announced. "Eligor will answer when I call. We've been together for nearly a decade. I will find both of you after I speak to Eligor."

"Both of us?" Sabien objected. "This princess is *my* target."

"You're wrong," Viette replied. "This princess may be all of our problems. Mine included."

Sabien shifted closer. "Is there something you aren't telling us?"

"Get out," Viette said, ignoring his question. "And don't lay a hand on this girl until we speak to the First Prince." She jerked her head in Dagmara's direction.

"You can't tell me what to do," Sabien objected.

"Yes, I can," Viette snapped. "We may need her."

Junne let out a sharp exhale. "I'm not going to sit around and wait for you to speak to the First Prince." The wind around her began to spin violently until she began to levitate. Her eyes glowed red. "If Magdalena and Kiran are truly the only two left, then we kill them. I'm done wasting time waiting for Magdalena to find this girl," she shot a deadly stare at Dagmara, "and I will not wait nearly a decade like you, Viette."

"You know nothing. Being impatient will get you killed," Viette stated. "A Spirit Guardian can't take out a Soul Guardian let alone... this Magdalena girl." Viette swallowed, and her throat bobbed.

Junne let out a sharp laugh. "Watch me." Then she flew away, vanishing.

Viette snapped her head in Sabien's direction. "Do you need anything else?"

He shook his head. "You can release her."

Viette met Dagmara's gaze. "*You're free.*"

For some reason, she didn't feel free. Nothing that transpired made any sense. Magda didn't have Life magic—that was the entire reason Aleksy orchestrated the coronation. But then...who was on that ship?

Sabien grabbed her by the arm and yanked her toward the exit. "Come on," he said. "Looks like we need to prepare a welcome party for the princess." He glanced over at Dagmara, and his lips creased into a grin. "And once I kill her, I can finally kill you too."

CHAPTER 14
Magdalena

Princess, your time is running thin. Come save your friend, and come meet my assassins. Eligor was back, his voice taunting.

Why are you doing this? Magda asked. As if she had opened an invitation, she was suddenly transported, her entire mind shifting and the world around her darkening.

They were once again together in the Void space. Magda watched him, curiously, with his glowing crown and flowing cape, trying to read the thoughts behind his mind, as he could often read hers. But he was a complete mystery to her, with his boyish face and blonde hair, a young man seemingly trapped in a cage for hundreds of years.

Eligor stood before her, and his head tilted, as if he was considering telling her the truth or not. He let out a chuckle, throwing his hair back. *So many questions.*

She repeated herself. *Why are you creating assassins? How do you create them?* The knowledge that she would gain by letting him in was worth every risk. She was running out of time to find out more about his powers and save Dagmara.

He stepped toward her, his smile tantalizing. *Does it bother you that we both are Master Guardians, but I know so much more? That I see everything that you see, that I lurk in your mind and penetrate your deepest thoughts?*

He raised his hand, letting a wisp of Soul magic channel through his fingers. The yellow color pierced his eyes, and a wisp of yellow magic stirred around his crown. Immediately after, a strand of violet light sparked from his palm, and his eyes turned deep purple. Like clockwork, the yellow color dancing around his crown turned violet as he played with the Void magic. As he did so, Magda watched the magical crown with curiosity.

A Master Guardian. A person with the power to control all magic. It was true...and he had just confirmed it...she was just like him. The thought made her shiver inside, but also filled her with intrigue. Why were they the same?

You offered me answers. Magda said firmly.

A wicked smile curled on his lips. *That is true. I am a man of my word, and enjoy our little...*he paused as his eyes roamed around her lips before flicking across her entire figure...*conversations.* He finished. *I guess I will have to entertain your questions.*

Magda sucked in a ragged breath and blurted out her first question before he could change his mind. *Being a Master Guardian... what does that mean?* She dared to ask.

Once in a millennia, a Master Guardian is born. Master Guardians can reset the magic, ensuring that there are guardians until the end of time. Master Guardians are a way to ensure our world always works, that water, air, earth, and more prosper and elements can always be channeled. To do so, Master Guardians can create new guardians.

Magda let the information sink it. She was finally getting somewhere, but she remained cautious, searching for any lies in the words. She assumed he had no reason to lie to her, as he expected her to die at the hands of his assassins soon.

If it was true, and if Eligor could make new guardians, it would make sense how he was able to create new assassins with magic to send after the current royals. But if he had the power to create new guardians...that meant she could too.

She asked her next question. *Why do Master Guardians need to make new guardians?*

A failsafe. We are our world's last resort if the guardian's bloodlines are severed from the land.

How do you create guardians? She was burning with curiosity, and his gaze and words only lured her deeper, to a place she wasn't sure she could return from.

He didn't answer immediately, and Eligor's hands went to his crown, which mirrored the yellow sparks in his eyes. When his fingers grazed the golden object, a wisp of bewitching Soul magic escaped from the crown to his finger tips, and he held the crown out in front of Magda, as if he dared her to touch it.

She warred with the emotions deep within her, tempted to take the crown and fall under his mesmerizing spell, but she remained still.

When she didn't move, he placed the crown onto her head lightly, while keeping his fingers firmly around the gold. Instantly, a shock of electricity swirled in Magda's veins.

Do you want a taste of the power? He cooed. *Don't worry, I'm still holding on.*

Magda looked at him with curiosity but didn't respond. She didn't know what to say. She didn't know if she should trust him.

Try it. He said. *Droplets of water surround my tomb, find them and hold them in your palm.*

Magda closed her eyes, doing as she was told. The intrigue growing in her core was too strong to fight. Each breath she took the power pulled her closer to him, as if she was succumbing to a new master, becoming more enraptured in his words.

She could sense the physical space, somewhere in the world where he was buried, and the droplets hitting the top of the tomb. Her hand sparkled, the cerulean glitter circling up her arm, and when her eyes opened, she could sense a blue glow emanating from the crown.

Magic thumped through her body, and she felt every vein, every muscle, on fire. Then, as if the magic was being sucked from her soul, the power trickled up to the crown, before circling around Eligor's wrists.

Isn't it powerful? He grinned. He closed his eyes in pleasure, letting the magic wash over him.

Something awakened inside her, pulling her to the power, stimulating and enlivening her senses. The power of the crown kindled a newfound feeling, urging her to release herself and be overcome with the freedom of relinquishing her magic to him.

Yes, let me have you. All of it. Eligor said.

No! screamed Magda, pulling away abruptly. She yanked away from the crown, and the glow stopped immediately. The magic retreated, and she felt a burst of power collide back inside her chest.

Magda snapped to Eligor. *You tricked me.* She seethed.

Eligor let out a laugh. *You wanted to know how I create guardians. I was only giving you what you asked for. A demonstration.*

You wanted me to give you more magic! Magda accused.

Eligor replaced the crown on his head. *I'm afraid it doesn't work like that, dear Princess. We are Master Guardians. We're different. Anything we try on each other with this crown won't make a difference.*

Magda gulped. *And why us?*

Master Guardians are different from everyone else. They are individuals that can come from any magical lineage, deemed worthy of holding the title. Originally, I belonged to the lineage of the Void, the Void magic having been controlled by my family for generations.

But you killed your family, didn't you? Magda confirmed.

When I was born, I was an anomaly even the most powerful guardians feared. A Master Guardian. My family excluded me from the trials, saying I was too powerful to inherit the title of guardian and continue the lineage. So, I killed my brothers, ensuring I would be their only choice. Their only heir. How did they repay me? By fearing me and locking me in a prison for all of these years.

Magda stared into his mysterious eyes, expecting to see a tumultuous storm. But instead, she saw someone hardened, emotionless to the factual information he was presenting to her.

A cold-blooded killer. Willing to slaughter his family just for power, just to ensure that he was the only one who held onto the void magic, when he had been gifted with so many other branches.

You're terrified of what I am. He spoke clearly, enunciating every word.

She couldn't let him sense her fear, and she couldn't make herself more vulnerable to his advances. *No. I'm not.*

Don't worry, you still have a bit more time to live. Enjoy it while it lasts.

The ship lurched as the Starway docked in Tydal. Magda slammed against the ship's railing, before snapping her eyes open. It was pitch black outside, and heavy clouds slinked over the moon.

"Lower the gangway!" a crisp voice yelled in Flaustran, and suddenly the commotion of the sailors brought Magda back to reality.

Ahead, Tydal was a quaint fishing village, with wooden structures making up the multi-tiered homes and buildings with triangular shaped roofs. A rock beach led into the water. All along the shoreline were fishing boats, and villagers were cleaning their nets and fishing gear in the cool evening. Some of the homes extended into the water, propped up on stilts. Up and down the shoreline, more wooden structures decorated with red lanterns dotted the rocky shores. The rest of the village extended inland, all the way to a dense pine forest at the base of a mountain range on the horizon.

Magda knew the Sapphire Pass was through the mountain range.

Yes, head to the Sapphire Pass. Eligor said. *Dagmara will be waiting.*

Fine. How? Magda retorted.

Get a map. Eligor said. *You will need it.*

"Ready?" Ravi came up behind her, interrupting Magda's thoughts. He passed over her winter cape.

Odie circled alongside Ravi, following his every move. Ishani and Kiran stood close behind, both dressed for the cold Celesta weather. Their hair was pinned back, and Ishani's axes were sharpened and attached to her waist.

"Yes," said Magda, taking the cape and buttoning it around her neck.

"Are you alright?" said Ravi.

"I'm fine," Magda answered.

Kiran gave Magda a hug. "Ishani and I are heading to the safe house. Thank you for everything, and for saving my life again. Be safe," she squealed.

"I will," said Magda.

They disembarked, and Ravi, Odie, and Kiran went ahead, heading down the gangway and arriving on the docks. However, Ishani grabbed Magda's arm, stopping her.

"Where will you go?" Ishani asked Magda. She had a backpack strapped to her shoulders, and Magda noticed some of the logbooks were sticking out.

Magda took a deep breath, wondering whether or not to open up further, but for some reason, she trusted Ishani when it came to the secret voice in her head. "Eligor will lead me there," Magda admitted.

"He's going to kill you," said Ishani, her voice low. "Are you sure you want to listen to him?"

"I don't have a choice. I'm afraid something terrible will happen if I don't get to Dagmara in time."

Ishani nodded. "I've been in many dangerous situations, and I know they're not always avoidable," she said. "I would do the same for Kiran. But as much as I want to protect my sister, I also don't want to see anything happen to you."

Magda's expression softened. "That's not what I expected you to say."

"You're a guardian, Magda," said Ishani. "Sometimes you just have to own it." She looked up to her sister, who was playing with Odie on the docks. Ishani added, "And sometimes the people in our life need us more than they even realize."

Ravi and Magda left the princesses at the dock and wove through the marketplace in Tydal. Odie followed them intently, curious as to where they were heading next.

The market was a packed space with symmetrical red and black stands that matched a tall, central tower with balconies on all levels and roofs that curved upward. Townspeople and shopkeepers rushed back and forth, trading extra supplies due to the escalating war between Celestaire and Ilusauri. In the distance, lively music filled the air, and wind instruments sang the native tunes of Celesta.

They had secured a map, and Ravi scanned the image. "The Sapphire Pass looks like only a few hours hike."

Once on the outskirts of Tydal, they began the long trek through the forest. As they traveled, the tree-cover became more dense, and the air became cooler, and the sky was blanketed with a thick fog. Snow dotted the landscape, becoming deep enough to leave a trail of footprints behind. At certain points, they hiked single file over slippery rocks and cliff edges, ascending through a sea of pines as they made their way toward the base of the mountains.

Magda couldn't get her mind off the conversation with the First Prince. It was terrifying knowing that Eligor had the power to create guardians, and only confirmed that more assassins could come after them. She committed their final moments together to memory, watching how Eligor pulled Soul magic from his crown, channeling it through his fingertips before replacing it. She remembered how it felt when he had placed the crown on her head, using it as a way to transfer the gift of magic.

"Where do we go next?" Ravi broke her thoughts, holding the map out in front of the two.

The lake. Eligor was back in Magda's mind.

What lake? Magda called into her mind, staring at the map before them.

It's rumored by locals to be haunted. Haunted by magic perhaps?

Magda stared at the map that Ravi held between them, putting her finger down on a clearly marked lake next to the exit of the Sapphire Pass. "There. Mirror's Edge. That's where we need to go."

Ravi gave Magda a concerned glance, but he didn't protest.

They continued walking, and slowly the path ascended. The passage was easy for Odie, who was used to long hikes across the fields and mountains of Azurem, while the other two panted behind the dog, struggling to maneuver in the thick snow. Magda ran her hands along the trees, feeling the pines underneath her fingertips. The branches bent with a sliver of magic channeled at her fingertips, as if they were bowing to the power.

Suddenly Odie stopped abruptly, the hair on his back prickling as he reared up onto his haunches. In the distance, an echo of howls reverberated through the woods.

"Did you hear that?" Ravi asked beside her.

Between them, Odie's teeth bared, and a low growl emitted from his chest.

"What do you hear, Odie?" Magda whispered, her eyes scanning the fog. She turned twice, hearing howling all around her, as if the sounds were bouncing off the trees in every direction. A petrifying fear fluttered through her body as she imagined facing whatever was lurking in the forest. She had been dreading facing off against another assassin, but the spine chilling sounds that pierced the fog unnerved her.

Then her entire body froze in terror.

In front of the pair, emerging from the fog, was a pair of monstrous hounds with a mixture of gray fur and purple scales. Their underbellies were gaunt, as if their ribs peeked right through, and their eyes alight with horror. Drool dripped from their teeth to their massive paws.

Magda held out her hand in front of Ravi, steading him before tensing completely. All around them, more howls sounded through the trees. They were the same monster she had seen in Flaustra—in Vex's hideout—something out of her nightmares.

Without warning, the massive beasts lunged.

CHAPTER 15
Dagmara

The trip back across Mirror's Edge was longer than Dagmara remembered. Dagmara was alone with Sabien once more, for they hadn't seen Junne since she flew away on her own. Dagmara's mind was still reeling from the conversation with the guardians and the information she had gathered. At the same time, she remembered Viette's playground and the hundreds of people imprisoned under her compulsion. Shuddering, Dagmara pulled her cloak tighter around her. The ice was seeping too deep, turning her stone cold.

She had revealed Magda's secret. Now the assassins knew. But it didn't make sense. Who did Junne see on the ship? Dagmara wanted to believe that it was Magda coming to rescue her, but Magda didn't have Life magic.

Regardless...Dagmara now had nothing else to hide. Sabien may keep her around to lure Magda, but in all honesty, he could get rid of her in a heartbeat.

"What happens now?" She voiced her concern.

Sabien met her gaze, his irises shimmering as he manipulated the water. It was as if she was gazing into the ocean itself—beautiful but dangerous, and full of the unknown.

"We kill Magdalena," he announced. "But what I don't understand is how you lied under compulsion."

"I didn't lie. Magda isn't a Life Guardian, she has Soul magic—that is the truth. You don't have to kill her."

"We will see about that," Sabien replied.

Maybe she could convince him that she was still necessary. Maybe she could manipulate Sabien—play to his ego and his heart like she had once in the library.

Who was she kidding? This man killed the love of his life for the First Prince. He had no heart.

She had to escape now.

Her entire body felt broken, and bruises painted her skin. Her heart rate was undoubtedly at its peak, her health faltering, but she was facing life or death.

And she wanted to live.

This may be her last chance to escape. She had to get off the water—far enough away from his source of magic to stand a chance. She remembered the panel in the foyer where the truth serum was hidden. There was a blade inside—

But if she made it back inside the manor, she may never make it out. She had to escape now. Could she even outrun Sabien?

The bank came into view, and Dagmara knew she was almost out of time to formulate a plan. She eyed his figure, seeing a single knife latched to his belt. The odds of her grabbing it without him noticing were slim. He was a guardian, and she had to remember that. He had magic—

Her eyes widened, a terribly reckless plan taking shape. She remembered seeing the hounds on the riverbank. They were close by. They would be able to sense Sabien's magic and awaken. If there was some way she could use them as a distraction...maybe she could escape.

That depended on the hounds not killing her first.

Death by the hounds would be swifter than whatever Sabien had in store for her. She would not be used as bait.

The boat ran aground on the sand, and Sabien jumped out first, landing in ankle-deep water. "Let's go." He didn't bother to help her. He didn't even pause to turn around.

She remained seated.

He barely glanced over his shoulder. "I know you heard me. I said move."

She folded her hands in front of her. "Come get me."

He halted in his tracks, whirling around. "Excuse me?"

"I know you heard me," she replied, flashing him an inviting smile.

He stormed back toward her, lunging for her arm. "I don't have time for this—"

Dagmara jolted up as he leaned toward her, leading with her elbow. The point of her bone met with the bridge of his nose, and she enjoyed the sickening crunch that followed. He roared in pain, his hands flying to his face.

She jumped out of the boat, splashing down in the frigid water. It cooled her boots, threatening to seep inside. The bottom of her cloak ran against the water, weighing her down, but she pushed through.

He yelled, swiping for her cloak, but she was too fast.

Racing up the sand, the treeline approached steadily. Her legs burned as she raced forward through the snow.

Almost there.

Ice cracked behind her, and she could sense magic rising in the air.

She dove for cover, rolling in the snow, as ice shards embedded into the trees around her.

"Dagger!" his voice roared.

She didn't pause for a moment. Scrambling to her feet, she tore off through the trees. Branches beat against her body, snow coating her clothing, but she wouldn't stop. The shadows and frosted trees made it hard to make out any direction she was heading. But it didn't matter. She had to run until—

She skidded to an abrupt halt. She gasped, clutching her chest as she stared at the clearing before her. A giant rift separated the earth, a stark darkness against the white snow. Trees collapsed into it, broken branches and logs scattering the area.

Her heart stopped as she saw four hounds lying on the ground at the top of the rift. They were larger than she remembered. The fur barely shielded their gaunt bodies, their jowls contorted and gruesome. Their slick underbellies were layered with iridescent scales, a beautiful violet.

The one in the front's ears twitched, and a single eye opened.

Her heart plummeted into her stomach, and for a brief moment, she couldn't move. Staring back at the glowing iris, a culmination of emotions fluttered through her, not only terror.

"Shhhh...." she soothed, backing away. "I'm a friend. No magic."

In fact, no weapons at all.

Then a twig snapped behind Dagmara. This time, Dagmara wasn't the only one to jerk back in alarm.

All four hounds jolted upright, landing on massive paws with razor-sharp talons. Drool coated their fangs, their attention set on the distant voice. Yet the voice was directly behind her, and she was in their line of attack.

Dagmara prayed this wasn't the stupidest plan she had yet.

CHAPTER 16
Magdalena

Magda and Ravi were stranded in the middle of the forest, facing a group of hounds. The first hound lunged forward, its jaws going straight to Odie's neck, while the other hound went for Ravi.

"No!" yelled Magda, using her powers to snap tree branches in the hounds' direction. The branches whacked the hounds fiercely, and the dogs flopped to the side.

Another hound leapt out of the fog, leaping onto Ravi's back. Its claws sunk into Ravi's thick jacket as Ravi struggled to escape from its grip. Quickly, he wiggled out of the jacket, pushing the hound off him.

At the same moment, three more hounds encircled Odie, and they stood at a standstill, all snarling at each other. Odie lunged for one of the hounds, while Magda found the soft spots in the earth, enclosing the hounds in small holes so that they were trapped.

Magda turned twice more, but she was disoriented in the fog. "Come on!" she screamed, heading in the direction of the tallest mountain.

The path ascended, and they ran up the hill as fast as they could, heading to the highest peak. The mountainside was littered with minuscule rocks that shifted under their feet, making it difficult to gain traction on the ascent.

Odie sprinted ahead even further, kicking the small rocks down the mountain behind him.

Ravi easily scaled the rock ledge, jumping up to a higher point. "Come on, Magda!" he yelled, reaching back down for her and grabbing her hand.

They found themselves on a path that ran along the side of the mountain, weaving around the ridge until it turned toward the Sapphire pass. The trio sprinted down the path, careful to stay close to the inside wall of the mountain, and not slip and fall to the snaking trails below.

Then, they stopped in their tracks. Directly in front of them, was a break in the path. They would have to leap over a six feet chasm to a lower platform before continuing their ascent. Easily, Odie leapt up on the right, finding an alternate pathway on the slippery rocks, before jumping down on the other side.

"It's too far!" yelled Magda.

"I'll jump over and then help you across," Ravi decided.

Ravi took a few steps back, before running as fast as he could toward the interior of the mountain. Then, he used his shoes to gain traction as he ran slightly up the rock wall, before grabbing onto a higher ledge. Ravi pulled himself up, before balancing on the side, on a space barely wide enough for his feet.

"Be careful!" yelled Magda.

As fast as lightning, Ravi ran across the thin ledge, before jumping across the chasm from the higher position, landing in a roll on the other side. He leapt up, holding out his hand, "Jump, Magda!"

Another group of howls sounded behind them, and Magda turned for a split second. A group of six hounds charged toward her. Quickly, Magda blasted a set of rocks toward the group, and one of the hounds tumbled down the mountainside, taking a companion with it.

As she watched the beast fall, Magda noted the view beyond. From this elevation, she could see a crack in the ground, with violet magic seeping out, as if pollution was seeping from the depths of the earth. More hounds emerged from the crevice, following the leader as if they all had one, unified mind.

These monsters lived in the ground?

Magda didn't have time to process the new information and turned forward again. Taking a running start, she leapt out across the chasm, hurling her body in Ravi's direction. At the last moment, he reached out for her hand, but she still was losing altitude. She felt herself falling, plummeting to the ground.

"Magda!" yelled Ravi.

Pure adrenaline surged through Magda's body. She reached for Ravi and interlocked her fingers with his. Her stomach slammed hard into the side of the cliff, and she gasped for air.

"I got you," he said, grabbing both her hands and using all his might to try and pull her deadweight to his level.

Magda let out an ear-piercing scream as a sharp force yanked on her neck, pulling her backward.

"Hang on!" yelled Ravi.

Magda choked on her cape as one of the hound's teeth smashed into it, attempting to pull her down. She tried to find her magic, but her hands were tight in Ravi's, and it was all she could do to fight the blackness threatening to consume her as she gasped for air.

A silhouette leapt over Magda's head, blocking her view of the moon, and the tightness on her neck released. She came to just in time to look back, seeing Odie tumble into the crevice and roll down the mountain, dragging the hound with him.

Quickly, Ravi lifted her upward, away from the hounds.

Magda stood next to Ravi, staring down the mountainside, but she was too horrified to scream. Odie and the hound tumbled down the mountain, sliding down a stream of minuscule rocks. In the scuffle, the beast's teeth sunk into Odie's side, and blood poured from Odie's black and white coat.

Odie was rolling toward a group of hounds, about to be slaughtered.

CHAPTER 17
Dagmara

Dagmara faced the ravine, peeking around the trees and at the hounds in the distance. She knew Sabien was pursuing her, and she didn't have much time.

The hound in the center sniffed the air, tasting magic on the breeze. With a chilling snarl, he leapt forward. Shrieking, Dagmara dove out of the way. She landed with a hard thud on the snow, the hound leaping directly over her. It hurled himself into the trees, and the three hounds followed suit. She heard Sabien yell, but she didn't waste another moment.

When blue magic lit the area, she was already on her feet. But there was no way forward. The rift was massive, spanning the entire clearing. She couldn't cross through it or else risk getting stuck at the bottom, and it would take too long to traverse around it. She would have to cut back into the protection of the trees and find another way past the obstacle. She didn't want to head back toward Mirror's Edge —closer to a source of water, but all the snow around them could be used by the Life Guardian. This was Sabien's playing field, and she had to escape before he won the game.

The crunch of bone and flesh sounded from the battle between Sabien and the hounds. Dagmara retreated back into the cover of the trees, trying to move swiftly around their battle. The rift wasn't only in a straight line, it zigzagged toward Mirror's Edge, causing her to cut back farther than she wanted. She had to head back in the direction of the manor. Then she could get past the rift.

The ground sloped underneath her shoes, and instantly she felt the change in pacing. Her heart lurched in her chest, a sharp pain igniting between her ribcage. She stumbled, catching herself on a nearby tree with one hand, the other gripping her chest. Gasping, she willed her health to let her run a little farther. She pushed aside the darkness dancing in her peripheral vision and continued ascending the hill. She barely made it a few paces before a whiz of a blade cut through the air.

A shard of ice flew by her, nicking the side of her ribcage before it impaled the bark of a nearby tree. She screamed, putting her palm over the bleeding wound, and only glanced behind her for a fraction of a second.

Sabien was like death himself, walking toward her covered in blood. His nose dripped crimson, his hands dark with red liquid. He wielded a large sword made entirely of ice, his body coated in a sheer ice breastplate covered in scratch marks.

There was a time when Dagmara was enthralled by the sight of Life Magic. She never imagined she would feel sick at the sight of a Life Guardian.

She refused to give up. Sabien had provided her with a weapon. She tore the ice shard from the tree bark before charging through the trees, stumbling out into the open once more. She could see the manor in the distance, farther up the ascending slope. However, she had reached a high enough point on the hill that the ground in the distance dropped off at a cliff edge. Mirror's Edge was beyond. Should she keep running back up toward the manor? Or cut back through the trees and hope to lose him? She couldn't keep going forward with the cliff edge in the distance.

There was another whiz, and Sabien's aim was perfect. A shard of ice caught the bottom of her cloak before lodging into the earth, pinning the fabric to the ground. It yanked against her neck, and she choked against the fabric. She tugged on the coat, but to no avail. Loosening the tie around her throat, she flung the cloak off her. The bitter cold chilled her bare arms, the dress from the masquerade covering little of her body.

Sabien's tactic had worked. He was too close now to outrun, but at least now she wasn't pinned to the ground.

She whirled to face Sabien and leveled the ice shard. His face was stone cold.

The game was over.

CHAPTER 18
Magdalena

Magda stood on the cliff edge, watching Odie and the hound tumble downward, heading toward a group of animals that waited at the crevice in the earth.

She had to do something.

Magda's eyes caught a large boulder that was teetering on the edge of the cliffs. In seconds, her eyes were glowing in yellow flames, and she thrust her hands out towards the boulder in anger.

The magic hit the large boulder with full force, cracking the cliff it teetered on. An explosion of dirt and rock blasted through the mountainside, as the boulder began racing down the hill toward the group of hounds.

"Odie!" Magda called out towards her dog, her eyes already filled with tears.

The hound Odie was tussling with stood up on alert at the sound of the cracking boulder. He released Odie from his grip, and both of the animals darted out of the way. Odie leapt upwards, skillfully maneuvering onto another ledge, however the hounds raced back together, retreating in one group down the mountainside.

A moment later, the rock rolled over the beasts before knocking them down the mountain to the earth. The sound of cracking limbs and bones echoed through the woods as their bodies crumbled. A loud reverberation shook the air, and their shrieking howls ceased.

When she was sure it was safe, Magda jumped down to a lower ledge, and then another, making her way over to Odie. Her dog was limping across the rocks.

"You're going to be alright!" she shouted, brushing up against him and hugging his soft fur. There was no water around to heal him, and she wasn't sure how far away the lake was. But the bleeding was coming too fast.

"That looks bad," said Ravi, bounding up beside her.

Magda took in a breath of fresh mountain air and outstretched her palm upward. Water came in many forms, didn't it?

Her eyes darted to the snow, and she grasped a pile of it in her arms, plastering it against Odie's fur coat and smearing it across the wound. The ivory-white snow turned crimson in seconds. Magda placed her hand against the snow, channeling the Life Magic in her mind, and letting the cerulean magic swirl through her nerves and up her arm. Power rocketed through her body, splintering her senses. She fought vigorously to control her emotions and channel the magic into Odie's body.

Her heart pounded in her ears, and adrenaline flooded her veins. The magic surged, channeling from her to Odie, and suddenly the power released from her body as an emptiness overcame her.

Odie's head perked up, his tongue hanging out of his mouth as he panted. His tail wagged as he rubbed his body up against Magda and Ravi.

"You're alive!" Magda exclaimed, hugging her dog.

"You did it." Ravi embraced Magda, pulling both her and Odie to him.

You're running out of time, Magda. Eligor was back in her head. *The time is ticking down to Dagmara's last breath.*

No! Magda screamed. She leapt up, calling to Ravi, "Come on, Dagmara's in danger."

Ravi jumped to his feet. As he did, he uncurled the map, struggling to read as they began sprinting across the snow. "The lake should be close. We're almost there!"

Magda pushed forward, her legs taking her as fast as she could. She had to save Dagmara in time. She could not lose her.

"Go!" Magda yelled at Odie, encouraging him to run ahead. "Go find Dagmara!"

CHAPTER 19
Dagmara

Sabien swung his iceblade, aiming directly at the shard Dagmara held, humorously small in comparison. A jolt of pain radiated through Dagmara's wrist, and her weapon went flying into the snow.

Before she could recover, Sabien lunged for her neck, his palm easily wrapping around her throat.

"I don't need you to lure Magda," Sabien said, his baritone voice husky. "I just won't let her know you're already dead."

She couldn't breathe. She threw her hand forward, connecting the ball of her palm to his already broken nose.

He yelled, releasing her, and her body collided against the snow. She choked for air on the ground, desperate for her lungs to expand once more.

He planted his boot against her chest, refusing to let her catch her breath. Blood streamed down his cheek, dripping from his sharp jaw. She struggled underneath him, trying to breath, but he only pressed his foot down on her harder. She prayed her ribcage wouldn't collapse under his weight.

"That's better," he said, watching as the struggle drained from her body. "I prefer when you're underneath me."

"Please—" Dagmara choked out.

"I gave you so many chances," he continued over her. "You brought this upon yourself. If only you agreed to work together."

Her mind began to falter, her desperation to breathe all-consuming. This couldn't be it. This couldn't be the end.

"I will admit, I am sad we didn't last longer. You were so much fun. But this little game is over."

The Life Guardian grabbed the iceblade with both hands, raising it above his head for a final blow.

She hoped he was kidding. She hoped this was another one of his games. His taunts. His lies.

But staring up at his ice-blue eyes, shimmering with magic gifted by the First Prince, she knew this was her end.

He sucked in a sharp breath, bracing himself to swing.

Then, the whiz of a projectile.

The sickening crunch of flesh and bone.

A single arrow protruded from the center of Sabien's wrist. His arm retracted at an awkward angle as he stumbled back.

Dagmara gasped, her chest free from his compression. She turned onto her side, choking for air. The ground began to shake, a rumbling reverberating through the earth, but her head was spinning.

Another arrow flew, making contact with Sabien's shoulder, and he yelled.

The rumbling...it was hooves.

Dagmara looked up as a brown horse emerged from the trees, ridden by a guard dressed in black stitched with silver. He held a bow and fired another arrow in Sabien's direction.

The world froze. This had to be a dream.

Dagmara's call was barely audible. "Pierre?"

The trees shook, and a group of horses broke through into the moonlight. One stallion was larger than the rest, a giant-like man riding him. Another was ridden by a female guard.

At the front, was a captivating man dressed in all black, his chocolate eyes sparkling with silver.

Dagmara's entire body shook as she sat upright, making sure she wasn't hallucinating.

They were truly here.

The Mad King was here.

Claude had come to rescue her.

PART TWO

The Reunion

CHAPTER 20
Dagmara

The Mad King was the first to swing from his horse, landing firmly in the snow.

"You'll pay for this, Sabien," Claude roared.

"I'm afraid you'll have to be more specific," Sabien replied. "Are you here to scold me for leaving my captain duties unannounced?"

A flash of silver lit the area, igniting magic. Claude glowered at Sabien. His eyes glistened, dancing against a stoic expression.

"I'm here for my wife," Claude retorted. As he extended his hand toward Sabien, his illusions emerged. Horrifying monsters manifested, ghoul-like creatures with razor-sharp talons. They swarmed Sabien in an onslaught of terror.

Dislodging the arrow from his shoulder, Sabien stumbled back. He dodged with precision, rolling onto the ground and catching his balance on his hands. He utilized the water from the blood-splattered snow to form more weapons. Meanwhile, the snow flooded across his body, reinforcing his armor and healing his wounds.

Martine was already at Dagmara's side, grabbing her by the shoulders and hoisting her to her knees. "Are you hurt?"

Everything hurt, but Dagmara was too struck with disbelief to form a response. She stared dumbfounded at Martine, who was grabbing her by the arm to make sure her friend was actually there. This wasn't an illusion. This wasn't a dream.

Pierre fired another arrow at Sabien, and Sacha swung off the horse with a hard thump, joining his king in the battle.

"Come on," Martine encouraged, grabbing Dagmara by the elbow. She pulled her out of the line of fire, dragging her toward the trees, moments before Sabien launched himself at Claude and Sacha.

Stumbling to her feet, Dagmara scampered out of the way, gasping for breath. She could still feel Sabien's grip around her throat. Suffocating her. Her hand flew to her side, checking her injury, and her palm was instantly coated in dark blood.

A shadow flickered from above, and the wind began to pick up speed, lashing against their faces. The wind sent a shower of Sabien's ice blades off course, and a few landed on the ground directly beside Martine. The shadow came into form, and Junne landed on the ground behind Martine, facing the four Ilusaurian men.

The Spirit assassin raised her hand toward Claude, summoning the wind to pummel him to the ground.

Lunging toward the dagger strapped to Martine's side, Dagmara withdrew it in one quick movement. She barely braced her throw before sending the blade flying in Junne's direction. It was far heavier than a throwing star, and not Dagmara's choice of throwing weapons, but the dagger made contact with Junne's thigh.

Junne screamed, stumbling from the impact.

Pierre switched his aim, letting Claude and Sacha attack Sabien and turning his bow toward Junne. He fired an arrow at her, which she barely blew off course before it lodged in her chest.

Withdrawing her own sword, Martine joined Pierre to take on Junne, both guards fighting the Spirit Guardian with no fear.

Flashes of silver, cerulean, and scarlet lit the space in front of the manor. Magic flew in all directions. Arrows whizzed left and right, and the glint of steel caught the sun from above.

A barrier of ice blocked Sabien from the onslaught, and Claude broke through it with a gallant swing of his sword. The loud shatter pierced the air with a thunderous echo. As the shards fell from the shield, Sabien reached forward, wielding all the minuscule fragments with his magic. They all responded to his summon, flipping in the air and aiming at Claude's chest.

"No!" Dagmara screamed, a surge of adrenaline coursing through her limbs. She saw the deadly incoming attack. She didn't care what it cost her.

Yanking one of the ice blades out of the earth, grateful Junne's landing had propelled them close enough for Dagmara to reach, she launched herself into battle. She raced toward Sabien, blade in hand, prepared for the strength of his armor to withstand the blow.

Sacha witnessed the scene simultaneously, yanking Claude back from Sabien's magic and shielding his king with his own body.

Sabien released the shards, and they all went flying, propelled into the giant guard's chest like hundreds of daggers.

Thrusting her own iceblade into Sabien's side, he was caught unaware. Sabien lurched back, reeling from pain as the blade shattered his armor and punctured his side. His arm came flying in Dagmara's direction, his elbow meeting her temple before she had the chance to dodge. She fell hard to the solid ground, stars dancing in her vision.

Another scream sounded in the air as one of Pierre's arrows found purchase in Junne's stomach. Dagmara barely could make out the Spirit Guardian grasp her stomach before launching herself into the sky. Her flight was uneasy, and she nearly collided with the treetops as she ascended, but she fled despite the weapons lodged in her flesh.

Sabien gripped the iceblade, halfway lodged in his side. He backed away from Dagmara, nearing the edge of the mountain close to Mirror's Edge.

A flash of light lit the space, an illusion jolting Sabien back farther and temporarily blinding him. Claude raised his sword in the air, his illusions dancing beside him as he charged at his former captain.

"I'll see you again, Claude," Sabien smirked at his former king.

Before Claude could deal a killing blow, Sabien leapt from the edge of the cliff. He disappeared, and Claude skidded to a halt before he teetered over after him. Snow fluttered off the side, cascading down to the lake far below.

Sabien had vanished, no doubt summoning the water from Mirror's Edge to bring him to safety.

He was gone.

Another wave of emotion assaulted Dagmara's senses, and she struggled to sit upright, her mind still swimming from Sabien's blow. Exhaustion cascaded over her. Every morsel of her being was at war with herself. She had been seconds from death, and the quartet from Ilusauri—who she was certain despised her—had rode in as her saviors.

And now, Sabien was finally gone—at least for now. She knew he would heal himself, would probably heal Junne, and return with a vengeance. She sucked in a ragged gasp, tasting blood, and enjoyed the first breath of freedom.

The silver apparitions faded, and Claude turned away from the cliff edge, bringing his attention to Dagmara.

Her breath caught in her throat as he finally met her gaze. She hadn't looked directly in his eyes since the night she had betrayed his trust. Now, he was standing before her, his face pristine and the scar hidden under an illusion. Blood splattered his clothing, and his chest shifted rapidly with each breath.

Her heart pounded against her chest, threatening to beat out of its cage. She stared up at him, her eyes wide, and a chill shuddered down her spine.

"Dagmara," he spoke, his voice strained but his accent exactly as she remembered. The sound of her true name on his lips sent a shudder through her body.

"Claude," she let out, barely audible.

His face softened, and the silver dissipated from his dark brown eyes. He took a step forward, closing the space that separated them, before dropping to his knees in front of her. His sword fell to the snow, adding to the blood around them. He immediately tore off his outer coat before draping it around her bare shoulders. The fabric cocooned her body, protecting her from the chill. The coat smelled of his cologne, wafting her senses and reminding her of Ilusauri—of safety.

Then he reached toward her, his palms grazing both of her cheeks, clasping her face in his hands.

"I found you," he exhaled.

Her breath hitched, and a reminder of what she had done to him collided with her emotions. She had betrayed him. She had lied to him, accused him of murder, and forced him into a marriage he may have never wanted. For all she knew, he was hunting her down to punish her. He could drag her back to Ilusauri and throw her in jail for her crimes. She could have been saved from one situation to be thrown into the next.

Pierre's voice rang out through the clearing, interrupting them. "Claude!" Pierre called. "It's Sacha!" His voice broke off in a crack.

Claude yanked back from Dagmara, whirling to confront their worst fear.

The burly man lay yards away. He was unmoving, his chest entirely still. The snow around him was a stark red, and dozens of shards of glass protruded from his chest.

Sabien had slaughtered the king's guard.

"No!" Claude yelled, his cry a guttural scream as he raced over.

But Sacha had protected Claude. If Sacha hadn't been there, it would be Claude on the ground, dead at Sabien's hand. Sabien didn't care that he was about to murder his best friend. He hadn't cared when he was moments from bringing his blade down on Dagmara's throat.

She knew that if she ever crossed paths with Sabien again, someone else would end up dead.

CHAPTER 21
Dagmara

The horror of Sacha's death settled into the atmosphere around them, thick and foreboding.

The king was kneeling at Sacha's side with Pierre. Claude clasped his face in one hand and reached his other palm to Sacha's chest.

It was overwhelming. There were too many emotions to process, and Dagmara was unable to compartmentalize the resounding relief of freedom, especially knowing it was still possible she would be brought back to Ilusauri and charged for her crimes against the crown.

The snow around her had officially begun to numb her body. Her dress was soaked. Her ribcage stung from the ice shard Sabien had thrown, and her side felt sticky with blood.

A soft crunch resounded as Martine approached. She was tentative, taking each step carefully. "Are you hurt?"

Dagmara met her gaze. It was unreadable. All of them undoubtedly knew of her betrayal by now.

"I'm alive," Dagmara muttered.

"And I'm so glad for that."

"Have you come to take me back?" Dagmara replied, breathless.

Martine's face flashed with a different expression, her head inclining. "We came to save you."

Dagmara hesitated, equally unsure of the direction of the conversation. "How did you know I needed saving?"

Her guard tilted her head. "We were able to piece together what happened with Sabien, and we knew you were in danger."

There was a pause in the conversation as Dagmara waited for a follow up, but she saw no malice in Martine's gaze. "But I lied to everyone." Dagmara blurted out. She could feel tears beginning to well in her eyes. "I'm a traitor. The only reason you would have come to rescue me would be to take me back and charge me for my crimes."

"What are you talking about? That's not the case at all." The guard took a seat beside Dagmara, their shoulders barely touching. "Look, I don't have any say in the situation and what transpired. It's all up to His Majesty..." Martine paused. "But I was assigned to protect you. I came to save you."

"You were assigned to protect Princess Magdalena. The Queen of Ilusauri. Not me."

"You are the queen, Dagmara," Martine replied. She cast a sidelong glance. "He married you, regardless of what name you used."

"It's not that simple. I could be charged with treason."

"I suppose," said Martine, "but what matters is you're safe now."

Dagmara pulled Claude's coat tighter around her shoulders, letting its warmth seep into her. "You don't hate me? For lying?"

Martine shrugged. "I...knew already."

Dagmara nodded, holding back a sob. "Why didn't you expose my secret?"

Martine grimaced before dipping her chin. "The first day you arrived, Pierre told me you saw a phantom bird. The same apparition that had been haunting the king. I thought...maybe if someone else can see it, the king isn't as mad as everyone says he is. It didn't matter who you were at that point. It didn't matter if you were Princess Magdalena or not. I knew if you stayed at the castle, maybe you could help His Majesty. You gave me hope that the king could be saved."

The tears could not be contained any longer. They broke through like a dam, cascading down Dagmara's cheeks in small waterfalls.

Martine reached out, and Dagmara fell into her friend's embrace. The guard hugged her tightly, and for the first time, Dagmara accepted that she was finally safe. No matter how long it would last, at that moment, she was alive and free.

"I thought I was dead," said Dagmara, her face buried against Martine's shoulder.

"I'm sorry we couldn't get here sooner."

"Sabien used truth serum torture," Dagmara whispered.

Her friend didn't respond, but only tightened her grip. A sharp jolt struck Dagmara's side from her wound, and she winced. Martine pulled back abruptly, a concerned expression on her face, but Dagmara cut her off before she could ask.

"Just a scratch," she said. "Also, remind me that you and Pierre don't keep any secrets from one another." Dagmara forced a laugh, wiping the tears from her eyes.

"No, we don't." Martine smiled. "Now, let's get out of the snow." Martine rose from the ground before extending her hand down to Dagmara and helping her to her feet.

A few feet away, Claude and Pierre were busy situating Sacha's limp body on the back of his horse. Martine approached, shortening the distance, but Dagmara was more hesitant to follow. She put her arms through the sleeves of Claude's coat, tightening it around her to cover the bodice of the red masquerade dress. She watched Claude carefully, trying to discern his expression. She couldn't imagine the pain of losing Sacha. She fiddled with the wedding ring on her finger, twirling it mindlessly. Why had Claude come to save her? Did he forgive her?

He spun to face Martine. "I want you and Pierre to take Sacha back to the border. He deserves to…" his voice cracked, and he cleared it abruptly before finishing, "he deserves to return home. He gave his life for me." He paused once more, swallowing, before his glossy gaze met Dagmara's. "You can join Pierre and Martine who will lead you through the port of Tydal and back to Ilusauri. Or, there are ships that leave for Azurem from there as well—if that is what you prefer."

Momentarily speechless, Dagmara stared at the king. That didn't answer any of her questions about his feelings toward her. "Will you not be joining us?"

"I must speak with Reon. I need to put an end to this war between our kingdoms."

Dagmara vaguely remembered Reon. He was the Spearhead of the Celesta militia. He had come to the engagement ball and to Sailonne when news spread of Guardian Sora's death. She remembered how he had used her as bait to speak with Claude, but the sharp end of the blade hadn't even been pointed at her throat. He never meant her harm. He and Claude were friends—or must have been before the war between their kingdoms broke out.

There was a moment of silence. Dagmara watched Claude carefully, trying to discern his thoughts.

"I'm free to go back to Azurem? I deceived a king," she blurted out.

"It is my understanding you were acting on orders from Princess Magdalena," Claude replied. "I won't punish you for what she did. She is the one that orchestrated all of this, and she is the one who must face the consequences."

Dagmara's brow furrowed. She could feel Pierre and Martine's stare on her, heavy and curious. This was neither the time nor the place for a longer conversation with Claude, though there were so many unanswered questions and things that needed to be said. He came to rescue her—and then he was telling her she was free? Dagmara didn't want to be sent away. She wanted to stay with him, one of the only people she felt safe with. She didn't even know if he forgave her for what she did to him.

She had to know.

"Let me come with you to speak with Reon," Dagmara stated. "I know you didn't kill Sora. That Spirit Guardian..." Dagmara pointed to the blood on the snow, "...she killed Sora. I can tell Reon the truth."

Claude inclined his head. "Do you have proof?"

"No," she admitted, realizing Reon wouldn't believe her any more than he would believe Claude. She changed tactics. "Then I can tell Reon his attack on Ilusauri is also a deliberate attack on Azurem. Celestaire cannot afford going to war with both our kingdoms."

"And why would he listen to you?"

She paused. "He still believes I'm Princess Magdalena." The words were difficult to say, catching in Dagmara's throat. She was dancing around the main topic she wanted to speak to Claude about. They both were.

"Your hair is no longer silver," Claude replied.

"You can cast an illusion, can't you?" It was a risky question.

Claude shifted his stance, rubbing the back of his neck. With a deep sigh, he finally said, "Alright."

She had a chance to make it up to him, and she desperately wanted to succeed.

"I brought things for you," Martine said, "just in case." She gave a faint smile, as though she too was hoping Dagmara would stay with Claude. Martine returned to the saddlebag on her horse, unfastened it from the buckles, and handed it to Dagmara. Flipping over the cover, Dagmara found a change of clothes, boots, and her makeup box filled with her hidden poisons.

"How did you..." Dagmara's voice trailed off, glancing up at her guard.

Martine smiled. "You're welcome."

"Are you certain you two can go on alone?" Pierre chimed. He shuffled awkwardly in the snow toward his king. "What if Captain..."

His face twisted into a frown. "Is he still our captain? Nevermind. What if he comes after you?"

"Then I will avenge Sacha. For all of us," Claude said. "Now go, and be careful. They still won't take kindly to Ilusaurians being in Celestaire."

Pierre and Martine nodded, flashed each other a glance, and then mounted their horses. Pierre tied the reins of Sacha's horse to his own. The sight of Sacha's limp body being carried by his horse once again sent a shudder through Dagmara.

Claude filled the silence. "Reon is at least another day away, so we should find a place to rest tonight." Then he gestured toward the horse. "You'll ride with me."

A lump formed in her throat. She approached Claude's horse uneasily, buckling the saddlebag Martine had just given her to the horse, and heaving herself up. She winced, a furious pain lacing through her ribcage. She clutched it uneasily, and her palm was immediately coated in sticky warmth, but she refused to announce her injury. It was a small cut, and the blood would cease soon enough.

Claude placed his boot in the stirrup before hoisting himself onto the saddle behind her. Her entire body froze at his proximity. His cologne wafted toward her, his warmth at her back. He reached around her to pick up the reins, his arms resting against her waist.

"Hold on."

She obeyed his command, taking the leather in her grasp. His coat was slightly too big on her, reaching to her fingertips, but she gripped the reins regardless. Her heart thundered inside, so loud she wondered if he could hear it.

As she held onto the leather, her hands on the inside of his, she noticed his ring. He was also still wearing the wedding ring that contained her blood. A warmth danced through her, an ember igniting inside her chest. As though he could sense what she was looking at, he spoke:

"Dagmara," Claude said, his voice strained and his lips at her ear. "I'm glad you're safe."

She closed her eyes briefly, letting the weight of his words settle over her. She wanted to lean back against his chest and fully relax into him, but her body remained rigid.

"Only because you arrived when you did. Thank you, Claude."

He sucked in a ragged breath before snapping the reins, and they set off down the trail into the darkness. The horse moved at a leisurely pace, but every step shifted her in the saddle, and she tensed at the friction between their bodies.

"I'm sorry, I guess I'm supposed to call you *Your Majesty*?" Dagmara called over her shoulder. The question was subtle. A question of where they stood with one another. It was as if she was reaching into the fire, hoping she wouldn't get burned. Stepping into the ocean and praying it wouldn't suck her out in a riptide. Jumping from a cliff and wishing she had wings.

His response was soft. His chest expanded against her back as he inhaled, and his lips were close to her ear as he answered, "I suppose that is correct."

She was burning, drowning, and falling, all at once into the tumultuous abyss that separated them. She clung to the image of their hands inches apart, both wearing matching wedding bands. Maybe that was the only vow that still held them together and the only connection that ever would.

CHAPTER 22
Magdalena

"There!" shouted Magda, pointing toward the lake.

Magda, Ravi, and Odie sprinted to the water, Odie taking the lead as he bounded across the soft snow. Within minutes, they had reached its shores and peered out onto the frosted waterline. The lake stretched as far as the eye could see, and beyond, was a perfectly symmetrical snow-capped mountain, dominating the horizon. Its turquoise waters provided a surreal reflection of the pines as they stretched up toward clear skies.

"This must be the haunted lake," said Magda.

"Mirror's Edge." Ravi had unfolded the map.

Magda nodded. She scanned the snow surrounding her, but it was in disarray. There were no distinct pathways leading outward from the perfectly still water.

BARK!

Odie called before he tore to the right, following the shoreline.

"What does he see?" Magda asked, running after her dog.

Ravi pointed in the distance to a small, black shape along the waterline. "What is that?"

Magda quickened her pace. She didn't want Odie running into a trap, let alone hurting himself again. For all they knew, there were still magical assassins, hounds, or bounty hunters lurking in these woods.

"Odie, wait!" Magda called, struggling to keep up in the snow.

When they reached the black object, all three skidded to a halt, but Odie continued barking. It was a rowboat, perched on the shore, but it had no oars. Odie put his snout on the wood, sniffing all around the boat and the surrounding snow. He kept his nose on the ground as he began moving further down the shoreline, as if begging the pair to follow.

Ravi inspected the boat. "With water this calm, it's useless without oars to get across."

Odie had already drifted paces down the shore, but paused to look back at Magda, letting out another bark. He began sniffing along the snow, following a scent.

The boat wasn't useless for someone who could control the water.

It is fascinating to see how your mind works. Eligor's voice was back.

Magda didn't respond. She peered down at her hands, before announcing to Ravi and Odie. "It's not useless if you have magic." She closed her hands to fists, and a ripple coursed through the water, lapping against the boat on the bank.

You're more intelligent than you think you are. You're a Master Guardian.

"Let's go," said Magda, heading after Odie. "He says it's correct."

"Wait, who said what?" Ravi asked, grabbing Magda by the wrist. "What do you mean?"

"I...," Magda knew she couldn't lie to him. "The First Prince. Eligor. He's in my head, and I'm letting him lead us to Dagmara."

Ravi flinched, jerking back. "Eligor's been leading us? Why didn't you tell me this? It could be a trap."

"You said that you would follow me wherever I needed," said Magda.

"I didn't agree to casually walk with you to your death!" Ravi said.

"If I had known, I would have asked some of Ishani's officers to come."

"It's the only way to save Dagmara in time," said Magda.

"Dagmara might not even be here," said Ravi. He held both her hands in front of him as he looked down at her. "I can't let you do this. Not if it's your life on the line."

"This won't be the last time I have to do something dangerous. I'm a guardian."

"But these people specifically want to kill you," said Ravi. "And you have no plan, and we have no idea what we're up against."

"Ravi, we don't have a choice."

Ravi sighed, "Magda, you don't understand. You're the only thing that has been in and out of my thoughts since the day I met you. If all this is ripped away, I'll have nothing left. Please, for my sake, can you promise me you won't be unnecessarily reckless?"

She sighed, hoping she wasn't lying to him as she replied, "I promise."

BARK!

Odie alerted the pair to his presence, and the dog perked his head in their direction as if he was waiting for them to follow.

Ravi and Magda followed Odie up a small hill, traversing through the pines once more. Odie turned right, jumping up a set of stones, and then switched back in the other direction, climbing up the side of a cliff. Ravi and Magda followed, and when they reached the top, they were met by a thick line of trees. Quickly, Odie disappeared underneath the pines, and Ravi and Magda followed, pushing prickly branches out of their way.

They emerged into a clearing, and Magda's mouth dropped open in shock.

Around the snow-covered landscape were large pools of stained blood seeping into the white powder. Large dents were imprinted into the snow, signifying where bodies had once laid. Snapped branches and scattered pine needles strewn across dirty snow depicted a gruesome struggle. In the middle of it all, was a cloak made for royalty held in place by an ice dagger.

"Dagmara!" Magda yelled, rushing forward to the cloak and picking it up. She pulled the ice dagger out of the snow and turned the red fabric over, searching for any kind of insignia.

"She was here." Magda whipped around to Ravi. "And this shard of ice is too perfect. It was created by a guardian. She's still in trouble."

Ravi examined the material before surveying the scene. Then he bent down, running his hand over the snow and blood. "This blood is fresh," he said. "Whoever was here was here recently."

"Do you think she's hurt?" Magda asked, and her throat closed in a striking burn as she fought back tears. She would never be able to forgive herself if Dagmara was injured—or worse.

Magda scanned the pattern of the footprints, discerning that three horses went off in one direction, while another horse exited in the opposite direction. It was clear someone had survived this attack, she just didn't know who, and which set of footprints to follow. She clutched the blood-red cloak tighter as her mind swirled through a series of possibilities.

You promised me that you would lead me to her! Now you have nothing to say!? Magda screamed, to no avail. She needed to find Dagmara this instant.

The wind was picking up, and the night was getting colder. Ravi placed his hand on her back.

"The snow will melt by morning," said Ravi. "We'll lose the footprints, so we have to hurry."

The blue magic swirled at Magda's palm, and she thrust her hand forward. A graceful blanket of dust blasted from her fingertips and settled in the melting snow, turning it into a more solid form. "There," she said, her voice hardening. If Eligor wasn't going to cooperate anymore, she would have to do this on her own.

"Odie, come," Magda said, kneeling down onto the firm snow and pressing the cloak into Odie's snout.

Odie sniffed around the fabric, and instantly his tail began wagging.

"Dagmara," Magda said, and the dog's eyes brightened. Then she gave the command:

"Go find."

CHAPTER 23
Dagmara

The sun was setting, casting orange rays through the towering trees. White snow fluttered down from the sky, and Dagmara stifled a chill, pulling Claude's coat tighter around her. She shuddered, pain lacing through her ribcage from the small cut left behind from Sabien's iceblade.

Her back was pressed against Claude's chest, his warmth radiating into her. Every move of the horse shifted their bodies, creating friction. All of her muscles were on high alert, feeling every inch of him taught against her.

"I see a place up ahead," Claude said, his voice soft against her ear.

Another chill shuddered through her that had nothing to do with the cold.

They stopped at a small two-story inn with ornate balconies and golden banners. The exterior was white, blending with the snow. An owl hung over the sliding front door, symbolic of Celestaire. Text was written above the door that Dagmara couldn't read, for the script was foreign to her.

Dismounting first, Claude landed softly on the snowy ground. He led the horse over to a hitching post and tied off the reins. Then he extended a hand up toward Dagmara.

"I'll help you," he said, his voice firm and leaving no room for question.

"Thank you," replied Dagmara, swinging her leg over the horse before Claude's hands slipped underneath her coat to grip her hips. He lifted her off the saddle, his palms secure as she slid down against his chest, landing on the snow directly in front of him.

A sharp pain immediately tore through her side and she winced, collapsing against his chest as she suppressed a shriek. She clutched her side, knocking his hand away in the process.

"Are you alright?" he asked, steadying her. He pulled his hand back, seeing the blood on his palm and the front of his shirt. "Why didn't you tell me you're injured?"

"I'm fine, really," she replied.

"Let's get you inside, I'll help you."

"I said I'm fine."

He shook his head before grabbing both his and Dagmara's knapsacks off the horse. He gave Dagmara hers before he started toward the entrance of the inn, lit by a single flickering lantern. As he slid open the door, boisterous laughter filled the air, followed by an onslaught of smells. A myriad of scents, such as liquor, sweat, and spices, flooded Dagmara's senses, reminding her of the Wilk tavern back in Azurem. However, here the air was lighter and the spices more pungent.

There were nearly a dozen tables filling the main space of the inn, all crowded with Celesta villagers. They clanked brass mugs together, and an intricate wind instrument filled the space with music.

A tall woman approached them, gesturing wide as she greeted them in Celesta.

Dagmara tightened Claude's coat around her, hiding her wound, though she knew her face was still reminiscent of the bruises Sabien had given her.

The king replied to the woman in her native language before pulling out a few coins from his pocket and extending them toward her. His hand retained some of the fresh blood from Dagmara's wound as he dropped the owl-stamped coins into the innkeeper's palm.

The innkeeper's eyes widened before she caught sight of the crimson smear. Her attention shifted to Dagmara, her gaze surveying Dagmara's appearance before addressing her.

Unable to interpret her words, Dagmara looked to Claude for advice.

Claude replied for her, his silver eyes glistening against the dimly lit room. The innkeeper nodded, pocketing the coin without another objection. Then Claude placed a hand on Dagmara's lower back and guided her toward the staircase.

"They have no room available on the first floor," Claude stated, pausing at the bottom of the stairs.

He *remembered*. Stairs were difficult with her health—a seemingly mundane obstacle was her worst nightmare—and not only did he remember, he had asked for a room on the first floor.

"That's alright," Dagmara replied, her chest tightening. She exhaled slowly before proceeding up the stairs. "Why didn't you disguise yourself?"

"That woman won't remember us in the morning," he replied. "And I'm trying to save my magic. The farther I am from Ilusauri, the harder it is to hold the illusion on the castle."

"But..." Dagmara started before stopping herself. She wanted to ask why he was using his magic to hide his scarred face, but she refrained, asking another question. "Isn't it exhausting to hold the magic that long?"

He gave her a weary glance. "It doesn't matter if it remains a beacon of hope for my kingdom. The longer guardians have their magic, the stronger it gets. I wouldn't have been able to do this a year ago."

Nodding, Dagmara didn't press the topic further, saving her energy as she struggled up the remaining stairs. She sensed the moment her vision threatened to drown her in darkness. She hesitated, clutching the wall for support, tightening every muscle in her body to keep her upright. The nape of her neck heated, her entire body going flush.

There were only two more stairs. She pushed herself on, ignoring the way Claude's hand tentatively reached out to prevent her from falling.

They arrived at the room shortly, and Claude pushed his way inside. Dagmara followed in behind him, surveying the chamber. It was spacious, with a fireplace, seating area, and master bed. A large glass door led to a small balcony, coated with a fine layer of snow.

"I think Martine packed clothes for you," Claude said, gesturing toward Dagmara's knapsack. "I'll start a fire, and then we should dress your wound."

"Is this...for both of us?" Dagmara stood in the threshold.

"They only had one room left," he said. "Don't worry, you can have the bed to yourself."

Nodding, Dagmara entered behind Claude and shut the door behind her. If she understood Celesta, she may have intervened in the conversation earlier, demanding they sleep in separate rooms, but she had no idea what conversation had transpired between Claude and the innkeeper.

Setting her bag on the couch, Dagmara fished through to reveal its contents. Both a sleepwear and daywear set of clothes were packed inside, along with her makeup kit and weapons pouch. Her dagger and throwing stars lined the weapons pouch and instantly made her feel relieved. She pulled the makeup kit from the bag, checking how much she had left of her potions, poisons, and antidotes. She didn't remember how many explosives from Teos remained. Lifting the lid, her breath caught in her throat as the vibrant purple liquid caught her eye.

Truth serum.

Her heart nearly stopped.

She slammed the lid closed, refusing to look through the contents another moment longer, flashes of the torture thrumming through her veins. Instead, she grabbed the sleepwear and stormed into the powder room, slamming the door closed before Claude could see her face.

She dropped the clothing on the ground and gripped the edge of the basin, catching her breath. In and out...slowly. She was free. She was safe. Then why did she feel so uneasy?

Catching sight of a stool in the corner, she let out a sigh of relief. She sat down immediately, letting her blood settle. Once more, the spinning world around her was coming to a standstill.

The door slammed outside, and she wondered if Claude had left. Maybe he was giving her space. Maybe it was for the best.

She pulled off his coat, wincing at every movement of her arms. The red masquerade dress she wore underneath was low cut, revealing far more of her figure than she realized. Tearing off the dress, she knew she never wanted to see it again. She changed her undergarments and hoisted sheer pants on that Martine had packed. The sleep shirt was also light and airy, meant for the weather of Ilusauri as opposed to Celestaire. She refrained from putting the shirt on right away, examining the wound in the mirror. It was a thin slice, running from the side of her ribs to her spine. She first tried to wash the wound, but couldn't reach far enough, every bend and twist sending another surge of agony through her.

There was a light knock on the door.

"Can I help?"

Her breath caught in her throat. She quickly grabbed the new shirt from the ground, holding it to her bare chest. "I don't need help."

There was a brief pause. "Just let me in."

Swallowing the lump in her throat, Dagmara crossed to the door and opened it. The king stood on the other side, leaning against the frame. He held a plate in one hand, filled with bite-sized meat and rice balls, and a large mug of water in the other. "These are for you."

Dagmara nearly dropped the shirt covering her chest at the sight of the food. "Thank you," she exhaled.

Claude was still for a moment, his eyes wandering.

Goosebumps ran down Dagmara's arms as she felt his gaze on every inch of her skin. She suddenly cleared her throat before taking the mug from his hands. Then she began to gulp down the water furiously, both relieving her parched throat and preventing herself from having to talk.

He entered the bathroom, immediately making the room feel half the size. He placed the platter on the counter before moving to stand at her side to examine the wound. "I hate that he hurt you."

She set down the mug on the counter, making sure one hand remained holding the shirt to her chest. "Only a few punches and truth serum, nothing I can't handle."

"But you shouldn't have had to handle it," he replied. "If I had only seen through Sabien's lies. I'm going to find him, and I'll make him pay."

Dagmara met his gaze in the mirror. "None of this is your fault." She slowly returned to the stool and sat, desperately clutching the shirt to her chest.

Claude used a washcloth to smear the blood, the movement causing more pain to lace through Dagmara's body, but she ignored it. Instead, she ate the food he brought her, not remembering the last time she had a full meal. Then the salt ignited her senses. She glanced closer at the food, seeing it decorated with small shaved salt crystals. Her heart warmed, and she finished eating.

"Why are you being so nice to me?" Dagmara asked. She turned her head to face him, realizing exactly how close he was to her. Her breath caught in her throat, and it was as if there was no air left at all.

Claude was like a chiseled statue, molded from the guardians themselves. The heat rose in Dagmara's cheeks as Claude scanned her entire face, pausing to look at her lips, before meeting her gaze once more.

He hesitated, his fingers still lingering against Dagmara's skin. "I don't think I'm the one who owes you any explanations."

And yet she wanted to hear from him. She wanted to know what he was thinking.

Recalling the late nights in his chamber, she remembered the game she once played with him. *A truth for a truth.* It had been a dangerous game at the time, for she was unable to share too much personal information while playing the role of Magda.

Now, the idea of truth tasted like bile in her throat. All she could think of was Sabien and the truth serum. It sickened her to the core... and yet...it may be the only way to speak with Claude as she once had.

"A truth for a truth?" Dagmara ventured.

There was a twinkle in his dark eyes as he remembered the game. His voice wavered as he replied, "Did you ever give me the truth?"

Her stomach flipped, as the question settled into her bones. Heat flushed her cheeks, and she parted her lips, but couldn't find the words.

Mostly. In the game they had played previously, she tried to share all truths until she admitted she would do anything for her brother—and had to pretend she was speaking about Aleksy instead of Teos.

Claude returned his attention to the wound, finishing it with a thick gauze.

"I'm so sorry for what I did," Dagmara blurted out.

The muscles in Claude's jaw tightened, his lips shifting to a thin line.

"You have to understand," she continued, "we thought you were behind the assassinations, so I came in Magda's place to keep her safe."

The king shook his head but didn't respond.

How could he ever believe her? There was nothing she could do to convince him she was being entirely honest.

Her heart plummeted in her chest, her stomach pivoting with

unease. There was one thing. But the thought of it froze her to the core. Every nerve was on edge. Simply thinking about the acrid taste caused her to choke.

Clearing her throat, she said, "What if I took truth serum?"

Finishing applying the gauze, Claude pulled back. He wiped his hands on the rag, washing them, as he gazed intently at Dagmara. His brow was furrowed, and his eyes slightly narrow. "Do you even have truth serum?"

"Yes," she said. She pointed to her makeup kit, visible through the open door. It was still hanging out the side of her knapsack. "I brought two vials to Ilusauri," she added, her voice barely audible.

The king tracked her gesture. "You would take it?"

"For you I would."

The king didn't meet her gaze. "No. It isn't right."

Swallowing the lump in her throat, Dagmara shoved her fear deep inside her chest.

"Claude, I need you to believe me. If that is the only thing that lets you believe me, I'll do it."

"I will simply have to believe you without the truth serum, even if it is against my better judgment."

"But will you? Truly believe me?"

He hesitated, and it was all the answer she needed. She rose from the chair, holding the shirt up to hide her body. "I'll go take it, but let me finish changing."

He rose. "If you are so adamant, I'll mix us a drink so you can't taste it. Take your time getting dressed."

After Claude exited, Dagmara finished putting the shirt on, covering the bandages. She was grateful that Martine had brought everything she needed. When she returned to the bedroom, Claude was already seated on the couch, and two mugs were placed on the table in front of him.

"You had two vials. I added truth serum to my drink," he announced. "You deserve the truth as well."

Dagmara took a seat beside him, and they both raised their glasses to one another.

"A truth for a truth," she said, not allowing herself any more time to think about it. She knocked back the mug, and the liquid poured into her throat. The taste of the alcohol concealed the noxious truth serum. Perhaps she was used to the burn, since it slithered down her throat in one gulp.

Claude grimaced, shaking his head from the aftertaste. He set down the mug and stated, "You first."

She thought of a question that didn't affect their relationship with one another. Something she had been wondering for a long time—something that made her doubt him.

"What were you looking for in Celestaire with Guardian Sora?"

"The First Prince's tomb," Claude replied. He shut his mouth quickly, a flicker of surprise crossing his face, before nodding and loosening his posture. "Each time all guardians of one branch die, the lock is broken, and the land begins to deteriorate without a guardian. I don't count since I didn't have my magic yet. I thought, if I found the tomb, I could maybe reseal the lock somehow. If I remade the Mind lock, perhaps Ilusauri would be restored."

It was both honorable and genuine. He had never been a malicious king, even when he had been framed for invading Celestaire. However, the idea of searching for the First Prince's tomb was risky, and no wonder he didn't want all of Celestaire to know his true intentions. Why did he think it was in Celestaire though? That was another question she held onto for later.

"Your turn," Dagmara said. She gripped her mug until her knuckles turned white, remembering the pain of the truth serum that increased the longer she spent trying to answer a question. She would have to answer him immediately, no matter what truth came out. Sweat dripped down her back as nerves raced through her.

The king shifted closer on the couch and placed his hand on the mug in her iron grip. "You're safe here," he said. He lifted the mug out of her hands and placed it down on the table. He was so close that their knees were inches apart.

Then he asked his question, "How long were you working with Sabien?"

Dagmara jerked back. "I was never working with Sabien."

Claude's eyes narrowed slightly.

A sigh escaped her lips, before she proceeded to tell Claude everything. She started with the night Sabien arrived in Gorzhelm, how she stabbed him and shoved him into the ravine. Then she explained how she and Magda made a scene at the coronation.

"Wait—" Claude interrupted. "Magdalena doesn't have Life Magic?"

"No," Dagmara admitted. "That's another reason I had to come in her place. No one could find out."

The king glanced at the empty mugs on the table, then propped one elbow on the back of the couch and leaned closer. "Go on."

So she did. She proceeded to explain arriving at the castle and being anxious about Sabien's ability to reveal her identity. She explained the letters from Teos had revealed more possible clues linking Claude to the Azuremi murders. Then she explained that on the night of the wedding, Sabien had planted evidence and pretended to read a letter in Flaustran.

"He took me because he thought I would lead him to Magdalena," Dagmara stated. "But he brought me to a Mind Guardian who forced me to reveal Magdalena's secret Soul Magic. They know everything."

"A Mind Guardian?" Claude asked. "What did she look like?"

Dagmara hesitated, understanding the motive behind his question. "She was the one who killed your parents."

"By the Guardians," Claude muttered. He ran a palm against his face, exhaling a sharp breath. "I was hoping she was gone for good." Shaking his head, he cleared his throat. "I have so many more questions, but I think I have asked far too many in a row. It's your turn."

For some reason, a weight was lifted from Dagmara's chest. Finally telling the truth to Claude began to clear the thick fog between them. All that was left was the stone wall to tear down.

After telling her story, a new question was at the forefront of Dagmara's mind. "I heard you talking to Madame Annette the night I arrived. You said you would use me and get rid of me. What was that conversation about?"

"That was my original plan," Claude admitted. "I only intended to form an alliance long enough to find the tomb and hoped to avoid a legally binding marriage. I figured once I found the tomb and restored my lands, I wouldn't need Azurem's food supply anymore. I selfishly wanted to use Magdalena to access her father's logbooks. I knew he was also searching for the tomb. But, I had to gain your trust first before asking for the logbooks, and you demanded immediate marriage...and then...there were other obstacles."

"Such as?"

His eyes twinkled, a spark behind a veil. The muscles along his neck tensed. He couldn't fight the truth serum.

"Such as my feelings for you."

Heat flushed through Dagmara's body, leaving her head in a dizzying spell.

Then he added, "It wasn't your turn."

"Didn't you just ask multiple questions in a row?"

"Yes," he replied, the truth serum slipping the answer from his lips even though it was rhetorical. His mouth creased—a hint of a smile. "I thought we were better at this game."

"I guess we're out of practice. Your turn."

"Tell me something about the real Dagmara." It wasn't exactly a question, but rather an open ended answer. She might get away with saying anything she wanted.

But what she wanted was for him to know the real her.

"Teos is actually my brother. He's smart, loves cards, and is my accomplice in everything," she began. "My mother was an assassin for the king and was tortured to death. She trained me to continue in her footsteps, but I could never be as good as her because..." Dagmara paused. What would he think of her if she admitted her condition? Did it even matter? She wasn't a princess. She would never be worthy of him anyway. There was no future where she and Claude ended up together. All that was possible was mending their relationship and hopefully her heart in the process. Then she could let him go.

Closing her eyes, she let out a deep exhale, focusing her clouded mind. "You know I'm not a guardian, but I'm not even normal." Finding her courage, she opened her eyes and met his gaze. "I have a condition, and I don't know if it has a cure."

He nodded, his expression unwavering. "And how does the condition affect you?"

"It..." she stopped suddenly. "Wait—you're not surprised?"

"No," he replied, his voice calm. "I noticed. I was waiting for you to feel comfortable enough to tell me."

Of course he noticed. He gave her salt. He had them all kneel during the wedding. He summoned a chair with a snap of his fingers at the engagement ball.

At first, disappointment cascaded over Dagmara as she realized she wasn't as good as she thought at hiding it. But then, as the wave crashed and withdrew back into the stormy ocean of her emotions, she found herself reassured. Calm. Content.

Safe.

He had paid attention. He had seen her.

"I..." She cleared her throat, suppressing her smile. "It affects me in a multitude of ways. Constant pain, inability to stand for too long, headaches, fatigue, an inability to run long distances, a cloud over my thoughts like a physical weight impeding my ability to think clearly—it's hard to articulate. Some days are better than others."

"And what helps relieve some of the symptoms?"

"Salt seems to help with energy. I have to make sure I sit, and—" she stopped. "You keep stealing questions!"

He smiled. "I was hoping you wouldn't notice."

"Well, it's my turn, Your Majesty," she said. She shifted the conversation away from her health. "What are your plans for after speaking with Reon?"

"I will keep searching for the tomb. I have to restore my kingdom. You?"

"I have to find Magda before Sabien does," she said. "Maybe...you can help me find her."

"I will need to speak with Magda eventually, and I suppose I will be indebted to you if this conversation with Reon is able to suspend the war. So...yes."

"Thank you."

"And after that?"

She hesitated. "I guess...I will return to Azurem."

"Why?"

"Because that is my home. My brother is there." She paused, shifting the wedding ring on her finger. "And you will be married to Magda."

"Is that what you want?"

"What do you want me to say?"

"I want you to say you will come home with me." Shock flashed across Claude's face, as though he wasn't expecting the truth serum to draw the confession out of him. He shifted forward on the couch, placing his elbows on his knees and diverting his gaze. "I should despise you after what you did. I shouldn't have cared if you were safe or not. And yet here I am—after you broke into my home, pretended to be someone you weren't, and threw poison at me. I thought I married you, and yet my kingdom thinks I'm married to Princess Magdalena."

"You still are. Once we find Magda, she can take my spot as was always planned, and I can go back to Azurem."

"I don't remember agreeing to this plan." He rose from the couch and paced away.

"I..."

"And that's what you want? To return to Azurem?"

No. She wanted to return to Ilusauri with him. But it wasn't possible. There was no alliance for medicine if Magdalena wasn't the one married to Claude. Could that be changed? Could the wedding be called off and the kingdoms could form a normal alliance between them?

She couldn't get her hopes up. She wasn't a guardian. She was a nobody without power. She served the Azuremi crown, and she would have to follow whatever Magdalena wished. She couldn't start scheming to break up the marriage. Maybe Magda wanted to marry her childhood friend. Maybe whatever Dagmara started between her and Claude was betraying her own best friend.

Dagmara said, "I want to return to Azurem and see Teos." It wasn't a lie. But it wasn't the full truth.

Claude nodded, rubbing a hand across the back of his neck. "And you'll continue to work for the Azuremi crown?"

Dagmara hadn't considered any other options, and she knew working for the royals was the only way to keep Teos safe and healthy.

She spoke, "Yes, I will."

"Will you ever return to Ilusauri?"

She hesitated at the question. "I doubt I will have another mission there. So...no."

He nodded, staring out the window. "Then I need to hear you say you hate me."

Dagmara stood to her feet. "Claude—"

He whipped around to face her, and the spark in his eyes had transformed into a flame. "You despised me once. Say it, I'm begging you. I need to be released from this turmoil. Say you hate me so much that I can think about something other than you." He approached her until he was standing a foot away. She gazed up at him, feeling as though she were choking from the emotions trying to drown her.

"I don't hate you," Dagmara started, "but the world thinks you're married to Magda. As soon as we find her, I'll step away and leave the guardians to do what they do best."

He reached out, placing his hands on either side of her face. His palms were rough and calloused, but his touch was gentle. "I don't care if you're not a guardian, Dagmara. It has never been required for guardians to marry one another. My mother wasn't a guardian. Queen Bernadette—"

"Claude..." she started to argue.

"Then tell me you hate me," he said once more. He leaned close, placing his forehead against hers.

She could feel his breath on her face, and it sent a chill down her spine. Her heart threatened to beat out of her ribcage. She ran her own hands up the front of his chest, wrapping her fingers in the fabric and holding tight. She closed her eyes, letting his words rush through her.

"You've ruined my life, Dagmara. Free me. Say you detest me. Otherwise, you will return to Azurem, and I won't know a day of peace."

Her stomach was catapulting inside her. His touch was electrifying. His lips were inches away.

She tried to fulfill his promise, despite knowing she could never return to hating him as she once did.

"I hate you," she whispered, surprised the truth serum would let her utter such a lie. Why wasn't she burning from the inside out? What else would it let her speak? "I hate how you put your people first. I hate how resilient you are. I hate how conscientious you are and how much you see me. I loathe the salt gifts and that you learned the Azuremi waltz for me. And most of all, I hate how guilty I feel for hurting you. You deserve someone better than me."

The truth serum didn't scorch her.

Claude sighed. "Oh, Dagmara," he said, his voice chilling. "It doesn't sound like you know the definition of hate."

"I was hoping to burn," Dagmara replied honestly, "but it seems the truth serum agrees with me."

Claude jerked away, but the magnetism between them was just as palpable as before.

"We should get some rest," he blurted out. "You take the bed. I'll sleep here." He gestured toward the couch.

Her guard was down, confused by his immediate withdrawal at the mention of the truth serum. "I'm sure there's room for both of us in the bed," she ventured.

The king only shook his head.

"If you change your mind, the offer still stands," Dagmara let in. She reached for her knapsack and makeup kit, removing it to give Claude space. As she went to close the makeup kit and shove it in the bag, she hesitated. A glimmer of purple peered back at her—truth serum. Each vial was a dose. Claude had said he had put one in each of their drinks.

"There was never any in yours," he announced.

She snapped her head up. "What?"

"You were tortured with truth serum, why would I ever let you drink another drop? Simply the idea that you offered to take it was enough for me," he stated. He clasped his hands, absentmindedly twirling the wedding ring on his finger. Dagmara tracked the movement, her heart aching. "And trust me, if anyone forces you to take it again I will personally rip out their throat."

Her face paled, before an instant heat pooled in her stomach.

She shoved the box into the knapsack. She had no other words. "Goodnight, Your Majesty," she finished before she climbed into the oversized bed alone.

CHAPTER 24
Dagmara

There was rustling in the room. A fast panting.

Dagmara's eyes fluttered open in alarm, staring at the ceiling of the Celesta inn.

"No, stop..."

The voice was barely a whisper.

Claude.

Shooting upright, Dagmara tried to focus her eyes in the darkness. The large balcony doors allowed the moonlight to pour through, illuminating the space enough to make out the figure on the couch.

The king's head was shifting side to side. He muttered words inaudible to Dagmara. He was far too large for the couch. The small blanket had already fallen to the ground beside him.

Slipping her feet out from underneath the covers, Dagmara rose to a standing position. Bracing herself against the wall in case a dizzy spell came over her, she approached the couch on the balls of her feet, remaining utterly silent.

"Don't..." Claude muttered.

Dagmara froze.

Then Claude sat upright, yelling, "No!"

"Claude!" Dagmara blurted out. She raced to his side, dropping to her knees at the edge of the couch and taking his hand. "It's alright, you're safe!"

The king jerked back, ripping his hand from hers. His eyes were wide, fear claiming his body. He withdrew a knife from underneath his pillow and aimed it at her.

Sucking in a breath, Dagmara raised both hands defensively. "I'm not going to hurt you. It was only a nightmare."

Claude's hand shook, the knife faltering in his grip. He released it abruptly, and it clanked to the ground. "Dagmara," he said. "I'm so sorry. Did I hurt you?" He shifted forward.

"No, you didn't, it was a nightmare," she repeated.

"I thought—"

He stopped suddenly, his head turning to the balcony doors.

Dagmara had heard the sound too. It was a faint fluttering of wings. She peered through the glass doors, seeing a blackbird land on the railing outside.

All the muscles in Claude's body tensed.

Rising from the ground, Dagmara approached the balcony doors. "Hey!" she shouted through the glass. "Get out of here!" She slammed the ball of her hand into the window, scaring the bird.

The blackbird let out a shrill call. The noise pierced Dagmara's temples. The creature took flight, soaring directly toward her.

Dagmara stumbled backward, distancing herself from the balcony doors. She slammed into a solid chest of muscle, but Claude held her upright. As the bird dove for her through the glass, it collided with the door in a bone-shattering crunch. Somehow, the glass held firm.

The blackbird careened to the side. Feathers dusted the balcony, and a smear of blood remained on the windowpane. The bird didn't attack again. It regained its balance and took flight. The creature disappeared into the dark of the night, leaving the two of them behind.

Dagmara let out a sigh of relief, turning around to face the king.

Claude had his gaze fixated on the dark sky beyond. The moonlight caught his figure, and she could see sweat beading his temple. His thin shirt was soaked through.

"Are you alright?" Dagmara asked, scanning his disgruntled appearance. What kind of nightmare had the king experienced?

He sighed, "I will be." He backed away from Dagmara, gripping the bottom of his shirt and pulling it off his head. He threw it to the side, and the sweat-ridden shirt landed with a splat on the ground. He ran the back of his arm across his forehead, every curve of his muscles catching the light. Then he bent down to pick up his knife, straightening with the weapon in his firm grip.

Dagmara couldn't help her wandering eyes.

"I'm sorry for waking you," he said before turning back to face her.

Her eyes snapped up to meet his. "Don't apologize." She waited for him to give her more. "Do you want to tell me about it?" She returned to the bed, climbing on top and sitting upright. She gestured to the wide open spot beside her.

The king hesitated a moment before finally conceding. He tentatively approached, placing the knife on the side table, before sitting on the other side of the bed. "There's not much to tell," he said, his voice wavering. "I can show you?"

She nodded.

Claude's gaze drifted to the center of the room. Three silver illusions came to life, dancing valiantly in the dim light. As bright as stars, a large man appeared with a young boy, both of them nearly identical. Beside them, was a stunning woman with her hair in a silk wrap and a silver, iridescent robe.

"I was only thirteen, and my father was supposed to take me to play a game of Soulaye the following morning," Claude narrated. The young boy vanished, leaving the king and queen behind. The king collapsed into the queen's arms, blood coating the ground in puddles. "In the middle of the night, I heard screaming. I raced into my parents room, but I was too late." The illusions painted the scene, the young boy returning to the painting before them, tears streaming down his face. "My father was dead. I raced to his side, trying to wake him, but then she saw me." Another figure appeared, tall and gorgeous, fizzing in and out of reality. "I don't think she planned to kill me until that moment."

"Viette?"

Claude nodded. "She attacked me," he gestured toward his face, and the illusion melted away. It was like a scratch in a once-beautiful painting, but to Dagmara, it made the painting more valuable. His disfigured eye was full of mystery.

The illusions played out the memory. The transparent reenactment of Viette lunged toward the young boy with a blade before the queen scrambled to her feet.

"Then my mom stepped in. My mom was the one who managed to rip the mask from her face. But the assassin didn't slay my mom. Maybe that would have been better."

"What did she do?" Dagmara asked, her gaze fixated on the silver memory in front of her.

He swallowed, pausing. "The assassin compelled my mother to walk off the balcony."

Chills ran down Dagmara's arms, a pit forming in her stomach. She watched in horror as a metallic set of doors manifested. The queen began to walk toward it, unable to control her mind or her body anymore.

"The assassin ran, no doubt thinking she had blinded me completely," Claude continued. "I could barely see through the blood in my eyes. But I got up. I grabbed my mother's arm, trying to stop her, but the compulsion was far too powerful."

The apparition of the boy clutched the queen's wrist, his bare feet slipping in the puddles of blood on the ground.

"She was dragging me closer to the edge of the balcony with her. I had to let go. I had to—"

His voice faltered, and he looked away, the manifestations evaporating.

Shifting onto her knees, Dagmara reached out and grabbed his hand. "I'm so sorry," she said. "You should never have witnessed that."

"People said I killed them. They thought I had the ability to do something like that."

Dagmara was one of them.

She had no words. She was about to pull him into her embrace, about to wrap her arms around him in a hug they both desperately needed, when he started to get up. His illusion slipped back into place, a mask covering his scar and blind eye.

Dagmara tightened her grip on his hand, pulling him back. "Stay."

The king didn't say a word. He merely gave her a gentle nod before pulling his hand from hers. He lifted the covers, sliding underneath.

She wished she could comfort him. She wished she knew how. She wished she could go back to before she had betrayed him.

However, she followed his lead, pulling back the blanket and making herself comfortable. They both lay on their backs, staring at the ceiling. An awkward amount of space separated them.

"How can you see the bird?" Claude asked.

Dagmara was quiet for a long moment. "I don't know."

"It belongs to the First Prince. Eligor."

"No," Dagmara muttered. "It doesn't make sense. Why do you think you can see it?"

"I thought it had something to do with being an heir to the Mind Guardian lineage," Claude stated. "I only started seeing it after my magic began to manifest—a few years after my parents were killed. But now that theory is debunked..."

"Because I'm not heir to any guardian lineage," Dagmara replied. She remained fixated on the ceiling, her mind whirling with thoughts.

She pulled the covers up closer to her neck, trying to protect herself from the unknown beyond.

"I want to get rid of it," Claude said. "I hate the Void. I hate Eligor's magic. I want it gone."

Dagmara swallowed the lump in her throat. She had no idea how to get rid of the bird and the Void that was tormenting the king.

"One thing at a time. Speak with Reon, find Magda, uncover the tomb, and restore Ilusauri. We can deal with the bird after all that."

Claude sighed.

Turning her head, Dagmara tried to read his expression in the darkness. "What?"

"Maybe we figure out the bird before finding Magdalena."

Dagmara turned her entire body, laying on her side. "We have to make sure Magda is safe."

He shifted, rotating onto his side to face her. He propped himself on his elbow, his muscles rippling across his naked chest. "Sabien may come after you," Claude said. "You think it's a good idea to lead him straight to Magdalena?"

"He may find her on her own at this point. Would you rather we go our separate ways and I find Magda on my own?" Dagmara countered.

"No—" he blurted out before exhaling sharply. "Maybe I don't want to find Magdalena."

Dagmara bristled. "Why? Do you need to look for the tomb right away?"

"You were the one who said, once we find Magdalena, you and her will swap places and you will return to Azurem," he reiterated. "So maybe, I don't want to find Magdalena. I don't want you to leave. I don't want to stop pretending that you, Dagmara, are my wife."

"We can't pretend forever. I'm not your wife according to the kingdoms. People as far as Flaustra know King Claude and Princess Magdalena are wed. When Magda returns, she will be your wife, and I will get as far away as possible."

"And you want to get as far away from me as possible?"

"It doesn't matter what I want. I was only fulfilling a duty to Azurem. You should hate me for what I did."

He shifted closer on the bed. "I have thought about it time and time again—I simply can't bring myself to hate you. And maybe I don't want to. I know why you did what you did, and I don't blame you. So forgive me, for not wanting to find Magdalena right away. I'm selfish, because I'm trying to postpone losing you completely."

The air vanished, and suddenly it was hard to breathe. She wanted to say, "I don't want to lose you either," or even, "I could never hate you," but neither came out. He was making this harder for her. She desperately wanted him, and every ounce of her body was drawn to him like a moth to a flame. But she was about to get burned. Unless he annulled the marriage with Magda, there was no hope for them. Dagmara wouldn't play pretend the rest of her life, and she certainly wouldn't be a mistress. And yet, she didn't want the marriage to sever. Ilusauri needed food, and Azurem needed medicine. Dagmara's desire for the King of Ilusauri—no matter how palpable—would never surpass her necessity to keep the people of both kingdoms safe. She would save her brother, no matter the cost.

But...there was still here and now. At least until they found Magda.

The king's expression softened. "I can see you thinking," he spoke quietly. He reached forward, his calloused fingers brushing a piece of hair out of her face. He traced his finger behind her ear and down her neck, sending a chill through her entire body. "Please, say something."

"We can't postpone finding Magda. Sabien will still go after her," Dagmara said. "But, we still have time until that moment comes." It was a terrible decision, but she was tired of putting everyone else first. She wanted Claude.

His hand stilled against her neck. His gaze drifted to her lips. "So you'll pretend with me until then? Pretend you and I have all the time in the world—only Dagmara and Claude. No obligations, no kingdoms, no guardian status, no Mad King."

"I like you for who you are, Mad King and all, but yes," Dagmara stated, her breath shaky. "I can pretend to like you a little longer, Your Majesty." A smile creased her lips, remembering the words they once shared before their first dance.

"Shall we pretend we're in love for one evening? Then we can return to disliking one another."

"I can pretend to like you for one evening, Your Majesty."

Claude returned the smile, no doubt remembering the moment as well. He shifted even closer, his forehead resting against hers. A burning desire coursed through her body, warmth spreading through her. She could feel his breath on her lips, and she could smell the faint remnants of his cologne.

"And what do you want in that time we have—before we find Magdalena?" he asked, his fingers trailing the length of her neck. "I want every second you'll give me. It is, of course, for the betterment of our kingdoms." He angled his head, drawing his mouth even closer until there was barely space between them.

A laugh escaped her lips. She opened her mouth to reply, knowing her answer and feeling comforted with the familiarity of it, when a soft tapping began at the balcony doors.

Her body tensed, every ounce of her on high alert.

"What is—"

"Shh!" Dagmara cut him off, jerking back and placing a single finger to his lips.

His lips were soft against her finger, his breath hot. She couldn't blink, staring back at his brown eyes, sparkling with a hint of silver. A spark of desire flashed across his face, mimicking the need flooding Dagmara's body.

A crash broke the silence.

Both Dagmara and Claude jolted upright in bed, their attention on the balcony. Dagmara fought the dizziness that cascaded over her from the quick movement. Instead, she fixed her eyes on the shattered pot on the balcony, visible through the glass doors. Dirt and leaves scattered the ground, the wind rustling the broken flowers.

Wind.

"I'll go look," Claude said.

Dagmara grabbed his arm before he could move. "Wait," she whispered. "Only a strong wind could've knocked a plant that large over. It has to be a trap. It's probably Junne and Sabien."

Claude's eyes narrowed. "Perfect. I'm going to kill him."

Throwing the cover off, Claude exited the bed and grabbed his knife from the side table. He didn't waste time throwing on a shirt or shoes before he approached the balcony doors.

Dagmara followed suit, flinging the blankets off. She didn't have time to collect her potions. Instead, she grabbed the dagger Martine had returned to her.

Before opening the door, Claude glanced once behind him, silver glistening in his eyes. Dagmara gave him a curt nod, keeping her distance. If Junne was about to fly in and land on the balcony, Dagmara wanted to take her by surprise.

Easing the balcony door open, Claude stepped into the night. He cautiously rounded the broken pot, his feet bare. He was not afraid. He glanced in each direction, holding the knife in front of him. His illusions could not kill. He needed the weapon.

There was nothing.

Maybe Dagmara was being paranoid? She shook her head from the thought. She couldn't let her guard down. She approached the balcony, inching the glass door open further to investigate for herself.

Claude reached the railing. He placed one hand against the barrier, staring into the darkness.

"Maybe it was just the wind," he whispered.

He spoke too soon.

Something shot up from the ground and attached to his wrists. It was far too fast for Dagmara to register what it was in the shadows.

The rope-like object yanked the king from both wrists, harsh and unyielding. The railing had no protection, and Claude was pulled over, careening off the edge before he could save himself.

"No!" Dagmara screamed. She raced forward, reaching out to grab him. Her hands were met with thin air. Gasping, Dagmara leaned over the rail, staring at the snowy ground below. Claude lay flat on his back, groaning from the impact. His knife was a few yards away. A few paces beyond the knife was a figure in black with a hood. And Claude was barely stirring.

No, no, no!

They were only on the second floor, but the drop was still too far to jump. Rushing from the balcony edge, Dagmara burst back into their room and charged for the door. She had to get down there. Gripping her dagger, she unlatched their door and flung it open. Charging into the hall, she started for the staircase, but didn't make it far.

A figure lunged out of the shadows, grabbing her around the waist. Her back slammed against the assailant's chest, and his other hand clamped against her mouth. His lips were close to her ear as he whispered:

"I have you."

Her body froze in his firm grip. He was speaking Azuremi—but it wasn't a Celesta or Ilusaurian accent. It wasn't even an Azuremi accent.

It was Flaustran.

CHAPTER 25
Dagmara

Flaustran? Who was kidnapping her from Flaustra? Did Sabien and Junne team up with another assassin?

Dagmara had no time to process her thoughts. Claude was in danger.

She elbowed the man in the gut, breaking free from his restraints. Whirling on him, she swiped the dagger at his face.

The man barely dodged, stumbling back and crashing into the hallway wall. His eyes were wide, and he blurted out a series of words in quick succession—none of which Dagmara understood.

She sized up her opponent quickly. He wasn't burly by any means, but slender and toned. She wouldn't have picked him for a fighter in any lineup. He was a few inches taller than her, but not by much. He had a knife on his belt, but it remained sheathed.

If she had her potions, she could take him down in one strike. Unfortunately, without her potions, it would take her two or three strikes.

Without hesitating, she lunged, driving the dagger toward his chest. He dodged, sidestepping the blade and grabbing her wrist. He bent it back, attempting to have her relinquish her grip. She would not yield. She kicked his knee, and he fell backward, dragging her down to the floor with him.

The world spun as she crashed against his chest. He tried to roll her off him, but the hallway was too narrow. Straddling him, she yanked her wrist free from his grasp, raised the dagger in the air, and plunged it toward his chest.

He caught her hands at the last moment, the tip of the blade barely grazing his shirt.

Words flooded his lips in Flaustran, no doubt begging for his life. Dagmara ignored every word and pushed harder. He was attempting to shift the tip of the steel away from his heart and toward the side. She had underestimated his strength—which made her question why he hadn't put up more of a fight. Why hadn't he withdrawn his knife?

Surging more energy into her body, she angled her entire weight into the attack. The dagger began to burrow into his shoulder, slicing skin and muscle.

The man screamed before finally blurting in Azuremi, "I'm good! I'm safe!"

His fear clearly stripped all Azuremi words from his vocabulary. He was neither good, nor safe. The dagger dug deeper, and his screams heightened.

A bark rang through the hallway, jolting Dagmara from her senses. She glanced up, seeing a black and white dog at the end of the hall, climbing up the last stairs and racing toward her. The dog was growling, his teeth bare.

Her mind went blank. Was that...?

No. It couldn't be.

The dog skidded to a halt directly in front of Dagmara, above the man's head. It suddenly stopped growling, and his ears pricked upright.

By the guardians.

"Magda! I know Magda!" the man underneath her yelled.

That made Dagmara's blood chill. She released the pressure

against the blade, and his strength won. He shoved her wrists back, sending a sharp pain through her hands. Now in his control, the dagger exited his shoulder and flew toward her face. Rocking back on her knees, she couldn't dodge the blade in time. The weapon sliced across her cheek, and a stinging pain tore across her skin. She reached up instinctually to feel the damage, and her palm met slick blood.

The dagger clattered to the ground beside her.

"Sorry!" the young man said, his eyes wide. His Flaustran accent was thick, and Dagmara thought she had heard him incorrectly.

The dog whimpered, rounding the dagger and coming to Dagmara's side. With one sniff at her elbow, the dog's tail began wagging vigorously.

"Odie?" she said under her breath.

Odie pranced on his paws, nudging Dagmara in the side. His wet tongue grazed her shoulder, leaving behind slobber.

Shock coursed through every part of her. How was Odie *here*?

The man jolted up to a seated position, shoving her off his chest and into his lap. He grabbed her chin to examine the injury, despite the fact that blood was gushing from his shoulder. He started rambling again in Flaustran.

Her knees on either side of him, his face inches from hers, Dagmara stared blankly at the man. She slapped his hand away from her face. "I have no idea what you are saying."

He cleared his throat as though that would help his translation. "We're saving you."

Dagmara shuffled off his lap, nearly colliding with Odie. The dog jumped up, licking her face, and she wrapped her arms around his neck, trying to hold him still. Trying to hold onto a piece of home. "I don't need to be saved. Who the hell are you? Where's Magda, and why do you have her dog?"

The man's brows knit together, and his head tilted to one side. Did he not understand her? Or was he as confused as she was?

Dagmara looked back at Odie, his tail wagging so intensely that his entire body was shaking. There was no way Odie would be content with a stranger if Magda needed him. He would run to the ends of the earth to find her. The only option was—

Her mind flashed to whatever had pulled Claude from the balcony. *Vines.* And it wasn't the wind that had knocked the plant over. It was the plant itself.

Guardians, no!

Dagmara grabbed the dagger and was on her feet in seconds. Her world spun, and her shoulder collided with the hallway wall, but she wouldn't stop running.

Magda was the one who had yanked Claude from the balcony. Did she hear Dagmara was missing? Did she think Claude was Sabien—a man with magic holding her hostage? Magda had come. Her best friend had come to save her!

And now her best friend was about to die at the hands of the man she loved.

Unless…Magda killed Claude first.

CHAPTER 26
Magdalena

The man lay in the middle of the snow, shirtless and weaponless—but Magda knew better. His magic was a weapon.

This had to be Sabien—the Captain of Ilusauri who had kidnapped Dagmara. All clues led here, and the innkeeper claimed there was an Azuremi girl who was being held against her will in this room. This was the man that had murdered Aleksy and her father.

At least, that is what Magda believed as she tightened the head-wrap concealing her silver hair and charged forward.

The man groaned, rolling onto his side and inhaling a sharp breath. He reached for a small knife in the snow that had cascaded over the balcony with him.

Magda reached for the stone holding up the balcony. She channeled her Soul magic, gold glistening at her fingertips, and yanked a piece loose. The rock came flying toward the man on the ground. She had to get to Dagmara, whether she had to incapacitate this man or outright kill him. Though she wanted to take slow revenge on the man who had killed her family, Dagmara was the priority.

The man barely dodged the giant slab of stone. He scrambled to his feet, but the stone collided with his hip in a sickening crunch. He let out a yell of agony, nearly collapsing once more to the ground, but he held firm. His gaze met Magda's for the first time, and his eyes narrowed on her before a hint of silver began to illuminate.

Shards manifested from thin air, surrounding him on all sides. They flew toward Magda, and her heart lurched in her chest. She dodged the weapons, but the air didn't stir as they flew inches from her face. They landed in the snow behind her, not leaving a mark or an indent.

Confusion rippled through Magda. The silver eyes...

She whirled back to face the assassin, but there was no longer only one of him. There were a dozen copies surrounding her, all of them a perfect replica of the last, holding knives in her direction.

A Mind assassin? She thought the assassin would have Life magic, but then again, she had to remember a Spirit assassin had just attacked her on Ishani's ship. She couldn't take any risks.

She staggered back, her eyes darting between each illusion. She had to find the real him. She had to cut him down before he cut her down.

One of the figures lunged for her and she slipped as she dodged, barely missing the blade. Was it real? Would that one have impaled her?

She couldn't waste her energy fighting phantoms.

She tried to reach for the soil, to pull more roots from the ground, but they were frozen. It was as though she were tugging on an immovable statue, covered in snow.

Snow.

Scrambling out of the way of another illusion, she reached for the ground, honing her magic. Warmth surged through her palms. It was like fire—so hot that she could mistake it for ice. Her head throbbed in pain, begging her to pace herself, but she would not listen.

The snow began to shift. Water droplets levitated. Life Magic was answering her call. There wasn't enough to knock him down, but there was plenty for her scheme.

Thrusting her hands forward, the liquid went flying, spraying the area in front of her. It soared through all the illusions, undisturbed. Only one figure disrupted the pattern. The water splattered against his naked chest, leaving behind droplets.

She charged forward, ignoring the other illusions that attacked, her gaze set on the real Mind assassin. He hesitated, a fraction of a moment, no doubt baffled by her dual wielding abilities. But his hesitation gave her the chance to strike.

She barreled into him, taking him to the ground. He grunted as his back met the snow once more. She had already withdrawn her dagger from her belt, poised to slice his throat.

His head came for hers before she could react. She heard a snap as his forehead met her nose, and instantly she saw stars. The dagger slipped from her grasp as he thrust her to the side.

He was pure muscle as he rolled on top of her. He easily snatched both her arms and pinned them above her head. His hand was large enough to wrap around both her wrists, restraining her with one arm. His other hand pressed the tip of his knife to her throat. The weight of his body against her caused her chest to tighten. She struggled to inhale a deep breath to quell her throbbing head.

"Who are you?" he demanded in Ilusaurian, her mind taking a moment to translate.

She didn't bother with an answer. She thrust her knee up, attempting to throw him to the side. She racked her brain with everything Ishani had taught her, but none of the moves could help her when this Mind assassin was twice her strength. Instead, she honed her attention on the roots below. She could find them. She could free them from the frozen ground, for she controlled the earth.

The blade pressed deeper against her skin.

"Don't make me ask again," he growled.

"You won't have the chance to ask again," Magda spat. She found the roots in her mind and yanked. The earth burst open on either side of her. Roots tore into the open air, cracking and splintering against the frozen earth. Snow whipped around them. She commanded the roots to wrap around the assassin's neck.

They latched to the Mind assassin's throat, wrapping around until she was certain he would release her.

But he didn't.

He pressed the blade deeper to her chin. Guardians, he was going to slit her throat as she strangled him. They both were going down together.

"Stop!" a scream rang through the night. "Magda!"

At her name, Magda jolted out of the bloodlust.

"Claude, please!"

Magda's eyes widened. Claude? The Mad King? Her childhood friend?

He jerked the knife back, seeming to snap out of the fight at the sound of the voice as well.

Magda released the roots' hold, and Claude gasped for breath. The roots snaked back into the earth, returning to the soil. Claude released her hands and slid off her, choking.

Similarly, Magda rolled out from underneath him, panting. She reached up to her neck, feeling blood. He was really about to kill her.

And she would have killed him.

"Magda!" the voice called again.

The voice.

Suddenly alight with a surge of adrenaline, Magda looked up from the ground. A trio was running toward her. Odie, Ravi, and—

"Dagmara!" Magda called, heaving herself to her feet.

Her best friend's face was covered in crimson, but her smile was clear. She didn't stop running. Dagmara barreled into Magda, embracing her in a hug. They held firmly, as though the other would vanish from sight if they let go too soon.

"You came!" Dagmara exhaled, her face buried in Magda's hair. "You're finally here."

"I'm so sorry I didn't come sooner," Magda replied. "I'm sorry that—"

Wait, was Claude the one who had kidnapped her?

Magda pulled away from Dagmara, but took her hand. She glared at Claude, fury behind her gaze. "What did you do to her?"

"Me?" asked Claude, his voice raspy. He was rubbing his throat, glancing once at a growling Odie, before meeting Magda's gaze. "I'm the one that saved her." He struggled to straighten, limping closer.

"Claude? As in...the king?" Ravi muttered under his breath in Flaustran.

Dagmara pulled her hand from Magda's, stepping toward Claude. "Are you alright?"

"What happened to your face?" Claude spoke over her. He reached out and touched her neck, looking closer.

"He took a dagger to it." Dagmara nodded in the direction of Ravi.

Ravi stood a few feet away, awkwardly staring.

Magda switched to Flaustran. "What did you do?"

"I didn't mean to!" Ravi threw up one hand defensively, and the other remained attached to a bloody shoulder. "She thought I was attacking her."

"Wait, I don't understand," Magda said, returning to Dagmara in her native language. "I thought you were in danger. I thought Sabien —the captain—had you."

Dagmara hesitated. "He did. Claude saved me."

Magda jerked her head to her childhood friend—her supposed husband. "I didn't even recognize you."

"Well, this is what I look like. I didn't send anyone to pretend to be me."

Magda heard the bitter edge to his voice. "Sorry," she muttered under her breath.

The king inclined his head. "For attacking me? Or for assuming I murdered your family whom I admired and respected?"

"Let's go inside," Dagmara cut in.

Magda ignored her, anger simmering in her stomach. She opened her mouth to reply to Claude when he shifted his attention to Ravi. His Flaustran was perfect as he asked, "And who might you be?"

Staring back at the king, Ravi was silent for a moment. Magda knew he wasn't prepared for this. *She* wasn't even prepared for this—she was planning on saving Dagmara and facing the Mad King later. She had no idea they would be together.

"I-It seems a lot of conversations are in order," Magda stammered, trying to shift the focus off Ravi.

"Who is he?" Claude insisted, gesturing toward Ravi. "If he's going to attack Dagmara again I will take care of him myself."

Ravi cleared his throat, straightening his posture before saying, "I'm Ravi Kalal, and I am—"

"My bodyguard," Magda blurted out.

Ravi blinked in surprise.

Claude looked unconvinced at best.

"Azuremi, please?" Dagmara asked, glancing between everyone, unable to understand Flaustran.

"The princess says he is her bodyguard," Claude answered Dagmara in her native language, his piercing gaze burning into Ravi. But Ravi didn't back down. He held the king's gaze, unwavering.

"Again, a lot of conversations are in order," Magda announced. "First, let me help you." She picked up a wad of snow and approached Dagmara.

"What are you—"

Magda pressed her palm to Dagmara's cheek. Her best friend winced but let the water seep into the wound. Focusing her magic, Magda summoned her ability to heal the scrape.

Dagmara's eyes widened. "Magda. What—"

"As I said, we have a lot to talk about."

CHAPTER 27
Magdalena

After nearly killing one another, rest was desperately needed. Magda quickly healed Ravi's wound before following Claude and Dagmara to their suite. The Mad King refused any healing, but the way he was limping signified that maybe he sustained a deeper injury than one Magda could heal. She suppressed her guilt from yanking him off the balcony, convincing herself she had done it to save her best friend.

"Now that you can heal..." Dagmara muttered under her breath, curiosity lingering in each word, "there's one more injury on my ribcage that is killing me."

"Anything," Magda replied.

As they entered the suite, Dagmara took Magda's hand and pulled her to the washroom. "We will be right back," she announced.

Magda flashed Ravi an apologetic glance as he stood aimlessly in the center of the room. Meanwhile, Claude grabbed a shirt off the ground and threw it over his head, not paying the girls any attention.

Odie scampered between the girls' legs, running into the washroom with them. As soon as Dagmara had tugged Magda inside, she closed the door and leaned against it.

"How do you have Life Magic?" she blurted out, maintaining a forced whisper.

"I didn't realize until I got to Flaustra," Magda admitted. "I've been so lost, Dagmara. I went to Flaustra to try and uncover who I was, only to get myself in more trouble and uncover more questions."

"I'm listening," her friend responded.

So Magda confessed everything—how Queen Sanyal had been killed, how she had traveled here with Ishani and Kiran, how Junne had attacked them on the boat, and how the First Prince had been communicating with her.

"I also learned that Claude is looking for the tomb, but I'm not sure why," said Magda.

"He is looking for it, but he's not with the First Prince," Dagmara confirmed. She pulled up the stool before taking a seat, lifting her shirt to reveal a bandage on her ribcage.

"That's all you're going to tell me about Claude?" Peeling back the gauze, Magda examined the wound, momentarily distracted from her question. "Ouch, how'd you get this?"

"Sabien," Dagmara replied. She kept her gaze on the mirror, her face calm. "When I tried to escape him."

Magda shooed Odie aside before running the water. She scrutinized her friend's expression, before finally echoing her earlier remark: "I'm listening."

As Magda healed Dagmara's wound, she listened in horror to the torture her best friend was put through. Dagmara explained Sabien's connection to the First Prince, his role in killing Aleksy and Bogdan, and the torture she had endured. Finally, she explained how all the assassins knew Magda's secret.

Hearing her story made Magda's heart ache. Dagmara had summarized a small sample of what she had experienced, no doubt withholding the most gruesome details. She did that often, always masking her emotions and her pain to put others first. Magda wished she could be as selfless and brave as her.

Magda rounded the stool to stand directly before Dagmara and took both of her hands. "Dagmara, I owe you a huge apology. I should never have asked you to take my place. If I hadn't gotten us into this mess, you never would have been in so much danger. I'm afraid I've made everything worse, and I don't know how you'll ever forgive me—"

"Magda," Dagmara cut her off, "It is my job to complete missions for the Azuremi crown."

Magda frowned. "You don't work for my father anymore. I don't want you to do things because you feel a responsibility to me or to Azurem. You're my friend, Dagmara. We're equals. And yet I made you jeopardize your life. What friend does that?"

"I don't blame you for any of this," Dagmara insisted. "I agreed to your plan when I could have said no. I could have left Ilusauri and returned home, but I chose to stay. I am as responsible for all of this as you are."

"So you forgive me? For proposing such a reckless plan?"

A soft laugh escaped Dagmara's lips, and she squeezed Magda's hands tighter. "What else are friends for?"

Relief crashed through Magda. She wrapped her arms around Dagmara once more, pulling her into a hug. There were moments when she thought she wouldn't make it here time, and she wouldn't see her friend again, but now, she could finally rest easy knowing they were together again.

"How did you find me?" Dagmara asked, her face buried in Magda's hair.

"My mother sent a Scribestone telling me you disappeared, so I got on a guild ship to come here."

"And you brought a Flaustran bodyguard?" Dagmara asked.

Magda withdrew from the hug and backed away, nearly tripping over Odie. The dog whimpered, scampering out of the way, his paws slipping on the tile. She thought of how to explain everything she had Ravi had been through over the past few weeks. "Well...he is not exactly my bodyguard." She knelt beside Odie, petting her dog instead of meeting her friend's all-knowing gaze.

"Yes, I gathered that much when fighting him. So, who is he?"

"He's...a friend," Magda mumbled. "I care about him a lot and...well...I don't know where everything is left off with the marriage." She looked up once more. This was the topic she was most nervous to discuss. Having to marry Claude and leave Azurem would change everything.

She asked, "You and Claude went through with it, didn't you?"

Dagmara's expression shifted. She clasped her hands in front of her, fiddling with a ring on her middle finger. "Yes."

"I'm sorry I didn't arrive sooner," Magda apologized. "I thought you were going to find out information that would lead to the cancellation of the marriage. Before I knew it, I heard an announcement. I tried to send a Scribestone."

"I didn't get any Scribestone," said Dagmara, before closing off again.

Magda wanted to ask more, but she didn't want to press Dagmara any further. Was the wedding so awful it couldn't even be discussed? What had transpired between her and Claude? Guardians, why had Magda put her through that?

"I will talk to Claude. Then we will return to Azurem immediately, and my mom can help us figure out what to do," Magda decided. "My mother also said Azurem is dying, and I know it has something to do with the First Prince and the breaking of the Life lock."

"Yes, Ilusauri has been dying since Claude's parents died."

"The Mind lock," Magda nodded.

"And there are rifts with—"

"Hounds?" Magda gasped. "You've seen them?"

Dagmara nodded. "But if you have Life Magic...why don't you count for the Life lock? Shouldn't Azurem be stable?"

"I'm not sure I count at all," Magda admitted. "I think I'm different. There's so much more we have to discuss, but I'm sure you're as exhausted as I am. Don't worry, I promise we will be home soon."

"I..." Dagmara's voice trailed off. She cleared her throat before continuing, "I promised Claude I would help him stop this war. He's on his way to speak with Reon, the Spearhead of the Celesta militia. I thought I—well, *you*—could dissuade this war or at least pause it. They're attacking because they think Claude killed Guardian Sora, when both you and I know it was the First Prince's assassins."

Magda rose to a standing position. "Eligor has caused a war between kingdoms, and he's not even out of the tomb." She exhaled sharply, shaking her head.

Azurem couldn't risk Celestaire turning on them either. Now that word had spread that Magdalena and Claude were wed, Celestaire would undoubtedly assume Azurem was siding with Ilusauri. Now that Dagmara was safe, Magda needed to make sure Azurem was safe, from zowach, the First Prince, and any attacking armies.

"Yes, you're right," Magda nodded. "I'll go with Claude and speak to Reon. Thank you, Dagmara, for always putting Azurem first."

"Always," Dagmara echoed.

For once, Magda couldn't read her best friend's expression. There was something she wasn't saying—something behind the facade she was presenting.

"To think we blamed Claude at one point too..." Magda spoke, filling the silence. "But you were on your way to speak with Reon on behalf of his kingdom. Is it safe to say you and Claude are on good terms?"

"No," Dagmara replied. "I was only repaying a debt since he rescued me."

"Oh," replied Magda, her voice drooping. She scrutinized Dagmara's expression, and her best friend instantly looked away, reaching out to scratch Odie behind the ear. As Magda waited, she could see right through her friend. Dagmara was lying—but why?

Magda opened her mouth to voice a follow-up question, but Dagmara cut her off.

"So how do we stop Eligor before he sends more assassins?"

Magda recognized the attempt to transfer the conversation away from Claude, and she hesitantly followed. "Eligor has a crown," Magda replied. "It's a magical crown he uses to give his followers magic. The only way to stop him from making more assassins is to get rid of that crown."

"Then we have to do that before he kills anyone else," said Dagmara. "Steal the crown, kill his current assassins, and then find a way to restore magic to the lands."

A smile creased Magda's face.

"What?" Dagmara jerked back.

"Nothing." Magda shrugged. "I'm simply glad we're working together again."

A soft laugh escaped Dagmara's lips. "Me too. How are we supposed to steal his crown though?"

It was a question that had also crossed Magda's mind, and truthfully, she didn't know the answer. If she could successfully rip it from Eligor's grasp in the void, maybe he would stop sending assassins. Maybe, it would render him completely powerless. However, she didn't want to burden Dagmara with anymore uncertainties tonight, so she said:

"I'm working on a plan," Magda replied, "but we should get some rest. We can finish this discussion tomorrow on the road to Reon's."

Dagmara nodded in agreement. "I'm sure the two of them are wondering what we're doing in here." She rose from the stool and swung the washroom door open, stepping back into the suite.

Magda glanced down at Odie who was sitting on the floor simply, looking back up at her with wide eyes. Magda said, "Come on," and ushered Odie out.

King Claude was standing before the balcony doors, his arms crossed. He was gazing into the darkness like a stone-cold statue.

He addressed Magda first in Azuremi, "So do you want to stay with your best friend or your boyfriend?" he said coldly.

Magda looked from Ravi to Claude in confusion. "I see you two have gotten to know each other," she said awkwardly. "I'll stay here with Dagmara, of course," she snapped back at Claude.

Ravi shrugged. He stepped closer, his eyes scanning Magda's face as he lowered his voice in Flaustran. "Is everything...alright?"

"I don't know yet," Magda replied, wishing she knew how to solve everything.

"So...I'm your bodyguard then?"

"I'm sorry. I just didn't know how Claude would react. Especially after I almost killed him."

"Well, he seems to already know." Ravi eyed Claude who was sulking at the balcony doors. "To be honest, he doesn't seem too happy that I'm here. But...he hasn't killed me yet. I think that's pretty good."

"He's not going to kill you," Magda shook her head.

"Whatever happens, I plan on fighting for you." He smiled, before touching her lightly on the shoulder. His eyes lingered on her lips, as if he wanted to kiss her, but he didn't. "I'll be in the next room if you need anything," he said, before heading out the door.

Magda wanted him to stay, to share the same bed and continue their conversation, but he had disappeared. Disgruntled, she crossed to the large bed. Odie jumped up first, and Magda struggled to slide her feet under the blankets with his weight. Glancing up, she waited for Dagmara to join her, but Dagmara was hovering near the balcony doors.

"I told you," Claude's voice was a low growl, barely audible from where Magda began eavesdropping, "I won't be sleeping tonight anyway."

Dagmara shuffled in her stance, continuing to fiddle with the ring on her finger. "I suppose you don't need to help me find Magda now,"

Dagmara said under her breath, an unamused laugh escaping her lips. "She found us."

Claude finally turned away from the balcony windows. The tension in the room was as taught as a violin string.

"Yes, she found us," Claude answered. "So everything has returned to the way it should be, just as you wanted. Right?"

A glint caught Magda's eye. Claude was wearing a ring identical to Dagmara's.

Dagmara nodded, finally answering the king. "Yes."

Magda knew the inflection in Dagmara's response. She had heard it a multitude of times in the past.

A bitter, cold lie.

Dagmara whirled away from the king and climbed into bed beside Magda, her gaze unfocused as she pulled the covers up to her neck. But Magda was the one who watched Claude stare at Dagmara longer than he should have. It felt like an eternity before the king finally tore his gaze away from Dagmara.

Then he crossed to the door, slamming it behind him.

Magda wasn't sure her heart was still beating. When she had been fighting Claude outside, he had been completely shirtless. He and Dagmara were spending a night together at the inn with one bed, long after he knew Dagmara wasn't Magdalena. Dagmara had swiftly dodged any questions about the king, and they both were still wearing their wedding bands.

The blood drained from Magda's face. She suddenly realized why Dagmara was being so evasive while talking about the king. It was as plain as day.

Her best friend was in love with the Mad King. And by his lingering stare...there was no doubt the King of Ilusauri reciprocated the feelings.

CHAPTER 28
Magdalena

Magda manifested in the black alcove that was Eligor's prison. He sat alone on a rock in the center of what was increasingly resembling a cavern. His back was to her, and this time, his navy cape was strewn on the floor next to him.

He ran his fingers through his hair so that it was disheveled. Then he replaced his golden crown on his blonde hair. It glistened, and Magda distinctly remembered the way the power had felt when they had held it together. She knew that it was a conduit for the passage of magic, for she had felt it with her own hands. The crown was the way he made new assassins by granting them elemental magic, and it was the one thing that still held power over her.

Eligor. She called to him.

Princess. He shifted his body towards hers. *Come to visit me once more in my cage?*

No. This time, she was here for the crown. If she took it from his possession, he wouldn't be able to create any more assassins. It may be the only way to save her and her friends.

He rose from his seat, crossing over to her. As he did so, he extended his palm outward, and violet magic swirled around it, matching the color of the sparks dancing around his crown. From only paces away, Magda could sense the vastness of his power—tempting, enchanting.

Now I see the truth about you, dear Princess. As much as I hate to admit it, we're similar, you and I. Eligor's cerulean eyes sparkled with mischief, as if there was more to the thought, and he was considering telling her the secret.

He moved his hand forward, encouraging Magda to touch the violet magic. Deep down, she had to know if he was real...if he was actually here. Or if this was all an illusion at the back of her mind, and with one touch, she would pass right through him. She needed to know if she could drive a dagger through his heart and feel him gasp for his last breath underneath the pressure of her knife.

She needed to hurt the person that had hurt her friends.

At the same time, his magic lured her toward him.

Magda placed her right hand in his, and his fingers clasped tightly around hers. He wrapped his other arm around her waist, pulling her forcefully into his chest, until she was pressed tightly against him. The grip of his forearm was like iron, trapping her against his strong body, while the magic intensified between their hands. Soon, the space between their palms was burning with bright light.

Magda's entire body was overwhelmed with power. The sparking magic flooded through her limbs, electrifying her senses and igniting a newfound magnetism between their bodies.

She ran her free hand up the front of his chest, hoping to inconspicuously reach for the crown. She needed to know if she could hold it, take it, and leap from the Void with the object.

He watched her hand run along his chest, trickling up to his neck. *You are like a burning fire that I cannot wait to suffocate as soon as I escape from this prison.*

Magda tensed in his arms. *Why do you want to kill me so badly?*

I was the last heir to a lineage of great power. But then you showed up. Another Master Guardian. Another heir to the Void magic. One more person in my way.

I don't care about the Void magic.

As a Master Guardian, you will have the power to control the Void once I am free. Before you, I was the only one with the Void magic. But now you have put a wrench in all my plans.

Magda's hand had made it to his neck, but she held her palm an inch away from Eligor's skin. If she wanted to, she could reach up and grab the crown, but he held her so tightly, she didn't know if she would be able to leave his prison. Or, if he would let her.

Touch me. He acknowledged Magda's hand hovering over his cheek.

Magda gulped. While she had confirmed they were somehow physically here together, and she didn't float right through him, something about touching his face made her heart race inside.

Softly, Magda pressed her hand to his cheek. Eligor leaned his face into her touch as her fingers caressed around his ear, twisting in his hair. She brushed against his gold crown, feeling the cold metal underneath her fingertips.

It has been too long... He sighed, and his breath sent a chill down Magda's spine. His powers flowed through every nerve of his body, a guardian that controlled all five elements, and Magda could feel the enchantments tempting her, stimulating her senses with invigorating magic. It was almost as if she could reach out and taste it, as if, through him, she could somehow learn how to channel her remaining powers.

Eligor's eyes were closed as he leaned into her so that their foreheads were touching. Magda's breath caught in her throat, but she was sure he was fully distracted. Quietly, her fingers clasped the edge of the crown.

Magda grabbed the crown off his head without waiting another second. He instantly released her to snatch it back, but Magda was too quick. She bolted away, attempting to escape the Void, but darkness surrounded her. As fast as possible, she tried to wake herself up, or escape from their mind-prison, but Eligor was more powerful than she was.

He didn't move, but rather called out to her. *You won't get that crown out of here, not while I'm locked away.*

Magda's heart was beating out of her chest, and she clutched the crown in sweaty palms, hoping to take it with her out of the void.

But as if he could read her mind, Eligor responded:

I can't escape, and neither can my crown. The only way you'll ever see that crown is by letting me out.

Why would I let you out if you've made it clear you will kill me once you escape? asked Magda.

Eligor approached her, snatching the crown back, and Magda was helplessly frozen in her shoes. He let his hand caress around her hair and cheek as he said. *Don't be scared, Princess. I'll let you go this time. It takes care to put out a fire. You have to make sure that you don't get burned. Or else you'll unleash a blazing storm, and all that will be left is ashes.*

Suddenly Magda sat upright in her bed. She looked down at her palms, but to her dismay, there was no crown on her lap. She snapped her head to the right, seeing Dagmara sleeping next to her, and Odie curled at their feet.

Understand something, Princess. Eligor's voice echoed in her head. *I will not have another heir make claim to my powers. I will kill you Magda. I killed my brothers, and you will be no different.*

CHAPTER 29
Dagmara

The following morning, Dagmara sluggishly rose and proceeded to get ready for the journey to Reon's. She could still taste the acid in her throat, feel Sabien's hands on her body, and remember the occurring nightmares that had happened during her captivity. She had to pinch herself to be reminded that she was no longer in danger.

The back of her neck ached, and a headache burned behind her eyes. It would take a lot longer to recover from the horror she went through over the past weeks, and she willed her health to be patient. As with every time her health was at its lowest, she reminded herself it would eventually get better, no matter how hard it was in the moment.

She exited into the rising sun, the chill seeping through her clothes. A single carriage was already prepared to go, resting in the open space outside of the inn. A light flutter of snow was descending from the sky, landing gracefully on the top of the carriage.

Magda's new friend—Ravi—was sitting on the wide step leading into the carriage. He held a notebook in one hand, reading the contents, while he used the other to casually throw a stick across the snow, which Odie would promptly return to his side.

When Odie spotted Dagmara, he sprinted toward her, delivering the stick to Dagmara instead of Ravi, wagging his tail happily in the process.

Dagmara grabbed the stick from Odie, before heading in Ravi's direction. Odie promptly followed.

"Have you seen Claude?"

Ravi glanced up from his journal, tilting his head curiously.

"King Mirage," Dagmara added. Odie nudged her knee impatiently, so she threw the stick again.

"Speaking with the innkeeper. And Magda?"

"Still getting ready," Dagmara replied, to which he nodded. "Your Azuremi is better than you make it seem. When did you learn?"

"I traveled to Azurem for music. I understand more than I can say," he admitted. "Also, I could not think when you attacked me."

"Sorry," Dagmara replied half-heartedly. "Next time, don't sneak up on someone who has just been through—" she stopped herself short. "Just don't sneak up on the person you're rescuing."

"Sorry," he returned the apology. Then he gestured to the open space beside him on the step. She graciously took his invitation, sitting down and relieving her body of the nausea.

Odie returned the stick to her once more, which she threw in the opposite direction. It didn't go nearly as far as Ravi's throw, and the dog trotted back to return the stick to Ravi the next time.

As Ravi continued reading from his notebooks, he started humming, tapping his foot on the ground in a rhythmic beat.

"I know you're not really her bodyguard," stated Dagmara.

Glancing up from his notebook, Ravi gave her a genuine smile. "No. I'm a musician."

Dagmara laughed.

"So...you and the king?" Ravi inquired.

Dagmara bristled. "There is nothing between the king and me," she retorted before turning the question back on him. "What about you and Magda?"

He shrugged. "I'm in love."

"She's a married guardian."

He inclined his head. "And I'm a musician."

"It can't be that simple."

"For me, it is," he replied. "Life is short. With time I have, I'll be with her because I'm happy."

Dagmara could tell there was more he wasn't saying—more he wanted to express, but couldn't translate. She wished she could hear him in his native language so she could fully understand. How could he have such an optimistic outlook on life?

"I'm..." Ravi continued, but then hesitated. "I don't know how to say it." He reached into his pocket, withdrawing a folded piece of paper. He opened the flimsy poster, showing Dagmara. The tattered page revealed a charcoal picture of Ravi. The wanted poster was smeared but still legible.

She scanned the page, unable to read the Flaustran words, but could make out the numbers. It was obvious he had a high bounty on his head.

"You're a fugitive?" Dagmara asked. "For what?"

"Murder."

"Fifty thousand is a lot in Azuremi coin," Dagmara mused. She paused, before adding to lighten the mood, "Maybe I'll bring you to Dreadmarrow myself. After, of course, all this guardian nonsense."

His eyes widened.

"I'm kidding," Dagmara said with a short laugh. "You don't need to worry. But...you're right. Life is short. I thought I was dead. I need to focus on getting back to Azurem. To my brother Teos."

Ravi smiled, translating the joke a few seconds too late. He folded the paper in perfect squares before returning it to his pocket. "Teos?"

"My brother," Dagmara repeated. "He's sick. A deadly illness only Ilusaurian medicine can cure. But honestly, I'm nervous that it won't heal him completely. He wrote to me a while ago and told me he still isn't well yet." She had no idea why she was rambling to this stranger, but a part of her felt obligated to fill the awkward silence.

"My sister was sick too," Ravi said.

"What?" Dagmara blurted out. "And she's healed?"

Ravi nodded.

"With what medicine?"

"Ilusauri, but many," he said.

"Which medicines?"

He opened his mouth, but then shut it quickly. His brow furrowed as he thought of the translation, but finally gave up. Leaning over to his bag, he shuffled through the contents to find a leather-bound journal. He shifted closer to her until their thighs were touching, before he placed the open journal across their laps. After paging through a few drawings, he reached what he was searching for and pointed.

Dagmara's eyes widened. She couldn't read all the words, but a few Ilusaurian medicine labels caught her eye. The concoction was simply genius. She wished she had come up with it herself.

"And your sister is healthy again? How did you come up with this?"

"Laila. My other sister." Ravi held his hands up defensively.

Dagmara laughed. "I know the feeling. My brother is the one who concocts so many explosive variations."

Ravi nodded, although the blank expression on his face insinuated he had no idea what she had said.

She returned her attention back to the book. Flipping through the pages, she noticed it highlighted more than just Ilusaurian medicine. She stopped when she recognized one. "You use bilans in Flaustra?"

Ravi nodded. "It was a mess."

"Well, you have to concentrate it with a pinch of kaspin," Dagmara replied.

Ravi stared at her blankly.

"I'll show you, let me find it," Dagmara said. She began paging through the journal once more, skimming every picture until she saw one that resembled a name she understood. The Flaustran language made no sense to her, making it even more admirable that the guardians could speak all the languages.

Odie dropped the stick at Ravi's feet, but they were both preoccupied with the notebook. The dog placed his chin on the journal and both Dagmara and Ravi absentmindedly reached out to shoo him back from the page. Their hands touched briefly, and Dagmara jerked back.

Ravi glanced at her, but didn't stop brushing his palm against Odie's fur.

"Bilans?" he asked, returning her to the previous conversation.

She smiled and started explaining the mixture she normally used, flipping back and forth between pages and using wild hand gestures. She tried different vocabulary to explain the process, often saying words Ravi didn't understand and having to start over. He would say the Flaustran version of the word, and Dagmara would repeat it back, knowing there was no way she would remember it tomorrow.

Bottles were drawn in the journal that Dagmara didn't recognize. "What is this for?" She pointed to one and waited for Ravi's response.

He opened his mouth and then shut it. He pointed to his head.

"Headaches?"

"No, no." He passed the journal fully onto Dagmara's lap before he stood up from the stairs and spun.

"Spinning...?"

Dramatically, he stopped the spin and fell to the ground, holding his forearm against his head.

"Dizziness? Vertigo?"

Odie was already joining in the game, nuzzling Ravi's face and barking.

Laughing, Ravi pushed Odie back to sit upright. "Yes!" he exclaimed, beaming.

A new idea had formed. She never thought there would be medicine to alleviate her symptoms. A medicine that could ease her health condition. Her gaze found the drawing on the journal, the foreign words, and the tiger label announcing it was from Flaustra. It wasn't a cure, but what if it helped?

Ravi hopped up from the ground, brushing snow from his pants and smoothing his shirt.

Smiling, Dagmara flipped the page, finding another drawing with a tiger label. Unable to read it, she held the book up, showcasing the page. "This one?" She smiled up at Ravi, wondering if he would take the bait.

Ravi inclined his head, his mouth slightly open. Finally, he laughed, before reenacting another condition.

It was an elementary word, one he should've known. Secretly, Dagmara wondered if he was only continuing the charade to make her laugh.

Regardless, it worked.

CHAPTER 30
Dagmara

The Celesta tower was an expansive complex, with lodging for the militia, the everyday operations of the council, as well as Celesta priests. The walled tower was enclosed in a military complex, surrounded by a large moat, and a wooden door with a curved awning blocked the entrance. On either end of the wall, was a six-story guard tower with square balconies on all sides. The wall was steep and slanted, made up of perfectly placed stones, so that anyone attempting to ascend would slide down into the moat. Tree branches and a small forest could be seen peeking over the edges, providing a glimpse into the complex.

In the center, the massive Celesta tower rose above the rest of the complex below.

The carriage rolled to a stop, and all four got out, facing the Celesta tower. Dagmara, Claude, Magda, and Ravi stood along the outer edge of the moat, facing a smaller, side bridge that extended to another gate.

"This way. This is the entrance I use when I visit Reon," said Claude, beckoning the group across the small bridge. His voice was commanding, making Dagmara's heart lurch in her chest as she thought of his arms around hers. It was all that had been on her mind during this journey. Her heart ached, but she quickly shoved her feelings to the side, realizing the royals were here for a political discussion, nothing more.

Odie pressed up against Dagmara, nuzzling his body against her knees. He whimpered, sensing Dagmara's anxiety and attempting to bring her some comfort. Dagmara patted Odie back, letting her fingers run through his fur, knowing that the dog often predicted if she was going to pass out.

When Claude approached, two men stepped outside of the wooden gate through a smaller door carved in the center. The men wore the standard Celesta uniforms, indicating they were low-ranking members of the militia.

Upon recognizing Claude as the foreign King of Ilusauri with whom they were at war, they immediately withdrew their swords and pointed them at the king.

Claude held up his hands in surrender, replying immediately in Celesta, which started a yelling match between all of the men. Ravi jumped forward, in an attempt to help, but Magda held her hand in front of him, encouraging him not to intervene.

"What are they saying?" Dagmara asked Magda beside her, unable to understand.

"They're calling him a murderer," Magda explained.

Dagmara's heart sank.

Odie let out a series of barks, although it was clear the dog wasn't defending Claude, but the girls.

Then Claude's eyes turned silver, and he whispered a few curt words before the soldiers obeyed instantly, sheathing their weapons and retreating back into the tower.

Magda continued to translate, "Claude is asking them to get Reon."

"No, he compelled them," corrected Dagmara. A shudder raced down her back as she remembered Viette. She was quickly comforted by Odie, who began licking her hand.

"Who is Reon? What do you know about him?" asked Magda, seeming to ignore the magic that had been displayed before her.

"Reon came to the engagement ball," Dagmara explained. "Supposedly they were friends, but not since the war broke out. Last time I saw Reon, he was invading Ilusauri and held a knife to my throat," Dagmara admitted. "Also...Reon thinks I'm you."

Magda nodded. "Barging in and telling Reon that we have been lying all along about my identity is not a great way to end this war." She paused before saying, "Claude. Can you give Dagmara silver hair again?"

Claude glanced over his shoulder, his brow furrowing.

"I don't think confessing we tricked Reon is a great way to start negotiations."

After a long pause, Claude nodded. He extended a gentle hand toward Dagmara, and before their eyes, the blonde shifted to silver. The king sucked in a ragged breath before abruptly turning away.

Soon, the soldiers returned, and they beckoned the group of visitors to enter the complex. The four passed through a smaller door that was a cut-out of the larger gate and stepped into a large courtyard. Along the right wall were barracks that housed the lower ranks of the Celesta soldiers. Additional rows of guard houses lined the courtyard ahead, leading up to another gate, which concealed the tower grounds beyond.

Approaching quickly was a man with black hair tied into a bun, and a crimson, Celesta uniform. Unlike the other men, the armor and helmet he wore wasn't for battle, but was decorated with ornate red and black details, as if it had been hand-made especially for the Spearhead.

Odie became alert as the new stranger approached.

"Claude?" Reon asked, stepping forward.

When he saw Dagmara standing by, he proceeded in Ilusaurian.

"Your Majesty," he bowed slightly to Dagmara. Dagmara's eyes shifted, taking a sideways glance at Magda, but her friend didn't say anything.

Reon's hand moved to the handle of his sword. "Why are you here? I can't protect you here."

"I came to tell you that I am not responsible for Sora's death," Claude stated.

"I would like to believe you, I really would," said Reon, "but you're the only one who knew about Sora's location."

"It was Sabien," Claude admitted, his voice cold. "He was working with the assassins."

Reon inclined his head. "And you have proof?"

"He took me hostage," Dagmara admitted, "along with the woman who killed Sora. Her name is Junne, and she has Spirit magic."

Reon's expression wavered. "Someone other than a guardian has magic?"

"They're being sent by the First Prince. Honestly, Reon, who else reached Guardian Sora except for someone that could fly to her?" Claude asked.

"The council doesn't know there are assassins with magic," replied Reon. "If word gets out—"

"We can't keep that information from them," Claude responded. "They have to know it wasn't me. So get me an audience with the council. That is why I'm here."

Reon ran his hand against his face. "This is now a full blown war. The council wants your head—and you want me to deliver it on a silver platter?"

"I will talk to them about keeping my head. Your armies were on Ilusaurian soil, and you killed my governor."

"A governor is not the same as a guardian," Reon countered.

"Ilusauri is not responsible for Guardian Sora," Claude repeated. "We all know the militia holds heavy influence here. So don't make excuses and get me an audience."

Reon looked over the group, scanning Magda, Claude, Dagmara and Ravi. Then his face scrunched as he took in the black and white dog at their side.

His attention refocused on the king. "I'm sorry, I can't bring you unannounced. I can put in a formal request."

Claude's jaw ticked. "In that formal request, you can tell them that Azuremi troops are reinforcing Ilusauri, and this continued war on Ilusauri is a direct attack on Azurem as well."

"You can't speak for Azurem." His narrow gaze eased, and then he parted his lips as a new thought formed. "However, there is one person they would talk to." He cleared his throat before staring at Dagmara. "Her."

CHAPTER 31
Magdalena

The air was suspended in silence. All eyes turned to Dagmara, waiting for her response. This wasn't the time to announce to Reon the girls had swapped places—what if they lost the opportunity to speak with the council? What if they lost the chance to stop this war which would inevitably bleed over into Azurem? Magda wouldn't be responsible for taking that chance away.

More thoughts spun through Magda's mind. What if the council asked questions about Dagmara's time in Ilusauri? Or about the governor that was killed? Magda had no idea how to answer those questions—she barely had been able to speak to her friend about everything that had transpired.

There was only one solution. They had to keep the charade going just a little longer.

Dagmara opened her mouth to object, when Magda intervened. "Seeing as the council will accept an audience with the Princess, can't she bring Claude as her guest?" Magda vaguely remembered her foreign lessons years ago with Aleksy. The council was filled with rules —but also loopholes.

Reon shifted his weight, adjusting his grip on his sword handle.

"Yes..." he mumbled, as though it pained him to admit. "And who are you?"

"Just a friend." A thin smile spread on Magda's face. This was going to work.

Turning over her shoulder, Dagmara flashed Magda a wide-eyed glance.

Magda didn't even have to nod. She was used to silently communicating with Dagmara at every event growing up. This glance was no different.

"Alright," Dagmara stated. She cleared her throat. "Take me to the council. With King Mirage as my guest."

Reon sucked in a large inhale, before finally conceding. He spoke to his soldiers, "Search them for weapons, they're coming with me. And don't any of you say a word about this. If I find out information about my guests has leaked around the tower, I will exile you."

The soldiers nodded in agreement, before moving to the four and searching them for any weapons. Then the group were led deeper inside the complex. They passed another elite group of Reon's soldiers, getting closer to the central tower that was Celesta's unique landmark. Finally, after a third checkpoint, they arrived at a massive building.

Ahead, the Celesta tower rose above them, the most intricate structure that Dagmara had ever seen. It rose high, ten stories in the air, with outer balconies on all levels. Sliding doors led into interior rooms, and trees and greenery were interspersed in a series of intricate gardens and courtyards on all floors.

"Wait here," Reon held his hand up. "They're in session right now. I'll notify them of your spontaneous arrival." He adjusted his breastplate before a set of soldiers slid the central doors open for him, and he disappeared into the tower.

"Why can't we tell them the truth?" asked Dagmara. "I don't speak Celesta."

"We have to keep this up," said Magda, "I wasn't in Ilusauri at your engagement ball, and I can't really make this partnership...," she awkwardly gestured to Claude and Dagmara, "...convincing."

"You were the one who met Lionel," Claude added.

Dagmara opened her mouth to respond, but she didn't have time to voice her opinion, because Reon returned in the sliding doorway saying:

"They've agreed to see the Princess of Azurem. You may enter."

CHAPTER 32
Dagmara

The council room was on the ground floor of the Celesta tower, and it was far more magnificent than Dagmara had imagined—not that she gave herself much time to picture it. A month ago she would have never thought she would find herself here, conducting negotiations with Celestaire on Azurem's behalf.

However, she had gotten a rundown on all of Ilusauri's hierarchy with Martine when she was searching for the three aliases that crossed into Azurem on the night of the coronation. She had met everyone at the engagement ball, including representatives from all around Ilusauri and some from Celestaire. Dagmara even had the opportunity to meet and speak with Lionel—she had been there the day he was murdered. Magda was right. She had to do this on Azurem's behalf.

The Celesta council room took up the entire floor of the tower, and gorgeous, hand-painted gold and red murals lined the canvas walls, which Dagmara knew were concealing hidden entrances and panels. Only two columns on either end held up the space, and the ceiling was arched with ornate squares covering every inch of the curves. A large, semi-circular table was centered in the room, framed by nineteen chairs, all on a higher platform than the soldiers and guests.

Walking side by side with Claude, Dagmara's heart was already beginning to race. She didn't know how she would make it through this. It was so exposing, not having any weapons on her person. If only she was somewhat comforted by Claude beside her, but falling back into the role she played before felt like betraying him once again. Reon was on her opposite side, leading them toward the confrontation.

As soon as they were close enough for the first council member to recognize Claude, the room broke into a commotion. Shouts rang through the space in a language foreign to Dagmara. Some rose from their chairs defensively, while others leaned back, their eyes wide with terror. One council member even jumped up and raced to hide behind her chair.

Reon extended a hand, shouting something in Celesta. Finally, the room seemed to settle, however, the councilman in the center remained standing. He had gray hair, deep wrinkles, and a thin beard that elongated his face.

"Let us speak in the language of our visitors," Reon announced in Ilusaurian.

The man standing in the center echoed his statement, translating for the rest of the council. Then he addressed the two of them, "What is the meaning of this?"

"I have come to clear Ilusauri's name," Claude announced.

"We are not talking to you, son," the man said. "*You* were not invited." His pointed gaze fixated on Dagmara, and her blood turned cold. "I am councilman Lin. Explain your business. Why have you brought this murderer here?"

"Hello," Dagmara began, dipping her head in respect, though she wasn't certain what was customary here. "What His Majesty says is true, I have come here to clear his name. He is not responsible for the horrible death of your guardian."

Lin muttered under his breath the translation, and the entire room broke out in another frenzy. Claude flinched at their remarks. Reon exhaled slowly, and she could almost hear the silent "I warned you."

"Your attack on Ilusauri was what started this war," Dagmara called over them. "Your troops killed our governor, when we are not to blame for Guardian Sora."

Lin held up his hand, and the council settled. "*Our* governor? Do you claim Ilusauri as yours now?" he echoed. "We know this is only a marriage contract for trade routes. You don't have to support this murderer."

"I am not a murderer," Claude said, his voice booming through the space.

More remarks flew through the council, but Dagmara kept her attention on Lin, seeing as he was the only one that could translate for her.

"You're right, I don't have to support him," she replied. "But I want to." Then she buried all her feelings, swallowed the lump in her throat, and took Claude's hand. It was as if lightning sparked between their fingers. Her stomach curled inside her at his touch. Then, when he squeezed her palm back, she found stability. Security.

"Trust me when I say I once thought as you all did," she started, pausing intermittently to let Lin translate for the rest of the council. "I thought he was behind the assassinations of my own family. It is easy to toss blame around, as opposed to admitting there could be something worse out there. It wasn't until I arrived in Ilusauri and spoke to His Majesty when I began to understand."

An elderly woman shouted something, and Claude stiffened. Lin did not translate, keeping his attention on Dagmara.

Reon leaned toward Dagmara to whisper, "She believes you are under his compulsion."

Dagmara sucked in a breath. She lifted her chin, channeling every ounce of Magda. "Guardians can't be compelled," she stated. "I am not under his compulsion."

Another woman opened her mouth, but Dagmara wasn't finished.

"Nor am I being forced to have this conversation with you," she stated.

When Lin translated, the commotion intensified. They barked back responses, some louder than others, some under their breath.

"Council!" Dagmara called over them. They hushed, their eyes widening. "I urge you to give me five minutes of your undivided attention. Simply hear me out."

A tense silence spread through the room. The air was suffocating. Lin spoke, "We are not going to negotiate with the Mad King. Have him leave, and we will speak with you alone, otherwise, this conversation is over."

Claude's grip instinctively tightened on Dagmara's hand. She looked up at him. Tumultuous emotion racked his expression.

"I can do this," she told him, although she was more so trying to convince herself.

He gave a curt nod, though his jaw ticked in anger. "They'll never see me as anything but the Mad King."

Then he looked up at the council. "I need a chair."

The entire council was silent, until Lin finally spoke. "You're not staying."

"It's not for me," Claude snapped.

"We don't have chairs for guests."

Dagmara opened her mouth to intervene, but Claude was insistent. "Then give her one of yours."

Lin's face paled. "I will do no such—"

Claude started forward, ignoring the rush of insults. He proceeded to the closest of the nineteen, who quickly scrambled out of the way, rushing to the next council member for safety.

Picking up the oversized chair, the seams of his clothing straining,

Claude muttered a half-hearted thank you before returning the chair to Dagmara. He set it on the ground beside her. "For you," he said, his gaze fierce.

She swallowed the lump in her throat, both gracious and embarrassed. "Thank you," she said, taking a seat awkwardly. But as soon as she was settled, a rush of relief flooded her body. Her mind sharpened. She felt stronger.

With once glance at Reon, then at the council, Claude turned on his heel and exited.

The door slid shut abruptly. Now that he was gone, she had nothing to hold on to. She had no rock to keep her afloat. But she was stable in the chair he had given her.

Clearing her throat, she lifted her chin slightly and crossed her legs, finding her own courage.

"Now will you listen?" she asked.

The room was still. The seconds felt like years, until finally, Lin sat down in his own chair.

"Proceed."

CHAPTER 33
Magdalena

Anxiety raced through Magda's body as she waited for the results of the council meeting. She had faith in Dagmara, knowing she would be able to keep this hoax going, but what if Celestaire banned them from the kingdom?

Deep down, she didn't know if she had agreed to continue the charade for her own behalf. Speaking to Claude about their marriage and future—as husband and wife, or something else—was somehow more daunting than facing the council or the assassins. The decision they would make together affected the legitimacy of the crown, the trade routes, and their hearts. And she had no idea where Claude stood on the matter.

She knelt beside Odie, stroking his fur as her mind wavered between her multiple futures.

Ravi leaned against the wall in the hallway, playing with a loose string on his bag.

Then the council door slid open, and Magda jumped to her feet in alarm.

Claude stormed out, glancing once in their direction, before shaking his head. He moved down the stairs and into the courtyard, distancing himself. The doors slid closed behind him, leaving Reon and Dagmara inside.

"I assume it isn't going well," Ravi muttered under his breath.

Magda kept her gaze focused on Claude's retreating figure.

"I should talk to him," Magda said.

Ravi nodded.

Magda looked into Ravi's eyes with admiration. This conversation with Claude was inevitable, but she couldn't bring herself to break Ravi's heart, for in reality, she would be breaking hers. Truthfully, Magda didn't know what was going to happen with the marriage or if they all would even survive this.

Magda stepped away from Ravi, after she instructed Odie to stay and wait for her. Then she followed after Claude. The courtyard was full of rocks, creating designs in beds of sand. Between these, were red-leaved trees, a small pond, and a gazebo, decorated with scarlet lanterns.

Claude stood in the middle of the courtyard, facing the gazebo.

"How was the council meeting?" Magda asked in Azuremi, cautiously approaching.

The king exhaled sharply. "Not going well, clearly," he grumbled. "They won't negotiate with the Mad King. Who would?"

Magda nodded uneasily, not knowing what to say. Finally she let out a deep breath, "I would."

He looked at her, disgruntled. "Don't insult me."

Magda's face twisted in confusion. "I'm serious. I think of you as my closest childhood friend."

"No, you don't. You believed that I was mad, like everyone else did. Our friendship meant nothing to you," Claude growled, his hands turning to fists.

"It did," said Magda, reaching out to him, but he abruptly pulled away.

"Then why did you send Dagmara in your place, if it wasn't for judging me in the way everyone else has?" Claude asked.

Magda was taken aback and attempted to explain herself, "Assassins had just killed my brother and father, and I thought you were behind it. I hadn't heard from you until the day of the proposal. I had no way of knowing who you really were after all those years, so I decided to keep myself safe by not accepting."

"I was never a murderer. I didn't kill my family or yours. You were the one that I wanted to keep safe," said Claude.

"Then why didn't you tell me the truth?"

Claude's eyes shot through hers like daggers. "You never asked. You assumed I was behind everything."

Magda's heart dropped to the pit of her stomach. Asking for the truth seemed so easy, but over the years they had lost the undeniable bond of trust between them, whether it was due to malicious rumors or the passage of time. Even if she could go back, she knew she wouldn't have accepted the proposal.

Magda took a deep breath before asking, "Tell me...when you proposed...was it only political? Or somewhere, deep down, did you actually want to marry *me*?"

Suddenly, the silver magic sparkled from his fingertips, and Magda was drawn to his silver-tinted eyes. Before her, the small, garden ponds iced over, and snow darted the area. Above, a light breath of snowflakes flurried down upon them, and Magda was left in awe of the magic. When they were younger, Claude still hadn't obtained his gift.

It was breathtaking.

Magda's eyes were drawn to the pond, where she saw two young children playing on the ice. Suddenly, the memory flooded back, sending fear through her heart.

In an instant, the ice cracked below Claude's feet, and he was pulled underneath the frigid surface. Magda watched herself as a young girl, screaming hysterically for the servants. Suddenly, she was right back in that moment with all of the pain and terror that came with it. Then, Magda watched herself jump into the water next to

Claude, pulling him out of the icy-pond, and dragging him up toward the bank.

"Claude!" the young version of herself screamed as tears streamed down her face.

"Make it stop," Magda said.

In an instant, the illusion had vanished.

Claude's tone hardened. "That day has stuck with me just as that freezing water chilled me somewhere to my core. Throughout childhood, it was one of my recurring nightmares. You saved my life, Magda, and the girl from back then was the girl I thought I was proposing to."

"I had almost forgotten...," Magda's voice trailed off.

"Yes, I was trying to save this world. I wanted information from your father's archives to find Eligor's tomb, and I used the guise of marriage to get us to meet once more. But honestly...that girl from back then was someone I could have seen myself falling for. But you..."

Claude didn't finish his sentence.

"What?" Magda prompted him.

"You're no longer that girl."

"What does that mean?"

"While I made a noble gesture to protect you from the impending assassins of the First Prince, you ran away from your responsibilities as a guardian."

"I needed answers. I didn't know about the First Prince or my magic because my father and brother kept me in the dark."

"Then why go to Sanyal and not me?"

"I..."

"Because you didn't trust me. You thought I was mad and a murderer like everyone else did," Claude said.

"No, I went to Sanyal because she had Soul magic. I needed to know how and why I had Soul magic and not Life magic."

"So while I proposed to you to protect you, in return, all you did was protect yourself. I became the Mad King to save my people, keeping them in the dark about the dangers we face, while you deserted yours."

"That's not fair," Magda protested. "Dagmara told me you proposed marriage to get into our archives and find information. And you created a facade around the Ilusaurian castle to lie to your own people."

"Yes, to protect them. Ilusauri is on the brink of death, and now Azurem is too. But at least I'm saving Azurem with medication. One of us should."

Magda gasped, feeling as though he drove a physical dagger into her chest. "How dare you. I love my kingdom."

"I believe that. But I also believe you put the role of guardian over the role of princess."

"Says the man who put the role of king over being a guardian. You shut everyone out. You're the reason meetings between guardians ended. You pushed everyone away—including me. What friends do you have left who aren't your servants or guards?"

"And what about your friends? You claim Dagmara is your best friend, and yet you sent her away, as if she was only your servant."

"I came here to save Dagmara," said Magda.

"No, *I* came here to save Dagmara," Claude's words cut through the air. "And she wouldn't have needed saving if it wasn't for you."

Magda's face flushed in anger. She took a forceful step toward him, standing face to face with the king. "You can hate me and blame me all you want. But the truth is, we both care about Dagmara. We both care about our kingdoms, and we need to work together to save them. All of us. Can you do that?"

"I don't know if I can even look you in the eye," said Claude. "Thanks to your deception, every kingdom and citizen believes we are wed, and your actions have only caused me pain."

"For that I'm truly sorry," said Magda.

"Now we could be forced to remain together for the sake of our kingdoms," Claude said angrily, before his tone softened. Then he took a deep breath before admitting, "When it's clear we both have feelings for someone else."

Magda nodded. She had already seen Dagmara and Claude interact with one another, and hearing Claude's words only provided the final confirmation she needed. She knew they were dancing around the real topic that needed to be discussed—their future together. If Dagmara and Claude truly had feelings for one another, maybe with Magda out of the legal picture they could be happy. Magda didn't need Claude to be her husband, she only needed him to be her ally.

"Can we work together without a marriage?" Magda proposed.

Claude nodded in agreement. "I'm willing to continue the trade agreements if you are. They were important to Dagmara."

"I'd like to review them, but it does seem, according to my mother, that they have benefited us both," said Magda.

"But it doesn't solve everything. All because I wanted to marry her, I'm now bound to you."

Magda's thoughts churned, for she knew the importance of preserving the crown. She spoke, "We can find a way for this annulment not to look bad for the face of the kingdoms. We will say we parted ways, then you are free to be with Dagmara."

"My governors met Dagmara already—while she was pretending to be you. They will know I was fooled as soon as I introduce her for who she is." He shook his head, rubbing his palm against the back of his neck. "That is…if she even wants to return to Ilusauri." He cleared his throat abruptly. "Regardless, I don't see a way forward for us."

Magda let out a sigh. "You're not a bad person Claude, and I think, maybe, we can still be friends somehow. But the world needs us, and so does the rest of the group. Maybe we could have been a good match, but both our hearts are in other places, and I don't think I would have said yes in the first place."

"Then I'm sorry for not trusting you and proposing the marriage without an explanation," he replied.

"Thank you," said Magda. "I know I saved you from drowning that day, but it's clear Dagmara has saved you over and over again, from so much more. You need her."

Claude was silent.

Magda continued, "And she needs you. I see the way she looks at you."

"I don't know if she wants to be with me anymore," Claude admitted. "She thinks I fell for the idea of Princess Magdalena. She doesn't understand that I truly fell for her."

"I'll speak with her," said Magda, assuringly. "She is the one thing we have in common. We both want what's best for her."

"I just hope there's a kingdom for her to return to. Whether or not she chooses Azurem or Ilusauri," Claude admitted.

"If Azurem and Ilusauri are dying, we have to work together."

"Then we have to find the First Prince's tomb," said Claude.

"Why would we go there?" Magda questioned.

"That is where the locks are that hold Eligor in the tomb," Claude said. "Once a guardian dies and the locks break, the land deteriorates. So if we restore the lock, we restore the land."

"Then we will find the tomb together," said Magda, giving him a soft smile, "but not as husband and wife." She looked deep into his eyes, and said, "Friends?"

"Maybe someday, we will be."

Someone cleared their throat loudly, and both Magda and Claude turned to see Ravi, now standing in the courtyard and waiting patiently to jump into the conversation. Odie circled his feet, staring up at him.

"King Claude Mirage," he announced in Flaustran. "I have something to say."

Claude blinked, shifting his gaze to Ravi. He frowned before stepping closer, clearing the distance between them. "Yes?"

"Ravi—" Magda started, but he had already proceeded into his speech.

"I understand I am not royalty. In fact, I know I will never be enough for Princess Magdalena. But she is a beacon in a storm, a harmony I can't live without. I will fight for her until the day I die," he stated. "And if that means I have to fight a king and a guardian then—"

Claude held up his hand, effectively silencing Ravi. "No need. She's all yours."

Ravi's mouth parted, searching for words. "O-Oh," then he straightened his posture. "Good. Now Magda has the freedom to choose what she wants."

Magda could feel the heat of embarrassment. She suppressed her smile and her desire to lunge forward and kiss Ravi then and there.

She opened her mouth to speak, but was interrupted by the door to the council chamber sliding open once more.

CHAPTER 34
Dagmara

Dagmara faced the council members, and her heart hammered against her ribcage. This was her moment to make a difference. She had forgotten everything she had accomplished in Ilusauri while being captured. But this...*this*...was bigger than her. She wasn't only negotiating with Ilusauri to get medication for Azurem...now she was negotiating for the safety of both Ilusauri and Celestaire.

She folded her hands on her lap, holding steadfast as she began to speak.

"I originally went to Ilusauri to track down my family's assassins," she began. "It is a group of supporters who believe the First Prince will rise, and they must kill all guardians. When I uncovered their identity, they took me hostage. To lure other guardians to me. I met the woman who took your guardian's life. She was one of my captors, working with the man who murdered my family."

Hushed murmurs rang through the council.

"The First Prince?" Lin chuckled. "That is a legend."

"Not anymore. If we are able to call a truce," Dagmara said, "I plan to take revenge on the man who killed my family, and I will gladly hunt down the woman who killed Sora as well."

"Even if what you say is true," Lin began, "what of the rumors that Ilusaurian troops were invading parts of our kingdom months ago?"

"That was an agreement between Sora and Claude," Dagmara announced. She glanced up at Reon. "Is there any written agreement between you two that can be shared?"

"There may be something here," Reon said. "I know they exchanged letters."

Nodding, she turned back to Lin. "We will provide proof that Claude's encroachment into Ilusauri was approved by Guardian Sora herself."

Lin leaned forward in his chair. "How do I know this isn't all some convoluted lie to buy this murderer more time?"

Dagmara leaned forward in her own chair, mimicking his movement. "I guess you will have to trust me," replied Dagmara. "Let's not forget your people murdered Governor Lionel, unprovoked. I was there, and they could have killed me as well. You started this war, and we are more than capable of ending it. However, I am trying to negotiate peace, as we have all lost people important to us."

Lin glanced at the council members on either side of him, muttering in Celesta. When he returned his attention to Dagmara, he said, "Princess, you must understand my hesitation. For all I know you could be luring us into a standstill only to attack us once again."

"I give you my word Ilusaurians will not cross into your kingdom, but we do have a right to defend ours," Dagmara stated.

"And you can speak for Ilusaurians?" Lin asked.

She held his stare, resolute. "I am the Queen of Ilusauri." The words settled into the space, and Dagmara's heart skipped a beat. In one abrupt onslaught, the title felt like her own. She wanted it. Manifesting more courage, she continued with more urgency, "If you are not interested in a peace treaty, at least consider a ceasefire. Give us a month to track down Sora's assassin. Otherwise, I will not hesitate to fortify Ilusauri's troops with my own."

My own. As if Azurem's troops belonged to her. But she couldn't deny loving the power her words held.

When Lin translated, gasps rang through the council, followed by sporadic whispers. There was a hushed discussion, all of which Dagmara remained silent during. She held her composure. Although every nerve on her body fluttered with anxiety, she refused to show it on her face.

Lin shook his head, before stating, "We need time to discuss your proposal. This is difficult without definitive proof. However, we would like to prevent losing more lives. You have immunity here until we make our decision."

At first, Dagmara couldn't move. They were going to discuss a truce. That was all she could ask for.

Dagmara exhaled sharply, rising to her feet. "Thank you."

Reon dipped his head to the council before gesturing toward the exit. It wasn't a victory, but it was close. And *she* had done it.

As soon as they exited the door, Reon abruptly slid it shut. "That went better than expected," he stated.

"What happened?" Claude asked, running toward them with Magda and Ravi close behind.

"They need time to discuss it, but they're open to a ceasefire, and they're giving us a month to find Sora's real assassin," Dagmara replied.

"You did it," Claude said, taking her arm. "You..." he scanned her face, pausing to find the words. "You're..."

Before he could finish his sentence, Odie nuzzled against Dagmara's knees, knocking her away from the king.

A smile creased on Magda's face. She glanced at Reon, watching him carefully, before she told Dagmara, "You make a good queen, Your Majesty."

Dagmara's heart warmed at the compliment, but she was unable to bask in it. Claude was like an immovable statue beside her, his gaze drifting to something beyond. Following his gaze, Dagmara saw a black bird circling the air above the courtyard. Her blood turned to ice.

The bird let out a call, and the sound scraped against Dagmara's temples.

"What..." Magda followed their gaze, her face contorting in confusion. "What are you looking at?"

The bird dove toward them.

"Get down!" Claude yelled, pulling Dagmara to the ground below him.

With a shriek, everyone else followed suit, dropping to the stone immediately.

Then the courtyard lit in silver flames.

CHAPTER 35
Dagmara

Screaming rang through the air. Both Ravi and Magda dove to the ground beside one another, Magda grabbing Odie by the scruff and pulling him toward her. Reon jerked back, his hand flying to his belt lined with weapons. Silver fire fluttered on the ground, snaking up the walls, the illusion dancing like a beautiful nightmare. The loud fluttering of the bird's feathers became one disorienting cacophony.

"Go away!" Claude yelled, thrusting his palm forward. Silver sparks exploded from his hand, spiraling in the direction of the bird and causing it to careen off course.

"What is going on?" Magda yelled, but Dagmara couldn't bring herself to answer.

Beside Magda, Ravi shouted in Flaustran, but the words were foreign to Dagmara's ear.

The bird looped back toward the group before diving at its victims.

Odie jumped up, barking frantically, attempting to snap at whatever was harming the group. He darted back and forth, his nails sliding on the wooden floor, as he struggled to decipher where the danger was coming from.

The bird was flying straight toward Claude.

Without taking the time to think, Dagmara rose from the ground, her forearms covering her face, intercepting the bird's path. Its talons raked across her forearms, causing searing pain to soar through her entire body. She couldn't contain the scream that erupted from her throat. She bent over, clutching her arms to her stomach.

There was no blood, but the pain was undeniable. It was as if the phantom talons pierced through her flesh and created caverns in her bones.

Hands gripped both her shoulders, hoisting her upright and turning her body. She came face-to-face with the Mad King, his expression stoic and his eyes glistening with silver.

"Eyes on me," he said.

It was impossible to look anywhere else.

A rush of wind flew by them, and Dagmara jumped, the sound of the flapping wings sending a chill through her entire body. But Claude held her firm. His eyes scanned her lips, and Dagmara's stomach flipped inside out. She didn't want to pull away. Somehow, they were both tormented by whatever entity the phantom bird came from.

They were both mad.

"Damn it!" Reon cursed. "Get out of here!"

The king was the first to break out of the trance. He snapped his head toward the Celesta soldier, releasing Dagmara to allow her to do the same.

Odie was attempting to help the Spearhead, jumping and snapping his teeth exactly at the space where the bird had just been, although it was unclear if the dog could see it.

The bird curled around the group before taking off back toward the sky. Reon sent a throwing knife hurling in the bird's direction. His aim was impressive, slicing the side of the animal, and a few feathers fluttered down to the ground.

Claude extinguished the fire illusion as the bird soared away, but the tension was still heavy. The rattle of armor alerted Dagmara to soldiers approaching, their weapons drawn, prepared to protect their spearhead.

"By the Guardians," Reon grumbled. He peered beyond his shoulder, attempting to look at his back. "That stupid bird hurt worse than a whiplash. How bad is it?" He turned, showing off his back to the group.

Ravi asked a question in Flaustran, scanning the courtyard as he slowly rose to a standing position. He helped Magda up, and her eyes landed on Dagmara, yearning for her friend to explain what had transpired.

But Dagmara was too shocked to do anything but stare at the head of the Celesta militia. He had thrown the knife directly at the bird. He had *seen* it.

Dagmara's eyes widened. "Have you seen that bird before?"

"I don't keep a tally of how many times I see birds," Reon replied. His accent disguised his sarcasm, and Dagmara was unsure how to proceed until he added, "I've never been attacked by a blackbird before, no."

"That is a phantom that only Claude and I are able to see. Notice how it injured you but left no visible wounds? How can you see it?" Dagmara insisted.

"I have no idea. Maybe you two brought it here with you."

"No one else saw it."

"I don't know what you want me to say," stated Reon.

"The night of the engagement ball, when I ordered you to leave the room, did you see it then?"

Reon's eyes narrowed. "I don't remember."

"You would have if you saw it," Claude interjected.

"Then I guess I didn't."

"But that doesn't make sense," said Dagmara.

"Listen, I don't care about this bird, phantom or not," said Reon.

Suddenly, he held up a hand to the approaching soldiers. "I'm unharmed," he said. "Go back to your posts."

Each one nodded abruptly before turning on their heels and obeying his command. However, one individual remained. It was apparent by her outfit that she wasn't one of the Celesta soldiers. She had dark hair and held the handle of an axe at her hip.

She muttered in a foreign language, staring at the group.

Odie leapt forward, rushing up to greet the mysterious woman with a wag of his tail.

"Ishani?" Magda blurted out.

The woman's face flashed with confusion. She greeted Odie before responding with a slight accent in Ilusaurian. "Magda? What are *you* doing here?"

"You know this woman?" Reon asked Ishani. He did a double take as he said, "Wait, Magda? The princess?"

Magda feigned a smile, "Surprise."

CHAPTER 36
Magdalena

"What?" Reon gasped, staring right at Magda. "I helped you lie to the council!" he shouted.

"Shhh," Claude quieted Reon. "Let me explain."

"I don't need you to explain anything. You all deceived me plain as day when I genuinely thought you wanted peace." Reon looked as if he was about to barge into the council chamber once more, but Claude swiftly grabbed him by the forearm, pulling him deeper into the gardens.

Magda, Dagmara, Ravi, and Ishani stood outside the council chamber, watching as the two men argued. Their voices were crisp in Celesta. No one dared to intervene, afraid to further upset the one person providing them sanctuary.

Finally, after a few minutes, Claude and Reon returned to the group, neither admitting what had been spoken between them.

Reon grumbled, "You can stay with me, and we will keep this quiet until the council makes a decision on the ceasefire. You'll be safe here just like Princess Ishani and Princess Kiran."

"Reon, I'm extremely sorry...," Magda began.

Claude shot her a glare, and Magda instantly knew to keep quiet.

Whatever had transpired between him and Reon was a precarious agreement as is, and she didn't want to jeopardize that.

Then Reon led the group to another floor of the tower, with angular roofs and a porch-like balcony that wrapped around the entire designated area for the spearhead. To the right, was a wing for living quarters, and to the left was a garden, full of ponds, flower beds, and bare trees that had lost their leaves in the cool air.

"Floor eight is my personal floor," Reon grumbled. "You'll be safe here."

Magda exchanged a glance with Ravi, who walked beside her. She quickly translated for him, and he nodded in understanding.

As they walked, twisting through the paths of the complex, Magda hung back with Dagmara and Odie, keeping her voice low. She waited until the rest of them were far ahead, before she started.

"I talked to Claude," Magda whispered. "I told him I can't be with him. We will annul the marriage, and it was a mutually agreed upon decision."

Dagmara stopped walking. "Why?"

"I don't know the entire story, but it's clear he cares about you."

Dagmara shook her head. "Don't annul the marriage for me. I won't be the reason the kingdoms look like fools and the trade routes end."

"He agreed to continue the trade. He said it is what you would want. And it isn't entirely about you. I don't want to be married right now, let alone to him. I want to return to Azurem and rebuild what Aleksy and my father created. I've been gone for too long, and ever since getting Life magic, I finally feel like I'm worthy to carry my father's legacy. I don't care what the kingdoms think when they hear the marriage is over." Magda reached out and took her best friend's hands. "So, Claude and I are ending the marriage today. I wanted to let you know. You're free to do whatever you want with that information. And...you're free from the royal assassin position too."

"Magda—"

"No, listen, please," she said. "I know it's never what you wanted. I know you only felt obligated to follow in your mother's footsteps and protect Teos. But after Eligor is dealt with, Azurem doesn't need a royal assassin right away. I only need my best friend. Alive and happy, preferably."

Dagmara laughed. She pulled Magda close, embracing her in a hug. "I'm not making any decisions yet. But no matter what happens, you will always be my best friend. I would have switched places with you over and over again. And honestly...I wouldn't have met Claude if we hadn't swapped."

Magda frowned. "You wouldn't have been tortured either."

"And Ravi wouldn't have introduced me to medicine that may save Teos, as well as medicine that may help me."

Beaming, Magda's eyes widened in surprise. Her gaze shifted past Dagmara, landing on Ravi. Her expression melted, her cheeks reddening. The group was already far away, and they would have to hasten their pace to catch-up.

"Thank you for what you did with the council," said Magda. "You will have saved not only Ilusaurian and Celesta citizens, but Azuremi ones too. It was remarkable."

"I was only being you," said Dagmara.

"No, you weren't," Magda assured her. "I couldn't have done that. It was all you."

Dagmara grinned, giving Magda another hug.

Odie let out a bark, encouraging the two to keep up. "Come on, we can't lose them," said Magda.

They followed the rest of their friends. Reon was in the middle of sliding open a door, leading into a hallway that was lit faintly by scarlet lanterns that cast red glows from their circular shapes. On all sides of the hallway were more sliding doors.

Then Reon stole a look at Odie, who was padding in beside them. "Dogs aren't usually allowed inside."

"I promise he's friendly," Magda said.

"Wipe off his paws then." Reon gestured to a towel hanging by the wall.

Magda nodded, before taking the towel and wiping Odie's paws after the long journey.

It wasn't the first time that she had been to the Celesta tower, although the last time had been with her father as a little girl during one of the embassies between the guardians. Claude, Aleksy, and Kiran had all been in attendance. Back then, the spearhead was another man, who was rumored to have died at sea.

Magda stole a glance at Ravi, knowing he hadn't understood any of the conversations in the other languages, but he only returned an assuring smile.

Where are you off to, Princess?

Eligor's voice slithered into her mind like a serpent. She shuddered against his words as they penetrated her thoughts.

Get out of my head. She called back, trying to shield her mind. She didn't want him to know where they were. He could send his assassins after them.

I'm everywhere. He replied, before a low laugh scraped Magda's temples.

Finally, Reon approached a final door, sliding it open and beckoning them all to enter.

Inside, was a low table and chairs, as well as carved, lacquer furniture. The walls contained hand-drawn paintings depicting a Guardian of the Spirit blowing Celesta's iconic red leaves in a vortex, before soaring over the Celesta mountain side and blessing dozens of fishing boats with the gift of wind in their sails.

Kiran was seated in the center of the room, around a table, sifting through some of Ishani's logbooks.

"Magda, you made it!" Kiran blurted out when they entered. "I'm so glad you're safe, there are horrible creatures out there!" She wrapped her arms around Magda and engulfed her in a hug.

Odie leapt up, attempting to get Kiran's attention, his tail wagging furiously.

Kiran withdrew from the hug and knelt before Odie, scratching behind his ear. "Good boy." Then her eyes went wide, seeing Dagmara and Claude. She straightened to her feet, her mouth slightly agape. "You found her! Oh, Dagmara, I've heard so much about you. I'm so happy you're safe."

Dagmara gave Kiran a gentle smile, "Nice to meet you, Your Highness."

"And you're Ishani, one of the guild leaders?" Claude put the pieces together.

"Yes. I've been helping you search for the First Prince's tomb, haven't I?" she asked.

Claude nodded, "It's the only thing that will save Ilusauri."

"And Azurem," Magda added.

"I'm beginning to see the shifts in our lands too, ever since Sora died," admitted Reon. "Rifts have also sprung up all over Celestaire, and more of my soldiers are being slain by the hounds each day."

Magda cut in, "The problem is, we still don't know where the tomb is."

"It's not in Ilusauri," Claude admitted, "I've searched everywhere."

"Or in Celestaire," Reon said, filling everyone in. "Sora had an alliance with Claude, allowing him to search for the tomb in secret. All leads were exhausted."

"What about Flaustra?" Magda asked.

Ishani shook her head. "I searched all my trade routes, and even copied all of the other guild leaders' logbooks. You, Claude, and I have all scoured those notes."

"What about Azurem?" asked Claude.

"I don't know," said Magda, "My father and brother never told me about any of this."

"So it looks like it's a lost cause," Kiran said, her eyebrows drooping.

"No, it's not," Claude stated, "I've been searching for years, I won't give up yet. I know it is underground, maybe the Azuremi salt mines?"

"I know where it is."

All heads snapped to the voice. Dagmara stood in the center of the group, her eyes wide. "When I was captured, they were talking about going to Eligor. They said both Sabien and Junne could get there... but only Viette could get out."

Everyone waited for her to finish, leaning in closer.

She let out a shaky breath before announcing:

"The tomb is at Dreadmarrow."

"Dreadmarrow?" Ravi echoed the familiar word in his own language.

Claude leaned closer. "I've considered Dreadmarrow before and sent spies to scour the prison, but no one has been able to get inside."

"Think about it," said Dagmara, "Only a Life or Spirit Guardian can get in. Dreadmarrow is on an island in the middle of the ocean..."

"Built on towering mountains," Reon added.

"The only entrance is a cove for ships," Ishani mused.

Dagmara continued, "...and only a Mind Guardian can get out."

"They say no one can leave the island alive," Magda said. "How would a Mind Guardian get past thousands of guards and prisoners?"

Claude spoke up, "An illusion."

"Or compulsion," Dagmara finished. "Think about it. Dreadmarrow's at the center of all four kingdoms. It's impenetrable."

Hmm... Eligor mused. *I like this friend of yours.*

Magda's face paled. She stepped back, pressing a palm to her forehead. She had to shut him out. For good. If he really was at Dreadmarrow, he couldn't sense them coming. Refocusing her brain, she exhaled slowly, imagining walls surrounding her on all sides.

Eligor? She called, testing her thoughts.

There was no answer. Only silence.

Claude ran his hand along the back of his neck. "It's a high possibility," he said. "That prison is centuries old."

"It must be there!" Kiran squealed.

"My spies couldn't get past the front gate," Claude stated. "Maybe I have to take matters into my own hands and go myself. If Viette can get in and out, I should be able to as well."

"You're not going there alone," Magda objected. "Ilusauri isn't the only land that is dying. I have to restore Azurem. I'm going too."

Ishani cut in, "Dreadmarrow is one of the most secure places in all the kingdoms. You can't just walk through the front door without a reason. You need specific papers, but there's no way the prison guards will let anyone into Dreadmarrow without a legitimate reason. No one cares about royalty or guardians."

The entire group began speaking loudly over one another, all shouting out ideas to enter the prison and sneak past the thousands of guards. One by one they presented their ideas, talking in furious succession to come up with a viable plan.

Ravi tapped Magda on the shoulder. "What are they saying about Dreadmarrow?" he asked curiously.

Magda whispered, "We're trying to figure out a way to get inside."

Ravi nodded. Then he withdrew the wanted poster from his bag, holding it toward Magda. "I know a way," he said before turning to the group and announcing:

"Me."

CHAPTER 37
Magdalena

"No, Ravi you can't!" Magda shouted over the commotion, and all eyes turned to her. Thinking of risking Ravi's life for their plan overcame her with frantic emotion. "I won't let you do this."

"Do what?" asked Claude.

"I'm going to turn myself in so you all can have a reason to get inside Dreadmarrow," Ravi announced, presenting the poster once more. "One of you can 'deliver' me to the prison."

Magda watched as the poster was passed around the group, and each person nodded in turn, while some eyes widened at the reading of Ravi's crime. Magda's thoughts raced as she tried to think of an alternative plan before everyone agreed to this one. She was against using Ravi as bait, revealing him to the Dreadmarrow guards and risking that he would carry out his sentence. The entire reason he had left his family behind in Flaustra was to guarantee his safety from the bounty hunters.

Magda decided, "No. It's not an option. We'll find another way."

"Apparently, if all you guardians can't figure it out, there is no other way," protested Ravi, "and we're running out of time. Who's to say that Eligor doesn't know where we are right now? He could be sending more assassins after us."

Magda gulped. She hadn't told everyone about the voice in her head, and she especially didn't want Reon to know. The trust between their group and the council was precarious as it is.

"Ravi's right," Ishani said, understanding the connotation placed in Ravi's voice. "This place is barely a safe house anymore."

Magda scanned the group, and everyone's eyes were on her, as if they were waiting for her to make a decision. If Eligor really was at Dreadmarrow, this could be their only chance to try and reseal another lock, ensuring he stayed trapped. If he wasn't, she could be leading all of her friends into a death trap. She was tempted to reach Eligor in the Void space, seeking a confirmation of his whereabouts, but she feared her scattered emotions would accidentally reveal their current location.

Magda turned to Claude, "This wanted poster could be a way in. Can you disguise yourself as Ravi?"

Claude mused over the suggestion before shaking his head. "It's risky," he paused, his thoughts churning, "I don't speak Flaustran natively, and I'm taller than him. It won't be believable, and I'd rather not put us in more danger."

Ravi stepped closer to Magda. "Please, Magda," he said. "I'm the only one here that's not a royal or a guardian. I have to do what I can and play my part."

She still couldn't move, couldn't think. The thought of using Ravi in a plot to infiltrate Dreadmarrow had paralyzed her decision-making.

When she didn't answer, Ravi turned her toward him, away from the group, and lowered his voice. "Nothing is going to happen to me," he whispered.

"How can you be so sure?" she looked up at him.

"I'm not. If I told you I wasn't scared, I would be lying to you. I'm also terrified. But if I thought there was another way, I would take it. I can't bear the thought that you are constantly looking over your shoulder for Eligor, and if he escaped, he would come after you. If this is the only way I can help prevent a future where I would have to go through each day without you, then I will do it."

Magda's heart melted, her entire body flushing with heat. She wanted to embrace him right there, pulling him to her and holding him in her arms, but everyone was staring at them. They all were looking to her to lead the group. She needed to project confidence in a definite decision.

Magda nodded before turning back to everyone. "Will Ravi's plan work?" she asked.

"It could," Ishani mused over the situation.

"It will get us closer than any other plan," Claude nodded.

Magda stole a glance at Ravi before speaking, her voice unfaltering. "Alright, let's do it. Reon, do you have a map of Dreadmarrow?"

"Yes. Let me find one," said Reon, heading out of the room for the adjacent one.

"How will we get there?" asked Ravi.

"Oh, let's take your ship!" Kiran exclaimed, looking at her sister.

"Wait," Ishani blurted out, "*You're* not going anywhere. Your life is the most important."

"I can't sit here and wait," Kiran objected.

Ishani shrugged. "We're not sitting here and waiting. We will have to find another place to hide."

Kiran shook her head in protest. "Please, Ishani. I'm the Queen of Flaustra, and I think helping the other guardians in this quest is important. I've never felt so strongly about anything before in my life. We have to do something."

"Are you ordering me to take you all on the Starway?" Ishani raised her eyebrows.

"No," Kiran said, "I'm asking you. As my sister. Please help me do this."

Ishani hesitated. "It feels wrong. We came here to keep you safe and going to Dreadmarrow is the biggest danger there is."

"I understand the risks," said Kiran. "I really do."

"I...," Ishani's voice trailed off.

"The Starway is not the only boat we can commission to take us," Claude cut in. "I have my own resources."

"But there's no other crew you can trust to transport a group of guardians," Ishani said, shooting a glance at Magda in concern. Then she looked at her sister. "I'm sorry, I just don't think it's safe. We came here to stay away from this nonsense."

Kiran continued to protest, "You don't know what type of magic will be required, and since I'm the only Soul Guardian, they might need me to reactivate the other locks. We won't know until we get there."

Ishani's brow furrowed, unhappy with her sister's words.

Dagmara intervened with a solution. "Can you disguise Kiran?" she asked Claude.

Claude answered, "I can change her entire appearance so no one will ever know she's with us."

"That relies on Claude not getting killed," said Ishani, shooting him a death glare.

"No one is getting killed," said Claude, "a few prison guards are nothing I can't handle."

A long moment passed, as Ishani considered her decision. It seemed like the seconds turned to minutes, as the elder sister considered all of the options. Finally she announced, "We'll take my ship. I'll chart the route and prepare my officers, and we'll leave at dawn. But no one will believe that the Starway—a trading ship—suddenly is delivering Ravi for a bounty. We need someone to pose as a real bounty hunter."

"I've had my fair share of bounty hunters," said Dagmara. "I can pose as one."

"It's smart," said Magda. "It may be the only way in."

Claude looked as if he was about to interject, and exchanged an intense glance with Dagmara. But at the last moment he conceded, staying silent.

"Will this work?" asked Dagmara, "Are you sure you can restore the magic?"

"We will find a way," said Claude.

Magda spoke clearly summarizing the plan for everyone, "Alright. We get inside using Ravi, and Dagmara will claim the bounty. Once we find the tomb, Claude will try and reset the Mind lock. Kiran stays on the ship, and Claude will disguise her."

They all agreed on the plan, and soon Reon promptly returned with the map in hands. He placed it down on the table, announcing:

"A map of Dreadmarrow island."

The entire group gathered closely around the table, examining the intricate drawings of the deadly island.

"I pulled this from Sora's archives," explained Reon, unrolling a large parchment. "Initial construction of Dreadmarrow was completed nine hundred years ago. Over time, more and more floors and wings were added to keep up capacity for an increasing population of prisoners." His fingers flipped the piece of paper over, pointing to a section at the center of the map. "The oldest part of the prison is here."

"Maybe the prison was constructed around Eligor's tomb, to hide it," said Dagmara.

Reon continued, "You should study these blueprints and commit them to memory. I'm inclined to agree that you should search the oldest wings of the prison first."

Magda leaned over the table, attempting to remember everything on it. The prison was a labyrinth of tunnels, wings, and towers, connected by various elevator shafts. "Alright," she answered. "I'll study everything tonight."

"I'll memorize it as well," Claude agreed. "Reon, are you coming?"

"No, I need to stay and oversee the militia given the recent unrest," Reon said.

A voice sounded from the adjacent room through the curtained entryway. Everyone jerked upright. Odie barked from his spot in the corner, jumping up to his paws.

Leaving the table, Reon approached the curtain and threw it open. One of his men stood in an identical space that was adjacent to the hallway, though this soldier was barely older than Teos.

"Kenzo," Reon acknowledged him. "I told you not to interrupt."

"There's a man and woman here," the boy announced. "They say they came for Claude and Dagmara."

The air shifted, a tense atmosphere filling the space.

Dagmara and Claude exchanged a glance, and he quickly translated for her. Her voice was nearly a whisper as she asked, "Sabien and Junne?"

Upon hearing the names of the assassins, Magda's heart clenched. She had tried incessantly to block Eligor out and to conceal their location. Had he still been watching them this whole time? She braced herself, a faint hint of yellow magic swirling at her fingertips, mirroring Kiran's own stance.

Claude's hands turned to fists, and a silver glint shimmered in his eyes. He crossed the room and threw the curtain aside violently, brushing past Reon on the way, unafraid. Then he ran to the sliding panel at the end of the next room, ready to meet whoever was on the other side.

Magda barreled after Claude, unable to restrain herself. She was aware of Dagmara and Ishani following after her, anxious to see who were the visitors in the doorway.

They all slid through the panel door, rushing through the hallway, and skidding to a halt at the front entrance. Standing before them was a man and woman, just as the soldier had announced—but the woman wasn't Junne.

Magda took in the appearance of the strangers. The man had a young face, with tight ringlets and a bow strapped to his back. The woman was strikingly beautiful, with cropped hair and dark skin. She was slightly taller than the man beside her, with a toned figure. They both wore uniforms that indicated they were part of the Ilusaurian royal guard.

"If I didn't know better, I'd say you were about to fight us," the man said, adding an awkward laugh.

Claude's silver magic dissipated. "We thought you could be someone else," he admitted.

Before the man could respond, Dagmara's voice rang out. "Martine! Pierre! You made it!" She skidded to a halt. "Magda, meet Pierre, Claude's first guard, and Martine, my..." she paused, "my friend."

"Oh," Magda stuttered, the yellow in her eyes fading away. "Nice to meet you," she said, not knowing how it was customary to greet Claude's guards.

"I'm not introduced as a friend?" Pierre asked, pouting.

"Princess?" Martine mused, scrutinizing Magda.

A silence spread through the space, and Magda felt as though she were being judged. She swallowed hard, calming her racing heart, overcome with gratefulness that the strangers were Dagmara's friends and not the assassins. Even though she and Claude had decided to annul the marriage, it still felt as if she had much explaining to do.

Suddenly Pierre broke the silence. He reached into his knapsack, withdrawing a small box. He popped it open, revealing globs of...cake?

He extended them toward Magda. "Caramel squares?"

CHAPTER 38
Magdalena

Magda headed to the Celesta archives, which was a large, one-story room with scrolls on all of the walls. Sliding doors with golden, hand-painted designs marked each corner, and a large table with a map of the kingdoms was in the center. Compared to Azurem, Celestaire hosted a wealth of information in the various towers that were spaced within the complex, information that had been safeguarded for many years.

For hours, Magda poured over pages and pages of documents. She was scared to drag her friends into this and knew a million things could go wrong during their mission at Dreadmarrow. If any piece of information could help them during their attempt to reseal the locks, she wanted to find it.

Ishani was with her, charting the way to the prison, using maps of the stars, currents, and the logbooks of former captains or daring Celesta fishermen who had made the journey to the prison. Servants checked on them every so often, bringing dinner, snacks, and tea.

Ishani shut the logbook she was studying, "I think I'm done here. You coming to dinner?"

"No, I need more time," said Magda.

"You'll have time on the ship."

"And I have time for a few more before we set sail."

"Suit yourself," said Ishani, heading for the door.

Magda examined maps of Dreadmarrow from all centuries, committing them to memory. She even secured a copy of the letter from the original excavator that was commissioned to create Dreadmarrow. He was a man from Ilusauri, who worked with the family of the Mind Guardians to envision the prison, and included a preliminary sketch book of ideas for the structure.

According to the archives, Dreadmarrow could hold one thousand prisoners, and only had one entrance—through a cove that was heavily guarded by an outer wall, only allowing ships to pass through. The guards kept a list of ships, assassins, guild leaders, or bounty hunters that might come to deliver prisoners or make claims for their release.

Dreadmarrow scared her. It sickened her that Ravi was risking his life, especially after he fought for her, professing his feelings in front of Claude. His proclamation had almost brought her to her knees with the weight of its emotion, and all she had wanted to do in that moment was run away with Ravi, leaving her problems behind.

Her throat burned and she fought back tears, for she knew Ravi was only agreeing to help them at Dreadmarrow for her benefit, for he felt as if he needed to do his part. The thought raked her chest with guilt, which came over and over in continuous waves.

She steadied her heart and convinced herself that Ravi would survive. Then she attempted to think of a back up plan if restoring the locks didn't work. If she and Claude couldn't fortify the locks, then Eligor would only be closer to escape, and the land would continue to die.

She sifted through more papers, searching for anything about the locks that the original guardians had commissioned. But even though she looked through notes from architects, royal advisors, and letters from the guardians' descendants, absolutely no one mentioned the magical locks.

She unrolled another scroll, finding some information about spells and curses tied to family lineages, but it wasn't enough. It only spread more unease through her body. Doubt crept through her mind, and she wondered if heading toward the tomb was even the right choice. She would be going closer to where the murderous First Prince had been encased for eternity.

Am I really that terrible, dear Princess? Eligor laughed. *It seems like your mind is begging for my presence.*

Or you're begging for mine.

Come to Dreadmarrow and find out.

There it was. His confirmation. He was still calling to her, leading her through this journey. She had to make sure that the destination was her choosing, and not his. But where was she trying to go?

The door creaked open, and Ravi entered. "You should come eat something,," he said.

"I can't," Magda rubbed her hands over her face. She looked at him with glossy eyes, and he instantly made his way over to her, wrapping his strong arms around her and holding her to his chest.

"What's wrong?" he asked.

"Everything," she said, letting out her emotions.

"It will be alright, don't worry," he said, stroking her hair.

She looked up at him, "I don't know if it will. I don't know if I'll be able to do this. I've tried. And...," she hesitated, "I'm so scared—no, I'm *terrified* of going to Dreadmarrow, possibly failing, and having to face Eligor. I'm terrified that tomorrow will be the first day on a journey to something horrible. I don't want to wake up tomorrow and have all of this," she leaned up to kiss him, savoring the taste of his lips on hers, "end."

Ravi nodded, holding her close. "There were times in my life when things seemed hopeless. There were moments when I truly thought my sister Prisha was going to die, or when I thought we would starve without my father's income." His eyes drifted as he remembered the memory, and Magda gripped him tighter, encouraging him to continue.

Ravi spoke, "And I realized that there was something, deep down, that willed me to survive and fight for the people I loved. I embraced deception and betrayal by selling secrets to the guilds, which were things I never thought I would do. But the people in my life gave me the strength to continue fighting for them."

Magda relaxed into his embrace. "I want to fight for the people that I love, but it doesn't make me any less scared."

"I wish I could take away your fear," said Ravi, "but hopefully it gives you comfort knowing I'm also scared, and you're not alone. And if anyone can do this, it's you."

"How can you be so sure?" Magda asked.

Ravi paused, choosing his words carefully. "Because, I truly believe there's a reason our paths crossed that day in the marketplace. And maybe, after everything we've both been through, we survived our pasts for this moment. I know it doesn't make sense, but being with you makes me believe that we can take on any challenge, and we will survive it. So it's alright if you're scared, Magda, because if you weren't, you would have nothing worth fighting for."

"Ravi...," Magda didn't know how to respond, her emotions boiling inside her.

"But if this is our last night together..." he began.

"It won't be," Magda cut him off, breathless.

"But if it is," Ravi continued, "You should know I love you."

A warmth spread through Magda's chest, the words seeping into her, confirming the feelings she had been having for so long.

She reached out and placed her palm on his cheek. "I love you too."

He took her face in his hands, kissing her with passion as she let her body melt into his. She needed to feel him against her. She wasn't close enough to him.

He withdrew briefly, taking her face in his hands and wrapping his arms around her. His tongue swooped into her mouth, and she savored every moment of their embrace. She let herself relax into his body, needing him closer.

He spoke softly, "I think you've studied enough tonight."

"You're right. I think we have some time to ourselves before dinner." Her fingers lingered, catching his sleeve. "You coming?"

He met her gaze and grinned. "Do you think I would ever say no to that question?"

She laughed before pulling him along with her.

CHAPTER 39
Dagmara

The night was quiet, the impending danger of Dreadmarrow resting heavy in the back of everyone's minds. After dinner, they all sat spaced throughout the small, adjacent rooms, each breaking off into their own individual groups. Reon instructed the servants to open all of the interior panels, creating a large space that connected all the guests' rooms and contained the guest beds, the dining room, and the living area combined into one.

Ishani and Kiran spoke in hushed tones together on their bed, while Reon, Magda, and Ravi were grouped on the opposite end of the room. Odie sat at Magda's side, his tail wagging.

Dagmara sat on the floor with Martine and Pierre while she finished filling them in on the plan. Both stared at her with blank expressions.

"There's no...underground tunnel?" Pierre ventured.

"Not that we know of."

"Are you going to throw sleeping potions on all of them?" Martine asked.

Dagmara rolled her eyes. "I said I was sorry."

"Mhmm," Martine mused, her lips creasing into a smile. Then her expression froze, her gaze fixated on something behind Dagmara. She straightened her posture, coming to full attention. "Your Majesty."

"I'm glad you two are back," Claude said. "Sacha...?"

"He's home." Pierre nodded.

"Thank you." The king cleared his throat awkwardly. He glanced at Dagmara. "I have something for you."

Heat rushed through Dagmara's body, but before she had a chance to reply, Claude pulled a small pouch from his pocket.

"I stole this from Reon." He dropped the pouch in Dagmara's palm.

"Oh?" Dagmara could feel her heart pound faster against her chest. She tore open the top of the velvet pouch, peeking at the contents.

Her stomach flipped, her throat instantly feeling like sandpaper. The granular white fragments sparkled.

Salt.

She couldn't look up at him. She couldn't tear her eyes away from the salt. The room was hot and sticky, all the air sucked from around her. And she couldn't speak.

The silence tore on for an eternity, until Pierre finally broke through the lull in the conversation.

"Did you try my caramel squares, Claude? Oh—I don't know where that came from. Can I call you that now? I feel like we're close...enough. Maybe."

Martine put her hand on his knee.

"Yes, I did try them," said Claude. He glanced once more at Dagmara before dipping his head and departing from the conversation.

Pierre leaned toward Martine. "He either doesn't like that I called him Claude, or he doesn't like my caramel squares."

"At least they're better than the first ones you made."

He jostled back in his chair. "You said you liked those."

"I liked that you made them for me."

Pierre's mouth was agape, staring at Martine.

"Go." She jerked her head in the king's direction.

"Right. Excuse me," Pierre said. He stumbled to his feet and chased after the king.

Still lost in the tantalizing glow of the salt, Dagmara barely noticed when Martine put her hand on Dagmara's.

"You alright?"

Snapping back to the present, Dagmara tied the pouch closed once more, tucking it deep in her pocket. "I'm fine. Overwhelmed thinking about tomorrow and..." her throat ran dry.

"The fact that the marriage is being annulled?"

"How could you possibly know that?"

Martine inclined her head. "You think Pierre can keep his mouth shut?" Her friend waited, her expression wide-eyed and hopeful.

"That's good, right?" Martine asked.

"I don't know," Dagmara admitted. "It was never a choice before. Magda was marrying Claude, and I had to return to Azurem to serve. Everything in my life...my role...my family...especially my illness, has told me what I can and can't do. For the first time, I get to choose."

"Well...that's good right?" Martine repeated. Her smile didn't reach her eyes, fading more at Dagmara's silence. Martine's expression grew somber as she asked, "If you don't come back to Ilusauri, what will you do?"

"Return to my brother. I love potions, and I've started to love what medicine can do for people...maybe continue something with that."

"And what about bringing your brother to Ilusauri?"

"I...didn't know that was an option."

"That's the fun thing about having choices, Dagmara," Martine said. "There are endless options. Have you spoken to Claude?"

"Not alone—"

A loud screech echoed through the room. At the threshold to the dining hall, Pierre stood with an instrument in hand and a bow aimed at the ceiling. "I found this in the hall, and I think we deserve some livelihood before we all potentially end our livelihoods tomorrow!"

Reon snapped his head up from his conversation, the knuckles on his mug turning white. "That's only for musicians."

"I can play!" he exclaimed. He started sliding the bow back and forth on the strings, tapping his foot unrhythmically on the wood.

Cringing, Dagmara forced herself not to cover her ears, even though the sound was deafening. Odie whimpered, and Ishani closed her eyes, shaking her head.

Kiran hopped up from her chair. "I do believe we have a proper musician in the room?" She eyed Ravi before saying something to him in Flaustran. Dagmara was uncertain whether she was begging him to save them from the torture of Pierre's playing, or if she was actually invested in this last hurrah before Dreadmarrow in the morning.

Ravi hesitated, looking to Reon for confirmation.

The spearhead grumbled, letting out a sharp exhale, before finally giving a single nod. A hint of a smile creased his lips.

Rising to his feet, Ravi crossed to Pierre. Though from different worlds, the two gave each other amicable nods before Pierre passed off the instrument.

Ravi counted—or what Dagmara assumed—to three in Flaustran, before he started playing. His fingers skimmed the neck of the fiddle, flying across the strings. The sound filled the room, the dining hall echoing with joyous revelry.

"Oh, you're good!" Pierre exclaimed, clapping his hands off beat.

Kiran laughed, pulling Pierre's sleeve. "Let's not do that." She smiled at him, and he heard no malice in her words. It was impressive how persuasive she could be and still maintain a perfectly kind inflection.

"Follow me!" Kiran called before executing a beautiful twirl, her arms high above her head and bending to hit each beat in perfect succession. Odie maneuvered in between their legs, finding his own role in the dance.

Magda stood up next, following Kiran in the rhythm of the Flaustran music that she had heard at her birthday ball. Magda danced with grace, repeating Kiran's move almost identically while Ravi's music continued to crescendo, moving with the girls as if the sound was a dance itself.

"Come on!" Pierre called, gesturing with wild arms to Martine and Dagmara. His energy was infectious.

With a glance at her friend, Martine shrugged. "This could be our last night."

"Don't say that!" Dagmara scolded, but then broke off into a laugh as Martine pulled her up to her feet.

Then Magda looped her arm into Ishani's before the captain could object. With a roll of her eyes, Ishani begrudgingly trudged along beside Magda, allowing herself to be pulled to Martine and Dagmara. The four girls continued to follow Kiran's movements. She shone in the glistening light of the lanterns, like a true queen dancing on a stage. It was as if Ravi was a royal musician, his music heightening her elegance with every turn.

"Join us!" Kiran flashed a smile to Reon.

"Absolutely not," said Reon, crossing his arms and holding his mug to his chest.

Ishani cut in, "Kiran, leave him alone. He doesn't want to dance."

"Oh, he will," Kiran said.

"He won't," retorted Ishani.

"I'm *very* persuasive." Kiran flashed the girls a grin.

"Kiran!" Ishani scolded, but Kiran was already heading toward Reon, her feet floating across the ground in perfect rhythm.

Dagmara couldn't help but laugh as Reon was pulled into the dance, joy bursting from her soul for the first time in a long time. She wanted to capture the fleeting moment of freedom—live in it forever. Then Magda grabbed her hand, twirling her in a circle. Odie stood beside them, circling around himself three times, as if he was mimicking their movements, making the girls burst into laughter. Dagmara was about to spin Magda, but her eye caught a figure in the threshold.

Past one of the outer panels, in the darkness of the hallway that encircled the interior space, was Claude. A stark contrast to the jubilant energy in the room, he was frozen as ice. A shadow beyond the light. A man longing to be a part of something, but unable to take the step himself. He turned his back on the false celebration, on the deceptive hope of happiness, and disappeared.

"Excuse me," Dagmara told Magda. Without waiting for a response, she slipped from the merriment and stepped through one of the open panels into the shadowed hall. A winter breeze rustled her hair from the open doors that marked the entrance to Reon's quarters. Beyond, she saw Claude crossing the quiet solitude of the gardens.

The cool night air did little to quell the embers burning inside Dagmara. She jogged faster to catch up to his retreating form.

"Claude?" she called, her voice careful as she approached.

He froze, turning over his shoulder to look at her. The snowflakes fluttered to the ground around him, as miniature as the salt in her pocket.

The salt he gifted her.

"Why aren't you inside?" he asked.

Her thoughts answered, *"Because my heart calls to yours." "Because I can't breathe knowing you're hurting."*

Instead she said, "I needed some air. Where are you going?"

"The Scribestone." He gestured to a raised tower, on the opposite side of the small gardens. "Ilusauri has no captain. Reon informed me the council will suspend attacks for one month, and I need to communicate with my kingdom."

"One month?" Dagmara exhaled. "That's good."

He didn't respond. He simply inhaled through his nose, taking in the night air, closing his eyes briefly. She sensed the turmoil beneath his stoic mask. She knew there was so much left unsaid between them.

"I'll come with you," she said. "I want to send a message to Teos."

He hesitated, but eventually nodded. He turned back to the path without another word, and she fell into step beside him.

They crossed the interior garden, stepping over a small bridge that arched over the ponds. As they headed to the Scribestone on the upper floor, they passed numerous soldiers, and Dagmara was aware of the tower's security.

At the corner of the tower was a wooden staircase looping up in a spiral formation along the outside wall. Dagmara's heart sank as she took in the staircase, leading them to the top floors. But she had to get to the Scribestone, for Teos.

Every step felt as though she was hoisting a bag of stones upward with her. Every joint in her body screamed, her mind swirling with dizziness. Claude paused briefly, slowing his pace for her, but she knew she couldn't stop halfway up—otherwise she would never make it.

They finally reached the top of the tower. Dagmara immediately leaned against the wall, catching her breath. On the right was a mural of a guardian with dark hair, flying above the land's lush rivers and fishing villages, while their people watched in awe. Below, the wind bent to her fingertips, pushing the fishing boats across the calm lakes and seas.

In the center, was a large pedestal with a red tablet on top. Ahead, out the window, one could see the incredible world within the complex's walls, full of soldiers, homes, and a forest of trees. From the second-to-top floor of the central Celesta tower, the people below appeared miniature. The jovial music distanced but never faded. Every note and strum was as cheery as before, if only minutely softer. Ravi shifted to a new tune, and she knew everyone was continuing the small celebration only one story below.

"You first?" Claude gestured toward the magic-imbued stone.

Dagmara beamed, racing to the Scribestone. She quickly

summoned the magic with the touch of her palm. She jotted down a quick sentence before sending it to her brother.

T, it's me. Long story, but I'm alive and I'll be home soon. Are you alright?

She could feel Claude's gaze on her. She stepped back from the stone, her face heating. "It's all yours," she said.

He paused, waiting in the doorway, blocking her exit down the stairs.

"I know your brother means a lot to you. I'm glad you are able to speak to him after all this time," he said, but the words were so formal. So reserved.

"Me too," Dagmara replied, before she ventured with her own statement, "And I'm glad you and Magda were able to speak about the marriage."

"Annul the marriage," he corrected.

"Right."

He hesitated. "And?"

"And I'm happy you both decided to keep the trade routes open."

"That's it?"

She shrugged.

Exhaling, he proceeded further into the room, approaching slowly. "What about us?"

"Yes, what about us?" Dagmara echoed. "You're a king, and I'm…"

"The woman I'm in love with."

Dagmara's breath caught in her throat. The world felt too small for the confession settling in the space before them.

"There. I've said it," he stated, coming to a stop directly before her. She was forced to tilt her chin back to gaze up at him. "You've officially driven me mad. You, Dagmara. You and only you."

"Claude..." she panted, unable to form words. He was captivating, and her love for him was all-consuming.

"Yes?" he asked, inching even closer, waiting for her to say the words in response to his—waiting to confirm she felt the same way for him. For all he knew, she was still acting. Still playing a role in his life. Their faces were inches apart. The magnetism between them was undeniable. His lips were a whisper away, and her breath hitched.

The silence lengthened between them, her heart hammering against her chest, urging her to admit her feelings. No fear of the future. No using his marriage with Magda as an excuse not to confront her feelings for him. She was undoubtedly, hopelessly in love. And it was a territory she had never stepped into before, daunting, emotional, and unknown.

She opened her mouth to say something...then shut it tight, glancing at the ground.

He let out a self-deprecating laugh. He pulled away, breaking the intensity between them. "Please go back to the party," he asked, gesturing to the staircase.

"I can wait for you to send your message."

He exhaled, but didn't argue. Stepping around her, he placed his palm against the stone and summoned his own message. Dagmara stepped back, approaching the window to give him space. The music from below still saturated the night sky. Snowflakes continued to flutter down, casting a blanket of white against the red trees.

After sending the message, Claude approached her against the window. He was careful not to touch her with his shoulder as he stood directly beside her, watching the night sky.

"Shall we head back?" she asked, listening to the distant music and laughter that carried through the air.

"You should."

"I want you to come with me."

"Dagmara," he said, his voice guttural, desperation pulling at every syllable of her name. "I don't know what you want from me.

I've told you how I feel. I can't breathe when you're near me—I can't breathe when you're gone. You have ruined me. I can't go anywhere with you and not desperately want to..." his voice trailed off and he fixed his gaze on the sky beyond, refusing to look at her. "Go back without me."

She waited for him to continue, but he was silent. "Claude," she started.

He exhaled, a puff of smoke escaping his lips into the night sky, but he didn't move.

"Claude..." Dagmara attempted once more, stepping toward him.

She didn't remember reaching out to him. She barely felt the graze of his shirt underneath her fingertips before he snapped.

At the faintest touch, he whipped away from the sky, and as his eyes fell on her, it was as though nothing else existed. His hands flew to her hips, gripping her body. She let out a slight gasp as her back met the wall, trapping her between the cool stone and his chest. A shudder tore through her, and she was frozen in place, her lips parted slightly.

Claude towered over her, his fingers digging into her with need.

"Don't torture me with your touch. I am only a man," he said, breathless. His eyes locked on her lips, and his hold softened. Yet his hands remained on her hips, sending her stomach into a rupture of butterflies. His proximity caused her heart to race, and her breath increased to catch up, her chest expanding in rapid movements. His eyes dropped lower, skimming her bare neck and chest, before he squeezed them shut and released her.

Stumbling back, he created distance, but she couldn't move. If her back wasn't against the wall, she was certain she would liquify right then and there.

He shook his head before saying, "I can't be cordial with a woman who holds my very being in her hands. So either tell me you detest me, and walk away now, or—" he paused, quelling his trembling voice, "Or marry me. Dagmara Zosia. We will do it all over again. I will add more of my blood to your ring," he gestured to the jewelry she still wore on her hand, "I would marry you a thousand times over. But I will no longer waver in this unknown with you. I have given you all of me, and I want all of you in return. No masks, no false names, no reservations. Now, with the marriage annulled, can't you tell me how you truly feel?" he begged. "I'm sorry if this marriage ruined your life. I'm sorry if every moment you've spent with me has been pretend. But please, say it out loud. Say you despise the Mad King."

"I can't, Claude!" she blurted out, every inch of her aching.

The music shifted downstairs. The melody rearranged into a tune they both recognized. A tune they both remembered.

The Azuremi waltz. The dance she had taught him under the stars in the ballroom. The dance they performed on their wedding night.

Her world shattered in that one moment, with that one tune. She couldn't return to Azurem and not think of him. She would never be the same, all because of the Mad King.

And she didn't want to return to who she once was.

"I can't tell you I hate you," she stated, "Because I'm hopelessly, madly in love with you. I'm scared that as soon as I admit it, I'll lose you somehow. Because that's what happens to people I love. But I can't lose you. I can't..."

He stepped toward her, cupping her face with his hands, forcing her to look directly into his eyes. "You can't lose me, even if you tried. I will always find you, because you are my heart, my home."

She shuddered, placing her hands on the front of his chest. "And you are mine."

"Then marry me."

She tightened her grip on his shirt before saying, breathless, "Yes."

Claude's lips collided with Dagmara's. She closed her eyes, letting the kiss consume her. It tore through every inch of her body, alighting her in flame. A fire ignited inside, her heart pounding against her ribcage. There was nothing sweet or gentle about the kiss. It tasted like desperation, a need to be closer and a fear that there would not be another chance to. She cursed every moment she hadn't spent kissing him exactly like this. As though there was no more time in the world. As though the world were burning and they were the only two left alive, and the kiss was the spark that lit the final flame.

She couldn't get enough. Pressing her palms against his chest, she walked him back against the Scribestone. His lower back met the stone pedestal, and she deepened the kiss. Wrapping her arms around his neck, she swooped her tongue into his mouth, meeting his.

His hands glided down her body, following the outline of her curves. He traced every part of her, memorizing her figure. Then his hands moved to her backside, and he tugged her tighter against him. She could feel his need, every inch of him pressed against her. A low rumble escaped his throat, and heat pooled in her core at the sound of it.

In one swift motion, he wrapped one arm around her waist, lifted her off her feet, and spun her around to the opposite side. Her back collided with the Scribestone, now in the place he was moments before, and her breath caught in her throat.

She broke the kiss briefly, her lips tingling with pleasure. "I'm not giving your ring back, by the way," she said, panting, "In this little interim before we get married again."

He grinned, his gaze filled with desire. "Then, in this interim, I will not stop referring to you as my wife—Queen of Ilusauri."

She smiled. "Let's not get ahead of ourselves."

A laugh escaped his lips, low and beautiful. "As you wish, my queen."

His lips met hers again, and she whimpered at the sheer intensity. She tried to memorize the rhythm of it, tried to remember the feel of his hands on her. She wanted to freeze time and hold onto this moment for eternity. A single moment of comfort—of home—before heading into the lethal storm that awaited them come dawn.

Pulling back from the kiss, he traced his lips across her jaw and down her neck. He tugged at her clothes, needing to touch her skin, until his hand found the edge of her dress. His lips continued down to her collarbone as his fingers trailed up her leg. She tilted her head back, bracing herself against the Scribestone with one hand as she gasped.

The Scribestone lit up against her palm, a gold light igniting the room. Her thoughts came rushing back, her surroundings coming into focus. Her touch against the stone summoned a message.

"Wait," Dagmara managed, though it wasn't more than a whisper.

Claude pulled back, meeting her gaze. As he withdrew, her mind reeled as the absence of his touch made her body desperate for more. He guided her away from the Scribestone as they both turned to read the glittering words that appeared.

One message from Teos Zosia, Azurem.

CHAPTER 40
Dagmara

Staring down at the incoming message from Teos, excitement and relief ricocheted through Dagmara's body. She could hardly move, her heartbeat intensifying.

"Read it," Claude encouraged, his voice sending a chill down her spine.

She brushed past the initial greeting, uncovering the message below.

Dagmara! You're alive! Thank the founding guardians!

Not that I had any doubts—my badass sister can take down a whole army, especially if she has my superior explosives. You still have some left right? You've been gone for way too long. I can make more!

Before you ask how I am, I'm not in bed anymore, the zowach has improved, but I'm not cured. Something is wrong, or the medicine isn't strong enough. Also, Azurem is a mess. The ground is breaking apart, the diseases are getting worse, and the water...is disappearing. I can't explain it.

"Azurem is dying," Dagmara said aloud as she read the message. "I don't understand. I thought it took Ilusauri years to get the way it is."

"We were also the first branch to be severed," Claude replied. "Maybe Eligor and the Void gets stronger the more guardians that are killed."

They needed to get to the tomb in Dreadmarrow as soon as possible. If Claude could rebind his magic to the land of Ilusauri, Magda would be able to do it for Azurem too, right?

She continued to read the message.

Bernadette has asked me to help her sort through some information about who King Bogdan was assassinating. It has something to do with guardian lineages and people with magic who shouldn't have it. What is going on out there? (I think I remind Bernadette of younger Aleksy. We both miss him, and she's really scared for Magda. Is Magda with you?) I'm getting sidetracked. Bogdan's assassinations.

I stumbled on something that I maybe shouldn't have. It's about mom.

King Bogdan was noting instances of people that exhibited magic, and sending mom to take them out. He claimed to be in correspondence with Claude. Apparently, Claude had told Bogdan that anyone who had magic and wasn't a guardian had been tasked to take out the reigning guardians. I don't know how much of that I believe, especially since the intel came from the Mad King himself. However, regarding mom's death—sorry to share this with you but I can't shoulder it on my own—there's evidence she was tortured by someone with Life magic. It was one of the assassins she had been sent to kill. Then, directly after she was found dead, an intruder with Life magic broke into a home in Frostmere and murdered two children. It was a young boy and his older sister. Luckily the intruder was killed on the scene, so at least we can rest easy knowing our mom's killer isn't on the streets anymore? But somehow...I can't rest easy with this story.

Also, what are you doing in Celestaire? Just visiting each kingdom one by one? Should I send my next message to Flaustra?

Oh who cares, I'll send my next message to every Scribestone in the land!

Your favorite partner in crime, T

Dagmara stumbled away from the Scribestone, her heart hammering in her chest. The news of her mother was like a blow to her chest.

Claude's hand slid against Dagmara's back, his other grabbing her arm to hold her upright. "Are you alright?"

Days after her mother was assassinated, her killer went to Frostmere. The assassin murdered a boy and his older sister.

"I think…two kids died in our place."

"What?" Claude adjusted his grip, rotating Dagmara to face him. His hands were firm, holding her steadfast.

She stared back up at him, her eyes wide, as she explained, "My mother worked for King Bogdan, tasked to take out the First Prince's assassins, but was caught by the Life assassin prior to Sabien. After my mother died, her murderer went to kill a young boy and his older sister. I think…my mother sent him to kill them…to protect us."

"Why would she do that?"

"She was being tortured…maybe it was the information he was trying to get out of her."

Claude scanned her face, seeking the answers. "Maybe the assassin had a list of people to kill and it just so happened he took them out in that order."

"I don't know," Dagmara shook her head. "But I suddenly have a strong feeling…" she gazed up at Claude, his concerned expression giving her comfort, "that I'm supposed to be dead."

PART THREE

The Tomb

CHAPTER 41
Magdalena

Magda stood at the helm of the ship as it soared toward Dreadmarrow.

The journey had taken a week, but they were ready to find Eligor's tomb and reseal the locks so that he would be forever trapped inside. During the journey, Ishani had drilled her and Kiran over and over in practice battles and magical duels, strengthening their magic day by day. The captain had also replaced the flags of the Fowler's Guild with those of pirates known for carrying prisoners.

Magda's thoughts drifted, knowing that she would do anything to keep Eligor trapped, but she worried that he would continue poisoning her thoughts if he remained in his prison. Each conversation they had, Magda could feel him growing more powerful, and he continuously latched onto her mind, poisoning it with his perfectly-crafted words and sensual voice.

Yes, that's right. Let me consume your thoughts. His voice curled against her ear as if he stood next to her.

She shuddered, thinking of the magic. Magda had not exhibited the Spirit or Mind powers, but if she continued down this path, unearthing more power, would she turn into another version of the First Prince?

Then come to me. If you are afraid of what you are, let me extinguish your fire.

A streak of lighting cracked through the sky, followed by a thunderous boom. The light illuminated other vessels that were anchored at sea but appeared to be abandoned. Around the graveyard of ships were piles of spiked wood and debris, and the remains of prisoners floating in the shadows. Not a breath or sound of life traveled through the wind.

Magda sensed Ravi's approach, and her fingers curled around his on the railing. For the first time, she was scared. There were a million things that could go wrong, and they had no back up plan. Her friends were putting their lives on the line for her, and she couldn't fail.

The Starway soared through the menacing sea, navigating around shipwrecks and death, until the island came to view through smoke and fog. Here, the ocean was still, and the sky was completely blanketed in a thick cloud. In the distance, tall structures poked through the mist, indicating that land would soon be in reach.

Ahead was an intimidating structure, built of black, square shapes and towers. The prison was built on a series of mountainous pitons, and a maze of layers and floors sprawled from the shores to the peaks. Flickers of torchlight whispered in the towers, acting as lighthouses in the dark haze.

They passed more ships, sparsely dotting the still waters, and this time, inhabitants populated the decks, but their faces were gaunt like ghosts.

"Who are they?" Magda asked Ravi, fear laced in her voice.

The lighting crashed once more against the dark clouds.

"Pirates. Bandits," Ishani approached them at the railing, getting a better view.

The ship soared to the main gate, which towered three times its size. On either side was a watchtower, and through the bars, was a cavern carved into the side of the island, revealing a cove docked with ships. A thick, stone wall circled the outside of the prison, and guards with longswords and crossbows patrolled the parapet, scanning for prisoners.

Violent waves crashed against the gate, smashing debris against the bars, before the water was sucked back out again. Suddenly, shouting was heard in the watchtowers, followed by a loud clanking. The click of the chain began, and another flash of lighting lit up the sky, fully illuminating the terrors of Dreadmarrow.

Magda stepped over to a crate, grabbing a rope from on top of it. Then she crossed to Ravi, and he held out his wrists.

"There's still time to change your mind," said Magda, swallowing a lump in her throat. She had never imagined Dreadmarrow to appear this intimidating, and her hands shook as she extended the ropes. "We can find another way to get inside."

"Magda, we talked about this. There is no other way," Ravi said.

Magda nodded. "Don't be scared, we'll both make it to the other side of this."

Ravi leaned in and gave Magda a kiss on the lips. "We will."

Then he held out his wrists once more as she tied them together, before saying, "Let's do this."

CHAPTER 42
Dagmara

The oversized gate rose with an excruciating scratch. The clank of the gears turning collided with the tune of the iron as they scraped against their tracks. The gate lifted slowly, water cascading from the metal as it rose from the water. Mist sprayed Dagmara in the face as it continued into the sky until the ship mast could clear the opening.

Dagmara suppressed a shudder, pulling her cloak tighter around her. She could feel hundreds of invisible eyes on her from the watchtowers above, coated in thick fog. The hair on the back of her neck prickled, making her feel exposed.

"If it takes that long to open the gate we can't make a quick getaway," Ishani said under her breath. "We need it to already be open."

Pierre's eyes were on the bridge high above them where the pulley system for the drawbridge no doubt resided. "I will take care of the gate."

"And I'll be with you," Martine stated, coming to stand beside Dagmara.

She nodded at her friend. "Thank you."

"Kiran and I will wait on the ship for you all to return," Ishani continued. "But hurry."

"Please be careful," Kiran pleaded. Claude had transformed her entire appearance, reassuring the group that the illusion magic would work at a distance. It was odd to see Kiran in the disguise, looking nothing like the princess Dagmara had met a few days earlier.

The ship lurched forward, catching in the wind once more and entering the cavern. It sailed forward, entering the dark cove in the center of the island and heading to the daunting prison docks. In all her life, Dagmara had never had an assignment of this scale before. Breaking into the prison was one feat, but getting back out? Nearly impossible.

"You have what you need?"

The voice calmed her fears. Claude stepped up to the helm beside her, his shoulder brushing hers as he surveyed the impenetrable death prison.

"My dagger and throwing stars. I couldn't conceal all my potions in my corset though, only a few would fit." It was too dangerous to carry an entire pouch of potions.

"We won't be separated," Claude announced.

But Dagmara didn't know if that would be true.

The ship was now fully in the cavern, and the only lights in the space came from dim torchlight, making it impossible to see how large the cove was, or where the exits were. The Starway approached the wooden dock, and Ishani's officers began shouting down to the sailors below. Ropes were thrown down to the deck, and the ship was firmly secured, coming to a stop.

Ishani called out orders to her crew to lower anchor. After the gangplank lowered, Dagmara was the first to exit and cross to stable ground. Claude and Martine were close behind.

Magda exited the ship next, tugging Ravi along with her. He stumbled across the plank, nearly tripping into the water below.

"Odie, stay," Magda called out to her dog, who sat on the main deck, watching the group disembark.

The dog wagged its tail, curiously examining its surroundings, but remained on the ship with Kiran.

Dagmara stepped onto the dock where a burly man was waiting for them. He was dressed in a long, worn trench coat and a bandana circled his throat. Far ahead, at the front gate of Dreadmarrow, nearly two dozen guards were lined up.

The warden asked a question Dagmara couldn't understand.

"Ilusaurian," Claude replied.

"On a Flaustran ship?" the warden asked, switching languages effortlessly. His speech revealed rotten teeth, and a single earring swung haphazardly with the movement of his head.

"The prisoner speaks Flaustran," Claude replied smoothly. "We prefer not to have our prisoner listening in."

The warden assessed Ravi up and down before saying, "Who is cashing in?"

"I am," Dagmara stated, lifting her chin higher. "I caught him."

The warden smirked, his eyes roaming Dagmara. "And you might be?" he asked. "How do I know you're an honest bounty hunter? If you're Flaustran, then we expect you to hand over your identification card."

"Zosia," Dagmara gave only her second name. "And I'm not Flaustran, but my prisoner is."

His eyes lit up as if he recognized the word. "Zosia," he said. "Welcome back to Dreadmarrow. You haven't aged a day."

Dagmara caught her breath in her throat. What was he talking about? She had never been to Dreadmarrow in her entire life. She instantly thought back to the note from Teos, and the fact that there was more to her mom's life than she had realized. If only she could speak to her brother.

Dagmara withdrew the wanted poster and Ravi's identification card from her back pocket before handing them over. The warden accepted the papers, unraveling them in front of him.

"Name's Barr," he said. He let out a low whistle, grinning at Ravi. "Killing a guild leader? Wow, that's a new one, but a nice sum. We will take him to his cell. You will have to wait until the man who posted the bounty arrives, identifies the prisoner, and gives you your reward."

"Absolutely not," Dagmara stated before Magda could open her mouth to object. "I know better than to turn over my prisoner before getting paid. How long will it take for the reward to get here?"

Barr shrugged. "A month, but for you, Zosia, I'll do it in a week."

"We don't have that kind of time," Claude said through gritted teeth.

"I can give you half the reward, and you can be on your way right now."

"So you can profit off my prisoner?" Dagmara inquired.

Barr gave her a crooked smile. "That's business. Surely you would know that by now."

Claude took a small step forward. "Are you in charge here?"

"I oversee the front gate and watch posts," said the warden. "Why do you ask?"

"Just confirming you're the one in authority," Claude said. "*You will allow all four of us to accompany you as you escort this prisoner to his personal cell.*"

A hint of silver twinkled in the warden's eyes as the compulsion settled in. Then he blinked, the compulsion washing over him and the urgency to listen to Claude rooting in every fiber of his being. "Aye, sir. Follow me."

Barr turned on his heel and proceeded to the front door. The group of five followed closely behind, none of them fazed by Claude's use of compulsion. It was the only way they would get inside.

They walked down the docks and stepped down onto the rocky shore of the cove. Ahead, was a large, barred gate with three disfigured faces carved above in stone, with glowing torches for eyes. Two, enormous braziers roared with flames on either side of the gate. Like statues, a row of guards was poised next to the gate, standing with their hands behind their backs. They were adorned with knives, hatches, and other weapons.

"Open the doors!" Barr announced. "These few are with me."

A few guards gave each other speculative glances. However, two moved to open the double-story door. It was on another pulley system, much like the iron gate for the ship. It raised vertically, and the two ropes holding it up framed the threshold.

Dagmara made a mental note of possible escape routes. There was one iron gate that would lead them out of the prison into the cove. From there, the ship would still have to make it through the main gate before it would soar across the ocean once more. She remembered the blueprints that Reon had shown them back in Celestaire and knew that other tunnels and passageways also poured into the cove, as if it was a central basin underneath the prison. They just had to find them.

The front door grew higher and higher, and Barr turned around to give them all a smug grin. "Welcome to Dreadmarrow," he chuckled, his yellow teeth on full display.

Dagmara shivered, exchanging a glance at Claude, who returned a reassuring stare, before doing the same with Magda, Ravi, and Martine.

"Are you ready to deliver your prisoner, Zosia?" Barr asked her.

Dagmara gripped Ravi by the arm. She tried not to let her voice waver as she said, "Yes."

Then Barr passed under the gate and disappeared into the depths of Dreadmarrow.

The island that no one escaped alive.

CHAPTER 43
Dagmara

Dreadmarrow was carved into the inside of the mountainous piton. The ceiling was sky-high, with rows of cells covering every wall. Hundreds upon hundreds of cells extended upward, like twinkling dots, until they reached a domed skylight that allowed moonbeams to strike the floor. The room continued forward into the next piton, and the next, like a series of endless chambers holding ghostly prisoners.

Around the sides of the walls, were caged elevators, extending to various heights, and a pulley system transported the elevators like gondolas to reach all of the cells. Next to the elevators, were thousands of guards stationed on various platforms, walking back and forth and surveying the main gate to make sure no one got in or out.

Dagmara gulped. With thousands of eyes on them, there was no way they could leave the same way they came. They had to find another way. She pictured the map in her head again, remembering the series of passageways dumped into the cove.

Barr turned around to face Dagmara. "All your weapons must be left here."

"No," Magda answered coolly. She looked at Claude. "Tell him."

Claude shook his head, unbuckling the sword from his belt. "We should do as he says."

There were too many people around. Too many witnesses. It would be suspicious if the guard kept agreeing with these strangers. For all Dagmara knew, they had already raised an alarm.

Magda obeyed, unlatching her blades and dropping them to the ground beside Claude's sword. Martine was next to follow, unsheathing her sword and throwing knives before placing them at her feet. Ravi stood watching the group.

Dagmara unlatched her dagger, dropping it to the ground, but she kept the throwing stars sewed into her corset along with the few potions she was able to cram in the lining.

"Check them!" Barr called, and a guard approached.

The guard roughly grabbed Claude by his shirt, feeling for any hidden weapons. He then went to Martine, finding a knife in her boot. He found no additional weapons on Magda. Finally he reached Dagmara. He yanked her cloak off, throwing it to the ground.

Dagmara opened her mouth to object but bit her tongue. Inconspicuous. She had to remain calm like she had nothing to hide.

Ice skittered through her veins as the guard began to feel her body. He started at her ankles, tracing her pants and trying to find a hidden blade. He then worked on her arms, before his hands found her hips.

Her breath caught in her throat. If he was too meticulous in his search, he would undoubtedly feel the weapons stashed in her corset. And yet she couldn't move as his hands traced her back, slowly grazing her.

"That's enough," Claude demanded.

The guard's hands froze inches from her ribcage. "I'll say when it's enough," he replied, his voice hoarse.

Claude's eyes narrowed. "Search her any further and tonight your friends will be searching for your corpse," he growled.

"No need for threats," Barr stated. "Enough on the search. Follow me." He turned on his heel once more and headed for an open side door. There were still at least two dozen guards surrounding them, watching their entrance with attentive stares.

They passed through the door, which was held up and open by a series of ropes. They stood at a crossroads, with a path leading to the left and a path to the right. Before them was another giant railing with the entrance to a spiral staircase, circling down into the depths of the prison. Beyond the railing, Dagmara could see a huge space, at least a hundred feet deep, with prison cells on every surrounding side.

"Alright, we'll take him from here," said Barr. "He'll be processed and assigned a cell in the next few hours."

"Grab the prisoner." A new voice rang through the entrance. A commander sauntered into the space, flanked by four guards. Two of his inferiors answered his command, brushing past Martine and lunging for Ravi.

"Wait!" Magda yelled.

"We want to see that we get our reward!" Dagmara shouted.

But the two guards were already dragging Ravi down the hall, despite his lashes and screams.

"Stop!" Claude called, but without eye contact, he couldn't compel anyone that wasn't already under his control.

"Barr should know the rules. No one but prisoners allowed in the front gate," the commander stated. He revealed a crossbow from behind his back and aimed it at the burly warden. With one loud release, an arrow went flying, burying into Barr's chest. He crumpled to the ground, his head smacking against the stone.

"Now," the commander turned his crossbow on the four before him, reloading another arrow. "Who are you and how do you know Barr?"

They had to act first, before this commander reloaded his bow and before the other guards withdrew their swords. Dagmara trusted either Magda, Claude, or Martine would follow her lead.

She reached into her corset, feeling for the silky marble ball she had grown familiar with. She pulled it from the binding on her chest and thrust it at the commander's feet.

"Smoke!" she yelled in Azuremi, hoping that the group was faster at recognizing the word than the three Dreadmarrow guards.

Instantaneously, the jasny ball exploded, and a huge pillar of smoke flew up from the ground. Both Martine and Claude dove into the smoke, no doubt going to retrieve the swords from the guards. Meanwhile, Magda raised her hand to the ceiling, dislodging a slab of stone. It hurtled down from the air, making contact with the commander's head in a sickening crack.

By the time the smoke cleared, all the enemies were corpses, and both Martine and Claude had new weapons.

"We're under attack!" a voice called.

Dagmara turned, seeing a crowd of guards behind them in the great entranceway.

Before Dagmara could react, Claude lunged forward, slicing his sword at the rope that held the door open. The door fell back to the ground in an abrasive punch that shook the floor.

"What was that for? Now we can't get out!" Magda yelled.

"You want to take on hundreds of them right now?" Claude snapped.

There was a loud thud, and the door reverberated against the impact of the guards on the other side.

"They'll break it down for us," Martine said. "We have to get Ravi."

"They've sounded the alarm," Dagmara stated. "We're going to run out of time, and they will kill us on sight if they killed one of their own that easily."

"I will not leave Ravi!" Magda shouted.

"You and Claude are the ones that need to get to the tomb to reset the Mind lock. Martine and I will save Ravi and meet you back on the boat."

"I hate to say it but Dagmara's right," said Martine. "Let us save

Ravi. The tomb has to be underground somewhere. They're taking Ravi somewhere on this floor."

"Please save him, Dagmara," Magda begged. "Claude and I will go underground."

Claude sheathed his new sword before stepping forward, portraying an illusion onto the floor. It was a series of intricate lines, which Dagmara realized was the map from Celestaire. He had it memorized.

His fingers traced the floor. "Magda and I will head to this space, the oldest part of the prison, underground. You can get out here, and here," he said, showing Martine and Dagmara the other ways to reach the cove. "We'll meet you on the ship."

"Got it," said Martine, committing the pathways to memory.

The map disappeared and Claude took a step toward Dagmara. "I didn't want to be separated from you."

"We have to," Dagmara assured him, despite the fact she didn't want to leave his side either. "Ravi is the reason we got in here, I have to at least try to save him. Save Ilusauri." She paused, before adding, "I want a kingdom to return home to."

"I will," he promised. "For the safety of our people."

Dagmara smiled. "And the betterment of our kingdoms."

Claude gave her a rare, hopeful smile. "I'll disguise you both as guards," he said.

"No, save your magic for Kiran," said Dagmara.

Suddenly, the sound of footsteps pounded along the hallway. "Guards are approaching. Come on," Martine called, heading down the hall where Ravi had disappeared.

"Be safe, Magda," Dagmara said.

Magda nodded. "You too."

With one last glance at Claude, Dagmara tore off in the opposite direction, reassuring herself that he would be safe.

He had to be. He would see her at the end of this, alive.

She wouldn't let her thoughts entertain the other option.

CHAPTER 44
Magdalena

Fear coursed through Magda, spiking her adrenaline. The ear-piercing alarm blasted through the corridors, signaling that intruders had invaded Dreadmarrow. All she could do was trust Dagmara and Martine to save Ravi.

Magda and Claude raced in the opposite direction, rounding the corner. At the sound of metal rattling against armor, she skidded to a halt. Claude nearly slammed into her back at her abrupt stop.

"This way," Claude said, grabbing her by the wrist and yanking her onto another floor of the prison.

Before Magda could examine where they were, Claude grabbed her around the waist and tugged her against his chest, slamming them both into the wall.

Her breath caught in her throat as she saw two guards standing in the hall. They whipped around to face Magda and Claude, withdrawing their weapons.

As Magda met their gaze, she reached for her magic, but Claude's other hand clamped down on her mouth, pulling her tighter against his firm body. In response, Magda froze.

"I thought I saw something..." one of the guards mumbled, inching closer to Magda, his gaze directly on her.

A flicker of silver danced in Magda's peripheral. That's when she noticed a translucent stone wall.

By the guardians, Claude was hiding them behind a fake wall. His magic was unmatched.

"Let's go, idiot!" the other guard yelled before taking off down the staircase.

Finally, the guard directly in front of Magda's face turned away and followed his companion into the depths of the prison.

Claude flashed another illusion onto the floor, revealing the map once more. "Where to now?" he asked.

"Here," said Magda. Putting her finger on the oldest part of the prison, she traced the map as if she was solving a maze. She let her hand swirl through the labyrinth, finding the entrance, and then retraced her steps back to where she and Claude were standing.

"We have to go down eight more levels," Claude noted. His silver eyes tracked Magda's hand, following the route.

"There has to be a faster way," said Magda. "Remember the elevators and pulley systems in the entranceway?"

"There," Claude said. The silver flashed once more, and the illusion changed. All of the sudden, a series of elevators were lit up in red, changing against the rest of the map.

"This elevator goes down the farthest," said Magda, pointing to an elevator across the prison.

"It's across the entrance hall," said Claude.

"How do we get there?" asked Magda.

Claude stood up and the illusion vanished. Then he began running through the space, past other doors and rooms, while Magda followed.

Suddenly, they turned another corner and found a staircase. They rushed up the stairs, climbing four stories, before coming to a screeching halt at the top.

They stood in an empty arch, looking out over the entranceway that housed the cells on every wall. Thousands of guards scoured the room, keeping their posts at all levels.

Ahead of them was a pulley system and a gondola to take them to the other side of the entryway.

"Let's go," said Claude, getting inside.

"Won't they see us?"

"We'll stay down."

His hand braced the crank, and he began turning it, rotating the gears. The gondola slowly crossed the entranceway. Magda sat on her knees, daring to peek her eyes and her silver hair over the edge of the gondola's railing. They flew through the hauntingly massive space, keeping their heads down so as to not be spotted by the guards above.

All around, eerie voices could be heard echoing throughout the center of the piton. Shouts came from the guards, and the stink of death hung in the air, making Magda's skin crawl. What was she thinking bringing her entire group of friends here? What if the tomb wasn't even here? What if they were wrong?

They said no one left the island alive, and now Magda understood why.

The gondola clanked to a halt on the other side of the space, and the two raced onto the other ledge, disappearing into the depths of the prison once more. At the end of the hallway, they came to the elevator that would take them to the bottom floors.

Magda raced in first, followed by Claude. Quickly, she pulled the crack until it clicked, and the doors slammed shut. The elevator began lowering, flying past floor after floor.

It was pitch black in the elevator except for a tiny crack of light spilling out from underneath the door. She couldn't even see Claude if she wanted to.

"Do you think this is going to work?" asked Magda. She could feel his presence beside her.

"I don't know, I just wish my life was the only one we were risking," said Claude coldly. "All we can hope is we all get out of here alive."

"We will," said Magda, attempting to convince herself.

The elevator clanked to a stop. They must have traveled down twenty floors, and the doors opened to reveal another series of hallways. This time, more doors and pathways extended in all directions.

Claude and Magda scoured the hallway, peering into unlocked doors and turning each way, trying to find the correct path they had seen on the map. A few minutes went by, to no avail, and they realized they were going in circles.

"Wait," said Claude, pointing to the right. "Down there. That wall. It's not real."

"How can you tell?"

Claude shot her a look that only a Mind Guardian could give.

Magda shrugged. "Lead the way."

They stepped further away from the elevator and the escape above, slinking their way through the labyrinth of tunnels. When they reached the end of the corridor, Claude held his hand out first, and his arm went through the mysterious wall until only his shoulder was apparent.

"Come on," he said. "This has to be the way. It must be an illusion to keep people out."

"Who would have created this illusion?" asked Magda, more curious than afraid.

Claude acknowledged the green light rippling through the wall as he waved his hand through it. "Ancient magic. A spell that lives on long after the guardian is dead. It's the most difficult to master."

"So this trap was set by the original guardians that sealed Eligor inside?" asked Magda.

"Yes."

They both pushed through the wall, stepping onto the other side. They emerged in a damp tunnel, filled with vines. Water dripped from the rocks above, and green and purple magic glowed from the crevices.

"This is it," said Claude. "Remnants of ancient and Void magic."

"We must be under the sea," Magda mused. "Let's hurry."

The two walked side by side, heading down the tunnel. As they continued down the pathway, it narrowed, forcing them to stand closer together. They followed the dim green and purple lights, which faded into oblivion as they continued their journey along the path.

Finally, they came to a door, sealed shut with a wheel. Around the edge of the wheel, were decrypt paintings, portraying four branches of magic—Soul, Spirit, Life, and Mind. The stone door was glowing with remnants of glittering powers.

"This has to be what we're looking for," said Magda. "Can you open it?" she asked.

Claude hesitated, sizing up the scale of the vault-like door. "What if this is Eligor's tomb, and we're inadvertently letting him out by opening this door?"

"No, that's impossible," said Magda. "As long as Kiran's alive, he can't escape."

Claude nodded, "Right, right, but something about this makes me uneasy."

The Mad King? Uneasy? It was a contradicting thought, but Magda took his apprehension seriously. Whatever was on the other side of this door, they had to be prepared to face, whether it was Eligor or not.

Then Claude gripped the wheel, begging for it to turn. As he did so, the door lit up, and silver magic extended through the mural, going from Claude's fingers to the outer rim. A clunking sound was heard as the gears loosened.

"It's activated with magic," Magda deduced.

"That means only guardians can enter," Claude added.

"Because when the guardians locked him here, only guardians came out."

Claude returned his attention to the door. After a forceful tug, it began to spin, all the way until a loud clank rang through the tunnel. The edges of the door loosened, and it started to swing outward in one slow movement.

"This is it," said Claude, "This is what I've been searching for."

CHAPTER 45
Dagmara

Lurking in the shadows, Martine and Dagmara were pressed against one another in the darkness. Glancing around the corner, they could barely make out the guard that threw Ravi into the cell and locked it with a large iron key. He said something to the man outside the cell before starting off down the hall.

"We need that key," Dagmara whispered.

"You get him, I'll take out the one watching the cell," Martine instructed, readjusting her grip on her newly acquired sword.

Withdrawing a throwing star from her bodice, Dagmara held it gently in her fingers. She next withdrew a small vial of smierc, adding drops on the edges of the blade. The poison steamed against the metal, and Dagmara was careful not to burn herself as she shoved the smierc vial back into her corset. The guard was retreating farther down the corridor, and if he went any farther, she wouldn't be able to reach him.

"Ready?" Dagmara asked.

"I'm waiting on you."

"Now!"

Stepping out of their hiding spot, the two women acted in sync. Taking aim, Dagmara thrust the throwing star in the direction of the distant guard. The throwing star lodged perfectly in the back of his neck, burrowing into flesh and muscle. The poison seeped into his bloodstream instantly.

He whirled around, withdrawing his sword in preparation to attack. The blade glinted in the dim light of the prison tunnel. But the guard stumbled, his hand reaching to yank the star from the back of his neck. He coughed once, a trickle of blood staining his chapped lips. Then he collapsed face first onto the stone, sputtering and gasping for breath.

Approaching him, Dagmara picked up his sword, easily removing it from his fingers. She positioned the steel against him and put him out of his misery. With only a drop of smierc in his bloodstream, it could take hours for him to die—a death filled with suffering. She didn't wish that on anyone.

His choking ceased, and his body officially fell limp.

She dropped the sword and yanked the iron key from his belt. A sickening crunch rang through the hall, and Dagmara turned in time to see the second guard dropping dead. Martine wiped her bloodied sword against his clothing.

"Once we got inside, this was easy," Martine stated, grinning at Dagmara.

Dagmara let out a short laugh, "We're leaving a lot of evidence."

She shrugged. "I'm a guard, not an assassin."

"Dagmara!" Ravi called, racing to the bars, his hands still bound.

Dagmara was quick to reach the cell bars, inserting the key into the oversized lock and releasing Ravi.

"Magda?" he asked.

"With Claude," Dagmara replied. "They'll meet us back on the ship. We have to move."

She pulled open the cell, and it shrieked on its hinges. Martine cut the ties binding Ravi's wrists, and the three of them tore off down the corridor toward the Starway.

CHAPTER 46
Magdalena

Magda and Claude emerged into the dark space. Here, the alarm above was faint, and they could barely hear the blaring horn that alerted the guards to their presence.

A large oval room appeared, with four distinct columns framing a stone floor. Above, a glowing, purple light illuminated the room, depicting a circular mural in between the four columns. In the distance, the sound of dripping water hitting the stone echoed through the musty, rot-filled space.

"Is this it? I don't see a tomb," said Magda.

Claude pressed forward, stepping close to the circular mural, but not on top of it. In the purple light, a design of four distinct colors all met in the middle, before the colored stones rippled towards the columns. On the ground were distinct emblems depicting water, air, earth, and the mind.

Claude's gaze focused on the emblem of the Mind, and his eyes trailed to the corresponding column. The colors of the stones were muted, as if the magic had faded over time. Contrastingly, the stones that fed towards the earth column glowed with a yellow hue between their cracks, as if whatever lay beneath them was still alive.

"Kiran's magic is still intact," said Magda, approaching the column for the Guardian of the Soul. Magda ran her hand along the stone, wondering if she had the power to reseal all of the locks, considering her gift. Or, would her magic not count for anything?

Claude crossed to the Mind column. "Help me find anything that could help me reset the Mind magic," he demanded.

"Already looking," Magda called, crossing to the faded, blue-stoned column that marked the Life Guardians. Upon approaching it, her heart lurched as the sight of the dim stones sank in. When Aleksy had taken his last breath, the colors had dissipated, mirroring his own life. Magda's throat burned, and she held back tears.

No. She would not cry in front of the Mad King.

Magda circled the column, searching for a lever or a space to put her handprint. She had never encountered a magical lock before—one that was powerful enough to trap a guardian that controlled all of the elements and was the last heir to the Void lineage in existence. It didn't matter if Eligor was evil or not, she knew that this world didn't need anyone else with that much power.

What? You don't want to see me in person? The sound of the prince's velvet voice intoxicated Magda's mind.

No, I'm going to see that you stay locked away and that you never get that chance.

What a shame. said Eligor. *Just when I was beginning to admire you.*

Magda distinctly remembered the feeling of his body against hers. But she quickly shook away the mental image. *You don't admire me. We're enemies. You said it yourself that you wanted to kill me.*

You can't run from power, and neither can I. No matter if we are destined to kill each other, we might be the only equally matched souls in a millennia. Doesn't that kind of intimacy intrigue you?

Magda shivered and shut the First Prince out of her thoughts. She wasn't going to let him manipulate her.

Even though she spoke to Eligor in her mind, she still had the feeling the conversation was private, so Magda pulled further away from Claude. She crossed to the curved walls that surrounded the room. Painted onto the stones were a series of murals, but they were too faded to make out their contents. She continued running her hands along the shapes, feeling the excess grime rub against her fingertips.

Directly opposite the door, she came to another painting. This time, she could make out five figures, all holding hands, while their magic shone above them, depicting the five branches. In the sky above the five figures, was a golden crown which appeared exactly like the one that Eligor wore. However, the magic didn't flow from the crown to the guardians, as Magda had suspected. Instead, it seemed to flow both ways, in a constant circle. If the crown was so important, why did the guardians lock it away with Eligor in the tomb? Surely, they wouldn't have given such a powerful object to someone that was so evil. Unless, there was more to the story?

Still want my crown?

Is it a gift or a curse? asked Magda.

Both. But not for anyone.

Just us. Magda finished his thought.

You're catching on beautifully. She could almost see the wicked smile that accompanied his voice. *Maybe I will have to keep you alive...*

"Magdalena!" yelled Claude from the column.

"Coming," Magda said, shaking out her head. She darted in Claude's direction while her eyes lingered on the mural. When she reached Claude's side she asked, "What did you find?"

"I think we need to examine Kiran's lock," he said. "It's intact, so it will be easiest to understand the magic and what we need to do. Hopefully, we can assume the others are identical."

Magda nodded. "Let's hurry."

Are you sure you don't want to see me, Princess? Eligor's soft, sultry voice was back. *You're so close to me I can almost feel you again.*

Magda answered this time. *You'll have to wait another millennia.*

CHAPTER 47
Dagmara

Dagmara, Martine, and Ravi had run down another corridor, retracing their steps on the map and heading for another exit. They decided to make their way to a water drainage pipe, large enough for them to sneak through and retreat back to the cove and the ship.

They could still hear shouting coming from the main entranceway, as guards rushed back and forth on the elevators and pulley systems. The alarm was still ringing, pounding against Dagmara's senses.

The trio rounded the corner, seeing a few guards blocking their path. Just beyond was the grate that would lead down the pipe, signifying their way to safety.

"We need to sneak past them," Martine whispered, her shoulder pressed against Dagmara's in the shadows.

"A distraction?" Ravi suggested.

"I got this," Dagmara announced. She had a jasny bomb, and she simply had to throw it far enough. Withdrawing it from her corset, she aimed and threw. It soared over the guards' heads, landing on the stone ground. It immediately ignited, a flash of light as brilliant as the sun. The sound reverberated and billows of smoke filled the air. Then the two guards turned in the direction of the distraction, prepared for the worst.

Martine tore off out of the hiding spot. She swooped to grab one of the guards' knives from their hips, before slipping behind them. Dagmara and Ravi followed, sprinting along the outer wall to remain concealed in the shadows.

Dagmara's breath caught in her throat, and immediately her heart threatened to pound out of her chest. Her heart rate intensified, attempting to keep up with the pace of her movement. She willed her health to remain steady. She was so close to freedom, and she didn't have time to stop for a breather now.

Skillfully, Martine killed the two guards before the trio raced forward to the grate.

"Ravi, help me," Martine said.

Ravi and Martine pulled the grate off, letting it clatter to the side.

"That was loud. They'll be here," said Ravi.

The three ran through the pipe, making their way around the corner. Soon, a streak of light came into view. They emerged back into the cove as the getaway ship appeared. It was still there.

At the front gate, there were no longer any guards stationed. Dagmara guessed they had been called into the prison in the attempt to search for the intruders. At least that meant they could make it to the ship without being spotted.

They finished their sprint along the rocky, cove shore, and leapt onto the slick dock. Then they headed down it, Martine in the lead, before ascending the gangway.

All Dagmara could think about was Claude. Had they succeeded? Were they back? Were the locks refortified?

Martine stopped in the center of her ship. "Pierre?"

"Magda?" Ravi echoed.

Unable to breathe, Dagmara collapsed onto a wooden crate, panting as she tried to quell her racing heart. She had made it out. She was safe.

"Here!" Kiran's voice resounded as she raced down from an upper platform. If it wasn't for her voice, Dagmara wouldn't have recognized her. Claude's magic was wondrous.

Odie raced down after Kiran, trotting up to Ravi and Dagmara with a wagging tail.

"Thank the guardians you're safe!" Kiran exclaimed.

"Where are Claude and Magdalena?" Martine asked.

"Are they back yet?" Dagmara asked, though she knew the question was unnecessary. Of course they hadn't returned. Anxiety settled in Dagmara's chest.

Then Odie went up to Dagmara, pressing his body into her legs as if to offer her support. The dog looked up at her with big, pleading eyes, before pulling at her sleeve and attempting to force her to lay down.

Dagmara steadied herself, gripping Odie's fur as she struggled to maintain focus on the group.

"We can't wait long," Ishani was saying. She had descended from the upper deck, her axes attached at each hip.

"We have to," said Ravi.

"We're not leaving without them," Martine objected.

"We won't," Dagmara concurred, feeling for Odie's fur as she stood, "but they can take care of themselves. They will return soon. If not, I will go in after them."

"You won't get in a second time," Ishani replied. She wandered to the railing and peered over the edge to the front gates. Through the iron bars leading into Dreadmarrow, a commotion could still be heard. Guards raced back and forth with patrol lights. "It won't be long before they start checking the ships." Her head shifted to the large gate that kept their ship from leaving. "We need to get that open, now."

"I took care of it," Pierre replied, holding up a large key. "Whenever we want to open it, I can now access the control deck. Should I go now?"

"Yes," Ishani said. "Take someone with you, and hurry!"

"Let me help," said Ravi, as he and Pierre bounded off the ship, heading onto the docks. They sprinted in the opposite direction, making their way to the main gate, so that they could open the passage for the Starway to escape.

Odie barked in Ravi's direction, but Ravi held his hand up to him. "Stay, Odie. Stay with Dagmara."

Odie turned his head to Dagmara as if in agreement.

Martine looked out at the docks once more. "Do you think they're in trouble?"

"I don't know, but I'm starting to feel uneasy." Kiran's usual smile had ceased.

"Time is ticking," Ishani shrugged, leaning over the railing and staring back at the gate.

Dagmara joined the other three girls, so that all four were now watching the entrance to the prison. "Magda, where are you?" she whispered under her breath.

"I was wondering the same thing."

The new voice drew all of their attention. On the bowsprit was a tall, balancing figure, his tan skin glistening with drops of water and his black hair drenched. He jumped and landed on the upper ship deck with a loud thud. The light from the prison cast dark shadows across his face, but it was the light blue glow to his eyes that gave him away.

Sabien Renaud.

Dagmara's blood turned to ice, her entire body freezing in his presence. Beside her, Odie let out a series of barks, snapping his head in Sabien's direction. The dog positioned himself in front of Dagmara, letting out a low growl.

"I was waiting for you all to show up," a smirk creased his face.

Ishani withdrew one of her axes, and Martine pulled out her sword.

"Get off my ship," Ishani snapped.

"Hmm...no thank you. I'm here for your sister."

"She's not here."

"Liar," Sabien replied. "I don't believe you would leave her side." Then his gaze met Dagmara's, and his grin widened. "Hello again, Dagger."

"Sabien," Dagmara replied, and her hands turned to fists. This was the man that betrayed her, manipulated her, tortured her, and nearly killed her. She wanted him dead.

Odie barked again, this time with more force.

"We can take him," Martine whispered under her breath.

Even though they only had one guardian on their side, Kiran, they had more fighters. The girls could take Sabien. Although he could heal himself, he stood no chance. Behind the group of four, some of Ishani's crew began to file out onto the deck to make them seem more well-equipped than they were.

However, if Sabien were here, that meant Junne was close by.

"Hand over Kiran, and I will be on my way," Sabien said, stepping closer.

Ishani reacted. She launched her axe toward him, and it soared through the air. He tried to dodge, but Ishani's attack was too fast. The axe sliced his bicep as it passed him, immediately drawing blood.

"That is your final warning," Ishani stated, gripping her opposite axe.

A low laugh rumbled in Sabien's throat as he watched the blood pour from his arm. "You're going to have to do better than that." He summoned the water underneath the ship. It rose over the edges, trailing the ground before reaching him. It spiraled up his body, creating a glistening suit of ice armor. The water cleansed the wound on his bicep, and he was healed.

Behind them, they heard the gruesome clinking once more. A few guards poured out of the prison, beginning to search the cove and the docks. Their torchlight moved in the distance. It would only be a matter of time before they reached the ship, and then they would be trapped on the island.

"Last chance," Sabien repeated. "Queen Kiran, now."

Nobody moved. Everyone remained utterly silent, waiting for Ishani to give the command to attack. Dagmara reached for her belt, Odie's teeth were bared, and Martine had a hand on her sword. Kiran was the only one to shift, glancing at Ishani with worried eyes.

Ishani looked at Kiran for a brief moment before telling Sabien once more, "No."

But Sabien tracked the swift glance between the sisters. His cheeks creased as his smile deepened. "Oh, Claude is good with his illusions, isn't he?" He watched Kiran like a predator eyeing their prey. Then he whistled loudly, calling out for any guards in the distance. "They're over here! The escaped prisoners are here!"

Dagmara's heart plummeted in her chest as a horn blared out followed by the stampede of boots on the dock. They might have been able to take Sabien, but not an entire group of Dreadmarrow guards too.

The Life Guardian summoned the water below them to collide into the side of the ship. They all lost their balance as he raced toward Kiran.

"No!" Ishani screamed, withdrawing her other axe.

Dagmara charged toward Sabien. She had to stop him. Kiran was the only one holding Eligor in the tomb. Odie raced at her heels, scampering after Dagmara to engage in battle alongside her.

"Hide!" she screamed at Kiran, who instantly fled to the opposite deck.

In the distance, Dagmara could hear the clanking of the gate, meaning Ravi and Pierre had reached it. They were turning the key in the gears and ensuring that the main passageway to Dreadmarrow remained open for the ship to pass through.

Suddenly the Dreadmarrow guards reached the ship, boarding and attacking instantly. When the guards breached the deck, they swung at Martine and Ishani, who began engaging in the fight with their weapons drawn.

Dagmara glanced at Odie. They had to hold off the attack—at least until Claude and Magda reinforced the Mind Guardian lock.

Hurry! Dagmara pleaded in her mind before lunging at Sabien with her dagger.

CHAPTER 48
Magdalena

Claude and Magda crossed to Kiran's column. Despite Queen Sanyal being gone, the stones still shone brightly. Vines with yellow flowers wrapped around the column—the only column left with magic. Claude made quick work of searching the area for more ancient magic that could be concealing one of the locks. The room was massive, and the lack of light made it only more difficult to scan the area for false stones and walls.

Magda ran her hands along the bottom of Kiran's column, including the different parts of the mural, but to no avail.

Finally, they approached the circular mural in the middle of the room once more, standing above the four emblems that depicted the mind, water, air, and earth magic.

You're getting closer.

Magda tried to put the voice out of her head. She knew that she and Eligor had different goals, and she didn't want to take any of his advice.

"Do you hear him?" Claude asked, watching her face carefully. "Is he talking to you now?"

"Yes. He said *'we're getting closer'*," said Magda.

"We shouldn't listen to him," said Claude.

"But what if he's right?" asked Magda. "What if it's about this mural, the one thing that's right in front of our faces?"

"The emblems are the locks?" Claude clarified. "Then how can I reseal mine?"

"You could try stepping on it, for starters," said Magda.

"What if that's exactly what Eligor wants?" Claude snapped.

"Then he wouldn't have killed so many guardians. He would have lured us here instead."

Claude's jaw tensed as he pondered Magda's words. "I have a bad feeling that we're running out of time. Either we try this or not."

"Alright," said Magda.

Claude took a deep breath, before stepping onto the Mind emblem.

Magda braced herself with her hands, hoping she wouldn't have to use her powers, but nothing happened. The room was perfectly still.

Think. Take your time, Princess.

"Try to do something with your magic," Magda encouraged.

Claude let a small spark of silver form at his fingertips, and suddenly, the stones underneath him flickered, as if they were trying to spark back to life.

Magda's face beamed. "Do something else, something bigger!"

Claude nodded, before letting a burst of flowers shoot up from the center of the room, twirling upward to the purple light until he and Magda were enclosed in a magical gazebo crafted out of pink and red roses. Twinkles of silver magic made the entire space glitter. The enchantment was like nothing Magda had ever seen before, and she remained captivated by the illusion.

However, despite the glorious display of magic, the emblem underneath Claude barely flickered.

Claude mused, "It's as if the lock knows I'm a guardian, but something is incomplete."

Magda's eyes trailed to the remaining locks.

Kiran's was glowing brighter in dazzling yellow. Across from her lock, Claude stood on the mind emblem. The water and air lock remained untouched.

"Magda." Claude thought of the idea at the same time she did. "Go to the Life lock."

Magda's heart beat faster, and she crossed to Claude's left, standing on top of the water emblem.

She took a deep breath, before letting the sparkling blue magic light her fingertips and the surge of power electrify her body. She could feel the small water droplets throughout the room, seeping through the cracks in the rocks from the ocean above, and she drew them to her. All around the room the tiny drops surged to the top of Claude's magical greenhouse, before falling around them in a cool mist.

Claude's eyes widened, looking up as the rain fell around them, coating them in a light spray underneath the roses.

Below Magda, the emblem flickered slightly, but then died down once more.

Nice try, said Eligor. *But you're missing something. Until then, you'll never keep me here or reignite the magic.*

Claude spoke first, "We need something else."

In front of them, as if screaming the answer, was the remaining lock for the Spirit Guardian.

"But Guardian Sora is dead," said Magda. "There are no existing Spirit Guardians."

"You haven't exhibited Spirit magic yet?" asked Claude.

"No," Magda confessed. "And I can't stand in two places at once."

Claude continued, "What are we going to—"

A whiz of a projectile alerted the two. A knife flew through the air, glinting in the glowing light from the Soul lock. A hint of crimson magic accompanied the blade, guiding it toward its target. Claude tried to dodge at the last moment, but wasn't fast enough. The knife buried into his side.

"Claude!" Magda screamed.

The force of the blade knocked Claude back, and he grunted in pain, his hands flying to the handle.

Magda snapped her attention to the entrance, confronting the threat. The assassin from the ship—Junne—was hovering above the ground, her irises the color of blood.

"I thought I'd find you in here," Junne sneered. She summoned the wind, and it began to spiral around her form. Her cascading hair flew in all directions, and her clothing fluttered against the beating of the air.

Channeling her Soul powers, Magda braced herself against the assassin, reaching for the thick stone that surrounded them.

Then Claude fell to the ground hard, gasping. She had to save him. She had to protect him against Junne and find water to—

"Magda," Claude choked. "The Spirit lock..."

Glancing at his pained expression, Magda interpreted his idea. She glanced at the emblem on the floor, representing the power of the air. The last remaining Spirit Guardian was also the First Prince's assassin. But, if she could trick Junne into landing there, then Claude and Magda could still use their magic on Mind and Life. They could reseal all the locks with Junne.

Summoning her magic, the plan swirling in Magda's mind, she faced the Spirit assassin as a pummel of wind collided against her chest.

CHAPTER 49
Dagmara

The dagger bounced off Sabien's armor of ice, barely chipping the breast plate. Sabien whirled on her. "You can't get enough of me, can you, Dagger?"

A flicker of steel glistened in Dagmara's peripheral. Ishani's axe came flying down on Sabien's arm, shattering the armor. Sabien roared in pain, reeling back and bracing for another attack. At the same time, Odie snapped at Sabien's calf, drawing blood as his teeth ripped into his flesh.

Sabien let out a yell of pain as the water rose from the sea beneath them, congealing into spears of ice.

"Get down!" Dagmara screamed, hoping others would hear her. She launched herself to the ground as the ice rained from the sky like sharp arrows. Odie mimicked her movements, falling to the slippery wooden deck.

Clearing her vision with a shake of her head, Dagmara peered at her surroundings. Bodies littered the ship, mostly guards and crew members who didn't make it out of the way in time. In the distance, scarcely hidden behind a large barrel, was another familiar face. Her long black hair cascaded down her back, and she peered around the barrel at the battle that ensued.

Junne.

She knew it. Dagmara knew that Junne and Sabien had arrived together.

"The other assassin is here! The Spirit Guardian!" Dagmara yelled, warning everyone. She yelled until her voice was hoarse, attempting to warn Ishani who was fighting off the Dreadmarrow guards who tried to board the ship. Martine was slashing her way through the guards who had already boarded, making her way over to Magda.

Scrambling to her feet, Dagmara turned back to face Sabien. He was stepping back, scaling the stairs, and preparing to launch another assault with his Life magic.

"Behind me," Martine called, grabbing Dagmara by the arm and yanking her to her feet. Martine positioned her body in front of Dagmara's, assessing the newfound danger now that another assassin had arrived. She addressed Dagmara sternly, "No matter what happens you stay behind me."

Odie barked as if in agreement, bounding forward in front of the two girls.

"You can't fight all of us," Sabien taunted them, his eyes glowing with magic as he sauntered forward.

All? Who else was with Junne and Sabien?

Ishani slashed another Dreadmarrow guard, a shard of ice protruding from her shoulder. Her face was pained, but she held her axe determinedly.

"Where is the other assassin?" Ishani asked Dagmara, desperate.

Glancing over her shoulder at the barrels, Dagmara could no longer see Junne hidden there. "She was there a second ago."

This ship rocked again, knocking the three of them off balance. Sabien had control of the sea beneath them. A large wave ascended, threatening to collide with the side of the ship. Withdrawing a throwing star, Dagmara chucked it at Sabien, but it bounced off his armor pitifully. He couldn't be stopped.

The wave barreled into the side of the ship, snapping the railing and pelting Dagmara against the side of her face. Dagmara slid to the opposite side of the deck near a Dreadmarrow guard and thrust her dagger into his throat, killing him instantly. When she looked up, she saw that Martine and Ishani had been thrown to the ground, choking in the water from the assault.

"There!" Ishani yelled, seeing a retreating figure. Ishani was the first on her feet, completely soaked

Dagmara's head was in a daze, but she was alerted by Odie standing next to her, licking her fingers. She broke out of her stupor, snapping her head upright to spot Junne. The barrels had been knocked to the side by Sabien's magic, revealing her hiding place. Her eyes were not full of the crimson magic, but rather, they glowed with a tinge of yellow.

Wielding her axe, Ishani wound up for a throw.

"No!" Dagmara yelled.

The axe went flying across the deck, creating a perfect arc despite the wavering ship. The tip dug into Junne's stomach in a sickening crunch, blood splattering the deck.

The Spirit assassin stumbled back, the blade buried in her abdomen.

A silver glow illuminated Junne's body, and then, the vision shifted. Her facial features moved in silver hues, her hair molding into a different shape. The transformative magic revealed the true identity behind the facade.

Kiran.

The world seemed to stand still. Kiran's mouth was agape in a silent scream, the axe blade protruding from her stomach. Blood poured from the wound like a crimson waterfall, before she stumbled back and collapsed onto the ship deck.

"Kiran—" Ishani choked, rushing forward. She dropped to her knees and touched Kiran's face as though she didn't believe it were real. None of them did. Dagmara couldn't comprehend what had happened—it was all a blur. It was Junne—wasn't it?

Then the terrorizing realization dawned on her. Scrambling to her feet and steadying herself against Odie's body, she saw Viette standing on the railing, dancing effortlessly close to the edge. Her pristine appearance seemed to glow in the night, her irises as silver as a polished sword.

"Claude isn't the only Mind Guardian." A soft smile creased Viette's perfect face.

But how was it possible? How was Viette more powerful than a true guardian? How had her illusion overridden Claude's?

Viette read the thoughts in Dagmara's head as though they were written on her face. "I didn't overtake his illusion," she paused before emphasizing, "His was no longer there."

In another split second, an arrow went right for Viette's chest. Dagmara turned to see that Martine had grabbed Pierre's bow, sending a deadly arrow for Viette's heart.

At the last second, the arrow went right through Viette's body, and the illusion burst into colorful fragments.

"Until next time!" Viette's voice called, this time from the entirely opposite end of the ship. With a small step, she dropped off the edge of the boat and disappeared.

"No!"

Ishani's scream lit the night. It was raw and desperate, but also futile. She clasped Kiran tightly to her chest, rocking her on the ground. The Flaustran Princess was choking, blood sputtering from her mouth. Her arm dangled limply at her side, and her eyes were unfocused.

The boat lurched to the side and Dagmara stumbled, barely catching herself against the rail. Odie lunged for her shirt, snatching it between his teeth as he pulled her back, so that she didn't succumb to the sea. Dagmara whipped over her shoulder, prepared to defend herself.

Martine equally took up a battle stance, reloading the bow.

"That wave wasn't my doing," Sabien smirked, feeling the tide of the water churn underneath them before dropping his blade to the ground. It shattered against the wooden planks. "That was the tomb."

A rumble quaked the earth, and the ship swayed to the side once more. Screams from guards in the distance joined Ishani's cries for her sister.

Sabien flipped his hair out of his eyes and sent droplets of water flying in all directions. "We finally killed the last guardian. My work here is done, and it's time to unite with Eligor. This is your last chance to join the winning team." He held out his hand toward Dagmara, which was soaked in blood.

Shaking her head, Dagmara struggled to remain standing against the slick rail while the ship continued to sway. Water pelted her as the ship careened against the sudden waves, rippling from the shattered earth underneath. "We will never be on the same side, Sabien."

"What a shame. We look so good together." Sabien winked at her before hoisting himself on the rail, and the water churned beneath him, beckoning him.

"Don't move," Martine said, aiming the reloaded bow at Sabien's neck, seconds before he leapt over the side. Odie growled next to her.

"Oh, Martine," Sabien chuckled. "Don't you remember that I'm the one who gives orders around here? Until next time, Dagger." Sabien dove from the ship in perfect form, missing the arrow by seconds and landing in the black water with grace. He didn't resurface, but he was alive, carried off by the current generated from a Life Guardian.

She could only assume Sabien and Viette had disappeared to return to their master.

Martine rushed to Dagmara's side first. "My queen, are you alright?"

Odie padded up to the girl and nudged Dagmara's leg.

Dagmara acknowledged Odie, but she didn't have time to think about herself. Viette's departing words replayed in Dagmara's mind. *His was no longer there.* There was only one other time Dagmara remembered Claude's illusions failing—when he was gravely injured when Celestaire first attacked Sailonne.

He was hurt. Somewhere inside the tomb, Dagmara could feel it in her core.

"Claude needs help," Dagmara announced.

An ear-piercing crack rang through the night. Turning to the source of the noise, Dagmara witnessed the first structure begin to collapse. A high tower snapped, the foundation crumbling in a heap of stone, colliding with other sections of the prison.

A gasp escaped her lips. "Claude..."

Pierre was charging down the dock, returning from the gate. "Ravi has it open, we have to leave now!" he called.

"They're still in there!" Dagmara replied, sprinting down the gangway and onto the docks for a better view. "Odie, come!" she yelled frantically. The dog followed her command, sprinting after her as she barreled down the planks.

A rush of air beat against Dagmara's face as someone flew up beside her. Martine and Pierre were instantly on either side of her. They all watched the prison begin to crumble before them in a heap of gray smoke and debris.

"His Majesty!" Pierre exclaimed. He met Dagmara's gaze, a burning intensity in his eyes. No words were needed. They both knew what they had to do.

"Ishani!" Dagmara shouted, but she didn't appear. One of her officers leaned over the railing, blood coating his clothing. "Gather the crew and be prepared for a quick escape," Dagmara instructed. He gave her a curt nod before disappearing once more.

Then Dagmara charged down the gangplank, Pierre and Martine flanking her and Odie on her heels. They charged the opposite way of the crowd, the majority trying to escape the heaps of rock falling from the prison.

A trembling sound ricocheted through the earth once more, spreading from deep underground and through the stone. A sharp pain surged through Dagmara's chest. She clasped her stomach, unable to catch herself as she fell to her knees. The air had been stolen from her, and anguish tore through every fiber of her being.

Pierre was already hoisting her up underneath the arms.

"Are you alright?" Martine asked, her expression concerned while Odie pranced between them.

"I'm fine," Dagmara choked. A fleeing guard bumped her in the shoulder, and her weight tipped against Pierre's chest. He was surprisingly strong, holding her on her two feet with ease. "It's only my heart," she told him with a thankful nod before pushing away. Only her health, threatening to prevent her from saving the ones she loved.

And yet, as Dagmara, Odie, and the two Ilusaurian guards continued their way into the crumbling prison, retracing their steps through the pipe, she couldn't shake the feeling that it wasn't only her health.

It was the tomb, breaking open with Kiran's last breath.

CHAPTER 50
Magdalena

Magda's back slammed against the stone, yards away from the locks. Pain ruptured every part of her body, but she channeled it into her attack.

The Spirit assassin landed beside Claude, the wind expanding around her in bursts. She reached down toward the handle of the blade protruding from his side, prepared to rip it free. He sat up abruptly, smashing his forehead against hers, screaming in agony as the blade shifted inside him.

Junne clasped her hand to her forehead, reeling in pain.

This was Magda's chance. Junne was so close to standing on the Spirit emblem.

Magda reached for her Soul magic, stealing a large rock from the earth. It ripped free, her mind throbbing as she channeled the power. She thrust the stone toward Junne, commanding it to shatter into smaller pieces. Claude extended a shaking hand, casting silver magic to hide the rocks from Junne's sight. She didn't see them flying toward her. The rocks slammed against Junne's frail form, and she flattened on the stone beside Claude, a crack of bone reverberating through the space.

Scrambling to her feet, Magda raced toward the emblems,

ordering the vines that wrapped around the Soul column to bind Junne.

Junne screamed as the vines slithered around her, clasping one of her arms that was bent at an awkward angle beside her.

Closing her fist, Magda ordered the vines to drag Junne toward the Spirit emblem.

"Let me go!" Junne screamed, lashing against the restraints.

Magda reached out to Claude, still holding onto Junne with the vines. She attempted to focus on the earth, but her mind was distracted seeing the knife protruding from Claude's side. "I need to heal you," she blurted out.

"The locks first," Claude grunted, using his forearms to pull himself onto the Mind emblem. "We're so close, Magda, now!"

Nodding, Magda staggered back onto the Life emblem. She summoned the Life branch inside, channeling her father and brother. This was *her* magic. She belonged to the Life lineage whether or not she was like the First Prince.

The Mind emblem began to glisten. Claude winced, his blood soaked hands pressed to the ground as he surged his magic into the lock.

Magda glared at Junne, who thrashed against the vines. "Use your magic, Junne, or I'll kill you!"

"Then kill me. You're too late anyway!"

Anger vibrated through every ounce of Magda's body. For the first time, she felt both branches of her magic igniting, Life and Soul, as she ordered the vines to tighten their grip. They constricted further, eliciting another ear-piercing scream from the Spirit assassin.

"Now!"

Suddenly, the stones underneath them began vibrating. Magda gasped, releasing the vines as her gaze darted to the ground. The floor was shaking...but there was no red light coming from the Spirit lock. No...it was the golden lock that was twinkling. The yellow light that burned through the earth emblem retreated from the central mural, disappearing back into the column, until it had faded into nothing. The emblem flickered, until the light peeking through the rock had extinguished.

"No!" Magda screamed, letting her body collapse onto the stone. She knew what the light represented. The dimming of the light meant that there were no more Soul Guardians.

Kiran was dead.

A wave of despair pummeled against Magda's chest. She screamed in agony. They were so close—they had almost resealed the locks—and someone had killed her friend.

"Kiran!" Magda screamed, pounding the Soul emblem. Tears burned her eyes.

"That's right," Junne said through gritted teeth. The vines around her disintegrated, flaking to the ground as dead as their guardian.

Claude struggled to push himself to his knees, reaching for his sheathed sword. Silver glistened at his fingertips, but a thunderous explosion hit the room. The noise was deafening, and Magda covered her ears from the pain. The ground began to shake, jerking the three of them violently. Around them, stones fell from the ceiling, smashing into the ground.

Magda couldn't breathe, and she couldn't see through the tears that streamed down her face. She felt as if her entire body was being torn apart with excruciating grief. They had failed. Kiran was dead, and that only meant one thing. Magda screamed as anguish overcame her, and she froze, unable to move or think.

All around them, the room shook furiously as if new life had been ignited inside it, and beneath them, the mural began to open at its centermost point.

"Magda!" Claude called.

Blinking the tears from her eyes, Magda saw a stone falling from the sky. She reached up, finding her magic, and barely guided it out of the way before it collided with the floor next to her. She scrambled back as the mural began to open around them.

The First Prince was rising.

Magda didn't know whether to run, hide, or stay. The tunnel to escape seemed so far away across the room. Terror consumed her body, and she struggled to control her gasping breaths and shaking hands. She saw Claude, desperately clutching his side, the dagger still protruding from his skin. He wasn't going to make it without her help.

She needed to heal him, and she needed to do it fast.

All four emblems began to tear apart, creating a giant opening at the center. She was drifting further away from Claude and Junne, as the fragment underneath her tugged back by an invisible force. Pushing herself to her feet, Magda launched herself over the opening, despite the shifting of the ground. She landed near Claude, saying, "We have to get out of here."

Behind her, the chasm continued opening, and Junne was strewn on the opposite side of the hole, in complete disbelief. The violet smoke continued to rise, clouding the central area.

Magda attempted to pick up Claude, but he was deadweight. Claude let out a scream of pain, clutching his side.

Magda knew she wouldn't be able to carry Claude out of the room, so she dropped to her knees and closed her eyes once more. She remembered when she was with Eligor in the Void, and how she had found the droplets of water that surrounded every crevice of his tomb. She attempted to gather them towards her, and the magic ignited.

"Hold on!" Magda yelled to Claude, holding firm to the handle of the dagger. She was not leaving Claude. Dagmara would never forgive her, and Magda would never forgive herself.

Out of the chasm, a flurry of violet mist snaked upwards, and the stench of death flooded the already musty cavern. An eerie silence hung in the space, and it was so still they could hear the sound of a single breath escaping from below.

The particles of water throughout the space swirled to meet her hand.

"Go, he'll kill you!" shouted Claude.

"He'll kill you too," said Magda.

"I don't matter. It's you who can make new guardians. It's you who can stop him."

"I can't make new guardians without the crown," Magda said in a forced whisper.

Suddenly a chilling voice sent a shiver down Magda's spine.

"Princess."

It was *his*. This time, he wasn't in her head.

The power snuffed out, and her eyes turned brown once more as she froze in terror.

Eligor stepped out of the violet fog, his navy cape flowing behind him. His face was glowing and pure, and his striking features were framed with golden hair. His metal armor snaked against his chest and arms in a swirling design, and jagged spikes protruded from his shoulders, collar and elbows. Violet and black wisps of power emanated from his body as if the magic was a part of him.

Eligor had eyes only for Magda. Ravenous. Insatiable.

"It's lovely meeting you both face to face," said Eligor. "I'm sorry you weren't successful with your little mission to trap me here for another millennia."

Behind the First Prince, another emblem appeared on the stone floor, and violet magic bled sharply through the rocks, as if the light cut straight through the stone. The purple, Void emblem shone brightly, and behind it, a column emerged from the ground, shaking the room even more violently. The stone column reached the ceiling, and settled in its groove. Now, there were five columns, and the Void was represented alongside the other elements.

Eligor took a step toward Magda, while Claude lay on the ground behind her.

Magda was speechless as she fixated on Eligor's golden crown. Every instinct in Magda's body told her to run, but she needed to save

Claude. Her thoughts spun out of control, and she attempted to devise a plan.

Eligor addressed Claude, "I told you the First Prince would rise."

"And you'll fall just as easily." Claude coughed.

"My prince. You're alive!" Junne called from the other end of the room.

Eligor turned around to address his assassin, his back to both Magda and Claude.

"Ah," he mused, "My Spirit."

This was Magda's chance.

In a mere second, she ripped the dagger from Claude's side. He painfully held back a scream, and Magda pressed her palm to his torn flesh, letting the water droplets sink into his skin. Magic swirled in her palm, and she could feel the healing powers soaking into Claude. But there were barely any droplets of water, and she frantically searched for more in the depths of the prison.

Eligor's attention was still on Junne, and he crossed to her, stepping on the Void emblem. As he did so, the emblem lit up with blinding magic, before a shockwave of purple fired into the corresponding column. The power swirled up his body, and the purple light remained ignited.

He had activated the Void lock just by standing on it. How? What had she and Claude been doing wrong?

Claude moaned on the ground, and Magda turned her attention back to him. She pulled the minuscule droplets from the room, drawing on every ounce of strength she had to continue healing the deep wound, but her mind burned in pain.

"Please," Junne was begging Eligor, "Make me a reigning guardian. Tie my blood to the land and restore my home. I promise to serve you, Master."

Eligor removed the crown from his head, before crouching down to Junne, who lay sprawled across the Spirit emblem. He reached out to place the crown on her head, and the Spirit emblem ignited. It lit up with glittering magic mirroring the vibrance of the Void emblem.

With the crown resting on Junne's head, the magical emblem surged with power when she activated her magic. The red magic remained ignited, swirling with a newfound intensity. The light trickled up the column, slowly making its way to the top.

"I always keep my promises," Eligor was growling.

Before Magda could finish healing Claude, Junne locked eyes with her. With a gush of wind, Magda was thrown backward. A force pummeled into Magda's chest, and she landed on the ground next to Claude. Magda reeled in pain, and she groaned, helpless to any more attacks.

Eligor turned around and put the crown back on his head. "Trying to save Claude?" he laughed. "Deciding who lives and dies is my job."

Magda winced. She knew Eligor was going to strike her—kill her—one way or another. At least she would join her father and brother, wherever they were. All that gave her any hope was that Claude's gash was partially healed.

In a flash, Eligor's eyes lit up with yellow magic, and his hand thrust outwards. Pieces of stone ricocheted out from the walls like sharp daggers.

"Magda, get down!" Claude yelled.

Time felt as if it passed in slow motion. Magda expected to be hit by the dagger-like stones, the shrapnel ripping through her flesh. This was it. The moment that Eligor killed both her and Claude, and she would never see Dagmara, Ravi, Odie, or her mother again. She held her breath as Claude's body covered hers, holding her close so that she couldn't move. The weight of his chest and arms pressed her firmly into the ground.

A scream lit the room, and it wasn't from Claude.

After a second, Magda dared to look up.

The shrapnel had pierced Junne's body, and her face had turned ghostly white. She crumpled to the ground.

She gasped for breath, before finally going limp. The red light beneath her flickered with her dying breath, before extinguishing entirely. Both Junne and the newly restored lock died together.

Magda gasped, her face going pale.

Eligor stepped toward Junne's lifeless body. He opened his chest to the sky and extended his forearms in either direction, as stands of red magic flowed from Junne's body to his. The crown on his head shone brightly with intense, blood-red magic.

Magda stared at Eligor in awe as the magic sucked out of Junne and went to him through his crown. It was clear the crown was a conduit, a way to not only give out magic, but also retrieve it back. Suddenly, it made sense why Eligor had only mastered two branches of magic. The Void and the Soul—because there were no Void or Soul assassins. Once he gifted the magic to an assassin, he didn't have it anymore. He had given his Spirit magic away to her, and now he was taking it back.

She had to make a getaway before he became more powerful. She needed to get Claude to safety. The violet fog of the Void coating the room would conceal them enough to make it to the exit. But...she needed that crown.

"Come on," said Magda, as the red and purple magic swirled in all directions, surrounding Eligor's body. She heaved Claude up to a sitting position and placed his arm around her shoulder.

Claude grunted as they stood, but he regained his balance. "I'm alright," he said, although he was still limping.

"Claude..." she whispered into his ear as she held him. "We need the crown."

The red lights were fading as Eligor's eyes became alight with red magic. "I missed this," he growled. Then he let out a low chuckle before he took flight. He launched through the room like a gust from a cannon, smashing into one of the columns as he went, and bursting the rocks in all directions. The sparkling, crimson magic swirled around him in a furious storm, carrying him on a menacing cloud.

He flew out of the tunnel, escaping the tomb.

He was free.

The room shook once more, dust scattering from the ceiling. A high-pitched scraping noise pierced the air as a talon scratched on stone. Another figure was emerging from the tomb. It was one of the hounds, massive and ready for blood.

"Go after Eligor," said Claude under his breath.

"No, I need to help you get to the surface—"

"We both saw it with our own eyes. We can't reseal the locks with magic alone, we need to be wearing the crown. If we ever want to restore Ilusauri and Azurem, the crown is all that matters!"

The hound surfaced, facing off against Claude. In a flash, the room was lit with sparkling illusions. Claude conjured his own hounds to distract the one from the Void, and the entire room shifted to conceal Magda's escape. With one hand on his bleeding side, Claude withdrew his sheathed sword, lunging forward and slaying the beast in one swoop.

Magda dashed to the door, stealing one glance back at Claude.

He gave her a nod. "I'll meet you on the ship!" he shouted.

There was no arguing with the king. Magda's eyes locked on the tunnel where Eligor had disappeared. They couldn't lose him now. They couldn't let him off this island, set to wreak havoc with his Void powers and his hounds on the world.

Without another thought, Magda raced after the First Prince.

CHAPTER 51
Magdalena

Magda sprinted through Dreadmarrow before she made it to the elevator. She peered her head into the shaft, looking upward, before realizing that it was already ascending. This time, she noted that the elevator climbed higher than before, to the upper floors of the prison.

Eligor had received his Spirit magic again, basking in the power. She was a Master Guardian herself, and she should have Spirit magic too.

She attempted to find the wind in her mind, channeling the particles of air that swept back and forth around her being. Magda squinted her eyes, focusing more intently than she ever had before, but the magic did not spark at her fingertips.

The elevator returned, and she dashed inside, attempting to use the Spirit Magic once more to speed up the ascent in the shaft, but to no avail. As she got closer to the surface, the sounds of clanking metal scraped against her ears, and the shrieking alarm intensified as she dashed out to overlook the main hall.

In front of Magda, Eligor's looming cape flowed as he soared across the entrance foyer like a bird, using his Soul Magic to crack open the cells. Guards below ran chaotically in all directions, some retreating, some fighting, and some overcome with confusion. Prisoners poured out of the cages, turning against the guards. Shrieking prisoners and guards let out deadly screams as they were pushed to their deaths from the platforms, elevators, and scaffoldings that ran around the outside of the prison.

Eligor used Spirit magic to thrust groups of guards away like tiny insects, or used more Soul magic to drop stones on their bodies, using no more effort than blowing a feather.

He was majestic. Invigorating. The epitome of evil.

Then Eligor swirled upward, blasting through the glass dome at the top of the inside of the piton, and letting shots of red, yellow, and purple magic explode like bursting fireworks.

She could follow him with magic, or die trying.

Magda ran outward, hoping to the guardians that her plan would work. She leapt out over the space, aiming for a small platform. She pushed the air to the forefront of her mind, letting the idea of the powers explode through her veins. Halfway to the platform, she began falling, and no blood-scarlet magic sparked in her hands.

Gravity pooled in her stomach as she fell dramatically fast, landing on a lower platform by one of the rows of cells. Excruciating pain shot up her legs and arms, but the worse pain was knowing the Spirit Magic had failed her. Why?

Without another moment of hesitation, Magda sprung up and jumped onto one of the elevator-like gondolas. She pulled the lever and it shot up immediately, taking her to the higher floors. When she got to the top of the prison, she dashed down the hallway and to a singular door, praying it would lead her to the top of the mountain.

She didn't know what she was going to do when she reached Eligor, or how she was going to get the crown, but if she didn't die trying, she had no idea when she would have the opportunity again.

Magda emerged into the dark night. In a second, rain pummeled her face, soaking her hair and clothes. She stood on a large rooftop, towering the gothic spires of Dreadmarrow and the haunting graveyard of shipwrecks that bobbed in the black ocean below. The roof extended from the side of the mountain, overlooking the other pitons in the dark night. Positioned around the roof were grotesque statues, providing perfect places to hide in the mist.

Above, lighting cracked, exploding into the night sky. A thunderous boom followed, and the rain became heavier.

Magda crept forward, keeping her head low and her thoughts on one thing only: the crown.

She traversed through the ghastly statues, searching for Eligor. Did he decide to leave completely? She had no idea if he had already taken flight, escaping the prison for good. She could not let him get away, for she had no idea where he would turn to, hurting more innocent people.

Finally, she reached the edge of the rooftops, where the mist thinned, to see Eligor surveying the vastness of the island of Dreadmarrow, like a divine being taking in its creation.

It was surreal witnessing him in the flesh. Magda wanted to call out to him, but something made her stay put, freezing in her shoes. Her entire being was overcome with a sense of dread as she laid eyes on the man destined to kill her.

Only one of them would survive. There could only be one Master Guardian.

"Come for my crown?" Eligor turned to Magda. "I didn't think you would run to your death."

Lighting flashed again, and a deafening rumble shattered the air.

Magda's teeth gritted. "You're a monster. You used Junne and discarded her once you needed the powers more."

"Are you really that surprised?" Eligor laughed. "It will only be a matter of time before I control every element, and everyone will revere me as the ultimate creator and master of this world's powers. And finally the Void will belong to me."

Magda's thoughts spun in all directions. What did that mean?

"Why? Why do you care so much about the Void?" Magda spat.

"All I wanted was to be the heir to my family's magic. But the precious guardians wouldn't let me participate in the trials, because of what I was. Because of what I still *am*!" Eligor roared. "Well, I'll show everyone what I am and can be. They locked me away for eternity and commissioned a prison to rise around my tomb so no one would ever find me. Those ruthless monsters didn't even have the mercy to put me to death, but rather had me suffer for one thousand years, as a shell of my former self, wallowing in a space where I could neither feel, smell, hear, see, nor taste. Do you know what that is like?"

"No," Magda shook her head.

"Then I felt *you*," Eligor said, his eyes burning into her, as if he could see her soul.

He lunged for her, tightening his fingers around her neck and pushing her up against one of the statues, so that her back was against the stone. His fingers pressed into her throat as his grip tightened, and her hands flew to his wrists, attempting to break free. But he held her in place, so that she was forced to stare back into his eyes.

"Touching you...," he growled, "...it's the first time in a thousand years I've felt skin underneath my fingers, blood pulsing through veins..."

Magda was speechless. She scratched at the fingers on her throat, while her heart pounded furiously in her chest.

Another crack of lighting. Another boom.

Eligor pulled her closer so that she was no longer against the wall, and they were face to face. She had to balance on her tiptoes to meet him at eye level. He spoke, "...and the breath that fills your lungs."

Magda took in his presence as she gasped for air. He was different too, outside the Void. He was more intense. Passionate. His touch electrified her, whether it was because he was the most powerful being in the world, or for some other reason, Magda didn't know.

"Do you know how easy I can break you?" he sneered. "How good it would feel to kill again, watching the life drain from your eyes and feeling the blood slow underneath the touch of my skin on yours?"

"Not...if I...kill you first," Magda retorted. Darkness was threatening to pull her under, and her only hope was to grovel at the mercy of the First Prince.

"But first I have to thank you," Eligor breathed. "I yearned for each of our next conversations in the Void, and how only you, the first girl in a thousand years, could satiate me. Another Master Guardian."

"We are not the same," Magda struggled. His words were pulling her under, hypnotizing her, as if he wanted to bring her close to death so that she remained under his spell.

"No, we are not equals. But, you let me indulge in your fierce mind, and I quenched my thirst for human contact," he remained transfixed on her. "You were the fire that fueled my bloodlust and helped me escape this prison."

"I will not be your inspiration for destroying this world," Magda said.

Eligor laughed, throwing his head back, and his golden hair flopped against the crown. "Now, all the guardians will see what happens when they are in the ground, and I am in power, and the Void is all consuming."

Another crack of lighting. Another boom.

Magda had to think fast. Her eyes were still on the crown placed meticulously on his head—the only way to make more guardians. The only way to repair this world.

"I can't let that happen," said Magda.

She stopped clenching his wrists, and yanked the crown from his head, slashing the points across his flesh. He reeled in pain, stepping back and grabbing his face, giving Magda a split second to dash into the fog.

"Princess!" she heard him roar, and a hint of yellow magic illuminated the mist.

CHAPTER 52
Dagmara

The cold air of the crumbling prison sent chills through Dagmara's entire body. They had no idea where to go or where to run. Martine was the first to point them to a rickety elevator. Magda and Claude had to be somewhere underground.

Pierre fired his bow, instantly killing the guard that was about to steal the elevator from them. Dagmara and Martine raced inside, Martine's sword drawn. The platform jerked to the left, but Pierre easily cleared the gap alongside Odie. Grabbing the lever, Martine set the elevator in motion, descending into the depths of the prison.

Kneeling beside Odie, Dagmara twisted the cap of her ring, revealing the blood from Claude, now weeks old. "Go find," she pleaded.

The dog inhaled a whiff of Claude's scent before turning his nose in the air, trying to pick up a trace. Screwing the cap back on, holding steadfast to the only object she still held of Claude's, Dagmara rose back to her feet. Another shattering pain laced through her chest, and she braced herself against the elevator wall. She was familiar with her health, but this...there was something else beneath her skin that crawled with unease.

The elevator lurched to a halt with an abrupt clank, revealing a dark hallway that branched in several directions.

With a single bark, Odie went charging to the right.

"Come on!" Pierre yelled before taking off after the dog. As the trio rounded the bend, Odie disappeared, leaping right through a wall.

Dagmara stopped short, before realizing an illusion was covering the path that Odie had taken.

"Follow him," said Martine.

They burst through the wall, not stopping to think twice, and ran to the edge of the tunnel. After she opened a vault door, they emerged into a room with five columns and a gaping hole in the floor.

All around the room, thick purple magic had twisted up the walls, like a sticky substance threatening to consume everything in its path. Specks of violet mist and dust twinkled in the air, coating the room in a haze of magic. Dark, cavernous cracks had split up the walls, expanding from the hole in the ground, just like the ravine in Nouchenne.

The ground was littered with two dozen hound carcasses. The room smelled of blood. Junne was sprawled out beside the deceased hounds, dead.

Then Dagmara spotted Claude. He was on his back, scarlet liquid puddled around him. He held his bloodied sword out, his entire arm shaking with exhaustion. Another half dozen hounds prowled toward him, readying their haunches to jump.

They were too far away. Dagmara could never reach them in time.

Dagmara screamed, the word escaping her throat in a guttural plea. She fumbled for a throwing star in her corset—anything that could prevent the hound from dealing a death blow. Anything that could keep Claude alive.

The hound lunged.

She was too late.

But there was a black and white blur in the corner of her eye.

Launching himself through the air, with the speed of light, Odie leapt for the hound. His jaw clamped around its neck, knocking the beast off course.

The monster howled as Odie drew blood. The dog wrenched his head from side to side, deepening his grip. Then an arrow flew through the hound's skull from Pierre's bow, killing it instantaneously.

Martine lunged forward, sliding on the blood-slick ground before decapitating the next hound. Both she and Pierre slaughtered the hounds one by one, defending their king.

Racing to Claude's aid, Dagmara slid to her knees beside him. His body was a canvas of bruises and cuts. His breaths were shallow and labored, fighting for air. He dropped the sword to the ground, falling onto his back. Blood pooled around him, dying his clothes red, but Dagmara couldn't tell where it was all coming from.

His lips parted in attempts to say her name.

"Shh, I'm here, you're going to be alright. Just hold on."

A whimper rang through the tomb. Odie was flung off a beast, but Martine was already sending her sword through the monster's scales.

"Where's Magda?" Dagmara asked Claude, desperation in her voice.

"She went after Eligor," he rasped. He tried to sit upright, but winced, letting out a shout before collapsing back to the ground.

Odie came up to Claude, licking his fingertips, while Pierre raced to Claude's other side.

"We have to go," Pierre said. "This place is unstable."

"Help me," Dagmara ordered, trying to heave Claude off the ground. He screamed again, the agony tearing her own heart in two. Pierre nodded, slinging his bow over his back before reaching out to assist Claude.

The sickening crunch of flesh and bone cracked the air as Martine killed another hound.

A growl rumbled in Odie's throat. His attention was steadfast on the hole in the center of the room, smoking with violet magic. The Void magic was seeping out, returning to the world.

The scratch of talons reverberated as the Void animals ascended. There were more. A thick paw was the first to scale the rim of the hole, before a massive hound followed.

Odie barked at the emerging hounds, but was retreating, backing up beside them.

Martine slaughtered another hound, the only line of defense. "Pierre!" she called.

There were too many, and they couldn't outrun them, not with Claude so injured. Even so, she wouldn't leave Claude behind. None of them would.

Pierre set Claude down, returning to his weapon. He raced forward, joining Martine in the battle, sending arrow after arrow into the oncoming beasts.

"Please, Claude," Dagmara begged, trying to heave him up, but she wasn't strong enough. Blood was gushing from his open wounds, coating her in crimson.

Odie barked as a hound broke through Martine and Pierre's defense. Its eyes were an iridescent violet, matching the scales that protected his chest. Drool dripped from its massive jaws as he showed his fangs. With eyes for Claude, it lunged.

CHAPTER 53
Magdalena

Magda raced away from Eligor, back into the fog, the crown in hand. The horrifying statues created a maze in the clouds, and she raced around each one, praying to escape this nightmare. She had the crown, now it was time to kill the monster.

She ran to the right, then to the left, trapped in a hideous labyrinth full of stones depicting gruesome figures. Magda burst through the mist only to stop dead in her tracks.

She gasped, finding her toes on the edge of the roof. She used all her strength to not topple below to the shipyard and mutilate her body on the jagged rocks. Below, the tumultuous waves beat the wooden frames of once-ships against the side of the prison, before the sea sucked the shapes back out again.

She turned around, running back in the opposite direction, away from the edge of the roof, but stopped dead in her tracks when she came face to face with Eligor.

Her heart dropped to the pit of her stomach.

"It's over, Princess." His chilling voice pronounced.

With all her might, she forced the earth magic through her veins.

She channeled the weapons that were placed in the grotesque statues that surrounded them. Stone shards from the statues flung in all directions, flying towards Eligor.

Eligor easily maneuvered out of the way.

Magda's hands curled into fists. She tried to hit the First Prince again, bringing down more stones, but this time Eligor used Spirit magic to fling them off course.

Eligor countered, ripping more shards from the stone that surrounded them. They didn't fly in random directions, but with his newfound Spirit magic, he aimed directly at Magda.

Magda swirled behind one of the statues, hoping the fog on the dark night would conceal her. She channeled the Life magic, her eyes turning icy-blue. She focused on the rain and puddles that were forming on the rooftop, turning the raindrops to ice.

She thrust them toward Eligor, but he froze the shrapnel-like daggers in their tracks. One by one, they bounced aimlessly to the floor.

Then a gust of wind knocked into Magda's side, thrusting her back with full force and slamming her onto her back as her fingers released the crown. Black spots spun in her vision, and she struggled to stay conscious. She couldn't breathe, and she gasped to reach an ounce of air. Then she attempted to push herself to her feet, but she couldn't move or make sense of her surroundings. She scrambled away, only for her hands to meet the edge of the rooftop once more.

The crown was paces away.

She reached out for the crown, but Eligor was equally as quick. He grabbed it at the same time that she did, and in his fury, he kicked her across the face. Magda reeled in pain as blood splattered across her nose, but she didn't relinquish the crown.

Then he grabbed her by her shirt, yanking her up to him, and she struggled to stand in a dizzy haze. He forced her backward, with one hand on her shirt, pushing her over the edge of the roof. His other hand held onto the crown high above his head. Magda careened over the edge on her tiptoes, and her only lifeline was a sweaty grip on the other end of the crown.

Eligor shook his head, "Killing you will be my first step in destroying this world and creating a new one. One where the Void overcomes everything else, and the rest of the guardians no longer exist."

"We've had multiple guardians ruling our kingdoms for centuries, and nothing is wrong with that."

Lightning cracked again, and a drop of rain slipped through her fingertips. She found the power in the rain, but she knew she had to act fast, before he saw the color blue ignite in her irises.

"Our powers don't lie in thrones and crowns. We are so powerful that we can light a fire in a generation and kill it in another."

"You think so highly of yourself." Magda spit the blood in his face that was trickling down from her nose.

Eligor smiled, and his tongue curled around his lips to taste her blood. "People have killed for me, for a taste of what it's like to be a guardian, and they will do whatever I ask of them as I am the only one that can give them the taste of being a god. And even so, I will always be more powerful, five times over. If that's not a sign that fate has chosen me to control this world's destiny, then what is? We are meant to be the world's gods, Magda, and gods were not only created to rule, but also they were created to cultivate and shape the fabric of our world. It's our duty to start anew when our creation doesn't obey, or when people rise against us."

Magda looked at him with newfound eyes.

"But unfortunately, as much as I want to give into temptations, you are not in that new world," Eligor announced.

"So you will kill the one person that can ever truly be your equal?" Magda clenched at his grip on her shirt, but it was like iron.

"Yes," said Eligor. "Because I would rather have you in the grave than let you be my undoing."

Then he pushed Magda backward with full force, sending another gust of Spirit magic into her chest, and she toppled over the edge of the roof.

CHAPTER 54
Dagmara

The tomb under the prison was overrun with hounds. Martine and Pierre struggled to hold back the line, but one had broken through. It dove for Claude, and Dagmara couldn't unsheathe her dagger in time.

"No!" Dagmara screamed, covering Claude's body with her own. She braced herself for the onslaught, to be ripped apart by the hound's fangs. She didn't care as long as it bought Claude a few more moments.

The hound skidded on the slick stone. It stopped its attack moments before ripping apart her face.

Every hound in the cavern stilled. Martine and Pierre froze, their weapons raised, panting to catch their breath.

The hound that had lunged at Claude was so close, its breath beat upon her, smelling like acid. Its glowing irises sent a chill down Dagmara's spine, but she couldn't move, watching the hound carefully. Maybe if she was utterly still, maybe it would spare her.

Tears pricked her eyes as she stared death straight in the face.

A dozen other hounds found their way to the surface, lining up beside one another. Their heads swiveled to each side, and their paws stamped the ground impatiently.

But they hadn't launched themselves forward. Everyone in the room, hound or not, was completely and utterly still.

Odie's stance shifted, his tail changing directions and beginning to wag.

A faint rustling rang through the tomb as Pierre moved to nock another arrow. In unison, all the hounds turned their attention to him, their ears pricked high on their heads.

"Stop!" Dagmara ordered Pierre, praying he wouldn't upset the hounds. Something was keeping them from attacking, and she wasn't about to jeopardize their hesitance.

Both Pierre and the pack of hounds froze at her voice. Her throat seemed to burn with the words, the command pounding at the back of her temples as fear overwhelmed her.

The hounds remained still.

Trying to quell the anxiety in Dagmara's heart, she spoke quietly, "The elevator."

Martine gave a curt nod, but didn't take her eyes away from the massive animals.

Attempting once more to lift Claude, this time more slowly than the last, she pulled his arm around her shoulder. He stifled his cry of pain, his eyes squeezed shut tightly. He was too heavy, there was no way she could get him back to the elevator.

"Help me!" Dagmara cried, unable to keep her voice a whisper.

Pierre obeyed immediately, but kept a cautious eye on the immovable hounds. He dropped to Claude's opposite side, slinging the king's hand over his shoulder despite his cries. But before they could heave him to his feet, one hound began to move.

Both Dagmara and Pierre froze once more, and Odie growled beside them. Martine leveled her sword, prepared to strike, but she didn't know which beast would lunge first.

The hound circled them, like it was circling prey. It was four feet tall, towering over them as they crouched beside Claude. Dagmara sucked in a ragged breath, unable to comprehend the hound's actions. It bowed his head low to the earth before nudging its snout against Claude's back. The creature was undeniably strong, the movement shoving Claude from the ground and elevating him enough for Dagmara and Pierre to pull him all the way to his feet. Once upright, Pierre held the majority of Claude's weight. He glanced at Dagmara, his eyes wide.

"You can...control them?" Pierre asked.

"No, I—" Dagmara couldn't respond. She felt sick.

"The elevator," Martine directed.

Dagmara and Pierre struggled to assist Claude to the elevator—the only hope of escape—while Martine kept her gaze attentive on the beasts. Blood smeared on the ground behind them, pouring from the Mad King's injuries, and he groaned as he attempted to walk with their help.

They entered the elevator and set Claude down on the ground, all three of them grunting in exhaustion. Odie bounded in last, continuing to glance over at the hounds that trailed them a few paces behind.

Claude panted, struggling to sit upright, wincing with every movement. Unable to stand longer, dizziness threatening every move, Dagmara kneeled beside him and took his bloodied hand in her own.

"You're safe, it's alright."

The king met her gaze, unblinking. "Dagmara...what...what are you?"

The air dissipated, the question like a knife to her chest. The betrayal on his face broke her in half, an expression she hadn't seen since the night he had discovered her true identity.

"All that matters—" Dagmara's voice broke off, and she struggled to form words. She gripped Claude's palm tighter, "is that I'm going to save you."

The elevator lurched as Martine slammed the lever.

Glancing over her shoulder, Dagmara eyed the hounds in the tunnel, their eyes glowing. She didn't understand what had occurred between her and the massive beasts.

There was only one thing she did know.

They had obeyed her command.

CHAPTER 55
Magdalena

Magda let out a scream as her body was in free-fall, about to be skewered against the sharp rocks and debris. Her body picked up speed as she flew toward the water, and she tried to open her eyes against the wind, but to no avail.

The wind.

She needed the powers of the Spirit or else she would be dead. If there was any time to find the swirling red magic and harness the powers of the air, it needed to be now.

As she continued falling, Magda put her hands out in front of her, picturing the air particles in her mind. She had already manipulated water and earth, now she just had to bend air to her will. Maybe, she could slow her fall.

The plunge picked up speed, and the jagged shipwrecks were in view. Magda screamed once more, surging all her energy into her hands and concentrating on the wind around her. Power flew through her body, sending electrifying pain through her nerves and shooting out in all directions. A twist of red magic flickered in her palms.

She continued falling, faster and faster, until the wind forcefully beat up against her body in the opposite direction, and her fall slowed as if she was wearing an imaginary set of wings. Her descent steadied, and the crimson magic spiraled from her hands up her arms. The magic glowed with intensity, and the wind bent to her will.

At the last moment, Magda pulled upwards, missing the rocks by seconds. The soft mist of the ocean splayed against her face as a white wave crashed against the shore.

Magda let out an exhilarating scream of joy as the wind propelled her forward, taking her higher in the air. She was flying! Just like Junne had. And there was no stopping her.

When she got her bearings, she made a wide turn in the air, looking back up to where Eligor stood on the roof, but he had gone.

Then she spotted the main gate, which was now open. They were going to make their escape. Through the gate, inside the dark cove, she could see Ishani's ship—the Starway—with one of the sails in flames.

Kiran.

In her pursuit of the First Prince, Magda had entirely forgotten. The only reason Eligor had been released from his prison was because the magical locks had been broken, meaning Kiran had died.

What about Dagmara? Ravi? Odie? Were they safe?

What about Claude? She had left him in the tomb.

Quickly, Magda took flight in the direction of the Starway, hoping her friends were alive.

CHAPTER 56
Dagmara

Exiting the same way they came, Pierre and Dagmara struggled to pull Claude to safety.

"Let me," Martine intervened, once they were far enough away from the hounds.

Dagmara gratefully accepted her help, unable to hold Claude's weight any longer. Martine filled in, assisting Pierre in leading Claude to safety.

The Starway was in sight, their escape in reach. The large gate was open to allow free passage beyond. Ravi had succeeded, and Ishani hadn't left them behind.

Ishani had no need to leave anymore. Kiran was dead.

"Odie!" Dagmara commanded, her breathing heavy as rain pelted her face. "Go to Ishani!"

Odie barked before charging ahead, far faster than the quartet. She hoped it would be the signal Ishani needed to get the ship moving.

Martine and Pierre reached the wooden dock, hoisting Claude between them, with Dagmara just behind. They were only paces from the ship.

"Stop!" a voice shouted behind them. Glancing over her shoulder,

Dagmara saw three guards racing out the front gate to Dreadmarrow. She cursed under her breath.

"Get Claude back to the ship," Dagmara ordered.

"But—" Martine started to object.

"Now!" Dagmara demanded.

Both guards gave Dagmara a curt nod, obeying, and quickened their pace down the slick dock.

Turning around, Dagmara faced the trio of guards racing toward her. She withdrew her dagger and gripped a jasny bomb in the other hand. Her vision blurred, stars threatening to pull her unconscious. She had pushed her body too far. She was beyond exhausted.

Hold on a little longer. She pleaded, shaking her head in an attempt to refocus. Her heart slammed against her ribcage, and a ringing pierced her ears. But she had to hold them off so Claude made it to safety.

"Please," she begged under her breath, willing herself to fight longer. When the men were close enough, she shut her eyes and thrust the jasny bomb at their feet.

The crack of the vial ignited the bomb, and smoke flew up from the ground. Dagmara lunged forward at the first guard, driving her dagger into the soft spot under his helmet. But as she yanked her dagger free, the weight of the guard's body caused her to stumble. The world careened on its axis, and Dagmara fell to her knees, gasping for breath.

She had to stay awake. She had to. She had to protect the people she loved.

Jolting her head upright, Dagmara braced herself with her dagger outstretched, but the world around her had transformed.

The vibrant colors that once existed were muted grays and purples. All around her, she realized she had been transported to a translucent cavern, with violet-tinted walls. Through the walls, the world existed in subdued colors, as if she was examining it from afar through a gray lens.

Fear curled through Dagmara's stomach, and she shuffled back on the ground, desperate to escape the glass-like cage that imprisoned her. The ground seemed to mold under her weight, darkness grasping her body. The purple magic clung to her, like sticky quicksand that adhered to her skin. It glowed in an effervescent light, illuminating the inside of the space.

The two remaining guards were waving away the smoke from the jasny bomb.

"Where did she go?" one yelled. Their voices were muffled as if something was covering Dagmara's ears.

The other glanced at his dead comrade before returning his attention to the ship in the distance. "Doesn't matter, let's get to the ship."

"No!" Dagmara yelled, scrambling to her feet. She lunged at the first guard, driving the dagger through his armor. He didn't have a chance to fight back. Then she whirled on the next. It was as if he didn't see her coming. He didn't block himself, but rather stood frozen as she sliced his neck. He hit the ground beside the other two guards, lifeless and unmoving.

The darkness around Dagmara began to lift, the hues of Dreadmarrow returning to normal and the smoke clearing. The world around her was saturated with its normal color, and she could hear clearly again. She didn't have time to process what had occurred and raced toward the Starway.

The sails were already raised, ready to embark. Martine was waiting by the gangway, encouraging Dagmara to keep running. Nearly slipping on the slick wood, Dagmara tore across the path and landed on the ship deck. She collapsed once more onto her hands and knees, gasping for breath.

Martine retracted the gangway, calling to the crew, but Dagmara's head was spinning. The entire deck was coated in blood from the previous battle. Claude laid in the center of it, Ravi at his side, pressing various cloths against his wounds.

"Where's Magda?" Dagmara rasped.

"We are out of time," Martine said. "I'm sorry, but my duty is to you."

All around them, rocks fell from the top of the cavern smashing down into the water. Another boulder crashed down, hitting the deck and bending the wooden boards underneath its weight.

Dagmara wouldn't accept that for an answer. "We have to wait for Magda! Claude will die if we don't!" she yelled, but by the breeze of the wind, she could tell the ship was already moving.

"If we don't go, we'll sink," said Martine, reaching out for Dagmara's hands. "Ilusauri can't risk losing both its rulers."

Dagmara's heart sunk in her chest. She looked around, seeing Ishani in tears, still at Kiran's side. Pierre was on the upper deck, commanding the sailors and crew to heave off. They couldn't leave. She wouldn't leave Magda to die and condemn Claude to death. There had to be another way.

A shadow flashed overhead, and a silhouette loomed toward the boat. The figure approached at a rapid pace, flying toward them until Dagmara could make out the shape of a person. The person careened toward the deck, falling until her feet collided with the wood. She crashed into an ungraceful roll, landing on her side. She groaned in pain, unmoving for a brief moment.

Sitting upright, Dagmara held her dagger out once more.

Odie bounded over to the fallen stranger, barking happily and wagging his tail. He began licking the stranger's face until they sat upright.

"Magda?" Dagmara asked in awe as her best friend lifted her head from the deck.

"Yeah?" Magda replied, wincing as she struggled to her feet.

"Oh, thank the guardians!" Dagmara cried. She wanted to run and embrace her friend, but she knew they were nearly out of time. "Claude needs help!"

Magda snapped upright, seeing the king a few paces away. She was on her feet in seconds, racing to his aid. She brushed Pierre and Ravi aside, kneeling next to the king and summoning her Life Magic. Water levitated from the sea below them, lifting over the side of the broken railing and floating toward Magda's palms.

Keeping her distance, Dagmara remained on the ground. A sickness churned inside her, and she was afraid if she stood up again she would pass out.

"You can fly?" Pierre asked in awe, gazing at Magda in disbelief.

Magda didn't respond but focused on the magic in her palm, her eyes transforming from scarlet to ice blue as the new magic answered her call. "Eligor got away with the crown."

"We will find him," Ravi said, his relief at seeing Magda written all over his face.

Claude gasped, his eyes flying open. He sat upright, pressing his hands to his body as though he were looking for more wounds.

Sighing, Magda sat back on her heels. "I'm glad—"

Claude jerked his head in either direction. "Where's—" his voice stopped as his eyes traveled past Magda. His expression was indiscernible as he met Dagmara's. Everyone followed his gaze, and Magda let out a gasp.

"Dagmara, your eyes—" Magda stopped short, covering her mouth with her palm.

Dagmara shut her eyes tight, unable to look at their faces.

She knew. She had known since Viette's compulsion hadn't worked on her, but she hadn't admitted it to herself. At one point, she had thought she was a Life Guardian, but she was wrong. She was something else entirely.

Claude finished Magda's sentence, his voice hoarse. "They're violet."

Violet. The hue belonged to the fifth branch of magic—the branch of magic that had been trapped away with Eligor for centuries.

"I don't understand how," said Dagmara, her voice breaking. Regaining her courage, she opened her eyes once more, hoping they had returned to their natural shade of green. However, everyone stared at her blankly as though they didn't recognize her. Her heart shattered, feeling like an imposter in her own body. Tears pricked her eyes, and her entire being threatened to become undone.

"The Void," Claude exhaled, his voice shaking.

He had every right to be afraid of her. She now possessed the magic that had been haunting Claude for nearly a decade. When the tomb opened, and the return of Void magic spread into the world, it had returned to her, a blood descendent of the Void lineage.

She possessed the same magic as Eligor's family. Because she was a descendant of Eligor, just as her mother was.

The truth settled in Dagmara's bones, weighing her down.

She was a Void Guardian.

PART FOUR

The Void

CHAPTER 57
Dagmara

The ship sailed for Azurem. Dagmara sat on one of the cots, across from Martine. They were sharing the small cabin with one another, and the space felt smaller than before. Dagmara struggled to accept the weight of her new revelation...of her new identity.

She was a guardian. After all this time. But how?

Nausea ate at her core, a sickness deep in her chest.

Being a guardian was a concept she had wished for and thought of time and time again—but she never imagined it would be true. She never imagined she would be cursed with Void magic of all things. She knew nothing about what it meant to be a Void Guardian. That magic had been locked in the tomb for centuries. She had no guide. No assistance. No mentor. There was only one person that knew what it meant to be a Void Guardian.

Eligor.

She shuddered at the thought. She was his descendant. A descendant of the First Prince himself. That is why her mother was assassinated—because Eligor was determined to get rid of every last descendant and be the only heir to the Void lineage. But if Dagmara was a guardian...then Teos...

Teos.

Her heart lurched in her chest, sending a radiating pain through her ribcage. She clutched it, sucking in a ragged breath.

The cot across from her creaked as Martine shifted forward.

"I'm fine," Dagmara blurted out, just as Martine was opening her mouth. "I just...I need to be alone."

"His Majesty asked me to—"

"I don't care what Claude ordered you to do," Dagmara said, hearing the disdain in her voice too late. She bit her tongue, fighting back tears. "I'm sorry."

"It's alright. But I want you to know I'm not doing this because Claude asked me. I'm here because you're my friend."

Dagmara gave her a halfhearted smile. "You're a great friend," she said. "It isn't you, I simply don't want to talk to anyone right now. Not Magda, and not Claude."

The vivid image of Claude's face seared into her mind. The way he looked at her when her eyes were violet...it was the same expression he had given her the night of their wedding when he had discovered her true identity. She wasn't ready to face him. She wasn't going to persuade him to forgive her again. He had been haunted by Eligor and his magic for years, and now Dagmara was a Void Guardian. She wouldn't blame him if he wanted to call off the wedding.

"How about Odie?"

A laugh escaped Dagmara's lips. "Maybe later," she paused, before quietly continuing, "It doesn't make sense. How is it possible? You were there. The hounds never woke up around me in Nouchenne."

Martine swallowed, pausing. "That's because there was no Void magic—it was locked in the tomb. It didn't return to you until the tomb was open."

Dagmara couldn't even meet her gaze.

"What can I do for you?" Martine asked.

"Everything hurts," Dagmara replied under her breath. Her head, her health...her heart. She slipped under the covers. "I just need to rest." Rolling away from Martine, Dagmara faced the wall, pulling the blankets up to her chin. She squeezed her eyes shut, but her entire body was heavy, as though she were being dragged down by boulders. She had pushed her body to its limit emotionally and physically. She was exhausted but wide awake, hungry but too nauseous to eat, and cold but sweat beaded her lower back. She may have wielded a hint of magic, but she felt far from being a guardian. The more she analyzed the idea of the Void, the more fear built in her chest. The unknown frightened her. Her ancestor horrified her.

Anxiety built in her chest, threatening to swallow her whole. She attempted to lessen the pain, to steady her gasps, but she was lost.

She didn't hear the door open over her labored breathing. Muffled voices floated through the room before Dagmara jerked upright, her eyes wide. She could barely make out a shadow on the opposite side of the cracked door. Martine blocked the threshold with her whole body.

"She's sleeping," Martine whispered, but her voice was crisp with authority.

"I don't care, I need to see her."

"Come back later."

"She's my *wife*."

"And she doesn't want to see you."

"She—what?" There was a brief pause. "Martine, let me pass. I am still your king."

"And you assigned me to protect her," Martine replied. "So I am actually acting on your orders by preventing you from entering."

Claude exhaled sharply. "I will break down this door."

Martine glanced over her shoulder, making direct eye contact with Dagmara. By the guardians, was Dagmara grateful for Martine and the friendship between them. Her heart hammered against her chest. She wanted to see Claude, she wanted to fall into his embrace, but she didn't know what would happen when he walked through that door. She didn't understand the Void magic. Now that it was out of the tomb and in full effect, could she accidentally hurt him?

"Dagmara, please," Claude's voice rang through the room. "I know you're awake."

Dagmara nodded at Martine before she could change her mind. Martine obeyed, opening the door wide, and Claude barreled inside. He froze in the center of the small cabin, his gaze fixated on Dagmara, sitting on the bed with covers pulled over her knees. He held a tall glass in his hands, gripping it tightly.

"I'll be right outside," Martine said, slipping from the room and closing the door behind her.

Suddenly there was no air in the room to breathe.

"Claude," Dagmara said, but her voice was barely audible.

"Hi," he replied quietly, but his accent added a comforting tone to his voice. "I'm sorry, but I had to see you."

Dagmara nodded. "I'm just resting. It was all...a lot. Physically."

"Right," he replied. "But you came back for me. You saved me yet again. I wouldn't be here if it weren't for you."

"Well, we both wouldn't be here if..." her voice trailed off, leaving the unsaid words to linger in the air.

...if I wasn't able to control the hounds.

He cleared his throat before extending the glass toward her. "For you."

"Thank you," she said, accepting it. Her fingers grazed against his, and she jerked back as soon as she had a hold of the glass. Taking a sip, she savored how cold it was, letting it reinvigorate her health, even only minutely.

"And this," Claude added, reaching into his pocket and revealing a small box. He set it on the edge of the bed, removing the risk of their hands grazing again.

Curious, Dagmara reached forward and opened the box.

It was a single caramel square, doused in salt.

She smiled. "Thank you."

He rubbed the back of his neck, looking at the ground, then took a step closer. "How do you feel about all of this?"

"I think we should keep our distance," Dagmara blurted out.

He froze once more, inches from the bed.

She set the glass and the box down on the floor before folding her hands in her lap, unsure what to do. "I have magic now, and I have no idea what that means. I could be dangerous, and I don't want you anywhere near me."

Claude inclined his head. "When I first started to get my magic, my dad was already gone. I had no idea what I was doing. I had apparitions chasing me without realizing I created the illusions myself," he let out a soft laugh. "It was awful. I was all alone. And I refuse to let you go through it alone."

"There's no reason for you to pretend, Claude," Dagmara objected. "I saw the way you looked at me after you discovered I have magic. You were horrified."

"No, I..." Claude was at a loss for words once again. He finally cleared his throat before explaining, "I was surprised. Taken aback, yes, but never horrified." He met her gaze sincerely, letting the statement sink in.

"I have the same magic as Eligor," Dagmara said softly.

He nodded, but remained silent, letting her continue.

"You fell for me because I *wasn't* a guardian. Now I'm a different person entirely, and I don't even know who I am."

"Let me be clear," Claude stated, closing the distance between them. He took a seat at the edge of the bed, meeting her at eye level. "I didn't fall in love with you because you were or weren't a guardian. I fell for your wit, your loyalty, your smile, and so many other things I could list that have nothing to do with magic. I admit I was surprised when you displayed Void magic, but it doesn't change my feelings about you. Do you still love me?"

"Of course," she said, breathless.

Claude reached out and touched her cheek, tracing his thumb

against her skin. "Then nothing has changed. Even if your magic unleashes and tears down our world, I will gladly tear it down with you if it means we can be together."

A shudder tore through Dagmara's body. "I'm scared," she whispered.

"I know," Claude replied. "I was too, until I met you."

"I don't know what has awakened inside of me, and it's terrifying," she continued. "Nobody understands the Void except for Eligor. I don't know when I'll unleash something I can't control. I could be a monster."

"Then be a monster," he said, his hand falling from her cheek. His fingers skimmed her shoulder before tracing down her arm. "Rip me to shreds, tear me apart if you have to. But be *my* monster. We fight this world together. I am yours." He paused briefly, leaning toward her. The bed creaked underneath their weight. "You are mine, right?"

Reaching out, Dagmara grabbed the front of his shirt in her hands. "What did I do to deserve you?"

A rumble escaped his throat, and his hands flew to her hips. His fingers dug into her thin nightgown, causing her breath to catch in her throat. "I need you to answer me."

"Yes," she whispered, tugging him closer. "I'm yours. Your wife. Your monster."

His mouth collided with hers. A fire burned in her chest, traveling all the way through her body. Heat danced in her core, her need for him intensifying with every kiss.

She trailed her hands down the front of his chest, feeling his muscles underneath his thin shirt. Simultaneously, his hands roamed across her body, appreciating every curve.

He shifted closer on the bed, and she tugged him toward her by the bottom of his shirt. Resting her head against the pillow, she guided him closer. He broke the kiss, hovering over her, his hands on either side of her head.

"You should rest."

She bit her lip, wrapping the edge of his shirt in her fingers. "I don't want to."

He smiled. "I want you to be fully awake when I have you to myself."

"You have me now."

A soft laugh escaped his lips. "You don't think Martine and Pierre have their ears pressed against the door?"

Laughing, Dagmara wrapped her arms around Claude's neck. "Can you stay longer?"

"Oh, I'm not going anywhere." He pulled back the covers, sliding beside her. "Didn't you hear? This is my room now." Wrapping a single arm around her waist, he pulled her flush against his chest.

Heat danced in her stomach, a shudder tearing through her body at his touch. She placed one more kiss on his lips. "I like the sound of that."

She met his gaze, basking in his eyes until she saw the shift in his expression.

Her smile faded. "What's wrong?"

He traced his hand against her back absentmindedly. "I thought finding the tomb would save Ilusauri. After nearly a decade I finally found it—but I wasn't able to restore the magic to my land."

"Not yet," she corrected. "We will find a way."

"The only way is to get the crown and bring it back to the tomb." He exhaled, shutting his eyes. "I don't care what it takes. I need to restore Ilusauri."

"We will together," Dagmara assured. She placed a single hand on his cheek. Her thumb grazed over the ridge of his scar, though it was invisible to her eye. "We will save our people together."

He nodded before pulling her tighter against him, placing a gentle kiss on her forehead. They remained in each other's arms, but neither was able to fall asleep, the weight of the world and their kingdoms resting heavily on their shoulders.

CHAPTER 58
Magdalena

Azurem was close. There, they would reunite with Queen Bernadette and Reon, and decide together how they were going to take on Eligor. Claude sent an officer back to Ilusauri as a messenger via a cargo ship, letting his guard know to await his orders on any future plans.

The entire plan had failed. They had not succeeded in trapping Eligor, restoring any magic to the lands, or getting the crown. And above all, Kiran had been killed.

Misery tore through Magda's body, feeling responsible for everything that had happened at Dreadmarrow. She kept replaying the events on a continuous loop in her head, wondering if there had been another way, but each time, all her mind focused on was Kiran's lifeless body, cold on the deck.

A few days into the journey back to Azurem, they held a small funeral at sea, each reciting their own personalized messages to provide blessings to Kiran as she became one of the stars. Then, they placed homemade lanterns on the water, decorated with flowers suitable for a Soul Guardian. The lanterns mirrored the twinkling lights of the sky.

The evening of the funeral, Ishani stood at the helm of the ship, staring at the black sea. Magda approached the guild captain slowly, standing next to her in silence, as they watched the sun sink against the pink and orange sky. Time passed minute by minute, and the only sound that could be heard was the cool breeze whipping against the sails.

"I'm so sorry," Magda finally said.

Ishani's throat choked up. She remained in silence for a long moment, before she said, "Getting up today was the hardest, knowing that it was the day of the funeral. Everything feels more finite, like she really isn't coming back..."

Magda didn't speak, waiting for Ishani to continue.

"...At the same time, it doesn't feel real. It's as if I'm on another trip at sea, and when I get back to Flaustra, she'll be there, waiting to see me when I return."

"I can't believe she's gone either."

"She didn't deserve this," said Ishani. "She was always the kind one, doing things for others. Why couldn't it have been me?"

"You can't change who she was, and why they targeted her," Magda offered, knowing nothing she could say would make anything better.

Ishani turned to Magda. "Laying my sister to rest is like ripping out a part of me. I don't know how I can ever be the same. I don't know how I can even get through another day. Without her, who do I have left?"

"You have us," said Magda firmly. Magda slid her hand over the railing, almost touching Ishani's, but stopped. "No one can replace Kiran, but I'm going to be here for you, every day. For me, there's a wound in my heart that I know will never heal. We'll always think of our siblings, but hopefully the passing of time will make it a little less painful."

"I know," said Ishani, "I've lost so many others, but this is different. It was my one duty to protect her, and I failed."

"I hope you don't blame me," said Magda, "I hope we're going to be okay, you and I."

Ishani shook her head. "I don't know, the pain is too much right now."

"Just know I'm sorry."

"You've done enough, Magda," snapped Ishani, "but I'm the one that should have had better judgment, for the both of us. I should have never agreed to go to Dreadmarrow. I should have kept Kiran far away from everyone."

"I understand," said Magda.

"In the end, Eligor's assassins are the reason that Kiran is dead. Not you."

Magda let the words sink in.

"If anything, you're the one person that understands," Ishani added. She continued watching the still waves that lapped underneath the sunset. "But now Flaustra has lost both its rulers in a matter of weeks. There's no one else."

"There's you," Magda smiled. "If there's anyone that could bring the guilds and the royal courts together, it's you."

"Maybe," Ishani wiped her eyes. "I always was the strong one. But I was strong for Kiran, and now, I don't know if I have any strength left. I don't know how I'm going to go on."

"It's okay. You don't have to be strong right now," said Magda, "You just have to let yourself grieve." Her fingers grazed against Ishani's, and they held hands for a brief minute, looking out at the waves.

Then Ishani let out an ear-deafening scream. Her fingers flew to her cheek, pressing the skin as if she was in pain. Ishani's gaze circled the sky, searching for an imaginary threat. Then she grabbed both of her axes, swinging them out in front of her, as if she was fighting off an invisible attacker.

"Ishani, what's wrong!?" Magda cried.

The sailors posted around the ship rushed to their captain's aid, but they held their weapons in all directions, also searching for the source of danger.

Ishani continued thrashing with all her might, letting out grunts of anger as she swiped at the air. "Help me! This bird is attacking me."

Ishani shouted again and stumbled back, her hand flying to her neck.

Magda scanned the deck, but there were no outlines of birds against the sky. But she had seen this behavior before. Dagmara, Claude, and Reon could all see the bird, and now, so could Ishani.

The officers ran in all directions, until the ship was in pandemonium as they sought out the attacker that Ishani had alerted them to.

Ishani threw one of her axes across the clearing, and then the other. Then, she dove at Magda, pulling her to the ground. "Get down!" she screamed. Ishani covered her head, before looking back up.

When Ishani was completely still, Magda rolled over. "Are you alright?" Magda asked.

Ishani sat upright. "It's gone. The blackbird."

"I still didn't see it," confessed Magda.

"I never saw it before either."

"It's Eligor's pet," said Magda.

"Why can I see it now?" asked Ishani.

Magda shook her head. "I don't know," she admitted. There was so much she still didn't know.

When the Starway docked in Azurem, Magda summoned two nondescript carriages to conceal her and her friends and escort them to the fortress. Magda didn't want to take any chances and wait for a royal escort, especially with Eligor, Sabien, and Viette still alive. Throughout the multiple-day journey to the Azuremi fortress, all

Magda could think about was where Eligor had gone, and how she was going to take his crown.

She remembered seeing him tempt Junne with the magic, almost appointing her as a new blood-line guardian for Celestaire. And he had done it all with his powerful crown. If she could take him by surprise, maybe she could attempt to steal the crown, but she had no idea where Eligor was. There was no doubt he believed he had pushed Magda to her death, for she hadn't heard a single word from him since their confrontation.

Magda peered outside the carriage as they traversed over Azuremi territory. As far as the eye could see were dried up rivers, and shriveled flowers dotted their banks. Frozen ponds had melted completely, leaving gaping, parched holes in their absence. The rotting smell of dead fish and animals, due to lack of water, hung in the air. At every curve in the path, gravestones dotted the edge of the forests, marked with colored pieces of wood.

"This looks just like Ilusauri when I arrived," Dagmara said.

Magda snapped back into reality. She sat next to Ravi in the carriage, while Dagmara and Ishani sat opposite them. Odie was at their feet, curled up on their shoes.

"The land is dying," Magda agreed.

"It's been years since Claude's parents died, but here it's only been months."

"The world is without its guardians. Maybe with more of them dead, it speeds up the world dying?"

They all looked at each other in confusion, but Ishani's thoughts were lost elsewhere as she stared out the opposite window of the carriage.

"You still have Laila's research, right?" Magda asked Ravi.

"Here," he patted the knapsack on his side. Magda grinned, for he was getting slightly better at understanding her Azuremi.

"We'll give it to the royal apothecaries," said Dagmara. "If there is a way as you said to make the medication for zowach stronger, we have to save our people."

Ravi nodded.

"And...can I get that page with the concoction for my symptoms?"

He hesitated, until Magda translated for him. Then he nodded briskly, tearing a single piece of paper from the journal and handing it to Dagmara who swiftly pocketed the recipe.

Then Ravi turned away from Dagmara and met Magda's gaze, speaking in Flaustran. "I know this is going to be a lot for you, seeing your mom again and being home. I know you're going to have a million duties. So if you need space...," Ravi reached across to grab her hand.

"No, I don't want space," said Magda. "I want you to spend time with my mom and with me. To meet the others in court. I'd sincerely like to know if you like Azurem."

"I'd like that too," Ravi smiled.

The fortress came into view, with its red-colored stones and pastel banners waving in the wind. However, instead of being greeted by the sound of rushing water, the air was eerily silent. Their entourage rolled up to the front gate of the fortress, before entering the small courtyard.

As soon as Magda opened the carriage door, Odie bounded out. He barked and leapt across the courtyard, running up to distract the knights. Magda stepped out next, followed by Dagmara, Ravi, and Ishani.

Claude, Martine, and Pierre exited the next carriage.

"Magda!" Queen Bernadette was running across the courtyard with open arms for her daughter.

"Mom!" Magda exclaimed.

Bernadette grabbed Magda forcefully, pulling her into a tight hug. Tears welled in her eyes as she yelled, "Don't you do this to me ever again!"

"I'm so sorry," Magda said, fighting back tears.

Bernadette held her daughter for another long moment, before she looked Magda straight in the eye, placing her arms on Magda's shoulders.

"What in the world were you thinking?!" Bernadette asked. "Sending Dagmara in your place to marry Claude? Running off to Flaustra?"

"I know," said Magda, "It was a stupid plan."

"You should have come to me."

"I didn't want to worry you."

"I couldn't have been more worried than I possibly have over the past few months!" yelled Bernadette. "I found out you had Soul magic, then I thought you were dead, and I constantly imagined the absolute worst!"

Magda had no more words. She couldn't justify her actions to her mother, and all she wanted was to rewind time, back to when her entire family was alive and when she didn't have to face the world's problems. But she knew there was no going back now.

Bernadette moved to hug Dagmara. "Dagmara, you're alive! I was so worried when you went missing the night of the wedding."

"I'm happy to see you too," Dagmara replied, her words muffled by the hug.

Pulling away, Bernadette found Claude.

"Thank you," she said, but the intensity in her gaze held many more unsaid words. "You can stay here as long as you need. I do hope to hear everything that transpired over dinner."

"Thank you for opening your doors to us," Claude said. "These are my guards, Martine and Pierre." He gestured to both of them in turn. Martine gave a curt nod, while Pierre waved.

Bernadette snapped at a nearby knight. "I need rooms ready, now."

The knight obeyed swiftly, going to retrieve the other servants.

"Captain Ishani!" Bernadette acknowledged the Flaustran

princess next. "It has been too many years since we last met. I'm so glad to see you, and I feel terrible about your family."

Ishani nodded. "My condolences to yours," she said, her voice breaking off.

"Your Majesty," Dagmara interrupted. "Excuse me, but I need to see Teos."

"He's not in the fortress," said Bernadette. "He went to Gorzhelm. There are a few villagers there trying to help those struggling with zowach, for it's the only town left with access to water. I fear the illness has only gotten worse."

Dagmara's face paled. "I'll go there now," she said. She glanced at Claude, not having to ask out loud.

"I'll go with you," he confirmed.

Without waiting another moment, she turned and departed, her pace brisk. Claude walked beside her, with both Pierre and Martine on their heels.

The knights finally arrived to escort everyone inside, but with the Ilusaurians off to Gorzhelm, Ishani was the only one left. She followed the knights into the fortress, leaving behind only Magda and Ravi with the queen. When Odie saw that most of the group was leaving, he darted back and forth, zooming around the courtyard at top speed and greeting every servant, who promptly squatted down to pass him treats and play with Magda's pet.

Magda approached her mother once more. "Mom, this is Ravi."

"Your Majesty," Ravi said in broken Azuremi, taking a small bow.

"Nice to meet you," said Bernadette, before snapping to another one of her servants. "Show him to his rooms."

"Actually, mom," Magda said, "he'll stay in my suite."

"Oh." Bernadette raised her eyebrows. Bernadette gave one look at Ravi, and then looked back at Magda, as understanding passed behind her eyes. "Magda, a word." She took Magda by the hand, pulling her in the direction of the fortress while Ravi waited by the carriages. "What happened between you and Claude?"

"The marriage is being annulled."

Bernadette inclined her head. "I understand the heart is a complicated thing, but think about the kingdom."

"I am," said Magda. "He said he'll honor the trade agreements. I don't want to marry him, mom. I think part of the reason I ran to Flaustra was to avoid my responsibilities. I didn't feel like I deserved to be Azurem's princess without the guardian magic. But now I am putting the kingdom first. I need to be here, not in Ilusauri." She paused, before adding, "Besides, Dagmara and Claude are in love, and I've never been happier for anyone else in the whole world."

"Well, regardless, I'm glad he agrees to honor the trade agreements. Without his medicine, we'd already be wiped out."

"How bad is it?" Magda asked.

"Almost the entire population under the age of twelve has been infected from zowach. A third of the teenagers. The other illnesses are also increasing in intensity, thankfully none as atrocious as zowach, though."

"I think I have something that could help," said Magda. "It's a journal of medicinal research from friends in Flaustra. Actually, from Ravi. I'll ask the royal translators to create an exact copy in Azuremi."

Bernadette shook her head. "Magda, right now, all I can think about is that you're alive and here in front of me." Her mother hugged her once more, stroking Magda's hair and brushing it behind her ear.

"I missed you so much," Magda replied.

"Never do that to me again."

"I won't."

Bernadette pulled away. "I'm serious. The grounds around the fortress are not safe. Besides the infection, the mountains are filled with ferocious beasts and chasms that have killed thousands. They were dormant before, but as of a week or so ago they're awake and vicious. We've tried our best to send knights to deter the attacks, but we are only losing more men."

"They're awake?" Magda clarified. "It must be because the Void was released when Eligor escaped..."

A soft gasp escaped the queen's lips. "It can't be..."

And like that, Magda poured out the entire story to her mother as fast as she could while still providing details. Her mother needed to know what Azurem was up against so that she could prepare the knights as well as the townspeople. She told her about Flaustra, the death of Queen Sanyal, their time in Celestaire, and finally, their near-scrape with death at Dreadmarrow.

Bernadette only interrupted a few times to ask questions.

"I'll take what I can to our advisors and knights right away," said Bernadette, before escorting Magda back toward the carriages. "Take the journal to the apothecary. I'll have the royal translators meet you there. A new shipment of medicine just arrived from Ilusauri. We must stop this illness before it's too late."

Magda nodded, and both mother and daughter crossed back to the carriages where Ravi was waiting.

Suddenly Bernadette ran to Ravi and embraced him in a hug. "Thank you so much for taking care of my daughter."

Ravi held his hands away from Bernadette, unsure whether it was appropriate to hug the queen, but finally settled into the embrace. He gave Magda an awkward smile over Bernadette's shoulder, and Magda smiled back at him.

Ravi replied, "You're welcome, Your Majesty."

CHAPTER 59
Dagmara

The cobblestone path to Gorzhelm was a mystery to Dagmara. She had traversed these streets nearly every night on one of her missions. But it looked entirely different to her now, and it wasn't only because of the broad daylight. Claude walked beside her, Martine and Pierre a pace behind, but they faded into the distance. Dagmara could only think of Teos.

The once familiar pastel blue and pink flags that lined the streets were foreign to her. She could feel her dagger strapped to her belt and her throwing stars lining her corset, but she still didn't feel as though she belonged.

She could see the town in view, simply past the bridge that led over the rapids. The bridge contained its own memories. She would never forget the night she had stabbed a blade into Sabien's chest and shoved him over the edge. If only she had killed him that night. If only she had waited to watch him take his last breath as opposed to pushing him into the water that inevitably healed him. Could she have changed history? Or would the other assassins have still made it to the coronation and killed Bogdan and Aleksy? How would life be different if that day had been?

Her legs pushed her faster, and her throat restricted as she bit back tears. She had pushed herself to the brink of exhaustion, but it was Teos that kept her going. It had always been for him.

Claude found her hand and interlaced his fingers with hers. She gave him a smile, thankful for his silent support.

She entered town and was surprised by the commotion. Villagers crossed left and right in a bustle of activity, and a cacophony of sounds and smells accompanied them. Many townspeople sat on the ground, their backs leaning against the houses as they coughed. Some were unmoving. Multiple people crossed back and forth, bringing drops of water or herbs to those suffering most. What had happened to Azurem in her absence?

"Teos!" Dagmara called, though her voice couldn't be heard over the commotion.

A man bumped into her absentmindedly, muttering an apology as he continued on. Then she noticed the blood. Claw marks raked down his back, leaving behind a torn shirt and caked, crimson liquid. The hounds. These weren't just sick individuals. These were men and women seeking shelter after their towns had been destroyed by the rifts.

With Eligor and the Void released, the hounds had fully awoken. They didn't need to sense nearby magic to attack. They were prowling out there, killing anyone and anything in their path.

Dagmara had to stop it.

But first, she had to find the one person she had done all of this for in the first place.

She turned to the three people beside her. "He has blonde hair and a crutch," she said, rushed. "He's here somewhere."

They nodded in turn before she pushed her way forward. She shoved through the villagers, uncaring. Calling his name, she continued slithering through the crowd, ignoring the rancid smell and the horror around her. Claude and the two Ilusaurian guards struggled to keep up with her pace but never lost sight of her. At this moment, she only cared about one person.

She saw the crutch first. The simple wooden beam supporting him.

Everything went still as she skidded to a halt. Her throat constricted. Her heartbeat stopped.

As though he could sense her presence, he slowly lifted his chin, rotating in her direction. He awkwardly held a canteen out to another villager, but then his movements froze. His blonde hair flopped on his head and his curls twisted in his face. He was thinner, his cheeks hollow from the illness, but his pale cheeks brightened as his gaze settled on his sister.

"Dagmara!" he cried, dropping the canteen from his hand. It clattered to the ground, forgotten.

Her breath hitched, tears meeting her eyes. "Teos!"

She ignored the three people she was with, taking off through the crowd. She raced forward as her brother limped toward her. She collided against him, embracing him in a tight hug. His arms wrapped around her. He swayed slightly on his one good leg, but she kept him upright.

Other nearby villagers shot glances in their direction, followed by longing smiles. It was no doubt that Dagmara and Teos looked like siblings reunited after a hound attack. In a way, that is what it felt like to her.

Dagmara clung to her brother, closing her eyes tightly as she buried her face in his messy hair. She had done it. She had gone to Ilusauri for medication to save Teos and returned home.

"You're here!" he cried, breaking off into a disbelieving laugh.

"You're alive!" she exclaimed, squeezing him tighter.

"Of course I am—but I won't be much longer if you strangle me."

"Sorry, sorry!" Dagmara pulled back and held him by the shoulders. "I'm sorry it took me so long to get back here. I tried I—"

"Sis," Teos laughed, his boyish grin revealing two dimples. "I knew you'd come back."

"You weren't worried?"

"I didn't say that." He rolled his eyes, refusing to admit anything out loud.

"Are you...taller?"

He shrugged. "Maybe you shrunk."

"Mhmm," she replied flatly. Dagmara noted his eyes were still pink, and there was a gruffness to his voice that she didn't remember.

"What are you doing out here?"

"I'm trying to help people," said Teos. "Ilusauri's medicine isn't the save-all it used to be. We thought it would help immediately but it hasn't. The disease must be stronger now."

"But you're sick too."

Teos dropped his voice to a whisper. "I have the nice amenities of the fortress. Food, warmth, a clean bath. Everyone out here...they don't have anything."

A pain radiated in Dagmara's chest. He only had the safety of the fortress because she had chosen to be an assassin for King Bogdan, following in her mother's footsteps. But now, Magda had set her free from her position. Somehow, she still had to find a way to provide for Teos.

"I know how to help you. I met a man from Flaustra who has experimented with mixing medicines with other herbs. He healed his sister, and it will work for you too."

Teos inclined his head, letting out a chuckle. "You don't ever stop, do you?"

A laugh escaped Dagmara's lips, and she shoved him on the shoulder. "Be glad I'm so paranoid about your safety. You aren't."

He shrugged. "One of us has to be the fun one."

"And I found this." She unraveled the piece of paper from her pocket and handed it to her brother. "It may help...me."

Teos skimmed the paper, his brow furrowing as he struggled to make out the medications in the Flaustran language. He met her gaze. "I can't read this," he replied, "but it's worth a try. We will get to the bottom of whatever you have." He gave her a gentle smile, a dimple reappearing on his cheek.

"Thank you for always believing me, even when the nurses said I was making it up."

His cheeks turned pink. "Yeah, whatever," he said, trying to suppress a smile. Then his gaze traveled over her shoulder.

Reading the surprise on his face, she whirled around to see Claude, Martine, and Pierre. Claude's head was inclined slightly, his hands folded behind his back. His clothing pulled at the seams, defining every contour of his body.

"Oh sorry," Dagmara blurted out. She turned back to Teos. "This is Claude, and my friends Martine and Pierre."

"Hi," Martine said warmly. Pierre awkwardly waved.

"Hello, Teos," Claude said, brushing past a villager to step closer.

Teos was silent, staring up at the king. His grasp tightened on his crutch. "King Mirage. I know who you are."

"Teos," Dagmara scolded under her breath. "Claude, this is my brother."

A gentle smile formed on Claude's face. "I've heard a lot about you. All good things."

"I've...heard a lot about you too," Teos muttered. "Not all good things, admittedly. Why are you here?"

"I arrived on the ship from Dreadmarrow."

"No...why are you *here*? Not at the fortress?" Teos insisted.

"I was accompanying my wife," Claude replied. His voice was so gentle, it took Teos a moment to process the statement. Teos jerked his head to Dagmara.

"Does he know or should I tell him?" Teos asked.

"He knows I'm not Magda," replied Dagmara. "That marriage is over, and we...," she took Claude's hand in her own, "are staying together."

Teos was quiet for a moment, pursing his lips as he looked at Dagmara and Claude in turn.

Then he laughed, blurting out, "Way to epically fail your mission."

Dagmara glowered at him.

"I know you mean a lot to Dagmara," Claude intervened. "I'm hoping we can...become friends."

Teos raised an eyebrow high on his head. "Do you play cards?"

"I'm a fast learner."

"Maybe friends are in the future," Teos shrugged. "We will see how you treat my sister. Then I'll decide."

Claude nodded. "Fair enough."

"And who are you two?" Teos asked, nodding at the guards. "Martine and Pierre, you say?"

"I'm His Majesty's first guard," Pierre replied with a smile.

Martine's expression was calm. "And I'm your sister's."

Teos pursed his lips. "You know my sister doesn't need an escort?"

Dagmara's cheeks turned bright red. She opened her mouth to reply when a loud bang reverberated through the village. Screams lit the area, and everyone turned to face the commotion. The wheel of a wagon snapped off, collapsing it to the side. A young child had his foot caught underneath the wood, yelling in pain.

As gasps scattered through the villagers, Dagmara started forward, but Claude was already moving as swiftly as lightning. He barreled through the townspeople, Martine and Pierre directly behind him. The King of Ilusauri lunged for the bottom of the wagon, piled high with crates, and attempted to lift it.

"Help!" he called, summoning other men to assist him and the Ilusaurian guards.

A stranger clobbered into Teos's side, running to get a better look at the scene. Dagmara caught him before he lost a hold on his crutch.

"Come on, they can handle that," Dagmara said. "Let's get out of the way."

Teos nodded, following Dagmara's lead as they pushed against the commotion. Slipping off the main street, they disappeared into an alley. Teos steered them directly to a stack of crates.

"So, what do you want to tell me?" Teos asked, raising an eyebrow as he plopped down on the wood.

He knew her too well.

As Dagmara watched him intently, she couldn't imagine that the same blood ran in his veins. He had Void magic too. Had Teos felt anything when the tomb opened? Or was he too young to channel magic?

"Actually..." Dagmara started, sitting beside him and easing her dizziness. "You're right."

"I know," he said. "So?"

She exhaled, steadying her breathing. The yells and cries from the villagers were only yards away, but she still lowered her voice as she explained, "The stories of the First Prince are real. After I got your letter in Celestaire, I went to Dreadmarrow to try and reseal the locks on his tomb."

"You did what?!" Teos blurted out.

"We all thought it could work," she admitted, "but his assassins were faster than us. They killed the last Soul Guardian, and the First Prince was released from a magical tomb."

"I knew something was wrong!" Teos insisted. "Monsters are climbing out of the rifts. It's awful. It's him, isn't it? The stories are true? He's evil and trying to take over the world?"

"More or less," Dagmara muttered. "There's more. When he was released, the fifth branch of magic that was dead for centuries also returned."

"The Void." Teos nodded. He cleared his throat, hiding a cough. "I read about it in some of the books Bernadette let me search, but there's not that much information out there."

"Yes, well...when the Void was released from the tomb, it returned to the lineage who had once controlled that branch of magic—back when the First Prince was alive."

"I thought the First Prince killed his siblings? Didn't he end the lineage?"

"I'm sure he had cousins," she said. "I supposed it was carried down through one of them. And now...I...exhibited this magic—Void magic." She hesitated, but couldn't stop herself in the middle of the confession. "And if I am a Void Guardian, then you are too."

Her brother stared at her blankly, and a silence spread between them. The distant bustle of the townspeople and the rushing rapids were the only sound for what felt like an eternity.

Then Teos burst out into a laugh. "Congratulations, you found a sense of humor out there in the world."

Her face was still. "I'm not joking."

"Well, I don't believe you."

"Why would I lie about something like this?" she snapped.

Teos slammed his palm on the crate. "Guardians can't be sick, Dagmara."

She jumped at the intensity in his voice, her body tensing.

"You really think magic was dormant in our veins? *Ours?*" He shook his head. "No, we are the farthest people from guardians."

His zowach, her chronic illness, none of it made sense. Weren't guardians supposed to be perfect? His fall at the cliffs was a different story, but everything Dagmara knew about guardians was crumbling around her.

Maybe they weren't perfect. Maybe she could change what it meant to be a guardian. Maybe guardians were just as imperfect and troubled as the next person.

A shadow passed at the end of the alley. Dagmara looked up to see Martine there, but upon recognizing Dagmara was safe, Martine made herself scarce once more. As soon as she was gone, Dagmara continued.

"Listen," Dagmara started, calming her voice. "I don't understand it either. It must be because the magic was dormant, and for a time, we were like everyone else. With the opening of the tomb, the magic has returned to our lineage."

Shaking his head, Teos looked away from his sister.

"Have you experienced anything...weird the past few days?"

"Weird?" Teos muttered. "Azurem is dying. Magical hounds are running around. Define weird."

"You," Dagmara insisted. "Anything different with you?"

"Just some medication side effects. I'm sick, remember?" He shot her a look, the redness in his eyes apparent against his pale skin.

"Side effects?" she urged.

"Dagmara—" he stopped short before letting out a sigh. "Look, I'm not going to discount that you wielded Void magic. If you say it happened, then I believe you. But I'm fifteen. Even if I'm also a guardian, I shouldn't be able to experience any magic until later, right?"

Dagmara shrugged. "Aleksy was able to use Life magic when he was young."

Teos's eyes snapped to his sister's. Aleksy's name created a blanket of grief between them. Then Teos pressed his fingers to the bridge of his nose. "'*This is what the guardians ordained for us.*'" Teos muttered, mimicking a higher-pitched voice.

Dagmara knew that line like the back of her hand. It was what echoed in her head every time Sabien had tortured her.

Be brave. Be selfless. Be loyal.

She was unable to speak, remembering the serum. It was Teos who filled the silence.

"When mom said that I had no idea she meant our own ancestors."

Dagmara found her voice. "I don't know if mom knew she was from that lineage."

"I understand you want to keep a perfect image of mom in your mind, but she knew she was part of the Void lineage." Teos paused, letting the words sink in.

"How?" Dagmara asked. "She wouldn't have had magic. The Void magic was locked away. No one has had Void magic since the time of the First Prince, even if they were descendants. I...am the first."

"She must have known her lineage was important," Teos argued. "It's the only thing that makes sense. Mom had no family. Her sister? Dead. Our grandparents? Dead. I don't think mom was the first one in our family that had been assassinated."

A sickening acceptance settled in Dagmara's bones. The thought had crossed her mind, of course. It had a million times. She spoke her thoughts, "A Life assassin was sent to kill her, not because she worked for the Azuremi throne, but because she was a guardian. Then, that assassin killed two kids in Frostmere—thinking they were us."

"Mom saved us." His brow was drawn in concern.

"And made the assassin think he exterminated the last of the Void lineage," she continued. Her heart began to pound against her ribcage. "The First Prince doesn't know we exist."

Teos scoffed. "I didn't even know we existed..." his voice softened, and Dagmara could sense him closing off.

She swallowed, before rising from the crate. "Let me get the others, and we will head back to the fortress. Alright?"

Teos nodded, giving her a smile that didn't reach his eyes.

Exiting the alley, Dagmara instantly noticed Martine leaning against the wall, only a few paces from where she was talking to her brother.

"Did you hear that?" Dagmara asked.

"Only if you wanted me to," Martine replied.

"I don't want to believe my mom was Eligor's descendant any more than Teos does," Dagmara replied. "Where's Claude?"

Martine nodded to the opposite side of the road before leading Dagmara. They pushed through a few villagers, cautious of those with injuries, as they reached the broken wagon.

The boy that was trapped underneath it was propped up against the wall. He couldn't be older than seven years old. His legs were extended in front of him, one twisted at an awkward angle and the shin bone protruding from his skin. He was screaming, clutching onto an elderly man as tears streamed down his face.

"It's coming out of my skin!" the boy cried, staring at his shin with wide eyes.

Claude was kneeling in front of the young boy. "It will be alright," he said softly. "My guard is going to find someone to help."

"B-But—"

"It's alright Henryk," the elderly man holding the boy said, trying to hold him still.

"Henryk, look," Claude told the boy, gesturing to his shin. In one soft move of his palm, the bone returned to the young boy's shin, the skin closing around the gaping wound.

The elderly man gasped, while Henryk calmed. "It...It still hurts," he stammered.

"A doctor is coming," Claude repeated. "But it's getting better already."

Henryk nodded, his brow beading with sweat, tears continuing down his face. "How did you fix it?"

The elderly man's mouth was agape. "You..."

"The doctor is here!" Pierre yelled, rushing back into the scene with a woman directly behind him. The woman dropped to the ground, unfolding a kit.

"I don't understand," the doctor said. "Where is the injury?"

"Henryk, look away now," Claude ordered.

Henryk nodded, burying his face in the elderly man's shoulder. Claude removed the illusion, and everyone else who had begun to watch the scene gasped in unison. A scream pierced the air, before a few villagers scattered away from the Mad King.

Rising to his feet, Claude backed away, turning and halting when he met Dagmara's gaze. His face was indiscernible, but he paid no mind to the townspeople running from him.

She extended her hand toward him, and he went to meet her. Before their fingers grazed, one villager intercepted them, slamming her hands against Claude's chest.

"Please," she cried. "Mad King, compel my pain away!"

Claude's brow furrowed, and he recoiled at her touch. "No."

"I'm begging you!"

"I don't use compulsion for that."

"That's enough," Dagmara said, cutting into the conversation. She slipped right between Claude and the woman, intervening.

The woman jerked back, her face aghast. "Please, Mad King!"

Her cry alerted others who hadn't witnessed the illusion on Henryk's leg. Dozens of eyes turned on them.

"Time to go." Dagmara grabbed Claude's hand, yanking him out of the center of the road. Pierre and Martine flanked them on either side as they dashed toward the alley. Pushing past villagers, they raced off the main street and into the shadows of the side street.

Then Dagmara froze. Claude's chest collided against her back at the sudden movement, before his body went taut.

"Teos?" she called.

He was nowhere in sight. An unease crept into her, her stomach churning in fear.

"Teos!"

"Are you sure he was right here?" Pierre asked.

"Maybe he went back to the fortress," Martine suggested.

Dagmara was already running. She raced down the alley, cutting back to the fortress. The quartet charged toward the edge of town, disappearing from the commotion in the process. She looped back onto the main street once the mass of villagers were behind them. Rounding the corner, the bridge back to the fortress came into view.

She skidded to a halt, gasping. Claude and the two guards followed her lead, coming to a standstill.

There were two figures on the bridge. Teos was on his feet, utilizing his crutch for support. Meanwhile, a large man towered over

Teos. They were talking cordially, Teos gesturing toward the fortress with wide arms. The stranger's back was to Dagmara, but she would recognize him anywhere. His broad stature—his dark hair and tan complexion.

A chill seeped into her bones. "Teos!" she called, racing forward. She cleared the few yards between them, and Claude followed. She stepped onto the bridge, her footsteps alerting the duo.

The man whirled around. "Oh, hello lovebirds," he said, his baritone voice melodic.

Sabien Renaud.

CHAPTER 60
Magdalena

Magda and Ravi reached the apothecary a few minutes later. It was an expansive room with a series of tables for scientists and doctors spaced throughout it. The walls were covered by wooden bookshelves, and candles were interspersed on their ends. Being back in the Azuremi fortress had overwhelmed Magda with emotion, whether it was relief or sorrow, she still didn't know.

The younger servants had begged Magda to play with Odie, and she agreed. At Magda's request, they took the dog inside to bathe him before getting him proper food to eat, and then they promised to play fetch with him in the courtyard.

Inside the apothecary, Magda crossed to one of the laboratory tables, Ravi following close behind, before spreading the journal out on the table. Around the table were bottles of smierc, and Magda knew it was here that Dagmara and Teos crafted their potions and explosives.

"Your mom said the royal translators are on their way, right?" Ravi asked.

"Yes, but I can't wait. I need answers now. I have to do something," Magda said. Frantically, she grabbed a fresh piece of paper, a quill pen, and ink. Then she leaned down on the table on her forearms, beginning the translations and carefully copying the notes from Flaustran to Azuremi.

Ravi crossed to stand next to her and picked up the journal, "At least let me read it to you, and you can write it down in Azuremi."

Magda nodded. "The faster I get this translated, the faster they can work on a cure." She wrote quickly, listening to the comfort of Ravi's voice. The time ticked by slowly, until her hand cramped from the pain of gripping the quill. She refilled the ink bottle twice, then three times, then once more.

Then she stopped writing, as pain clutched her chest.

"What's wrong?" Ravi asked, noticing her hesitation.

"I...," Magda said, as the grief hit her like a brick wall. "Being back at the fortress," she started, struggling to find the words. Her voice quivered as she said, "It's strange with my dad and Aleksy not here."

Ravi grew somber. "I'm so sorry."

"It seems so long ago, but at the same time it feels like it was yesterday." She paused, and then continued, "They were good people and loved by so many. I wish you could have met them."

"I wish that too," said Ravi. "I would give anything for that to be possible. But I am glad to have met your mom."

"She likes you," Magda grinned, "but be prepared for one hundred questions later."

"I'm the master of questions," Ravi laughed, "my mom didn't have any for you. She practically acted like we had been together for years."

"Sometimes it feels like that," Magda grinned.

Ravi raised his eyebrows.

"In a good way!" Magda giggled. Then she said softly, "You must miss your family too."

"I do," Ravi admitted. "I really hope they're alright. It's hard picturing my life without them, you know?"

"I understand," said Magda, the mood feeling heavy again.

Ravi reached out and lifted her chin to meet his. "All this loss won't be easy. And I'm sure you'll experience more of it as a queen, but you're the strongest person I know. Just promise me you won't give up."

She placed her hands on his chest and stared into Ravi's eyes. In all of this, Ravi had been her constant, despite the murders, the magic, and the First Prince. He was the one person that remained her sanctuary.

"Just don't let me go," she said.

"I'll never let you go," he said. "I'll hold you through the night, so you can finally have an ounce of sleep without the First Prince haunting your thoughts." He brushed his fingers against her cheek, before kissing her on the forehead.

Magda desperately wished she could pause the moment. She wanted to remain in Ravi's embrace, his warmth, and not have to worry about the weight or responsibilities of the world.

Magda closed her eyes. "I love you."

"I love you too," he said.

Ravi put his hand under her chin, and Magda's lips met his. A fire lit inside her, and thoughts of Ravi's body on hers cascaded through Magda's mind. She kissed him sensually, letting her lips linger on his, while his one hand moved up her bare neck, weaving his fingers in her hair.

His touch aroused her senses. Magda kissed him again, letting her tongue swoop into his mouth, tasting every inch of him, and letting him equally explore her lips and body. The intensity built inside her, heat pooling in her stomach.

Ravi's hand swooped down her back, caressing her figure, before hoisting her up onto the table in one swift movement.

"Ravi, we have work to do!" she laughed.

He pulled away. "Fine, you're right."

But she didn't want to let him go. Magda linked her legs around his waist and ran her hands down Ravi's chest, feeling for his shirt.

"Magda...," he teased. "What if someone comes in here?"

"Until they get here, I have you all to myself," she replied.

Her fingers grasped the fabric, and Ravi pulled it over his head, revealing his smooth skin. She was instantly drawn to his abs close to his pants line. Just the sight of his body and the mental images of him not fully clothed made her stomach flip.

Ravi's hand grasped the back of her neck, his fingers sliding into her hair as he arched her backwards, kissing her sternum lightly. She could feel the outline of his muscles, slick against her legs, and the perspiration on his chest against her as he drew his face closer.

Then Ravi backed away from the table, causing Magda to lock her legs around him so that she wouldn't fall. He held her tightly, before turning and pressing her up against the stone wall. His hands maneuvered underneath her, squeezing her thighs firmly to hold her upright.

Magda continued kissing him, letting his body consume her thoughts, and her grief melted into the background. She wanted to give him all of her, as if they had no cares in the world.

Footsteps sounded, and Magda was on alert.

"Ravi, stop. Someone's coming," Magda whispered playfully. She pressed down on his shoulders and set her legs on the ground.

Ravi scrambled away from her. As Magda stared back at him, she looked beyond him toward the window. Something about it was unnerving, as if it was different from the space she had grown up in, playing hide and seek with Aleksy and Odie. Ahead, as if she was looking at a pond, the colored potions on the table rippled.

Magda's eyes snapped to the torchlight, and she realized that the objects surrounding them cast no shadows on the floor. It was an illusion. Her muscles tensed as an eerie sensation petrified her body.

"Ravi!" Magda screamed to alert him.

Ravi turned around, preparing to go for the intruder, but the images before them shifted. The fake illusion faded away, portraying who was in the room with them.

It was a stunning woman with long, red hair and a beautiful face, although she appeared to be barely the same age as Magda's mother. Her eyes sparkled with a glint of silver, and the sweeping sparkles spun up her arms.

A Mind Guardian.

CHAPTER 61
Dagmara

Dagmara stood face to face with Sabien.

She had no weapons on her. She had nothing to protect herself from the man before her. She had nothing to kill the man she wanted dead.

"I was just getting to know your brother, Dagger. So this was who you were sending Scribestones to?"

"You asked...for directions," Teos muttered, his brow furrowed. "Do you know each other?"

"Get away from him," Dagmara ordered.

"I don't think so." A predatory grin spread across Sabien's face before he gripped Teos by the hair and yanked the boy against his chest. Teos yelled, his crutch clattering to the ground. Sabien had already unsheathed a blade, pressing it to Teos's throat.

Dagmara screamed.

"I'm going to kill you," Claude growled, storming forward with his hand outstretched.

"I wouldn't do that," Sabien remarked, yanking Teos by the hair harder.

Dagmara grabbed Claude's arm, preventing him from attacking. "You could hurt Teos," she said under her breath.

Pierre had his bow drawn, Martine had her sword unsheathed, and Claude was braced to use his magic, but none of them made a move.

Claude was reluctant to stand down, his eyes boring into Sabien like daggers.

Teos let out a cry of agony. Dagmara's heart shattered, watching Teos struggle to remain above the blade. Pain crossed his features as he stumbled on his injured leg. Sabien tugged his blonde curls, tipping his head back and exposing more of his neck to the knife. Teos's back was pressed against Sabien's chest with no way to escape.

"Let him go," Dagmara pleaded.

"I can't do that."

"Please," she insisted, hating the desperation in her voice. "I'll do anything. What do you want?"

"I want to see you beg. It has been too long since you've been on your knees before me," said Sabien.

"That's enough, Sabien," Claude snapped.

But Dagmara would do anything.

"Dagmara—" Teos attempted to object.

Dagmara could feel tears burning in her eyes.

"No, Your Majesty," Martine said under her breath.

But Dagmara wouldn't listen. She dropped to the ground, hitting her knees with a hard smack, never shifting her gaze away from Sabien. "Please."

Sabien grinned. "I see you bend to my requests so easily when it involves your brother." Then he glanced at Claude, a twinkle lighting his eyes. "Does she bend as easily for you, Your Majesty?"

Claude's hands turned to fists, silver igniting in his irises.

"Don't do that," Sabien warned. "One illusion, and I will drag this blade across his throat." Sabien shifted the blade against Teos's neck. Teos winced, gasping for air as he struggled to remain standing.

"I'm on my knees, Sabien," Dagmara said, breathless. "Let him go."

Sabien was quiet for a long moment. "Martine and Pierre aren't."

The two guards shuffled in their stance.

"Come now, you're only taking an order from your captain," Sabien encouraged.

"You're not our captain," Martine retorted.

"Please," Dagmara begged, tugging at Martine's leg. "Just do as he says."

Martine met Dagmara's gaze before finally letting in. She slowly lowered to one knee. Pierre followed her lead uneasily, but never lost the grip on his bow.

Sabien's vile grin only widened. Then he nodded his head at Claude. "You too."

"What?" Dagmara gasped.

Claude's face was stoic, his body as resolute as a statue. "No."

"No? I think it's time you listen to one of my orders," Sabien replied. His face hardened, his lips thinning. "Kneel."

"I don't kneel to anyone," said Claude.

"Even when it could save the life of our dear Teos?"

"You won't kill him."

"Is that a dare, Your Majesty?" Sabien spat the last word like it was a curse. Every muscle in his body grew taut as he tightened his grip on Teos. Her brother squealed, his leg twisting awkwardly under his weight.

"Stop!" Dagmara slammed her palms against the cobblestone. Her eyes welled with tears, threatening to pour down her face.

"You've lost it, Sabien," Claude said, his voice dangerously calm. "What happened?"

"Me?" Sabien countered. "Junne is dead thanks to you!"

"Like you care who lives and dies," Pierre spat.

"Eligor killed Junne," Claude stated. "Why are you still on his side?"

"Liar!" Sabien snapped, jerking Teos in his grip.

"I have no reason to lie about that," said Claude.

"Why would Eligor kill one of his own?"

"To gain his powers back," Claude explained. "You're being used, and after he's done with you he's going to kill you."

Sabien let out a bark of laughter. "Are you trying to protect me? You and I don't look out for each other, Claude."

"We did once," replied Claude.

"Not anymore." Sabien tightened his grip on Teos's hair, and Dagmara's brother let out another ear-piercing scream. "Now I work for Eligor. I know you killed Junne. You can't lie your way out of this one."

"Enough!" Dagmara yelled, her throat tight. "What do you want from us? Let my brother go!"

Sabien's attention finally shifted back to Dagmara on her knees. "Unfortunately, I can't let your brother go," he said without remorse. "Eligor discovered you were an heir to his lineage—which is hard to believe. You? Of all people?"

She could feel the magic simmering under her skin, heightening along with her rage.

"And when I told him you have a brother, he wanted to see Teos for himself," continued Sabien. "So I'm going to take Teos to him."

"No!" Dagmara yelled.

Eligor's goal had been clear from the beginning—to be the last heir to the Void lineage. If Sabien brought Teos to him—it would be all over.

She cursed under her breath, knowing Sabien must have looked into Teos's identity after seeing her Scribestones. She wished he had never been in the Ilusaurian library the night she had scribed Teos.

"Leave Teos out of this," Dagmara insisted. "If Eligor needs anyone, take me instead."

"Kind offer," Sabien pursed his lips, "but I'll decline. Unlike you, this poor boy won't fight me." He inched the blade up higher, and Teos gasped.

"Dagmara—" her brother muttered, before clamping his jaw shut, his eyes squeezing back tears.

A drop of crimson blood beaded on Teos's throat. It was the smallest morsel of blood, but it turned the tide in Dagmara's chest. Her rage snapped. Anger ignited in her veins, along with desperation. She needed to protect Teos. She needed—

The world shifted around her, transforming the pink and blue hues to a murky violet. Smoke flooded her vision, and crystals danced through the air in various patterns. She gasped, unable to process the sudden shift in her world, her gaze jerking in every direction.

"What the—" Sabien's voice stopped short.

A gasp escaped Claude's mouth as he whipped his head toward Dagmara, but his eyes were searching for her. Both Martine and Pierre shot up to their feet, looking in all directions.

"Claude, reveal her," Sabien ordered.

A shallow laugh escaped Claude's lips. He glared at Sabien, pure hatred in his eyes. He responded with a single word:

"No."

Then the realization dawned on Dagmara. They couldn't see her, and she was invisible to the real world.

"I told you no illusions!" Sabien yelled.

Scrambling to her feet, Dagmara withdrew a throwing star from her bodice. She launched it forward, her aim true. It whirled in the air, creating a perfect arc until it met its target. The tip dug into Sabien's palm, forcing his hand to relinquish the dagger.

She was already racing forward, withdrawing the dagger from her belt. She aimed it high, but Sabien tugged Teos in front of his body, using him as a human shield.

Skidding to a halt, Dagmara's dagger stopped inches from her brother's chest. The shock thrust her back into reality, for she was unable to control her newfound powers. The world returned, and she became visible once more, fractions from Teos's face.

Teos's bloodshot eyes were wide, and his mouth agape. He jolted back from his sister's reappearing form.

"Violet eyes. So you do have magic," Sabien said under his breath.

A silver flash ignited the air, and one of Claude's illusions attempted to distract Sabien. The whiz of an arrow pierced the sky, flying straight past Dagmara and grazing Sabien's shoulder.

A new flurry of strength surged through Sabien. He never loosened his grip on Teos, despite losing the blade. A throwing star jutted from the back of his palm, but he tugged Teos tighter against his chest.

"I'll scribe you soon, Dagger." His smile was vicious, his eyes twinkling as blue as the ocean.

She didn't hear the churning water over the distant rapids and the thundering of her heart. A huge shadow cast over her, a momentous wave blocking the sun. Nearly all the water had been pulled up from the valley below, creating a dark and ominous wall of churning water.

"Teos!" Dagmara yelled. She reached out and grabbed Teos's hand, despite Sabien dragging him back. Her grip was firm, and she wasn't going to let her brother go.

She heard her name, but didn't process where it was coming from. Not until a muscular arm swooped around her middle and yanked her away from her brother.

"No!" Dagmara screamed. Teos's hand slipped from hers. She saw the fear in his bloodshot eyes. There was no doubt hers mirrored the same emotion.

She was torn away. The arm was too strong, and she lost sense of reality as her world spun. She was being pulled off her feet, away from Teos, while Sabien was dragging Teos away from her.

Her back collided with the cobblestone, and Claude hovered over her, his body protecting hers like a shell. A thunderous boom pounded the air, colliding against her senses. The ground rumbled against her spine, and a ringing lingered in her hearing. Water and stones pelted them, bouncing off Claude's back and landing on either side of her.

"Get off!" Dagmara screamed, pounding against Claude's chest.

He rolled off her, setting her free. She sat up, and stars danced in her vision at the abrupt change. When her gaze cleared, the scene before her fully became visible.

The entire bridge was gone. The wave had taken out the entire structure. All that remained was a faint mist, dusting her from the sky above. The cobblestone path ended in jagged rock formations, leading to a deadly drop to the bottom of the ravine. The structure was gone.

And Sabien and Teos were gone with it.

Scrambling to her knees, Dagmara crawled forward, peering over the edge as far as she dared. She couldn't see anything but the churning rapids, hundreds of feet below.

Sitting back on her heels, she snapped her head in Claude's direction. "Why did you do that? I had him in my hands!"

Both Martine and Pierre were coming to their senses, brushing the water and debris off them.

"You didn't," Claude replied, sitting upright. "Sabien had Teos, you were only going to be killed by that wave. I saved you."

"You should've saved Teos!" she cried. She couldn't contain the tears any longer. They slipped from her eyes, streaming down her cheeks.

"I won't apologize for saving you," Claude said.

"Your Majesty," Martine interjected, but she was ignored.

Claude's tone was cold. "I will always choose you."

"Don't," she answered. "Teos comes first, do you understand? He always—" her voice broke off into a choked sob.

Claude reached out, tugging her away from the edge, but she yanked out of his grip. "Don't touch me."

He withdrew, giving her space. Instead, Martine knelt at Dagmara's opposite side, joining her at the edge of the broken bridge.

"We will save him," she said.

"How?" Dagmara asked, her voice breaking.

"I don't know yet," said Martine, her face hardening.

Claude was the one to finish the sentence, "But we will."

CHAPTER 62
Magdalena

"You're not Dagmara." The Mind Guardian squinted her eyes in the dim light, before approaching Magda and Ravi. Then she said, "My, my, my. Princess Magdalena. The First Prince will not be pleased to hear you are still alive."

"Who are you?" Magda asked cautiously, but the glint of silver in the woman's eyes had already given her away as a Mind assassin. This could only be the final, remaining assassin that had taken Dagmara hostage.

Viette.

"I'm surprised your friends didn't tell you about me," Viette laughed.

Ravi lunged for a glass bottle on the table, cracking it against the wooden edge, until he had a sharp piece of glass in his hands. "Stay away from us," he cautioned.

Viette threw her head in laughter. "This will be easier than I thought."

Magda stepped forward, blocking Ravi. "I'm not letting you get anywhere near him or Dagmara."

"You're incredulous if you think you know anything about my plans," said Viette.

Magda's teeth gritted. She knew Eligor was determined to rule the Void as the sole guardian and exterminate all the other Void descendants. Both Dagmara and Teos were in danger, and Magda would not let Viette get to them.

Magda thrust her hand forward, sending a gust of Spirit Magic in Viette's direction and slamming her into the far bookshelf. Glass shattered everywhere as potions and medicines toppled to the ground. The force reverberated through the wall, but Magda knew the sound would have alerted the knights.

Viette's arms lit up with silver, and her lips parted.

"Don't look in her eyes, Ravi!" Magda warned.

"I won't," Ravi assured her, still holding the glass bottle as a weapon.

Viette stood up from her position. "I'm surprised you want to kill me. And risk Eligor gaining back his Mind Powers?" she asked.

"And risk you killing Dagmara?" Magda shouted back.

Viette shook her head and let out a laugh. Then she withdrew her dagger. "Get out of my way. I don't have time for you or your little friend."

"No," said Magda, the magic prepared at her fingertips.

Viette rolled her eyes and lunged forward. She thrust the dagger toward Magda's stomach, but she quickly grabbed a bottle, slamming it against Viette as hard as she could. The force caused Viette to stumble back and clutch her arm as the potion signed her skin.

All around Magda the room shifted. The illusion took hold, and the apothecary warped into the room where she had her coronation —where Sabien had killed her family. She was standing in the center of the hall by the fountain, and all around her, the three-tiered balcony was decorated with pastel-colored banners. Guests examined her as they did that day, waiting for Magda to display her water magic.

This time, Aleksy stood in front of her, not on the balcony. He held a dagger in his hands.

Magda froze in shock at seeing her brother. For a moment, she was unmovable.

All of the sudden, Aleksy moved forward and put his entire weight into a swipe at Magda's face. She skillfully dodged, but blood instantly poured from a slash in her cheek. When he approached once more, Magda drove her knee into Aleksy's stomach, before using her shoulder to charge into Aleksy's chest, creating space between them.

Aleksy threw a few more swipes, but Magda leapt backwards. She knew it was Viette, merely taunting her, but Magda didn't have a weapon. She couldn't discern what was real and where the edges of the apothecary were.

Suddenly, Aleksy was thrown to the side, and the illusion dissipated. The door to the apothecary had swung open and someone had heard the noise. Ishani had lunged for Viette and slammed her body against a bookshelf. The shock reverberated through Viette's body, and Ishani punched Viette across the face, the crack of knuckles splattering across her cheek, but she was too stunned to block.

Then Ishani unhooked her axe, aiming it toward Viette's chest.

Suddenly the room around them shifted, bending as if they were in a prism, and Viette disappeared completely. The walls changed their shapes, slinking together so that the door and windows to the apothecary completely disappeared. Then, the four walls began moving in, as if to crush them together.

"Ishani! Ravi!" Magda called, spinning in all directions to find her friends.

"Here," Ishani called, bursting through the scattered colors.

"It's not real, Magda," said Ravi, floating through another illusion to stand next to her.

The trio seemed to be alone, for Viette was nowhere to be seen.

"She's another one of Eligor's assassins?" Ishani confirmed.

"Yes," said Magda.

"Where is she? She can't keep this up for long," Ravi cried.

All of the sudden, six versions of Viette appeared, flashing in a circle, surrounding the pair. Viette's apparitions charged with swords, but Ishani swung the axe, taking down the ghosts one by one, who all exploded into thin air.

Ravi held the glass in his hands, bracing himself for the real Viette.

Magda's Spirit magic was useless against the apparitions, and there wasn't enough water in the room. All she was aware of was the stone floor, feeling comfortable at her feet as the Soul magic rippled from her ankles to her hands.

Then Viette leapt out of the shadows, wielding a dagger that she thrust toward Magda's chest. Magda moved quicker, and with a flash of Soul magic, Magda thrust a stone at Viette's arm. Viette reeled in pain, and the room shifted to its normal size again. They were back in the apothecary, and Viette stood only a few paces away.

Magda, Ravi, and Ishani stood facing her, and it was unclear who would make the first move.

"Magda!" Ravi screamed, pulling her out of the way.

A dagger had been thrown in her direction, missing her by inches. Ravi's back hit the central table hard as they crashed into the wood, and the bottles shattered, spilling ink and potions all over the journal.

Ishani rushed forward, going for Viette.

Then the floor dropped, as if the three were in a cascading elevator. Magda, Ravi, and Ishani looked upward to see the ceiling grow twenty times in length, as arrows rained down on them. None of it was real, but merely a distraction. What was Viette up to? Where was she now and where would she attack next?

They were hopeless to think they would win this fight against her perfected illusions.

Magda knew what she had to do. She knew that there were glass shards all over the ground, even though she couldn't see them. A slamming sound was heard, and Magda could only assume Viette was preparing for her next move.

"Stand with me!" Magda ordered, and they instantly obeyed. Once Ravi and Ishani had their backs pressed to Magda's, she used a gust of air to draw the glass shards toward her, hearing them scrape along the ground. Then, she sent a forceful gust outward, exploding the glass shards in all directions, aiming toward the outside of the room.

All of the sudden the vision collapsed to reveal the apothecary as it once was. Bookshelves and tables were overturned. In the corner, Viette staggered back, shards of glass protruding from every inch of her body. With one last gasp, she collided against the floor, unmoving.

"She's dead," Ravi said.

"She was going to kill us. It was us or her," she said.

"You did the right thing," Ishani assured Magda as she attempted to catch her breath.

"But I've just made Eligor more powerful," Magda said, dreading the worst.

"Magda!" The door to the apothecary banged open.

The shrill voice caused a shudder to tear through Magda's spine. She turned to the entrance and Ishani braced herself with her axes.

Dagmara and Claude burst into the room, their two guards right behind them. The pain in Dagmara's expression was so palpable, it caused Magda's insides to roil. Her friend's eyes were bloodshot and puffy.

"Dagmara! What is—"

"It's Teos!" Dagmara cried. She skidded to a halt in front of Magda, gripping her hand. "Sabien took him. He's gone!"

CHAPTER 63
Dagmara

The throne room was filled with tension so thick it was suffocating. Magda, Dagmara, Ravi, Ishani, and Claude all paced inside. The cascade of the water behind the thrones was the only sound, for everyone was preoccupied with thoughts of Teos.

Magda sat at the edge of her throne, bouncing her leg and fiddling with the hem of her shirt. "Sabien must be bringing Teos to Eligor now."

Ishani stood in the shadows, her fingers tapping her axe handles in measured rhythm. Her breaths were shallow, her jaw clenched. "And where is this bastard?"

Claude paced, rubbing the back of his neck with his hand. "Which one? Sabien or Eligor?"

"Same thing," Ishani snapped.

Dagmara sat on the steps leading up the thrones, her knee bouncing anxiously. She could hardly think, her mind replaying the moments on the bridge over and over again. If only she hadn't left Teos's side. How did Sabien find him? He must've been watching from afar when they were talking in Gorzhelm—he had seen the letter from Teos at the Ilusauri Scribestone.

If only she had been faster. Maybe she could have saved Teos. She had no idea how to use the Void. She had no idea about the dark magic that was once dormant and now lived wildly in her veins. She could feel the magic simmering at her fingertips, flooding through her bones as it screamed to release once more. She couldn't control it. And somewhere, deep inside Teos, it lived too. That was the whole reason they were in this mess.

"I'm going to kill Sabien once I get my hands on him," Claude said under his breath, his growl barely audible.

"And make Eligor more powerful?" Ravi asked.

"No, we have to kill Eligor first," said Magda. "It is the only way. Now that Viette is dead, he has Mind magic too. The only branch he doesn't have is Sabien's. We have to make sure he doesn't get Life magic."

"I can't believe it," Claude said under his breath. He rubbed his hand along the back of his neck, staring at the ground. "The assassin responsible for killing my parents...dead."

"I'm sorry you didn't get your own revenge," said Ishani.

Claude shook his head. "It was never about revenge, otherwise I would have been spending my resources hunting her instead of the tomb. But...I am glad she is finally gone." He glanced at Dagmara, more emotions churning in his eyes that he wasn't going to share in front of everyone else. She gave him a half-hearted smile, silently communicating that they would finish this conversation later.

Claude turned to the Magda. "What are you going to do with her body? Will you bury her?"

"Don't worry," said Magda. "My knights and servants are taking care of it."

Claude didn't answer.

"So how do we get Teos back?" Dagmara asked, shifting the topic. The king gave her an appreciative nod.

"Eligor thinks I'm dead," Magda said, the conversation easily shifting back to the First Prince. "We could use this to our advantage."

"We don't know where he is," Ravi said. "We could be looking for months for the location where he has taken Teos."

"And what if he comes back here for Dagmara?" asked Ishani. "He has a whole army of hounds. We need to be prepared. You have Flaustra's support, of course."

"Is Reon still planning to come here?" asked Ravi.

"Dagmara was going to send him a Scribestone when we arrived..." Magda began, but then her voice dwindled out.

The last thing Dagmara was thinking about was sending a Scribestone to Reon.

The silence in the room spread like a thick fog.

Then Sabien's words echoed in her mind.

I'll scribe you soon, Dagger. Not 'I'll see you soon.' *Scribe.*

Dagmara jolted to her feet. "I need to get to the Scribestone." The urgency in her voice caused the other four in the room to perk up.

She didn't wait to explain. She took off toward the Scribestone, her heart hammering in her chest.

Scribe.

She could be overthinking it—she could have misheard him over the rush of the water—but a spark lit in her chest. Sabien was always playing games. This had to be another game. She could hear the clamor of boots on the ground, voices calling behind her. But she wouldn't slow her pace. Even as her heart threatened to break from her chest, she didn't stop.

Bursting into the royal library, Dagmara instantly crossed to the Scribestone. It was perched on a glorified pedestal, glimmering with magic.

"Dagmara—what is going on?" Magda asked, tumbling into the room after her. Ishani, Ravi, and Claude were directly behind her.

Ignoring all of them, Dagmara stepped up to the magical device. She blocked out the world as she pressed her palm to the cold stone. She waited...wondering if she had been wrong.

Until shimmering words ignited on the stone.

One message from Eligor Blaide, The Mystic South

CHAPTER 64
Dagmara

Gasps rang through the room, and all five of them stared at the magical inscription. Goosebumps traced Dagmara's arms, and the hair on the back of her neck stood on edge.

Eligor Blaide had sent her a message.

The First Prince.

Without another moment of hesitation, she swiped her palm against the cool stone, ordering the full message to appear.

My darling descendent, Dagmara Zosia,

I recently discovered that there are two more heirs to the Void lineage. Forgive my lack of introduction, but this does come as quite a surprise to me. Your brother is a darling. He reminds me of my own brother from a very long time ago.

I would love to properly meet you. I am throwing a celebration at midnight—I have amassed quite a few supporters over the centuries, you see. I would be honored to see you there. In fact, you should come. For your brother's sake.

Go to the Sea of Scarlet at midnight, and I will open a rift for you with the Void magic, taking you directly to my citadel, the citadel of our lineage, all the way in the Mystic South. Haven't you heard of it? The world tried to erase it. But I'm back now.

I would be mad to not invite your husband, Claude Mirage. Bring him, would you?

Your ancestor, Eligor

Forced to grip the edge of the stone for balance, Dagmara let out a shaky breath. She could feel the presence of the group hovering around her, reading the words for themselves.

"No," Claude said immediately. "It's a trap."

"He has Teos," Dagmara said. "He's going to kill him."

"King Mirage is right," Ishani agreed, finishing the message for herself. "He's using Teos as bait so he can kill you both in one fell swoop." She turned away from the stone, pacing.

"I have to go anyway," Dagmara said. "He said he's opening a rift just for me. It must be like some sort of teleportation for us, not only the hounds."

"Are you sure that's how it works?" asked Ravi. "The hounds teleport through the rifts?"

"If it is how it works, then send me through." Claude stepped toward Dagmara, taking her hand in his palm and turning her face to his. "I will go save your brother."

Dagmara took Claude's hand in hers, pulling it away from her face. A sudden dizziness overwhelmed her. This was all too much. "He wants me," she voiced before crossing to the spiral staircase. She plopped down on the second stair, relieving her nausea.

"He will kill you. That's what he wants, isn't it?" Ishani said. "And you have no idea how to use your magic to defend yourself. No one here has even been to the Mystic South besides me."

Claude shot her a glare. "Watch your tone."

"She's right," Dagmara admitted. "I don't know how to use my magic."

"But we have to do something, even if none of the options are good," Ravi cut in.

Magda had been awfully silent, rereading the message over and over. She then backed away from the stone, her eyes brightening. "Then...what if we change the plan?"

Intrigue sparked in Dagmara's chest. She could see the formation of a reckless plan on Magda's face, but she was desperate for any ideas. "How?"

Turning away from the message, Magda met her best friend's gaze. "Let me take your place," Magda proposed. "I'll be you."

Dagmara sensed Ishani, Claude, and Ravi exchange a glance, but she was waiting for Magda to explain further.

"He doesn't know I'm alive. He will never see it coming. When he tries to kill me, I can take him by surprise and fight him."

"Not to be rude," Ishani cut in, "But you two are not identical. He will know it's you. I was never fooled by your little swap unlike some other people."

Claude rolled his eyes. "Nobody asked."

"Claude can put an illusion on me," said Magda.

"I can't change your voice," Claude objected.

"I can do that part," Magda said hopefully.

"Are you sure?" Ravi asked, his voice full of concern.

Dagmara shook her head at Magda. "I won't let you go as me. It is too dangerous."

"You've put yourself in danger time and time again for me, Dagmara. Let me do this for you."

"Magda..."

"And while I'm distracting Eligor, you can sneak in and get Teos," Magda added. "You're better at that than me anyway."

A spark of hope ignited in Dagmara's chest.

"What if Eligor can't be killed?" Ishani voiced aloud. "Have we thought of that? There's a reason they trapped him in the tomb. What if that is the only way to stop him?"

"Even if we wanted to trap him inside the tomb," Magda said,

"We don't have a guardian of every branch to seal the locks. We would need Mind, Life, Soul, and Spirit."

"And what about the Void branch?" Ravi asked.

Claude filled everyone in, "A Void emblem appeared when Magda and I were down there. Eligor connected himself to it, and tried to tie Junne's blood to the land using the crown. Instead, he killed her."

"Exactly," Magda confirmed, "The crown is the way to appoint a new guardian to the land that will safeguard the magic and restore health to our kingdoms."

"Personally, I would rather focus on killing Eligor," Ishani spat. "Are you forgetting he also asked for Claude? He has plans to take him out too."

"Not if I kill him first," Claude replied.

"Fine," Ishani said under her breath. "We have to catch him off guard, steal the crown, and rescue Teos. Anything I missed?"

Magda let out a self-deprecating laugh. "And kill Eligor while we're at it."

"And Sabien," Dagmara added, her voice cold. "He will pay for this."

All of this was absurd. This entire plan was crazy. It was reckless—but what other choice did they have? Eligor was planning to kill Teos. They had to rescue him, and tricking Eligor was the only way they stood a chance. Killing Eligor or stealing the crown were mere afterthoughts in Dagmara's mind. All that mattered was rescuing Teos. If she killed Sabien in the process, that would be a nice upside.

Before the conversation could continue, there was a clatter at the door. All five of them jolted upright, turning to face a figure in the threshold. It was Martine, standing uneasily in the space with a giant violet box in her grasp.

"Dagmara," she said, "This arrived for you."

"What?" Dagmara rose to her feet, crossing the library to stand in front of her friend. Staring at the box, she saw a neatly hand-written note on the top.

For Dagmara Zosia. From Eligor Blaide.

"Don't open it!" Magda said instantly.

"I already did," Martine replied.

Dagmara shot her a glance.

"Sorry," she said, though she didn't sound remorseful at all. "You can scold me later. It is my job to protect you."

Dagmara brushed aside the comment. She tore the lid of the box and let it clatter to the ground beside her. Inside the box was a neatly folded gown, shimmering in violet gemstones. Layers of sheer fabric were folded over one another, and feathers protruded from the base of the box. Another handwritten note was placed on top.

Wear me.

"A—dress?" Magda stammered.

Withdrawing the dress from the box, she watched as the fabric cascaded to the ground. It was stunning, far more expensive than anything Dagmara had ever witnessed. It was as though it was woven with void magic itself. The bodice was made of scales—and Dagmara realized in stark horror that they were the scales of the hounds. The back of the dress had two large pieces of fabric that attached from the neck to the sleeves, as if a flowing cape was made to look like blackbird wings.

"Dress code noted," Ravi announced.

"We leave at midnight," Dagmara announced. "Magda," she looked up and met Magda's gaze. "Ready to swap places one more time?" She extended the dress toward her friend.

Hesitantly, Magda accepted the dress. She handled it as though it were glass, both fragile and deadly. She plastered a weary smile on her face. "Let's get ready for a ball."

Dagmara knew there was only one way this could end. They were either on their way to save Teos, or on their way to their own funeral.

CHAPTER 65
Magdalena

"Magda?" a woman's voice chimed.

Magda's eyes shot open to see her mother standing over her bed. Magda realized that Ravi had climbed into the bed beside her, and she had her head slumped onto his chest. Their fingers were firmly interlinked.

She had fallen asleep, attempting to get some rest before leaving for Eligor's lair at midnight. She had been going over the plan incessantly, hoping that she would be able to successfully impersonate Dagmara.

"Can you come out here, please?" Bernadette asked, holding a piece of paper in her hand.

"Yes," Magda rubbed her eyes, waking up fully.

Magda followed her mother outside of the bedroom, crossing into the parlor that was shared by the royal family. As she got up, Odie's head perked up from the pillow at the foot of her bed, and he dashed after Magda and her mother.

Once outside Magda's room, Bernadette's demeanor changed, and fear was laced in her voice. "I heard Teos was taken," she sobbed, dropping her queenly demeanor. "Please tell me you have a plan, Magda. Teos is like a son to me."

"I do have a plan," said Magda, attempting to reassure her mother. The two crossed to a sofa and sat down, while Magda quickly poured out the story. Odie jumped up next to the princess, putting his face in her lap. Magda scratched behind his ears, and she continued speaking with her mother.

While her mother didn't agree with Magda putting herself in more danger, she finally accepted that it was the only way. Bernadette's voice shook as she said, "I can't lose either of you like I lost Aleksy. I'll send as many knights with you as you need."

"No, you need to use those knights to fortify the fortress and be the queen that people need," said Magda. "Please, you need to keep Azurem safe while I help Dagmara save Teos."

Bernadette brushed a stray tear from her eye and nodded. "I'm sorry, this has made me very emotional. Well, now that you're back permanently, I'll be handing all the powers of the crown over to you."

Magda was silent.

"You are back permanently, aren't you Magda?" her mother prompted.

"Yes," Magda answered.

"What's wrong?"

Magda's thoughts drifted. She clutched Odie's fur as she opened up further. "As a Master Guardian, I have the opportunity to choose who will receive the powers of the guardians, and I don't know if I deserve that choice."

"Why not?" asked Bernadette. "You were clearly chosen to be a Master Guardian for a reason."

"But why me? Why should *I* have all this power?" asked Magda.

"Well, you're not meant to have all the power," said Bernadette, "You're meant to give it away when the lineage is broken. The question is, who is worthy of it?"

"I don't have much time to decide," Magda confessed.

Bernadette placed her hand on top of Magda's. "You were always meant to be a guardian and a royal, but you were meant to support this kingdom and hone the gift of water."

"I know," said Magda, "Even the First Prince has a stronger connection to his original gift. The Void."

"As for the other gifts, I can't tell you what to do. But, sweetheart, you've seen more of this world than anyone I know. I know you'll make the right decision."

"If I get the opportunity to make that choice, and give away one of my gifts, I need people that I trust," said Magda, "That can help me stop Eligor right away."

"Then I take it, you've decided?"

"About one of the elements."

"And the others?"

"Still thinking."

Bernadette reached over, giving Magda a hug. "I'm so proud of you, Magda. Please know that. I know it can't be easy to have these decisions on your shoulders, and I would tell you to stop all of this so you will be safe, but I know you won't. Whatever happens, and whatever you decide, I will support you."

"I love you, mom," said Magda.

"I love you too."

Odie barked loudly.

"Shhh...people are sleeping!" Magda whispered.

But Odie forced his way into the middle of the hug, pushing his snout between them. Specifically, he went for Bernadette, who released her daughter to give the dog attention. She pulled back as he slobbered his tongue on her cheek. "Odie, yes, I see you." She laughed.

His paws crumpled the piece of paper on Bernadette's lap.

"What's that?" Magda asked.

"Something for you," Bernadette answered.

Magda pulled Odie back, and he jumped off the sofa before circling and lying down at her feet. Magda unfolded the paper, reading its contents.

Bernadette continued, "I've granted Ravi a royal pardon and immunity in Azurem. He can stay here as long as he wants."

Magda's eyes widened. "Thank you, mom," Magda said, scanning over her mother's royal pardon for Ravi, which granted him sanctuary for saving the life of Princess Magdalena Krol. "I know this wasn't easy for you, and this means a lot."

"Well, I know how you feel about this boy," Bernadette admitted.

"I really love him," Magda admitted, "but do you think that guardians are meant for happiness? That we can have a normal relationship?"

Bernadette laughed. "Are you forgetting about me and your father? I fell in love with a guardian once, too. And he never looked at me any differently."

"It's not that," said Magda. "Did you ever come to resent that you didn't have powers? Or that you couldn't fully understand dad, or Aleksy, or me?"

"Not once," Bernadette shook her head. "I loved your father and that's all that mattered. In fact, I didn't even know he was a guardian at first."

"Really?"

"I met your father on one of his tours of the villages. You know grandpa oversaw the operations of the local salt mines, and my sisters and I gave your father and his men a tour of the town and mine. I thought your father was a royal bookkeeper, and little did I know, he was a young guardian. He was only sixteen, before the trials."

"Then what happened?"

"He came to visit me every summer, and I fell in love with the person he was, and not the person he could be someday. We didn't know if he would even win the trials against his siblings, and if he didn't we would have had our life in the countryside together."

"But he did win," said Magda.

"To both our surprise," Bernadette admitted. "What followed was months of horrible politics, but we got through it, and I moved to the fortress with him. We both agreed that the betterment of Azurem was more important than the life we had envisioned for ourselves."

Magda let her mother's words sink in.

Bernadette reached out to stroke Magda's hair. "I want all the happiness in the world for you, sweetheart, but sometimes what we were put on this earth to do is more important."

Magda nodded. It was up to her to steal Eligor's crown and use it to create more guardians. Her heart raced, concerned if she would make the right choices, and her entire body felt heavy with the weight of the responsibility. She feared that the rest of the kingdoms wouldn't agree with her decisions and that she only would be setting the world up for more political turmoil. However, stopping Eligor and ensuring their lands survived had to be the first priority, and any political ramifications could be dealt with later.

Her fingers clutched around Odie's fur, and in the distance she heard the clock strike eleven times, counting down the final hours before they would face Eligor.

Footsteps sounded along the hallway, and a maid approached, holding the black-scaled dress from Eligor and a make-up kit.

"Urszula?" Magda's face brightened upon seeing her handmaiden, and she shot up from her position.

Urszula gave a small curtsy. Then she smiled at the queen and her daughter before saying, "Good evening, Your Highness. Your mother thought you could use some help."

"By now I assume Urszula is a professional at disguising appearances," Bernadette explained, "And if you thought I was going to let you go to the First Prince's doorstep without everything looking exactly perfect, then think again."

Magda grinned.

Urszula walked into Magda's chamber. "Come, Your Highness. Let's get you ready for a ball."

CHAPTER 66
Dagmara

Dagmara's anxiety grew each minute that Teos was gone. Finally, midnight came, and it was time to go to the First Prince's ball, somewhere in the Mystic South. Eligor had explained in his letter that he would open a rift in the Sea of Scarlet, taking them directly to his citadel, but she didn't know how it would work.

The Void magic was still a mystery to her. She didn't know what to feel, how to feel, or how to channel the powers at her fingertips. Slipping into invisibility almost felt natural, as if her hidden form was another part of her. However, channeling the Void in order to rip a ravine through the earth that transported them across the sea seemed impossible.

It only reminded her how powerful Eligor was—how powerful the Void magic was. Could she someday open rifts?

Once the group had gotten ready for the ball, they made their way to the Sea of Scarlet. The once-glorious poppy field was ridden with ashes and debris.

Dagmara wore a sleek, form fitting, black dress, with matching jewelry she had borrowed from Queen Bernadette. On the other hand, Magda wore the scaled dress from Eligor with the crow wings that extended from her back to her arms.

Claude had disguised Magda as Dagmara perfectly. Her eyes were green, her hair was now blonde, and her body matched Dagmara's stature. On her head, she wore the midnight-studded tiara with a matching choker necklace that fanned across her sleeveless arms.

Claude and Ravi were also dressed in formal attire, equally as handsome. Next to them was Ishani, wearing a puffy-sleeved shirt under a corset and a high-low skirt. With her hair down for once, she looked strangely like Kiran. Martine and Pierre were out of their Ilusaurian uniforms, disguised as guests for the ball.

The seven stood in the Sea of Scarlet, waiting in anticipation. Everyone was expecting a mysterious passageway to appear in the ground, and if it didn't, Teos would not be saved. The thought threatened to consume Dagmara in fear, and she attempted to steady her shaking heart.

Claude put a hand on her shoulder, comforting her.

"We'll save him," he assured her.

Martine and Pierre flanked her, both of them nodding in encouragement.

When the moon soared high in the sky, a faint chiming could be heard from the town of Gorzhelm, signaling it was midnight.

"This is it," Ishani said, shifting in her stance.

As if on cue, a rumbling began beneath them. In the center of the ash-ridden field, a small cut ran through the earth, snaking its way between the group. The ground shook more violently, and Martine pulled Dagmara back, yanking her out of the way.

When the cut in the earth was almost three carriages long, the crack split open. Bright, violet magic flew into the night, illuminating the remaining blood-colored petals. The group turned away from the light that threatened to blind them.

When their eyes adjusted against the magic in the night, they all approached, staring down into the ravine. Below, was a mist of purple and gray fog, spiraling out of the crevice like a spurting geyser. It was impossible to discern what lay below the blackness.

Ravi's voice was laced with concern. "Are we really going down there?"

"How do we know it's not a trap?" Martine concurred. "The other side could be surrounded with hounds."

"Or he might not be leading us to the Mystic South at all," said Magda, "We could be headed back to Dreadmarrow, or worse."

"We shouldn't trust Eligor," said Claude, shifting toward Dagmara.

Dagmara stated, "We don't have a choice."

"I'll go," Ishani announced, and all eyes snapped to her. She shrugged before getting onto the ground and swinging her feet out over the crevice.

"Wait," said Magda, reaching out and grabbing Ishani by the shoulder. "Let me."

"I'm not scared," Ishani replied, before dropping down into the ravine without a second thought. In seconds, the fog had consumed her.

"Now we wait," Claude announced, crossing his arms.

Dagmara nodded, but one look at her best friend told her that Magda was stressed at the thought of letting Ishani go in alone.

The time ticked by, and seconds seemed like minutes.

"Maybe someone should go in after her?" Pierre asked.

No one was prepared to volunteer. Dagmara could only hope that Eligor had been telling them the truth, and he truly wanted to meet her in person. Was his citadel even a real place? Were there any rumors about a fifth kingdom where the guardians ruled over the fifth branch of magic?

Finally, a sound rustled from below, and they all snapped to attention. Claude's hand instinctively went to his belt, and they all crept closer to the ravine, peering below.

Ishani poked her head out, flipping her hair out of her eyes as she climbed up into the field beside the group. She grinned as she said mischievously, "It's all clear. While I don't have my ship, I hereby grant you passage to the Mystic South."

CHAPTER 67
Magdalena

Magda took a deep breath.

Ahead, was Eligor's gothic spired citadel, with purple and black flags spiraling from gruesome towers. The clouds were dark, with an aggressive burst of lighting cracking every few minutes. Gushing rain poured from the sky, and a thick fog blanketed the structure. All around, gleaming in the moonlight, was an endless patch of thorns acting as a natural wall surrounding the structure. A series of streams weaved through the thorny thicket, and small boats took guests through the maze to the entrance.

They all stood before a natural gate, made out of weaving thorns, and a small archway led into the labyrinth beyond. Four masked followers with formal attire and white gloves stood blocking the entrance.

After checking to ensure Dagmara's name was on the list of attendees, and commenting that she and any guests had been expected, one of the men approached. "This way," he said. The white mask startled Magda, with the striking image of the First Prince.

They settled into the boat, and the guard promptly set off into the dark moat. All around them, the black thorns that surround the castle provided a secluded tunnel for the vessel to pass through. Above, the sound of fluttering bats and owls could be heard screeching from the thorny brambles, and just a few paces ahead, they saw the trails of shadowy boats making their way to Eligor's lair.

The boat docked at a staircase, which extended into the brush. The oarsmen stepped out first, before helping the five and showing them up the steps. They melded into a sea of people, all wearing the masks of the First Prince and decadent clothing. The large crowd made its way to an enormous, violet door up ahead.

"Who are all these people?" Dagmara whispered beside Magda.

"Eligor's followers," answered Ishani.

Claude spoke, "Elites against the kingdoms that have been waiting for another guardian to come to power. They will pledge their money and services to Eligor, hence making him unstoppable."

Ravi piped up next, "Maybe, they're here out of fear. They believe it's the end of the guardians, and they want to be on the right side of this war when everything is over."

Magda shuddered. She didn't want to think about the possibility that Eligor could gain political power, on top of his magical abilities. She knew how delicate the game of politics was, and she didn't need a new opponent.

They continued walking up the staircase toward the violet door. On either side, snarling hounds were chained to the walls, barking and howling at the guests. However, the guests laughed in awe, pointing at the monsters as if they were pets on display.

When they got to the top of the staircase, they passed through the door.

The ballroom was painted dark purple from ceiling to floor. Four columns were spaced in a perfect square, all with the symbol of the First Prince. Black shadows fell over the guests, and voices murmured in all languages. An intoxicating incense burned through the space, mixed with the smell of alcohol and the wet fur of the hounds.

At the front of the room, on a raised platform, Eligor sat on a godlike throne. Women presented him with wine and treats, serving him from their knees, while he surveyed the room like a divine being judging his creation. His navy cape sprawled over the floor, and his magical crown was the brightest object in the room.

On Eligor's right, Teos was on the ground, his hands bound in front of him. His face was twisted with fear and anger.

Dagmara let out a gasp beside them.

"We need to get closer," said Claude urgently, referencing the dance floor.

"Spread out," said Ishani, moving forward through the crowd.

"We'll move up to the front," Martine announced beside Pierre, before hardening her voice. "Be careful."

Dagmara nodded, and both Ilusaurian guards disappeared into the crowd after Ishani.

"Claude and I will distract Eligor," Magda reminded Dagmara. "He's expecting us. Well, he's expecting Dagmara." Magda shot her friend a concerned look.

"I'll save Teos," Dagmara said.

"Don't forget the crown," Ravi added.

Promptly, Claude extended his hand to Magda, leading her on the dance floor first. Dagmara linked her arm with Ravi's, also pushing her way to the center of the group under the spiked chandelier.

Claude gripped Magda on her lower back, pulling her to him as they danced slowly, their faces close. She put her hand in his, letting the decadent wings of the blackbird dress splay out around her, flashing the beaded feathers to all in the room. The two couples swirled in a circle, following around the outside of the room in a monotonous rhythm with the other elites.

An uneasy feeling swept over Magda as they approached the throne, getting closer to Eligor and Teos, and she wondered if he would spot the dress that he had gifted Dagmara as it flashed underneath the purple lights in front of him.

As they passed, she was sure she spotted Eligor's eyes on her and only her. He snapped his fingers to his followers, not tearing his gaze from Magda's for a second. Then his lips curled into a twisted smile as if he was inviting her to the throne.

Claude and Magda swirled around the corner, away from Eligor, following in the circle of couples.

"You remember the plan?" Claude asked.

"Yes, you?"

"I...,"

However, before Claude could respond, a group of followers swiftly approached, grabbing Claude by either arm. Roughly, they yanked him away from Magda and toward the dais.

"Claude, no!" Magda yelled.

She went to follow him, but a man touched Magda on the shoulder. "Eligor's been expecting you." He nodded his head into a slight bow, before grabbing Magda's hand and pulling her out onto the dance floor.

Magda slammed into the man's chest, their lips almost close enough to meet if it weren't for his mask separating them.

"Doesn't this remind you of something?" he asked, swirling her around and dipping her back, until her head almost touched the floor. From this position, she could see Claude being pulled through the crowd of guests as they parted the way in annoyance. A third guard held a sword to Claude's back, forcing him to walk toward Eligor.

Then the mysterious man flipped her back up to him, gripping her around the waist tightly.

"Don't tell me you forgot what it was like to dance with me?"

Magda stuttered. It was obvious this man knew Dagmara, and she could only guess it was Sabien. Being in the arms of the man who had killed her brother and father only made her blood boil. She would take a meeting with Eligor over this murderer any day.

"Nothing to say?" he continued, "Where's the Dagger I know?"

Magda pitched her voice down, matching Dagmara's tone as she responded, "I have nothing to say to you. I'm here for Teos."

He stilled, before stepping away from her. His facial expressions were concealed by the mask. "Then I'll bring you to the First Prince."

Sabien held out his arm to Magda, as if to escort her like a princess to the First Prince's side. The guests stopped dancing, parting like a wave that rippled out to sea and creating a clear pathway to the throne.

Magda scanned the room, searching for Ravi, Dagmara, or Ishani, but they had disappeared into the crowd. At least they were safe and they knew the plan. Hesitantly, she took Sabien's arm, and a sickening feeling crawled up her skin. Then she let him walk her up the stairs to the First Prince.

Eligor sat in the middle, with Teos on the ground beside him. Upon seeing Magda, Teos's face twisted in confusion.

Magda's face hardened as she channeled Dagmara's voice. "Teos, are you alright?" she blurted out.

"Yes," Teos answered, his voice shaky.

"Let my brother go now!" Magda shouted, more forcefully now. She attempted to run forward, but Sabien held her back, gripping her around the waist and holding her to him as she thrashed in his arms.

At the top of the stairs, they forced Claude onto his knees in front of the First Prince, before yanking his hands behind him and tying them together. He wrestled with the guards, but they firmly bound Claude so that he couldn't move.

Eligor spoke first upon seeing the two, "I didn't think you'd actually be stupid enough to attend my gathering. The King and Queen of Ilusauri, the last remaining guardians, came right to my doorstep to be killed."

Then Eligor turned his attention to Magda, who was still fighting against Sabien's grip as he held her above the ground.

"Release her," he ordered Sabien.

Sabien pushed Magda down onto her knees, and she fell forward, catching herself on her hands at the foot of the throne. Then Sabien bent down, grabbing Magda's chin and forcing her to look at Eligor. As he did so, he whispered in her ear:

"Whatever you're planning won't fool Eligor."

Magda tensed, but she refrained from showing any reaction in her face. Anxiety flooded through her veins, but she stayed put and kept her eyes on the First Prince.

"Get your hands off her," Claude snapped.

"Claude's right," said Eligor. "That's no way to treat one of my descendants."

Eligor held out his hand, as if to help Magda to her feet. Magda almost took the offer, reaching out to him, but she remembered the way the powers surged between them when they touched and knew it would be an instant giveaway. Instead, she said through gritted teeth:

"Go to hell."

Eligor beamed upon hearing the response and shifted back in his throne. "I guess we are related, aren't we?" he laughed. "Dagmara Zosia. It's nice to finally make your acquaintance. I'm Eligor Blaide. First Prince and soon to be the last heir to the Void magic."

Magda only had to buy her friends enough time by distracting Eligor so Dagmara could get close enough to get the crown and free Teos. Then, Magda would use her own magic to create enough chaos for them all to escape. Her only hope was to keep Eligor talking and his eyes on her and Claude.

"I've heard all about your little charade. Impersonating Princess Magdalena and seducing the Mad King. You must be quite cunning," Eligor complimented her.

"I didn't seduce anyone," Magda retorted.

"If the world didn't know any better, they might say we were working together, and this was all part of some master plan designed by the void guardians themselves to take back control."

Magda's breath caught in her throat. She suppressed the magic itching at her fingertips, begging to be unleashed.

He lifted his hand forward as he eyed Magda.

Claude let out a yell beside them. "Get away!" He winced in pain, turning his face away and struggling against his bindings.

Then Claude's eyes fixated on Eligor's fingers, which were held outward like a perch. Claude eyed the invisible space above Eligor's hand. Magda noted Claude's tormented expression and could only assume that Claude had been attacked by Eligor's bird, which was now perched in front of them. She knew that Dagmara could also see the bird, so she watched the invisible space where the bird sat perched and gasped in fear, playing her role.

"Yes," Eligor stroked the invisible space. "Zerua here leads me to those who are blood-related to the guardians. It is supposed to guide me to candidates to reinstate a magical branch if it is severed. Zerua sensed that there was another individual out there, one with magic. Then, as soon as Sabien deduced that Dagmara could also see Zerua, I knew it was her."

"Remember, I'm the one that told you she had a brother," Sabien cut in.

"Don't worry, Sabien," Eligor said, "Your loyalty will be rewarded."

Magda's throat clenched, and she hoped that the bird couldn't sense that she wasn't really Dagmara, kneeling before them all. If Eligor's pet only interacted with guardians other than Magda, the bird could reveal their entire charade right now. If the bird went to attack Magda, and she didn't react, their secret would be revealed.

"And you're an heir too," Eligor's attention was on Teos now. "The two lost children of the Azuremi assassin."

"What do you know about our mother?" Teos snapped.

Eligor laughed. "I sent assassins to torture and kill her, as well as find out if she had any descendants. However, your mother lied, sending my assassin to kill two young children, and I thought it was the end to it," said Eligor. "I now see I was manipulated."

"How did you know our mom had Void magic?" asked Magda.

"My pet is quite cunning," said Eligor, stroking the invisible space. "He sensed her as well, when she visited Dreadmarrow many years ago. It only took recruiting a few assassins to get to the bottom of the mystery. Who would have thought that my mother had a baby out of wedlock so many years ago, and somehow the Void lineage continued?"

"You don't have to kill us to control the Void," said Magda.

"And you don't have to kill Teos. He doesn't have his powers yet," said Claude.

"That didn't stop you from gaining the powers after your parents were killed," Eligor said to Claude. "No matter what, Teos will someday exhibit the Void powers, just as you did, Claude. Meaning I will have to kill both Dagmara and Teos to ensure all the powers are mine."

"If you touch my wife, I'll kill you," Claude retorted. "Don't underestimate me."

"Unfortunately, you won't be able to see what I do to Dagmara once you're dead, Claude. But don't worry, I promise I'll give you a valiant death. Do you want to know why all these people are here? These people are here to witness your demise and my return as the last heir of the void kingdom," Eligor said. "All will see me take out the Mad King, and all will bow to me forever."

CHAPTER 68
Dagmara

Dagmara saw Sabien escort Magda toward the dais. She only had a matter of time to act quickly, free Teos, and get the crown.

Ishani had disappeared into the crowd, moving into position to provide back-up for both Magda and Claude once the plan was in motion.

Dagmara approached Ravi, stepping in close to him. "Come with me," she said, pulling him behind one of the large columns at the outer edge of the dance floor. Then she reached into the pockets on her dress, pulling out a smoke bomb, and pressing it into Ravi's palm.

"Go to the center of the crowd, and use this to conceal our escape," said Dagmara. "You'll know when."

Ravi nodded.

"I'm going up there," said Dagmara, indicating the dais. Eligor had forced Magda and Claude to their knees, and they were all having a hushed conversation. So far, he had taken the bait. It seemed as if Eligor's attention was all focused on the pair, as if he had already won. He would not be expecting another guardian to appear.

Dagmara continued, "Cover me so no one else can see. It's the only way it will work."

Ravi nodded, leaning toward Dagmara and concealing her against the column, eyeing the other attendants to make sure no one was paying attention.

This was a risky move. She didn't exactly know how to use her invisibility or how long she could hold it. She would have to move fast.

Closing her eyes, she exhaled, picturing the warped world she had visited before. She had slipped into it in Dreadmarrow and once again in Gorzhelm. Channeling every thought into her movement, she harnessed her newfound magic.

Just like that, Dagmara disappeared from the room. She was now invisible. Ravi moved like a muted, phantom beside her, as did the dancers. Ghost-like music filled the air, as sweeping, jeweled ball gowns took flight in all directions, smearing in Dagmara's vision like an expansive, water-colored painting.

Ravi backed away from her, but he moved like a wisp of color caught in slow motion. Her gaze settled on the dais once more, and she made her move. She remained on the outside of the ballroom, just in case she would lose her hold over her invisibility.

Her breath caught in her throat as she saw the blackbird swoop down and perch on Eligor's hand. She felt her blood turn to ice, and she forced her body to stay calm. Distracting herself, she continued moving, weaving through the attendants.

Slowly, she crept up the back of the raised platform, cautiously making her way toward Eligor. She remained behind him. She would have to time this perfectly.

Holding her breath, she withdrew the explosive from her belt. It was the concoction Teos had made and used to blow up the cathedral during Magda's coronation. That day felt like an eternity ago.

Magda and Claude knew what was coming and would get out of the way of the blast. Teos would recognize the explosive. As for Eligor and Sabien? She hoped they took on the full impact.

"If you touch my wife, I'll kill you." Claude was saying, although the sounds were muffled. "Don't underestimate me."

"Unfortunately, you won't be able to see what I do to Dagmara once you're dead, Claude."

Dagmara inched closer, gripping the explosive in her hand.

Eligor's voice continued, "All will see me take out the Mad King, and all will bow to me forever."

Eligor's eyes turned red as he used the power of the air to levitate a dagger from his belt, unlatching it and hovering it toward Claude.

"Ladies and gentlemen," Eligor announced to the audience. "Can I have your attention?" A cheer went up throughout the room. "First, I would like you to say goodbye to the Mad King, Claude Mirage," said Eligor. "You're about to witness the end of the guardians as we know them and the rise of the Void lineage."

Magic sparkled at Claude's fingertips.

This was it. Dagmara had to act now.

Eligor summoned his magic, and his eyes lit up with crimson as a gust of wind blew his cape and rushed to the dagger.

Dagmara tossed the explosive out from behind the throne, and it launched through the invisible barrier. It skidded across the ground before rolling to a stop at Eligor's feet. All eyes went to the small metal ball on the ground. The time was running out. She lunged forward, yanking the crown from Eligor's head. His hair tore as she ripped it free. She moved to slip back into the shadows and behind the throne to shield herself from the explosive.

But Eligor whirled around. His hand molded to her wrist like iron, his eyes ablaze. The rough grip jolted her out from the mask of invisibility, and she gasped as the ballroom readjusted around her.

Eligor's lips parted, his eyes widening in recognition. "My descendant."

"Eligor."

She thrust her leg forward, kicking him directly in the stomach. He stumbled back, relinquishing his grip on the crown, shock etched across his features. She dove for cover behind the throne just as the dais exploded.

The ground ruptured, throwing Dagmara from her hiding place. Her breath was taken from her as she landed on her back, yards away. The impact reverberated in her spine, and the back of her head throbbed in pain.

Ringing. The world was ringing, vibrating, and muffled screams filled the air. Smoke clouded her sight, and she rolled onto her side, coughing. Darkness danced in her peripheral vision, and she blinked rapidly, trying to make sense of her surroundings.

A shadow crossed behind the throne, and Dagmara could barely make out Sabien in the dust, striding toward her.

She was out of time.

Dagmara scrambled to her feet, her gaze searching the crowd. It was a mass stampede, much like the one from the coronation. However, there was one figure who had climbed onto the support structure of the column, who was waving his hands wildly.

Taking her chance, Dagmara threw the crown toward Ravi. It soared over the crowd, and Ravi jumped to catch it.

The hounds leapt down from their positions on the walls, breaking the chains that were clamped around their necks. Their beady eyes were glued on the guests, as if they had been instructed to not let anyone leave the ballroom alive.

Upon seeing the vicious hounds turn on the crowd, screaming sounded from the attendees, and the entire room burst into pandemonium as the guests sprinted to the door.

Using Dagmara's vial, Ravi thrust it into the ground. With a single shatter, smoke folded around him, concealing him from sight and aiding his disappearance into the sea of guests.

Dagmara prayed that the crown was safe. She whirled away from Ravi, about to rescue Teos, when she came face-to-face with her worst nightmare.

Sabien lunged for her, his hand lacing around her throat. "I knew it wasn't you," he growled, his fingers digging into her skin.

She choked, her hands flying up to scratch his palm away, but he only tightened his grip.

"You should have stayed away!" he roared.

She could see stars. Her breath was rushing out of her body, her head spinning.

Then, through the smoke and debris, a shadow emerged from behind Sabien. Claude stepped out of the dust. He had escaped his bindings and although he was stripped of his weapons, it didn't prevent him from striking. His elbow barreled into the back of Sabien's skull, clobbering him. Sabien immediately released his hold on Dagmara's neck, stumbling to catch himself against the wall.

"Hands off my wife," Claude growled.

Choking for air, Dagmara struggled to stand, but Pierre slid out of the smoke. He hoisted Dagmara up onto her feet in one swift motion.

"Are you alright?" he asked.

She nodded, and he flashed her a smile before whirling on his former captain. Claude and Pierre, side by side, charged at Sabien.

Dagmara knew she couldn't waste another moment. She needed to find Teos.

A flash of gold lit the castle. Soul magic. Magda was taking care of Eligor. Everything was going according to plan.

Bolting across the dais, avoiding the flashes of gold and crimson, she raced to her brother. Teos was on the ground, Martine already kneeling next to him and undoing his bindings.

"Dagmara!" he cried.

Dagmara skidded to her knees, assisting Martine with the tight rope. It burned against her palms, but she wouldn't waste any time. "We have to go," she said as soon as the last knot was undone.

Martine nodded, letting the rope drop to the ground, before slinging Teos's arm over her shoulder.

Dagmara grabbed Teos's other arm, and together they both hoisted him up to his feet.

"That was my explosive, wasn't it?" Teos asked, a dimple appearing on his cheek.

"We are partners, remember?" She gave him the hint of a smile before guiding him down the stairs. With Martine's assistance, they helped Teos down the stairs of the dais and toward the exit.

"Sabien!" Eligor's voice boomed over the blasts of magic. "Don't let them get away!"

"Faster, faster!" Martine encouraged, as the whiz of projectiles rushed by.

Dagmara yanked her brother along, trying to increase her pace. As she tugged, Teos tripped, his weight falling onto the two girls.

"Come on," she encouraged, grunting to hoist him back up on his feet.

A dagger met with an attendee's chest, and they went down directly beside Dagmara. She had to move faster, but darkness started to dance in her vision. She couldn't support Teos's weight. Her heart began to thump against her ribcage harder.

"I got him."

Claude appeared out of the chaos. He slid between Teos and Dagmara, relieving her of the fatigue. He hoisted Teos's arm over his shoulders and nearly lifted him off his feet as they increased their pace to the exit. Pierre emerged from the crowd, clearing the way to the exit.

The group burst through the castle doors and could see the boats in the distance.

"Almost there!" Dagmara yelled. "Hold on!"

CHAPTER 69
Magdalena

Magda knew that Dagmara was going to throw the weapon that would send a blast through the room. As soon as she saw the metal ball roll underneath Eligor's feet, she exchanged a glance with Claude.

Eligor turned, distracted, and Magda shot up, dodging Sabien as she rolled down the steps as quick as lightning.

Behind her, the blast shattered the room, and a sharp ringing pierced her ears. Faint, muted screams played in the background like a continuous song. All around her, fog clouded her senses and burned her throat, and she coughed up the smoke furiously. She touched her body, feeling for any wounds. Then her hands immediately went to her ears, holding them while her vision adjusted.

She saw Dagmara throw the crown to Ravi, before another smoke bomb went off. Guests shrieked as more smoke covered them. The sound of snapping chains and snarling breaths burst through the air, as the massive beasts wrenched themselves from the wall, ready to defend their master.

"Magda!" Ishani was at her side, helping her up. "He went this way."

Behind the dais, Eligor was limping away, holding his ribcage. He had been wounded in the blast, and this was Magda's chance to finish him off for good. She trusted Ravi to secure the crown, and she trusted Claude would keep Dagmara safe.

"Watch out," said Ishani, pushing Magda to the side, as a giant hound lunged in their path. As quick as lightning, Ishani skidded to the ground, grabbing one of the dead guard's swords and arming herself.

"Go after Eligor!" Ishani shouted to Magda. She tore off her shoe, throwing it at the hound's head, and it viciously turned to Ishani, disregarding Magda.

Magda ran after Eligor, looping behind the dais. She channeled the Soul magic, finding the sharp stones that made up the throne, before launching them in Eligor's direction. She only needed one good hit.

Eligor turned, his eyes glowing red. The shrapnel was pushed off course, flinging back into the throne. As he did so, Magda saw his chest, burned from the blast. Blood was gushing from his side, and he staggered to the wall, holding himself up.

"You tricked me," he said. "You're alive."

"You're finished, Eligor," Magda said, crossing to him furiously.

Eligor's eyes lit up with red magic again, but he couldn't take flight and escape. Then they turned yellow, but nothing came.

Magda leaned down and picked up his dagger, which had been thrown from the blast, stepping toward the First Prince. She raised it high, aiming for his chest, but at the last second, his eyes turned violet. She brought the dagger down, but Eligor had disappeared, and the dagger scraped against empty air.

He was gone.

Invisible.

"Master Guardians are always strongest in their original power," a phantom voice echoed throughout the space as if they were in a cavern.

Magda turned around twice, looking for the First Prince. All she heard was screaming and shouting from the other side of the dais, as well as the snapping of teeth. A burning pain rippled across her back as a dagger sliced against her skin, slashing the dress. Blood instantly poured from the gash.

"You can't see me, but I can see you," Eligor taunted.

Magda backed away, searching the space.

Slash. One of the wings was cut from the dress, followed by another.

"Where's my crown?!" the phantom voice roared.

Magda spun around, trying to get out of the way, but the dagger sliced again against her arm, drawing more blood. She let out another yell, clutching onto her forearm, feeling the blood underneath her fingertips and seeping down her back.

A force pulled on the choker necklace, yanking her forward, and suddenly the room shifted. Colors melted together like a waterfall, and the screaming became muddled to her ear. Then the world went black as she was transported into the Void.

She was standing before Eligor, his hands on her necklace, and he stared wildly into her eyes. His hair was unkempt, his cape slashed, and his body bloodied. "Now no one can come save you when I gut your body," he laughed, holding the dagger.

"No!" Magda yelled, thrusting him backwards with the powers of the Spirit, until he landed paces away in the blackness.

"You can't escape this place, Magda," Eligor laughed, rolling over to his side and attempting to stand up. "You're in my kingdom now."

He shot a gust of Spirit magic forward, and it swirled around her. The pressure of the air crushed against her body, holding her in place, so that she couldn't move. The world felt heavy on her limbs, and Magda collapsed to the ground as the air pressure flattened her cheek to the floor.

She gasped for breath, but the air was pushing against her chest.

Magda tried to control the powers of the Void, but she wasn't sure how to channel her powers inside it. She was technically a Master

Guardian, so she would be able to channel the magic as he was, but for some reason, she couldn't find the powers. As much as she concentrated, she could not slip back into the vibrant colors of the real world, visible to everybody else.

Eligor had managed to get to his feet. "Why don't you heal me so you don't have to spend eternity trapped here alone?"

"You can't trap me here," said Magda, choking.

"I can't?" Eligor sneered, walking toward her. "Want to test that theory?"

The air crushed down on her further, and Magda let out a scream. She steadied her frantic breathing before saying, "I'm a Master Guardian...I have the powers to get out."

"Do you know how to use them?" Eligor asked, spurting blood from his mouth. Then, on either side of the First Prince, a pair of hounds appeared, but now they were inside the Void with them. They moved slowly, approaching Magda with bared teeth, protecting their master. A few more moments, and they would pounce.

"Unfortunately, I am more skilled with the Void than you are. They will only listen to whoever is more powerful," said Eligor. He held his hand out, waiting to give the hounds a command. "We both walk out of this together, or we both end up dead."

Magda tried to ignite the Void magic, to send a spark through her body, to escape and leave Eligor in his prison, so he would die alone, but to no avail. Her breathing was raspy, and the wound on her shoulder and back burned, but no matter how hard she focused, she could not summon the Void powers with the terror flooding through her heart.

She could die here, and then who would restore the magic to the lands? Who would be able to use the crown?

Eligor reached his hand out to hers, "Heal me." he said.

An iron clasp of wind clamped around her wrist, and the air yanked her forward, pulling her up to a standing position, as if she was a light as a feather. Then the invisible chains pulled her wrist forward, causing her to stumble as the wind forced her hand in his.

When their fingers touched, it was as if a spark ignited inside her. Purple flashed from her hands, and she kicked Eligor in the groin, before tumbling backwards, falling over the dress to the floor.

Colors flashed around her, and loud screams pounded her ears. Eligor was gone, and around her the world came to once more. Behind her, one of the hounds lunged, raking its teeth across her back before its snout got caught in her cape. Magda let out a yell, her eyes turning red, as she spiraled the wind around the hounds body, before launching him away from her.

More hounds stepped forward, as if they were going for the kill, but Magda skidded around the throne, blasting as much magic as possible back at the beasts. On the other side, Ishani had just slayed another hound.

"Come on!" Magda said, grabbing Ishani's hand. Her entire body ached from the cuts and bruises, and her breath still came in violent gushes as if the wind had been forced from her chest.

She limped next to Ishani as they ran for the door, jumping over injured guests and hound carcasses. Ravi was at the exit, waving his hands furiously. He had the crown in one hand, and his other on the door handle. "Hurry!" he yelled. He was ready to slam the doors closed, trapping the vicious hounds inside so that they could make their escape.

A hound leapt up on Ishani's right, scratching her forearm. Ishani let out a scream, before plunging the sword into the hound's body. They both stumbled together, tearing through the crowd of shrieking guests and darting out of the way of the ravenous monsters.

Suddenly, about a dozen more hounds encircled them, blocking their path, and slinking their way toward Magda and Ishani. Behind them, another row of macabre beasts stepped throughout the room, bearing their teeth and glowing, violet scales.

"There's too many!" yelled Ishani, slashing the sword left and right as she slayed two more. "Can't you do something?! Don't you have Void powers?"

Magda closed her eyes, attempting to find the Void powers deep down, but she couldn't find the spark. She couldn't breath, for she still felt the crushing weight of the wind. The bruises on her neck and the blood on her clawed back only alerted her to excruciating pain.

Her hands turned to fists as she attempted to reach inside her, finding the Void powers, and her entire body felt like it was being splintered apart.

"Stop!" she called out to the hounds, attempting to use the magic, but instead, darkness clouded the outside of her vision like a dark curtain. It threatened to drown her in pain.

"I can't," Magda choked, spurting up blood.

It was clear this was going to be the end. All around them, the hounds crept forward, ready to pounce in one moment. There was no way the girls could fight all of them at once. Moreover, Eligor could be lurking in the void, completely invisible, at this very moment. How would they defeat the hounds?

Ishani had Magda's arm, pulling her away. Magda struggled to stay upright, sliding on the slippery tile. All around them, the sound of shattering windows blasted through the space as the thick, thorny brambles slinked into the ballroom like snakes. They coiled down the walls, the thorny vines extending closer to the girls.

Don't leave the party so soon. Eligor laughed.

Magda wanted to respond but she couldn't find her magic. None of the elements came to her, and she faded in Ishani's arms. The thorny vines and hounds slinked closer, as if they were waiting for a command. "Magda!" Ravi screamed.

Ravi's voice brought her back to life. Magda snapped her head up in time to see Ravi throw the crown into the air, and the golden object went flying, clearing over the spiked chandelier. Magda followed its projectile, before grabbing the crown in mid-air, gripping onto Ishani with all her might.

"What are you doing?!" Ishani asked, looking from the crown to Magda.

"Do you want this?" Magda struggled to ask.

"What?" Ishani clarified.

"Do you want the magic again?" she asked.

Ishani took only a second to pause and survey the approaching hounds and vines around them, before saying, "Do it!"

Magda put the crown on. The feeling of the earth and stone flew through Magda's mind, and Soul magic ricocheted through every fiber of her being. She focused on channeling the powers in her fingertips, and when she saw the yellow magic swirling through her hands, she closed her eyes. A pulse rippled through her body, seeming to crack it into pieces, as a jolt thrust from her core into her hands.

Suddenly the thorny vines grabbed onto the girl's ankles, digging into their skin. Magda let out a yell as she was flung to the ground, being dragged back toward the throne. But she never let go of Ishani or the crown as she wriggled in their grasp.

Using my crown, are we? The sounds of Eligor's luscious, deep voice rattled in Magda's head, but she held firm to Ishani.

You're only weakening yourself and making your friends into new targets. He laughed.

You're wrong.

Eligor continued. *While I grow stronger, you will only grow weaker.*

A flash of power ruptured through Magda's body, and she screamed as her hands became hot with white magic. All of the sudden, the surge died down, and Magda was filled with emptiness, as if the crown had ripped a part of her from her body, leaving nothing but a blank vacuum in its place.

Magda opened her eyes, still being dragged across the floor. Glass and debris tore through her clothes, ripping at her corset and skirt.

Ishani's irises were glowing, and her face and hair portrayed a newfound sense of health. There was no doubt she was a guardian once more.

The vines stopped moving, and dug their thorns further into the girl's flesh. Then the hounds reared on their haunches, ready to pounce and sink their teeth into their bodies.

In an instant, Ishani turned her hands into fists and let out a forceful yell. Explosions of magic sprung from her hands, and the vines released them. Even thicker ropes of thorns cracked through the stone walls, strangling the hounds like chains and pulling them back against the columns. At the same time, the stone floor flew outward, blasting the beasts in front of them, and splattering them against the edges of the ballroom.

Magda had to duck down and cover her head to avoid the force of the magic. When she came to, she saw Ravi at the door, beckoning them to run.

Ishani and Magda turned behind them, only to see more hounds flooding down from the throne.

"Where's Eligor?!" Ishani yelled, grabbing Magda's hand, and they tore for the opening. "We have to finish him off."

Running away so soon, Princess? Once my accomplice heals me, you will be finished.

"We can't let him get the crown!" Magda shouted, sprinting beside Ishani. Her entire body was in pain, but the only thing propelling her now was pure adrenaline. "We need to go!"

Ishani and Magda leapt through the door, and Ravi shoved it closed. A second later, the hounds smashed their snouts against the wood, snarling and snapping at the exit.

CHAPTER 70
Dagmara

Bursting through the barrier, they returned to the Sea of Scarlet. Pierre pulled Dagmara out of the rift and she resurfaced on solid ground. Reaching down, she helped lift Teos up before Martine and Claude scaled the side of the ravine. Rain instantly soaked them from the dark sky, the clouds having opened while they were in the Void. Pierre released Teos, letting him stand on his own, before whirling back to face the darkness. Martine and Claude panted, glancing at everyone in turn to make sure they were all safe.

Dagmara waited for Magda, Ishani, or Ravi to appear, but they were nowhere. "Where are the others?"

Teos stumbled back from the rift, regaining his balance, watching with wide eyes.

"They have the crown right?" Claude asked.

"They should," Dagmara said, wiping slick rain off her face. "Ravi should be out here already though."

"He must've gone back in for Magdalena," Martine suggested.

"Oh no," Dagmara breathed, starting forward, but Claude grabbed her by the arm.

"You can't go back in there."

"But—"

Before Claude argued further, a flash sparked in the rift. Ravi, Ishani, and Magda were climbing up the side of the ravine, pulling themselves out and over the rocks. The trio rolled over the edge of the crack, landing in the Sea of Scarlet, and the remaining hounds snapped at their heels.

They skidded to Dagmara's side, and the glint of Eligor's crown was vibrant on Magda's head.

Then Ishani raised her arm, creating a larger cavern in the earth. The ground shook, and Dagmara nearly lost her footing as the dirt separated. She created an obstacle between them and the hounds, and the creatures were forced to skid to a halt on the opposite side, but they didn't stop their prowling.

Utilizing the rain, Magda summoned the raindrops into ice. They flew down onto the hounds, slaying them. Within moments, Ishani and Magda had killed all the beasts that followed them out of the rift. No more appeared. It was silent.

Ishani bent over, placing her hands on her knees, and gasped for breath. Magda was already on the ground, bending over in pain.

"Is everyone alright?" Ravi asked, though his voice was winded.

Claude held Dagmara by the arm. "Yes. We saved Teos."

At the sound of her brother's name, a rush of energy surged through Dagmara's body. She straightened, knocking Claude's hand away to turn and face her brother.

He stood before her, his weight on one leg. His face was ghostly pale, and his lips were a shade of purple.

"Teos?"

"Dagmara..." he said, ending in a rasp.

"What happened?" Dagmara charged forward. She grabbed him by the shoulder, searching for the injury.

Then he collapsed into her.

"Help!" she yelled, and instantly the others surrounded her. Teos's face collided with her shoulder, and she saw the wound. Protruding from his lower back was a single dagger, ordained with Ilusaurian silver.

Sabien.

"No!" Dagmara screamed, struggling underneath his weight.

Pierre and Claude were already there, helping set him down on his side. He wasn't moving. His arms fell limply in front of him, his gaze nonexistent.

Magda skidded onto her knees, mud splattering the area. Bruises covered her figure, but she had already summoned the water all over her beaten body, and raindrops had seeped into the wounds on her skin. "I can use the rain. We need to remove the knife now."

Claude didn't waste a moment. He took the handle of the dagger and yanked it from Teos's back. He shook at the movement, but didn't cry.

"Stay with me, Teos," Dagmara said, gripping his hand. "We're going to save you."

Teos didn't blink, but she knew he heard her.

Leaning closer, Ravi placed his fingers to Teos's neck. "Magda..."

"Shh!" Magda scolded, pressing her palms to the wound. Her eyes began to change color, ice blue dancing in her irises. The rain fell hard, moving to her summon. It collected at her hands, washing the wound. The ground puddled in red.

The world seemed to still, and Dagmara waiting with bated breath as she watched the wound close. She gripped Teos's hands tighter in her own. "You'll be alright," she whispered under her breath, though her voice couldn't be heard over the cascading rain.

Leaning back on her heels, Magda pulled away. His shirt was still sliced through, but his skin was smooth.

"Oh, yes!" Dagmara said. She brushed Teos's curls off his forehead. "You're safe now, Teos." She shook her brother by the shoulder. "Come on, let's get back to the fortress."

The rain poured down Teos's face, streaming into his open eyes. He didn't answer his sister.

"Teos…"

The others surrounding her didn't speak. Ishani and Martine stood still in the rain. Claude, Ravi, and Pierre remained kneeling next to Teos. Magda reached a shaking hand toward Dagmara, but as soon as she made contact, Dagmara jerked back.

"No. Don't touch me." She shook her brother harder this time. "Teos!" she screamed, the cry erupting from deep in her chest.

"I'm so sorry…" Magda said under her breath.

"No!" Dagmara yelled, yanking her hands away. She shuffled back on the ground, away from the hands that tried to comfort her. The mud seeped through her clothes, but she didn't have the energy to rise. Every limb felt broken. She stared blankly at her brother, lying before her, unmoving.

He couldn't be gone. After all this time—she needed him. She needed him as much as she assumed he needed her.

A cough burst from Teos's chest.

"Teos!" Dagmara shouted.

Teos choked, spurting up rain water.

A collective sigh of relief passed through the group. Dagmara slid closer, helping her brother sit upright before tugging him into a tight embrace.

"Don't scare me like that ever again," she said, gripping him as strongly as she could.

"I will do my best to avoid the flying dagger next time," Teos muttered against Dagmara's shoulder.

A laugh escaped her lips, and despite his attempts to pull away from the hug, she didn't let him go.

CHAPTER 71
Magdalena

They made the short trek from the Sea of Scarlet back to the fortress. Magda held tight to the crown, which was still fastened to her head. Now, she had the power to create new guardians, not Eligor.

As soon as they reached the courtyard, Bernadette raced out into the rain to greet them. Odie was with her, sprinting at top speed across the open space. He reached Magda first, barking happily, and she knelt down to hug him around the neck.

"Yes, I'm fine, don't worry," Magda told her pet.

His tail continued wagging as he circled around her, and then the dog continued onto the rest of the group.

"Teos, I was so worried!" Bernadette shouted as she ran up to the group and embraced him. They stood together, exchanging a few words, before Bernadette pulled away.

"Promise me you'll go straight to the infirmary," said Bernadette.

Teos nodded.

Bernadette called out to Ravi. "Come with us, will you? My advisors and doctors finished putting the journal back together and translating it. They want to ask you about the potion you administered to your sister."

"Yes, Your Majesty," said Ravi. He was kneeling next to Odie, scratching behind his ears. He rose and gave Magda's hand a squeeze before they all began crossing the courtyard.

Bernadette called over her shoulder, "Magda, there's a man waiting for you. He's in the throne room."

"Who?" Magda asked, confused.

"He's Celesta. The spearhead," Bernadette explained.

"Reon," Claude's voice lifted.

Dagmara turned to Martine. "Can you both watch over Teos and make sure he stays safe?" she asked. "I don't know if they'll try to come back. I'll meet up with you soon."

"Of course," said Martine in full understanding, before heading after Teos and Ravi. Pierre followed Martine, and the two guards made sure to stay close to Dagmara's brother.

The remaining four raced to the throne room, still in their ball gowns. When they arrived, dawn was breaking, and sunlight poured in the cracks through the windows. Reon stood facing the throne, this time in muted armor, with his curved sword at his side. His hair was pulled back, and his metal helmet was fastened to his head.

"Princess," Reon addressed Magda first. Then he turned to Claude, greeting the king, Dagmara, and Ishani in turn.

"I came with reinforcements," said Reon, "As many men as I could spare. I hear we will have a great battle on our hands."

"Yes," Magda admitted, "Thank you for standing by Azurem."

"I'm standing by the guardians," said Reon.

"And the council allowed you to come here?" Claude cut in.

"It took some convincing," Reon admitted, "but since you left, the problem with the hounds has only increased. They certainly don't want Eligor in control, and they don't want their land to die either. They know the importance of having new guardians, whether they have political power in Celestaire or not."

"Well, when you go back," Magda started, "you can tell them that we found Sora's murderer."

"Where?" gasped Reon.

"She's dead," Magda confessed.

Claude continued, "Both Magda and I witnessed it."

"I see," said Reon. "I'll bring this information to the council, and hopefully we can make more progress with a peace agreement."

"Thank you," said Claude graciously.

Then Magda turned to the entire group, announcing, "Ishani has the Soul magic now." She gulped, knowing that Dagmara and Claude hadn't witnessed her split-second decision.

Reon looked to Ishani curiously, as did Dagmara, but Claude was silent.

Claude spoke first, "Once you give away your powers, there's no going back. You won't be able to wield the Soul magic again unless Ishani dies. You understand that, right?"

"Yes," said Magda. She looked at Ishani. "I know what these powers meant to you and to Kiran. I know the trials caused you a lot of pain, and you were always my first choice to be the Guardian of the Soul. You were a guardian, and you know how to use magic. It wouldn't have mattered if we were in danger of losing our lives or not."

Ishani didn't respond, but gave her a curt nod.

"I did this because you're one of the only people that I trust to fight alongside me, and you're the only one I trust to ensure the survival of Flaustra."

"I abdicated my right to the throne years ago," said Ishani.

"The people will accept you," said Magda. "Please, Ishani. I know I didn't give you any time to consider this, but I hope you'll think long and hard about helping Flaustra. Besides, Eligor won't stop, and we need all the help we can get to fight against him."

"You know I will fight with you all against Eligor," said Ishani. "I was just surprised. After everything you've done to master the Soul magic?"

"It was the only way. We have the crown now, and the whole point is to use it."

Ishani nodded. "You know I never wanted this."

"I know," said Magda.

"But I'll do my best to make Kiran proud. And try to make Flaustra better than it was under my mother."

"No one else could do it but you," said Magda.

Ishani gave a soft smile.

"So what powers do you have left?" Reon asked Magda.

"Void, Life, Mind, and Spirit," Magda admitted.

"I don't understand," said Reon, "Claude has Mind."

"A Master Guardian has them all, it doesn't matter who else has them," Magda replied. "Just like Eligor. He has them all. We're supposed to ensure a branch doesn't go extinct—like the Spirit for example, has no guardians. However, Eligor has decided to keep all the magic for himself."

"Why you?" Reon asked, though there was no malice in his voice.

"I don't know," she shrugged, feeling heat rise in her cheeks. "Any of the guardians could have become a Master Guardian. Kiran, Sora, Aleksy..." her voice trailed off.

Scared, Princess? Eligor's words slithered into Magda's mind, his voice slimy as oil.

The world shifted, and Magda did everything she could to stop herself from being transported into the Void next to Eligor once more, but she couldn't control the powers. All around her, she felt every inch of his emotions, a burning rage that fed his drive for retribution.

She stood before him, his gold and navy armor beaten and bloodied. A stained, red bandage was wrapped around his abdomen. His forehead was all sweat, and stringy, blonde hair plastered his face. But this time the crown wasn't on his head, but hers.

I'm not scared. Magda said, feeling confident for the first time.

You should be, he rasped. *I'm coming for you and my descendants.*

Then I'll kill the Mad King and your new Soul Guardian. I will be the only guardian this world knows.

You better stay away from them and out of their heads. Magda threatened.

Oh, Princess. He went to touch her again, but quickly conceded. He stumbled, clutching his side, before falling to his knees. Then he flipped his sweaty hair out of his eyes before looking up at her and saying, *How do you know I'm not already in their heads? How do you know your friends are people you can trust?*

I know you're trying to manipulate me. Magda retorted, attempting to hold onto any ounce of confidence. She tried to keep her voice from shaking as she said, *It's time you accept that I'm the new Master Guardian, and you have no power over them.*

Eligor reached for her in anger, grabbing her around the hips and pulling her to him, until his chin was pressed against her stomach. The magic pulsed through them when they touched, stimulating Magda's senses. He sunk his fingers into her body and growled as he looked up at her, wild and fanatic. *You call yourself a Master Guardian, but I think it's time you experienced how the world treated one. How they treated me. Trapped, helpless, and begging for mercy.*

You'll be begging me for mercy when I'm done with you. Magda retorted.

His eyes were aflame with wickedness. *I'm the one with plans for you.*

He released her, and Magda was back in the throne room next to her friends. She gasped, thankful to be free from the Void and the clutches of his stimulating touch.

"Eligor is coming," she announced urgently.

"Do we have any idea of how or where he will attack?" asked Ishani.

"Through the rifts," said Dagmara.

They all turned to her.

"Just as the hounds move through the ravines, he can too," she explained. "He could come from the rift in the Sea of Scarlet or any of the others. He could be anywhere."

"And he could come at any second," said Magda.

"We'll need weapons and reinforcements," said Claude.

"I'll get my men ready and prepared," Ishani said.

"Me too," said Reon.

"I'll head to the apothecary to get more potions and explosives," said Dagmara.

"I'm coming with you," Claude said strongly, and Dagmara gave a nod.

"Be ready," said Magda.

Enjoy your last moments. Eligor cooed.

Enjoy yours. Magda snapped before slamming up every shield in her mind.

CHAPTER 72
Dagmara

Quickly, Dagmara raced to her chambers. The rain had lessened, and only a few drops splattered against the windows. However, the day remained overcast.

She threw her mangled ballgown on the floor before putting on her fighting leathers, arming herself with a series of daggers and throwing stars. Claude changed as well, and she had to force herself to focus on the upcoming battle. They remained quiet as they got ready, both thinking of the worst.

Pain and grief pulsed through Dagmara's chest, for she was exhausted. Not only physically, but emotionally. They had almost lost Teos, and she wasn't even sure that she had the strength to get through the next attack. Any moment now, her health could cause her to collapse, and it was only pure adrenaline and the fear of death that kept her going.

Then she and Claude went to the apothecary, finding that it had been cleaned up after Viette's attack. The room was familiar, with a central table of potions and notebooks. The walls were covered with shelves of poisons, medicines, and Teos's creative explosions. Ahead, the large windows signified that the sun had peaked over the horizon, and the day was just beginning, although dark clouds covered the landscape.

Dagmara dashed to the first shelf, finding a hydration potion. Stealing a vial, she unscrewed the cork and drank it, knowing she desperately needed every ounce of energy for this battle. Then she grabbed a few jasny bombs, attaching them to her armor, before snatching a few of her favorite poisons.

She froze at the shelf of smierc and kaspin. The vials had been moved and over half were missing. She exhaled, frustrated that the knights had messed with her potions, but knew they had no choice after the disaster that had happened in the apothecary.

When she turned over her shoulder, she noticed Claude hunched over the table, his hands gripping the edge of the wood.

"Are you alright?" Dagmara asked, her voice soft.

"Is it wrong that part of me hoped Sabien would realize his mistakes and leave Eligor?" he asked. "I thought he would finally acknowledge he chose the wrong side. Eligor will hunt him down. And yet...on the dais...he fought me as though he truly wanted me dead. As though every day of our friendship was simply a long plot against me." He lifted one hand, bruised and bleeding along the knuckles, staring at it as though the marks were infected.

Dagmara approached him cautiously. "Sabien's mind is a twisted place. There's no way to rationalize what he's thinking."

"I wonder if he escaped. I wonder if Eligor finally killed him in order to take the Life magic. Eligor was badly wounded."

"I hope he did," Dagmara admitted. She leaned against the table, relieving her body for a brief moment. "Eligor may have ordered the assassination, but it was Sabien that killed Aleksy. I don't know if I can rest easy until I know he is dead."

Claude nodded. "Me too," he said. "Eligor killed my parents. My kingdom is dying. My best friend betrayed me, tortured you, and killed Sacha. I need this to end." He glanced up from the table, meeting Dagmara's gaze.

She nodded.

"But it won't be a victory if I lose you in the process," he admitted. He took her hand, interlacing his fingers with hers.

"I know," Dagmara replied. "Which is why we're going to stop him together. Don't worry. We're going home after this."

His brow furrowed. "Aren't you home now?"

She inclined her head. "You know I'm referring to Ilusauri."

He smiled. "I just wanted to hear you say it." He closed the distance between them, before placing his forehead against hers. "We will get through this together."

Before he could move in for a kiss, the ground began to rumble. The stone floor underneath them shifted, and an audible gasp escaped Dagmara's lips. She stumbled, clinging to the edge of the table to keep herself upright. "What is that?" she asked.

Claude released her. Then he raced to the nearest window and peered out.

"By the guardians..." he muttered under his breath.

Dagmara shoved her way past Claude, pressing her palms to the glass. Her heart plummeted into her stomach, every nerve igniting in her body as she gaped at the scene before her.

In the distance, past the rushing waterfalls, the Sea of Scarlet was barely visible. The ashen field, once full of life and poppies, was separating. The rift they had exited to get back to Azurem from the Mystic South was widening. The earth was opening up, swallowing the ground and breathing out gusts of violet magic. Darkness swirled out of the dust, a rift dividing the earth.

Thunder cracked in the distance, signaling that the rainstorm could start again soon.

She couldn't tear her gaze from the scene.

Out of the earth, a horde was emerging. From this distance, it resembled a swarm of insects, but the mass of creatures was only one thing.

Hounds.

They clamored out of the ground, scraping their way over one another. The hundreds of creatures emerged into the open air and tore off toward town. Their giant paws were like a stampede, and their numbers were endless.

"The hounds...Eligor..." Dagmara said breathlessly. "How? Did Sabien heal him?"

"Or did he kill Sabien?" Claude asked.

Dagmara shuddered, her breath shaking as she exhaled.

Dagmara turned to see Magda, Ravi, and Teos run into the apothecary.

"There you both are!" Magda said. "Are you seeing this?"

Backing away from the windowpane, Dagmara was one step ahead of Magda. "We have to save the town. We can control the hounds."

"I don't know how," Magda objected. "You're the only one who has successfully done so."

"He's stronger than me," replied Dagmara. "And there are far too many. I need your help. You have Void magic too." Dagmara reached out and grabbed Magda's hand.

"You aren't going alone," said Claude. He placed a gentle hand on Dagmara's back, stepping closer to her.

Teos was already at the shelves, grabbing mixtures and vials. "I'll keep making explosives," he said. "Maybe that will give you all an advantage. Ravi, can you help?"

"Show me how," said Ravi, reaching Teos's side and grabbing additional potions.

"I'll find the others," Claude said, running out of the room without another word.

For some reason, Dagmara's head clouded with doubts. Dark spots spun in her vision, and she struggled to keep herself upright.

"We can do this," Magda encouraged.

Dagmara agreed. "We'll do it together. For Aleksy, my mom, and your dad."

Letting out a sharp exhale, Magda straightened her posture. "Time to kill the First Prince."

CHAPTER 73
Dagmara

The horror had already saturated the entire town of Gorzhelm. Villagers ran haphazardly, desperately trying to escape for their lives. Massive hounds bolted through the streets, colliding against walls and tearing limbs and flesh. Blood trickled down the pavement, filling the streets with a putrid smell.

They were everywhere.

A burst of lightning cracked through the sky, but the ground remained dry. Dagmara hoped the rain held off to provide them a bit of visibility in the battle.

"Get the villagers inside!" Claude was ordering Martine and Pierre.

"Save as many people as you can!" Magda echoed. She whirled on an oncoming hound, sending it backward with a thrust of Spirit magic.

Reon slipped behind the hound and slayed it with his sword. He straightened, blood dripping from the blade as he rotated it in his grasp. "I'll see you all on the other side."

"Take count of how many hounds you kill, Reon," Ishani stated. "I think I'll have you beat." Golden magic danced in her irises, the reinvigorated magic lighting in her veins.

"I will be disappointed if you don't." Reon nodded. A hound lunged out of a side street, and Reon decapitated it with one swift blow of his curved sword.

"Remember," Claude announced at the center of the group. "As soon as one of us sees Eligor approach from the skies, we all go to meet him. We are stronger together."

Reon and Ishani both gave a curt nod before they broke off. A group of Celesta troops followed Reon, while the orange and turquoise colors of Ishani's officers flocked after her.

"Claude," Dagmara started, then stopped short. She didn't even have anything to say, but she simply wanted him to stay a moment longer. They had skirted death one too many times, and a piece of her was nervous that one of them wouldn't make it this time.

However, she wasn't forced to say anything.

Claude cleared the distance between them before she could blink. His hands swooped behind her lower back, and he yanked her flush against his chest. Her lips collided against his, her entire body igniting at his touch. His cologne wafted around her, his body heat warming the ice in her veins. He deepened the kiss, as though it was the last one they would ever share, and she whimpered at the sheer intensity.

Then he withdrew, meeting her gaze with an undeniable lust in his expression. He placed his palms against her cheeks, holding her face in place as he whispered against her lips. "I require you in my chamber after all of this is said and done. Do you hear me?"

Heat raced through her body, her cheeks turning bright red. "I think you mean *our* chamber?"

A slow smile creased his face. "I don't care what we call it as long as you're there."

"I will be." Dagmara returned the smile.

He pressed his lips to hers once more, short and sweet, leaving her wanting. Then he pulled away, withdrawing his sword and rotating to face another hound charging through the alley.

Skidding out of the way, Dagmara's back slammed against the wall beside Magda. Her best friend's eyebrows were raised so far on her head that they nearly disappeared into her silver hair. She was dressed for battle with two daggers and a canteen of water slung at her belt.

"We have to make sure you stay alive for *that*," said Magda.

"Oh, stop." Dagmara laughed.

The moment of reprieve was over as quickly as it had come about. She had to get to the Western edge of town. That's where Teos's explosive could safely go off, knocking out the hounds but keeping the villagers protected.

One of the beasts lunged out of the shadows. Dagmara whirled to face its snapping jowls, extending her dagger toward it. "Stop!" she cried, hoping to channel whatever power she had at the tomb.

The hound kept coming toward her. Suddenly the wet crunch of blade meeting bone rippled through the air. Martine skidded on the cobblestone, driving her blade between its underbelly scales. The beast collapsed to the side, dead.

"Well," Martine panted, rising to her feet. "Can't say I imagined we would be repeating this." A smile spread across her face.

Another dove from the alley. Dagmara already had a throwing star in her hand, chucking it toward the animal. It soared past Martine, nailing the hound between the eyes. It staggered against the impact, slipping on the cobblestone. Martine rotated and delivered a final killing blow. She continued into battle beside Pierre and Claude, all of them executing perfect Ilusaurian technique.

"We have one!" Ravi's voice penetrated the battle. He panted, holding an explosive in his grasp. "Teos is making more as we speak. We're trying to gather a whole team."

"Did you run all the way from the fortress?" Magda asked.

A lopsided smile creased Ravi's face.

"Come on, we have to set that off in the rift they're coming out of," Dagmara announced. The three of them turned to face the Western side of the town, but were confronted with carnage. The entire street was filled with hound carcasses, Azuremi knights, Celesta soldiers, and even Ishani's crew. Scattered villagers ran haphazardly, some of them attacking the animals with various homemade weapons.

"We'll never get through," said Magda.

Ravi inclined his head. "There is one way." He raced toward a stack of barrels, maneuvering up them with grace. With one jump, he grabbed onto the edge of the rooftop and hoisted himself up. He extended his hand down toward Magda. "Still trust me?"

Magda nodded before following his path. She reached for his grasp, and he helped her find purchase on the rooftop. Dagmara was last to follow, feeling uneasy as she scaled the barrels. As she launched herself upward, Ravi caught her. His strength was surprising.

When they were all safely on two feet, Ravi took off across the rooftops. Both Magda and Dagmara followed his every move. The roofs were slanted, an uneven surface underneath Dagmara's feet. And yet, they cleared the fighting below. They reached the border of town, dropping back to the ground utilizing wooden crates. The rift was in the distance, beasts pouring out. There was no way they would get close enough to drop the explosive in the rift itself. They would have to throw it from here.

"Would you like to do the honors?" Ravi asked Dagmara.

She couldn't respond, her heart hammering inside her chest and her pulse soaring through her body. She gestured forward, giving him the invitation.

The explosive soared through the air. Ravi aimed it perfectly, the ball flying toward the stampede of hounds. It bounced off one beast before landing in the center of the horde.

A blast lit the sky. Dagmara stumbled back, bracing herself against the crates. The explosive must've been one of the strongest Teos had made. Limbs, flesh, and scales flew in haphazard directions. The ground rumbled from the impact, and smoke ascended into the heavens.

As the smoke cleared, the devastation came into sight. At least two dozen hounds were lying in pieces. There was an indent in the earth from the center point of the explosion.

And yet, giant paws reached out from the ground, more beasts finding their footing on the land.

"We need more," said Ravi, backing up.

"We will hold them off," Magda said. "Go!"

Ravi nodded, turning and racing back to the fortress.

Magda looked to Dagmara. "We have to prevent more hounds from entering town."

Dagmara nodded, unable to tear her eyes from the creatures emerging. There were so many of them. They clawed their way out into the light, their talons scraping at the earth. How many were there? If they didn't stop this attack, the hounds would keep traversing through Azurem. They would take over everything.

Planting her feet firmly on the ground, Dagmara stared at the expanse. They were coming for her. She barely knew how to control them—she barely knew how to embody the new Void magic bestowed on her.

"I don't know what I'm doing," Magda said under her breath.

Dagmara reached out and grabbed her hand. "Together."

"You know what you're doing?"

"Nope. It's not like it is...that many hounds."

The earth practically vibrated under their feet, the stampede of the massive paws thundering closer. There were at least hundreds.

"One more may make it challenging," Magda quipped.

"Let's hope one more doesn't show up then," replied Dagmara.

They were close now. It was time.

Dagmara extended her hand toward the hounds, remembering the way she commanded them in Dreadmarrow. "Stop!" she called, meeting the gaze of one of the hounds in the front.

They didn't slow. The horde kept thundering toward them, snapping jaws and sharp fangs.

Magda squeezed Dagmara's hand tighter. "On three," she said

before holding out her own palm toward the wave of Void creatures. "One."

"Two."

"Stop!" they shouted simultaneously, their voices carrying over the clamor of paws and talons on the pavement. The creatures were mere strides away.

And yet they didn't slow. It was clear this was going to be the end. There were too many of them. Dagmara wasn't powerful enough, and Magda didn't know how to tap into the Void magic.

Another crack of lightning. Another burst of thunder. The storm was drawing closer.

"I don't need Void magic," Magda said under her breath. "I don't need to give it to anyone. But I can make you stronger."

"What?" Dagmara jerked back.

All of the sudden, the purple magic swirled around their hands and the crown lit up on Magda's head. The sky sparked with violet streaks and the remaining powers of the Void spiraled from Magda's body into Dagmara's fingertips. Magda channeled her glimmer of the Void magic into Dagmara's body.

"What are you doing?!" Dagmara yelled over the stampede.

"You're the only one who can do this," said Magda.

An abrupt jolt lurched through Dagmara, bursting through her heart before recoiling back to her fingertips. Her nerves were on fire, and her body was pummeled with all-consuming magic.

Dagmara released her fingers from Magda's, shoving her hand forward and screaming once more.

"Stop!" Dagmara yelled at the hounds.

As if the hounds were obeying a new master, they skidded to a halt, seconds from devouring the girls. Then, they promptly laid down, crossing their paws over their other.

"You did it," Magda panted, grasping her chest and leaning against Dagmara.

"Are you alright?"

"Yes," she replied, though still winded from the transfer of magic.

Behind them, they heard the howling of other groups of animals in the distance, who had not heard Dagmara's call. The roar of snarls and claws echoed through the city streets, and the rush of the stampedes beyond rustled the air. Had another rift opened on the opposite end of town? Even if Dagmara had temporarily stopped this group, hounds could be closing in on all sides.

"Don't feel bad," a sultry voice cooed. A shadow crossed over the sun before a figure landed on the rooftop on the opposite side of the street. "It took me years to be able to control all of them. You just found your powers."

As the man landed, his cape fanned around him, blowing perfectly in the breeze. His golden hair shimmered in the setting sun, his pale skin glistening in the light.

The First Prince.

CHAPTER 74
Dagmara

"Eligor," Magda said under her breath. She grabbed Dagmara, shoving her behind her.

Dagmara's hands clutched around one of the throwing stars in her corset, ready to throw. As she focused on his chest, prepared to take aim, his condition brought her a sense of hope. His brow was covered in sweat, and his shirt was still bloodied, with a bandage peeking out from under his armor.

The First Prince paid Magda no attention. His gaze was on Dagmara alone. The ice in his expression was chilling, sending a ripple of shudders through her body.

Then he waved his hand, and the hounds jumped back onto their haunches, now once more under his control. Distant screams and collisions echoed, reminding her that they were ever present in the town.

"My descendant. Dagmara Zosia," Eligor said. The name rolled off his tongue elegantly. He let the air stir around him, levitating him from the rooftop. He slowly descended to the street, landing across from the girls in the alcove. His eyes glistened crimson, resembling the Spirit magic he was channeling.

Dagmara braced herself, her fingers digging into the throwing star. "You've taken everything from me. My mother, Aleksy—" her voice broke off, unable to finish.

"And now you," Eligor cut her off.

The girls stepped back slightly, Magda still in front of Dagmara. "You'll have to go through me to get to her," she shouted.

Eligor continued approaching. "I have to admit it was clever. Magdalena is a Master Guardian of the Life lineage. She has a sample of the Void while you...a true descendent...your power is beyond your wildest imagination. You don't even understand what the Void encompasses yet, do you?"

Dagmara wasn't going to fall for his line of questioning. She didn't care to hear it from him. "Do all Master Guardians only have a sample of each magic?" Dagmara instigated. "So you only have a fraction of each power?"

His expression soured. "No. My greatest power is the Void. It is the same for Magda with Life magic. Regardless, I don't care for this idle conversation."

"You seemed to like it with me," Magda said.

"I'm done with this dance," Eligor stated, his hands turning to fists. "It is time for me to be the only guardian this world knows."

He barely gave them time to register his movement. His eyes instantly changed color as he thrust his palm forward, chucking a slab of stone toward Dagmara.

Magda screamed, desperately launching both hands forward to send a rush of Spirit magic toward the slab. The wind collided against the giant stone, slowing the movement enough for Dagmara to roll out of the way. The stone smashed to the ground where Dagmara had just been standing.

"Run!" Magda yelled.

Dagmara obeyed, scrambling to her feet. Then she tore off into town, disappearing around a corner and out of Eligor's view. She had to find more hounds so she could stop them from killing the rest of her friends. If she could get to a small pack, maybe she could control them and turn them against Eligor and help Magda. She needed reinforcements. She needed—

As she turned the corner, she slammed against something hard. Her entire body jolted against the impact, and she stumbled back, clutching her chest from the blow. She shook the stars from her vision, holding onto the wall for support, as she looked up—and up—at *who* she had just crashed into.

"Sabien—" she gasped.

His expression was like stone. "Dagger."

CHAPTER 75
Magdalena

The wind began to whip around Magda, lashing at her hair and clothes. It was nearly suffocating her, forcing her to channel her own branch of Spirit magic to alleviate the torture. She faced Eligor in the wide street, his eyes red as blood.

She wasn't sure how much of the wind was from Eligor's magic and how much was from the impending storm. All she knew was that the rain would flood from the heavens soon.

"Dagmara!" Eligor roared, watching as she escaped into the streets. Then his gaze settled on Magda, his voice venomous and dripping with contempt.

"You'll pay for all of this."

"This is your last chance, Eligor," Magda screamed, her eyes alight with power. "Stop this now."

"No. It's time for this world to be reborn. It is time for the void and this land to become one. And most of all…it is time for only one guardian."

"I don't think so!"

The voice carried through the streets. Magda barely turned in time to see Claude appear, racing down the street before silver beasts transformed from thin air. Behind him, Ishani was close, wiping the blood off her axes.

"Ah, your new creation," Eligor laughed, eyeing Ishani and then turning to Claude. "Let's see what they can do."

Eligor thrust his hand forward, and the hounds on the ground jumped up. They encircled Ishani and Claude, rushing forward with ferocious teeth. Both of the guardians countered, Ishani using her axes and her Soul magic, while Claude projected his silver beasts that snapped back at Eligor's monsters before decapitating them with his sword. Ishani and Claude were brilliant with their magic, with Claude manipulating the animals while Ishani took them down with rock, earth, and her weapons.

But the hounds didn't stop coming. More pounded into the square, overwhelming both Ishani and Claude.

Magda rushed forward, pummeling Eligor with Spirit magic. He countered with rocks and stone, and it was one burst against the other, over and over again. Magda's body weakened, using incessant flashes of magic, and she struggled to maintain absolute focus. Only one wrong move, and one of them would be impaled.

"Give up, Magda!" Eligor screamed, throwing more projectiles.

Magda's body clenched, and her entire brow was dripping with sweat, as was his. He only needed one distraction, and she would catch him off guard.

Suddenly, Magda was struck in the shoulder, a sharp rock piercing her body, and she was flung backwards. Landing flat on the ground, she felt the impact ripple through her spine and her breath vanished. Choking, she quickly opened her eyes to stare at the sun, her head spinning. Before she could recover, a sharp object pierced her right side, and she let out a deafening scream. Her hand flew to her side, coated in blood. Crimson liquid poured from the gaping wound, and she yelled in pain. Every nerve in her body was on high alert, agony ricocheting through her.

Eligor became visible again and was standing over her on her left, about to bring a boulder down on her chest. The first boulder smashed down on her, and Magda groaned in pain, before he reached for another. As he did so, Magda grabbed one of the sharp rocks, slashing it as hard as she could against him before rolling to the side. Eligor stumbled back, clutching a gash in his leg, and the boulder cracked into pieces where Magda had just been. He glanced down at the wound once, assessing the damage.

Then he thrust his hand forward, a sharp stone slinging forward and launching itself right into Magda's stomach.

Magda choked, her hands flying to the shrapnel, and she collapsed forward on her knees.

"Now who's begging?" Eligor laughed, raising his arm above his head as yellow magic swirled.

Claude and Ishani jumped Eligor from either side, Ishani taking the opportunity to slash at Eligor's right arm with her axe, while Claude used his magic to disillusion the First Prince. Eligor let out a scream, countering with his own magic, but it didn't deter the two.

Ishani's hands glowed yellow, and a rock was unearthed from the ground, smashing into Eligor and propelling him into a stone house. Then, she used her powers to crumble the house, so that the rocks encased him within Ishani's clutches.

Claude approached, his sword raised high, ready to strike a deadly blow, as Eligor was finally trapped.

In an instant, the wind around Eligor spiraled, picking up speed, and the rocks covering him blasted outward. Ishani and Claude dove for cover before Eligor launched himself into the sky.

"He's escaping!" Magda yelled, barely able to move. Searing pain tore through her body, for the sharp rock blade was still inside her. Seeping warm blood saturated her fingertips.

The hounds looked up to their master, pounding in his direction, dispersing through the streets.

"You're hurt," said Ishani, placing her hand upon Magda's sweaty forehead.

"The water...," Magda gasped.

Ishani grabbed onto the canteen that Magda had linked to her belt, before unscrewing it. Then she ripped the shrapnel from Magda's stomach and poured the crystal clear water over Magda's fingertips, letting the water slink up her arms and heal the cut. Instantly, the pain ceased.

Magda collapsed into Ishani, barely steadying her breathing. Her entire body was broken, and the surges of pain were beginning to be too much. Even though she could heal her wounds, the feeling of throbbing shocks lingered, causing a mental ache deep within her bones. Magda didn't know how much more she could bear.

"It's alright, we got you," Ishani said, holding Magda upright in a sitting position.

"Why didn't he heal himself?" Claude rushed up to the girls. "I thought he stole the Life magic from Sabien."

"I guess he doesn't have the Life magic," said Magda, panting.

But then...if Sabien was alive...

"Dagmara," said Magda looking up from Ishani's arms. "She's in danger."

"I'll find her," Claude said.

Magda nodded. She peered up at the sky, seeing the dark clouds, which illuminated a lingering trail of red magic. Claude and Ishani nodded in understanding.

"I'm going after Eligor," said Magda, pushing herself up on shaky knees. She knew she was the only person that could follow him through the skies.

"Here," Ishani said, handing Magda an extra one of her daggers. "Finish him for good."

CHAPTER 76
Dagmara

Breathless, Dagmara stared up at Sabien. Her heart pounded. Every nerve in her body was on edge. He was alive. He was here.

And she wanted him dead.

He was the first to lunge, but she knew his attacks by now. She grabbed him by the wrist, dodging his attempt to hold her by the throat. But he was faster. With one spin, he slammed her against the alley wall. Her back throbbed from the force of the impact, her breath stripped from her lungs.

"This is all your fault," he growled, wrapping a hand around each one of her wrists before slamming them against the wall on either side of her head.

"Which part?" she asked through gritted teeth, trying to wriggle free, but he only tightened his grip.

"Eligor just tried to kill me, after all I've done for him."

She couldn't help the smile spread across her face. "We warned you, and you didn't listen."

He scowled. "It would never have come to this if it wasn't for you. You thwarted me at the coronation. You showed up instead of Magdalena in Ilusauri. You're somehow a descendant of the lost Void lineage." He leaned closer, and his breath was hot on her lips. "I've given up everything to be a guardian, but *you* are granted powers you didn't even ask for?" he growled. "Why do you get to be better than me? Why are any of the guardians deserving of magic?"

"They're good people," Dagmara said, rising on her tiptoes to look him directly in the eye. "And you're not."

"So what about you? You get to be a guardian, and yet you've killed dozens."

"And you'll be next." She yanked down, trying to free herself from his grip, but it only angered him. He raised both her arms overhead, binding her wrists against the wall with only one hand.

He smirked, lifting his opposite palm toward her face. A single finger trailed across her cheek. "You can't kill me...because you still have feelings for me." His lips were inches away from hers, and the sounds of the fighting and hounds in the distance faded away. "You can't resist me, Dagger. I can see your pulse. I can hear your heart beating for me. You may be an assassin, but you could never kill someone you know. Someone you've tasted." His finger reached her lips, and he let it linger. "But I can."

She inclined her head, inching closer as she whispered, "You've always underestimated me." Thrusting her knee up, she found her target. He keeled over in a groan, loosening his hold on her wrists enough to break free. She didn't waste time, unsheathing her dagger, and driving it into his stomach.

He was a murderer. He tortured her.

It was time for him to die.

She wrenched the dagger back, and blood splattered the pavement. Sabien roared in pain, but he was undeterred. He lunged forward, grabbing her left arm with both hands and twisted.

A snap pierced the air, a nauseating crunch of tendon and bone. Dagmara screamed as a shattering pain laced up her arm. She fell to the ground, landing hard on her tailbone. The dagger scattered against the bloody pavement. She held her broken wrist to her chest, her body roiling with agony. The shooting pain threatened to pull her unconscious, and she struggled to clear the darkness from her vision.

She reached with her good hand toward the dagger, but her flesh only met wet blood. Stars continued to curl in her vision, masking her sight and taunting her into oblivion.

"I won't go easy on you anymore," Sabien said, his sultry voice turning cold. He stepped toward her and she scrambled back, her palm slick on the crimson pavement.

"You don't have to kill me," she blurted out, her voice raspy. "Eligor is hunting you. Run away while you still can."

"But then I will never stop thinking of you, Dagger," Sabien said, inching closer. He towered over her like a looming shadow ready to strike. "Regardless whether Eligor or Magdalena comes out of this alive, they will both hunt me down. I know my fate, and I know I will die, but I sure as hell won't let you live if I can't. You didn't win this one, Dagger. But I had a fun game." He withdrew his own knife from his belt, his palm sticky with crimson blood.

She had to survive, if only long enough to kill this monster. This would not be her end.

She lunged for her dagger on the ground, rolling out of range from his attack. Every ounce of her was instantly coated in the blood that ran through the street, but she didn't care. As she rotated to her knees, prepared to stand, the world before her shifted.

The vibrant hues of the town were muted, grays and greens surrounding her on all sides. Her distant vision was blurred, as though fog blocked her in a glass cage.

"Dagger!" Sabien roared.

He couldn't see her. This was her chance to run.

Gripping her dagger in one hand, the other broken against her chest, she tore off to the center of town.

She slithered through the alleyways, carefully and quietly slipping through town. Various bodies and carcasses littered the streets, both human and creatures alike. Door slammed as people ran for cover, and more hounds prowled.

She stumbled into the center of town, the central fountain revealing itself in the light. Her strength was fading, and she could no longer hold onto the cloak of invisibility. Her surroundings refocused as her body crossed back into the real world, becoming visible once more. The light returned, and she stood in front of the fountain with the rustling of the hounds around her. Some pawed at deceased carcasses, while others roamed the side streets.

Where were the Azuremi knights? Were they all already dead?

Glancing down, she examined her fractured wrist hanging limply against her corset. The pain came in waves, shooting through her entire arm in excessive agony. Then she noticed the ground beyond her broken hand.

Blood.

Her shoes were coated in blood.

She followed the tracks left from her boots, a direct path across the center of the main square...a direct path to—

Sabien emerged from the side street.

"You may be invisible, but your tracks aren't," he said. "And you led me right to water." He raised his hand toward the fountain, summoning crystalline water from the surface.

Bouncing back from the weaponized liquid, Dagmara drew away from the fountain. The water traveled to the Life Guardian, seeping into the dagger wound and instantaneously healing it.

The two hounds in the central square perked up, sensing the newcomer. They charged forward, their paws heavy on the ground.

It was far too easy for Sabien to decommission them. With one wave from the fountain, he sent an iceblade through the first hound's chest. Then he rolled out of the way, taking his own knife and plunging it into the other's skull. With a twist of the blade, the hound's bones cracked, and it dropped dead.

Rising from the ground, Sabien faced Dagmara, knife in hand. "Now, for you."

Dagmara was prepared. She had already gone for the poisons in her belt.

Barely clutching the dagger with her broken wrist, she was forced to use one hand for her attacks. She launched a jasny vial toward the ground, and it fractured in a plume of white light and smoke. In the brief distraction, she tore another bottle from her belt and chucked it forward. It soared through the dust toward its target.

Sabien easily dodged the bottle, sidestepping the bright orange liquid. The glass container shattered against the central spire of the fountain, all the contents scattering into the water.

"Missed me," Sabien smirked. He summoned water from the fountain. Ice shards manifested in thin air before they went flying in her direction.

A gasp escaped her lips as she dropped to the ground. She felt the slice of a single shard, nicking her side. She screamed as it tore through her shirt, slicing her flesh.

She was close to the ground, and Sabien took advantage. His boot collided with her chin, sending her sprawling backward. She landed on her back, the entire world spinning. She choked, gasping for air that had slipped from her lungs. She could barely breathe. She was fighting a Life Guardian, and she was nobody.

No. She wasn't a nobody.

She was a Void Guardian.

"Come." She whispered under her breath, unable to sit up. She reached deep into the earth, searching for the connection with the hounds, but she couldn't find the tether. It was as if Eligor had a hold of every one, cutting off her ability to interact with ones already assigned to him.

A shadow cast over the sky as Sabien loomed over her. "No one's coming to save you this time."

CHAPTER 77
Magdalena

It wasn't hard to follow Eligor through the skies. His movements were sporadic, his path nonlinear, and he left a trail of blood behind him. He moved toward the Sea of Scarlet, aiming for the rift the hounds were pouring out of, but he landed north of it.

Magda's flight was also haphazard. Her body burned from using too much magic, and she used all her remaining strength to channel the Spirit magic and follow Eligor through the winds.

Descending from the sky, Magda followed his lead. Ash spewed around her like dust. She landed uncomfortably on the ground, her knees buckling underneath her as she rolled to the earth, clutching her stomach. A snap resounded in her leg, and she let out a scream as it broke. She crash landed, a hot pain flooding through her shin under her weight. Another sharp pain jostled through her body as the earth scraped against her shoulder, drawing blood from her back. The crown fell from her head, landing a few paces away.

Magda fought back tears, and the darkness that threatened to pull her unconscious. She couldn't move, she couldn't stand, and there was no way she could fight in this state. Her eyes scanned the sky, pleading for the guardians in the stars above to help her now.

Just a short rest, and she would get back up again. She let her body sink into the poppies, into the ashes. But then, a drop of water hit her forehead, altering her senses. Her head turned to spot her enemy.

Yards ahead, Eligor lay in the center of dead poppies. His cape was sprawled around his figure, nearly concealing the wound in his leg. Yet a pool of blood began to spread around him, a miniature Sea of Scarlet. He held his chest as well, breathing unsteadily, as he fingered the bandage from his earlier injury.

Another drop of water splashed on her chest. Magda turned over, wincing in pain, and used her arms to drag her along the ashen field, heading his way.

"Seems like neither of us have much time left," he rasped. "The world will be free of all Master Guardians. The world will crumble to ashes, and a new one will be reborn."

Magda didn't respond. She didn't want to play any more games. She continued dragging herself along the earth, letting out another yell.

The sky above cracked with lightning.

"I would ask you to heal me," Eligor said, "but it seems like you can't even heal yourself."

Magda looked up, praying for an outpouring of rain, but nothing came. Only another boom of thunder.

Eligor coughed. "Your friends are about to kill Sabien, and then I'll be revived."

"No," Magda answered without a second thought.

A humorous laugh escaped his lips. "You're as cold-hearted as I am."

"I am not like you."

He looked up from the ground, his face paler than she had ever seen it before. "And yet you are. A Master Guardian, better than the rest. If you survive this without me, the others will grow envious. They will turn on you. Can you say with certainty they are supportive of your gift? That they aren't threatened—"

"That's enough!" Magda yelled, cutting him off. She could feel a few more drops of rain now, starting to fall. "You and I are not the same. I won because I had friends on my side. You're alone, Eligor. You always were and will always be alone."

"They threw me in a tomb!"

"After you killed your family! You know what I would give to still have my family with me now?" Magda's voice boomed. "You took them from me!" Her voice carried through the space, the scream erupting from deep in her throat. She caught herself, steadying her breathing as she continued. "You think as a Master Guardian you are the only guardian that needs to exist. And that's why we're different. I learned I am not enough as a Master Guardian. I need my friends. I can't do it by myself. Their powers are stronger than mine, and I can't control all five branches of magic."

"With practice—" he paused, coughing up blood and rainwater that threatened to clog his throat, "you could."

"But I don't want to," she stated. "I want to make my father proud. I want to live the legacy Aleksy should have lived. I didn't ask for this."

Eligor sneered, blood lining his teeth. "What a waste you are."

The skies opened up, and the rain fell in large gushes. They were surrounded in a downpour that clouded the space, and Magda knew it came directly from the stars.

Her face hardened, summoning the water to her body. When the rain washed over her, a new energy propelled her further. "And yet I'll be the one who's still standing," she told Eligor.

Her eyes sparkling blue, Magda's hand clenched around Ishani's dagger. She plunged the knife into his chest with a scream, feeling it pierce through his ribcage.

He sputtered, trying to fight, but he had lost too much blood already. His attempt was futile, and his life drained from his face. All dances of color vanished from his irises, until there was no more magic left in them.

Magda watched his skin turn even paler, and she pressed her fingers up to his neck, not feeling a pulse.

He was dead.

Letting out an exhale, Magda rolled onto her forearms. The rainstorm was furious, as if the sky was letting out all of its tears. She let the pounding rain wash the ashes and blood off her clothes and cleanse the poppy field in a light mist. Her head spun, and the world faded around her, but she held out her palm, letting the cerulean powers slink up her body and heal all of her wounds. The bleeding ceased, but her leg still throbbed in a furious pain.

She couldn't get up, so she pushed herself to a sitting position, noticing a red flower a few paces away. She went to grab it, barely reaching the plant with her fingers and wiping off the remaining ash. Somehow, this bud of life had survived the storm and rose out of the ashes. Maybe it was a new world, as Eligor had said, but maybe it was for the better.

A shadow passed her face, and Magda looked up. In the sky, a large blackbird swooped down from the heavens. As it passed across the sun, it shed its feathers. The black feathers fell to the ground, and as they caught the light, Magda saw the underside of them were lined with violet. The bird soared toward her, its new feathers a deep blue. For some reason, she was calm as it glided to her shoulder. It landed elegantly, letting out a shrill caw.

Magda reached up to touch a single finger to its wing. "And who might you be?"

A loud bark startled her, and she saw Odie in the distance, racing across the field. At the sight of the dog, the bird flew off into the clouds, disappearing from view.

Odie crashed into Magda's arms, licking her all over her face. His tail wagged uncontrollably, shaking his entire body.

"Odie, you found me!" Magda exclaimed.

Then Odie crossed to Eligor's golden crown, grasping the bloody object in his teeth, before returning it to Magda's lap.

"Good boy, Odie." Magda gave him another pet before placing the crown on her head. Then she gave the command, "I can't walk. Go find help."

CHAPTER 78
Dagmara

Sabien towered over Dagmara, approaching with predatory calm. She grabbed her ribcage, choking on the ground, her broken wrist useless in her defense. Blood seeped from the wound in her side, a result of the ice blade he thrust toward her with the fountain water. It coated the cobblestone, and she could feel her body becoming dizzy. Pain radiated from her gash, and she held back a scream as her blood burned.

Dark clouds rolled overhead. A rainstorm was approaching.

Sabien reached her with three strides before lowering to the ground and wrapping his large hand around her throat. He jerked her upright, and she gasped, unable to inhale with his fingers digging into her neck.

"Goodbye, Dagger."

But the ground began to rumble. A sudden pressure collided with Dagmara's chest as though she were carrying stones. She screamed, but Sabien cut off her supply to oxygen, and her cry was cut short. A rush of warmth flooded her body, and a shooting pain raked her temples.

Sabien shifted his attention, glancing once at the quaking earth underneath them before meeting Dagmara's gaze again.

His eyes narrowed, watching the shift of color in her irises. A violet hue danced around her palms, wrapping up her arms and coating her in magic.

Then a loud howl lit the main square.

Sabien released Dagmara, and she collapsed onto the cobblestone in a hard smack. He stumbled back, surveying the main square as a dozen hounds began to crawl out of the shadows.

"Eligor..." he said under his breath.

The hounds attacked, lunging for the Life Guardian. Sabien dropped his knife and manifested a large iceblade from the fountain. He defended himself against the onslaught, blood splattering the street.

Dagmara couldn't breathe, clutching her throat and gasping for air. It was as if the weight of the entire world shifted on her shoulders, and she struggled to remain sitting upright. She could feel every ounce of magic seeping into her bones.

Eligor...was dead.

She could feel it in her soul.

She could feel all the Void magic calling to its new master. All the hounds were turning to her to give them commands. The weight was nearly unbearable. *Her*—responsible for an entire new branch of magic.

Sabien decapitated the last of the dozen hounds that came upon hearing Dagmara's cry. He panted, his chest heaving up and down.

He held the bloody ice sword in hand.

"You'll never learn will you?" he asked, blood dripping from a gash in his stomach. It poured down his clothes, staining the silver stitching a crimson red. "You can't win, Dagger." He grunted, straightening his posture, the skin on his forearm peeled back in gruesome scratch marks.

Then, a smirk lit his face. "I am a Life Guardian. I can heal myself."

He extended a shaking hand toward the fountain, blood pouring from the teeth bites and puddling on the ground beneath him. His irises glistened, transforming into ice. The water began to levitate, rising from the fountain. It circled through the air, arching in majestic waves as it was summoned to Sabien. The water crested around his figure before gracefully landing against him.

She watched as the water slithered across his figure, dancing into every injury. "I know you can heal yourself," Dagmara said, her voice rough as gravel.

Sabien glowered, lifting his blade in the air as he approached her. The water fastened to his bloody wounds, mixing with the crimson liquid and evaporating. His skin began to mold together, the injuries closing.

He raised the weapon to the sky, prepared to drive it down in a death blow, when Dagmara added under her breath:

"I was counting on it."

He hesitated, inclining his head.

Then the poison began to fire through his bloodstream.

Sabien screamed, instantly losing his grip on the iceblade. It clattered abruptly to the ground and shattered into a million pieces. The Life Guardian stumbled back, grabbing at his now-healed wounds, yelling in agony. But he had already invited the smierc-poisoned water into his bloodstream.

"What—?" he gasped, letting out another scream. "How did you—"

He dropped to his knees, clutching his stomach. He started to gag, choking and gasping. No doubt the smierc was making its way to every inch of his body, burning him from the inside out.

"I never missed when I threw the bottle," Dagmara said, then she suddenly winced, holding the gaping wound in her side tighter. "I was aiming for the fountain."

He coughed, and blood splattered the pavement. He looked up, barely meeting her gaze. His eyes were red, filled with glossy tears.

"You—" He winced, sputtering up more blood. He grabbed at his throat, unable to alleviate his pain.

Dagmara was unmoving, watching as the smierc strangled his life.

Then he laughed. "I k-knew I liked you for a reason—" his voice broke off, nothing more than a faint whisper. "Nice move, Dagger."

Dagmara remained on the ground in silence. She watched as Sabien collapsed to his side, his breath labored. She couldn't tear her gaze away, afraid he would somehow survive this as he had survived every attempt on his life thus far.

"Dagmara," a voice said from behind. She knew that voice better than she knew her own.

Claude.

The sound of her name on his lips calmed her, easing her pain, but she still didn't tear her eyes away from Sabien. It was as if she looked away, Sabien would find a way to stand back up. He could sneak off and kill someone else she loved. Blood dripped from his lips when he coughed once more, his eyes searching hers and begging for mercy.

Mercy she would not give.

"Claude—" she gasped, nearly unable to speak.

Claude approached quickly, his boots light on the blood-slick pavement. He knelt behind her, and his cologne wafted over her, mixed with the foul tinge of blood. "I'm here."

A nausea roiled inside her stomach, and she felt sick. A sharp pain radiated through every limb of her body—but it wasn't from Sabien's blows. No, it was coursing through her bloodstream.

Tears burned her eyes, threatening to spill down her face.

She glanced down at the gash on her side from one of the ice shards.

A smierc-laced ice shard. It had met with her bloodstream. It was coursing through her body. It was burning her from the inside out.

"Claude..." Sabien choked.

Claude looked once to his former captain—his former friend.

Sabien's life was draining away by every passing moment. But Claude remained beside Dagmara, watching Sabien succumb to the poison.

Dagmara struggled to meet Claude's gaze. She let the tears roll down her cheeks as she forced from her lips, "It was smierc." Then she coughed, matching Sabien's dying breaths. Blood slithered down her chin, and Claude immediately caught her as she careened to the side.

Before she fell unconscious, she barely uttered the last words, "I'm going to die."

CHAPTER 79
Magdalena

Odie had raced back to the fortress, getting the knights' attention. Finally, some of the servants and knights had arrived at the poppy field with a horse and wagon, explaining to Magda that the battle was finally over. They helped her into the back of the cart, careful of her leg. Odie hopped in beside her, sniffing at her injury and whimpering, before the caravan emerged in the fortress courtyard.

Upon the sight of Magda, the townspeople froze. A unanimous gasp rippled through them, and they turned to face the royal.

"It's the Princess!" one of them yelled over the hushed murmurs. "She's alive!"

Magda cleared her throat, speaking from the back of the wagon. "The First Prince is dead," she announced, wincing through the pain.

The crowd let out a few exclamations, but stopped when Magda continued speaking.

"We're safe from him and his hounds. We are no longer under attack, and never again will the First Prince reign."

A scream of joy ruptured from the crowd, as soldiers, servants, and townspeople hailed their princess. All around, they embraced each other, celebrating their victory.

"Your Majesty," said one of the knights, helping Magda down and offering her support. Odie leapt down beside her, circling into the crowd, as each one of the servants took their turns petting him and congratulating him for finding the princess.

Magda hobbled on one leg, leaning against the wagon, and waited for them to find a crutch. Pain laced through her body, making her nauseous, but she forced herself to remain upright in front of the villagers. However, the crowd began to part, a figure barreling through them at top speed. "Magda!" he called.

As soon as she saw his face, her anxiety melted away. "Ravi!" she exhaled. He collided into her, and her arms flew around his neck. She buried her face into his shoulder as his arms wrapped around her lower back, holding her tight.

"You're alive!" Ravi said, relief flooding his voice. He held her closely, kissing her on the forehead.

"Eligor's dead," said Magda, her eyes welling in tears. "It's all over."

Ravi gasped. "What happened? Are you alright?"

"I broke something," Magda admitted, referencing her leg. "I feel like I'm going to pass out."

"We'll find you something in the apothecary," Ravi said, stroking her hair. "I think I've memorized everything I can about medicine at this point," he laughed.

"And then we have to restore the magic."

"Whoa, Magda, slow down," he said. "I'm just so glad you're alive."

Magda continued explaining what had happened in the battle, her thoughts running wild, "I gave the Void powers to Dagmara. And I plan to give the powers away to others too. Once I do, I'll be just a Life Guardian, and there will be no more Master Guardians," she explained.

"What?" Ravi asked, confused. "Is that what you want?"

"I didn't have a choice. We needed to be stronger to fight off

Eligor. But now, I realize that everything that I've ever wanted has always been right here in Azurem, and it's standing in front of me now."

A smile creased Ravi's face, and he pulled her close as his lips met hers. For a moment, she was soaring, the adrenaline and rush of the day consuming her. She grabbed Ravi's face in her hands and swooped her tongue into his mouth, their lips crashing together until her body was on fire.

She was finally free. They were finally safe.

Then Magda said, "I didn't have the chance to tell you, but my mom arranged immunity for you in Azurem. You can stay here as long as you'd like."

"Really?" his eyes beamed as the thoughts churned in his head.

"I'm sorry that it's all we can offer you. I'm sorry that you still can't go home yet or take this choice into your own hands…"

"Magda, I've always had a choice. Saving you in the marketplace, finding Odie, killing Vex, breaking into the Flaustran palace, were all choices, and I would never have done a single thing differently. I've been choosing you every single day."

"Back then you didn't know I was a guardian."

Ravi took Magda's face in his hands. "I've come to know you more than you know yourself. You're a woman who risks her life for her friends and her kingdom, a woman who saved my life multiple times, and a woman who will continue to captivate me as long as she'll have me. I told you I would always be here for you. Your battles are my battles, even if I'm on the sidelines."

"And you're the one I always want to return to," Magda pressed her lips to his, letting another kiss consume her. "So you're saying you'll be happy to stay in Azurem?"

"I can be a musician wherever I have an instrument," Ravi said. "Across Azurem or elsewhere."

"But in Azurem I'll be a queen. It's not just about choosing me, it's about understanding what my life means before you choose it."

"In Flaustra, I played the violin, but in reality, I was a listener. My job was to listen to the gliding of the bowstrings, the ascension of the melodies, and the rhythm of the streets. That's how I was able to notice you that day in the marketplace. And I truly saw you. If the life of being a royal means listening, I think I'm already a professional."

Magda laughed. "Well, I think you should listen to my first royal order of duty."

"What's that?" Ravi grinned.

Magda leaned in close, whispering into Ravi's ear. He smiled, before kissing her again and saying, "Yes, Your Highness."

"Help!"

The cry pierced the air, louder than the bustle of the townspeople.

It was Claude, stumbling down the street. His clothes were drenched in blood, and his forehead beaded with sweat. In his arms was Dagmara's limp body.

"Dagmara!" Magda screamed.

Claude collapsed to his knees, Dagmara jostling in his embrace.

Magda hobbled in Ravi's arms as he helped her to Claude's side. Then Magda dropped to the ground in front of them, wiping the hair off Dagmara's forehead. Her skin was clammy, and her lips a shade of purple. Blood trickled down her chin and to her neck. "What happened?"

"Smierc. In her bloodstream," Claude said through rasps for air. He wouldn't release Dagmara, holding her tight to his chest. He nodded to a gash in her bodice revealing an open wound in her side.

A breeze rushed by them, and Ravi skidded onto the ground. "We need to heal her, fast."

"Magdalena, please," Claude pleaded. His eyes met hers. Desperation dripped in every word. "I can't lose her."

"I-I don't know what to do," Magda muttered, pressing her hands to Dagmara's open wound. It was still raining, so water was available, but that wasn't the problem. "If I close the wound, the smierc will still be in her system. I can't pull the smierc from her blood."

Her heart sank in her chest. She was a Life Guardian...she was supposed to be able to heal people, she had healed her friends time and time again.

And yet, she couldn't heal her best friend. It was as if a knife had been driven through her stomach as the harsh reality weighed her down.

"Isn't there an antidote?" Claude blurted out.

Magda looked at Ravi. She had no idea. She was unfamiliar with potions and poisons...everything Dagmara was skilled with.

Emotions flashed across Ravi's face, his brow furrowing. "Yes, yes, I think so."

"You think so?" Claude echoed.

"I might have seen it in the book, yes, but I don't know for certain. Smierc is an Azuremi poison, we don't know much about it in Flaustra."

"So who would know?" Claude insisted, desperation laced in his voice.

"Teos," Magda stated. "He's our best option."

Claude didn't waste another moment. He rose from the ground, grunting under Dagmara's deadweight. Ravi extended a hand, offering to help, but Claude completely ignored him, heading inside.

Magda let Ravi support her as they followed Claude through the fortress, struggling to keep up with Claude's fast pace. She shouted haphazard directions to the apothecary as she hobbled on her good leg, putting her weight onto Ravi's shoulders.

Bursting through the apothecary doors, Teos jumped upright at the table, his hands filled with vials.

"Perfect, Ravi can you run these—" Teos stopped short, recognizing his sister in Claude's arm. "Dagmara!"

Claude raced to an empty table, setting her down on the wood. "She needs a smierc antidote. Now." He grabbed a rag and pressed it to her side, attempting to stop the bleeding.

"A smierc—wait, what about the battle? Is it over?"

"Yes," Magda said, panting. They had finally reached the apothecary, and she braced herself against the central table. Her leg throbbed in pain, her toes going numb. "The First Prince is dead, but Dagmara needs help."

Teos hoisted the crutch underneath his arm before racing to the wall of potions. "How long has she been unconscious?"

"Too long," Claude said. He brushed Dagmara's hair off her forehead, whispering something that Magda couldn't make out.

"Um..." Teos scanned the shelves, his face reddening. Then he shot forward and yanked two different vials off the wall. "It's one of these two." He extended the two vials, both filled with similar blue liquid, toward Magda.

"One of the two?" Claude asked, his voice raising.

Magda limped forward, accepting the vials from Teos. "They aren't labeled?"

"They don't explicitly say 'smierc antidote'," Teos stated.

She flipped them over in her grasp, only to find two different names written across each one. Both were foreign to her.

Claude crossed the room in three long strides. "Tell me which one," he ordered.

"I don't know for sure," Teos muttered. "I've only seen her use this color and bottle shape before as the antidote. Everything in here was moved when the knights cleaned it up."

"How do you not know?" asked Magda, leaning up against the bookshelf for support.

"She's the poison expert! If you were asking me about explosive powder, I'd be able to answer."

The tension only continued to elevate in the room. Magda could feel sweat beading against her forehead as she switched her attention to each vial.

Ravi raced to the table to where his journal lay. "Give me the names."

Teos limped over to him. "Eroxis and brixann."

Paging through the journal, Ravi moved at the speed of light. "Brixann!" He slapped his hand down on a page.

Teos leaned in. "What does it say?"

Ravi read the text in Flaustran, "A bitter tonic to induce paralysis and a heartbeat that cannot be detected, used to convince people you are dead. Results in many cases of being buried alive."

"Not that one," Magda cut in. "And eroxis?"

"I'm not finding anything," Ravi said, paging through his journal faster.

Then, Dagmara gasped.

All heads turned to her, watching as her chest expanded in rapid motions. She struggled for air, still unconscious. A gargle sounded at the back of her throat.

Claude returned to her side at once, holding her. "She's burning up, she needs something now!"

"Give it to her," Teos said.

"No, we don't know for certain if that's the right one," Ravi countered.

"We have to try something!" yelled Claude.

Magda had no choice. She limped back over to Dagmara's side, letting out a yell at the pain searing through her leg. Setting down the paralysis vial, she uncapped the other. She prayed to whatever guardian was watching over her as she parted Dagmara's purple lips and dumped the contents down her throat.

She gripped the table for support, waiting in horror. Her hand tightened around the empty vial in painstaking silence. What if it was the wrong one? What if Teos didn't even remember the color correctly? Her mind began to churn faster, her heart pounding against her chest.

One more sharp breath left Dagmara's lips. Her rapid breathing began to settle, her chest beginning to move slower and slower.

Claude leaned closer, holding Dagmara's hand, careful not to bump her injured one. He brought it toward his lips, kissing the back of her knuckles. "Please," he said, breathless.

"Now heal her," Ravi encouraged.

Magda nodded, dropping to the edge of the table. She grabbed a bucket of water and slowly mended the skin on Dagmara's side back together. After she was done, she stumbled back, her hands coated red. Dagmara still didn't move.

Teos came to stand beside Magda, his eyes glossy with tears. "It was the correct vial," he said, unassured. "The slow breathing means it's working, right?"

Magda remained unmoving, her throat closing. Tears pricked her eyes. If it wasn't the right one...if she had just given her something that accelerated her death—

She shuddered at the thought. The guilt would kill her.

"Right, Magda?" Teos insisted, his voice cracking.

"Right." Magda nodded, but she was only trying to convince herself. She couldn't lose Dagmara. Not after everything. She couldn't lose one more member of her family.

CHAPTER 80
Dagmara

For once, Dagmara didn't see only darkness, but a flicker of light. Her heartbeat was steady, her breath relaxed. There was no pain as the light drew closer, only disappointment. There was so much more in the world she wanted for herself. So much more she had yet to accomplish. Her life was only beginning, she could feel it as potent as the magic thrumming through her veins.

The light was drawing closer, and she could reach out and seize it.

This is what the guardians ordained for us.

Be brave. Be selfless. Be loyal.

Her mother's words floated in the space around her, as warm as a hug. But she could hear more than her mother. She could hear her brother, her partner in crime. The light sound of her best friend, assured and determined, even through the tears. There was also the soft melody of Claude's voice.

"Please."

His next words were barely audible, as soft as a caress.

"For the betterment of our kingdom..." he whispered, *"I need you to say the rest. I can't finish the sentence without you."*

Dagmara knew the response as though it were carved into her

heart, but she couldn't open her lips. The light was drawing nearer, her body floating on air. Her heart slowed. Her mind was calm.

But there was a single tether. It gripped her, strong as a lifeline. It was there for her to grab onto—to pull her back to the surface, only if she wanted. She could either stay in the light, resolve all pain, or fasten onto that single string. It would yank her back to the darkness. Tug her into the torture of the real world.

But also bring her home.

She reached for it, and it wrapped around her body. A sharp agony rippled through her wrist first, before a weight settled against her chest like stone.

Her body jerked, choking for air. Her eyes flew open, meeting a pair of brown eyes with flecks of silver.

"Claude," she breathed.

"Thank the guardians!" he exclaimed. His entire body relaxed, and his expression eased as he leaned forward and pressed a kiss to her forehead.

"Dagmara!" Magda squealed.

Claude stepped back, making room for Magda to grab her friend's shoulder. "I was so worried."

Coughing, Dagmara struggled to sit upright, but everything ached too much.

"Take it easy," Ravi's voice filled the room. "I'll go get you water," he said before racing out of the room.

"Even deadly poisons can't take down my sister." Teos came into view, leaning over his sister with a dimple in his cheek.

"Teos," Dagmara exhaled, before wincing at the searing pain in her wrist. It made her nauseous, and she was nearly going to pass out.

"I'll get a doctor," Claude stated. He whirled on his heel and stormed out of the room, calling in Azuremi for the nearest aide.

Magda picked up a rag and dabbed it to Dagmara's sweaty face. "You're safe now," she said.

"How?" Dagmara asked, touching her body to make sure she was truly alive. The smierc should have killed her.

"The eroxis antidote," Magda replied.

Dagmara nodded, but was still unconvinced. Eroxis was a weak potion.

"Sabien is dead, and I killed Eligor," Magda announced, the golden crown twinkling in her silver hair.

"We're all finally safe," Teos added, leaning against the table.

Dagmara let out a sigh of relief, letting her head rest.

"I thought guardians were supposed to be perfect," Dagmara said, staring at the ceiling. She had no energy to sit upright. "Perfect health was one of those things."

"I don't think they ever were perfect," Magda admitted.

Teos chimed in, "And maybe that's the entire point."

"I know that the Void is different from the other branches and that it was trapped away with Eligor until he was released," said Magda, "but it was never supposed to be that way. It was always supposed to be a fifth branch. Maybe there's a way to use the powers for good."

"These powers have caused the world so much pain, and the world won't easily accept it again," Dagmara paused, before continuing, "but it's a part of us." She reached out to grab Teos's hand with the one that wasn't broken. "It was a part of our mother, and there's so much more we need to learn about her—about how the Void can be used for good."

"And...," Teos laughed. "I think there's someone who wants to help you figure out that mystery."

"Partners?" Dagmara smiled.

"Partners." Teos grinned. "But that does mean I have to pack up my stuff, doesn't it? I'm coming with you to Ilusauri?"

"I don't know," Dagmara began. She looked at Magda. "Think you can handle Azurem without me?"

"Hopefully Azurem won't need a royal assassin for a long time...

but I will truly miss my best friend," Magda admitted, before leaning in to hug her. "All I've ever wanted is for you to be happy. And if you can find happiness with Claude, it means the world to me."

Dagmara gripped her friend tighter, not letting go. "We will be in close contact," Dagmara admitted. "After all, I will need to coordinate the medicine shipments."

Magda pulled away, smiling. "Of course, Your Majesty."

Heat rose in Dagmara's chest, her cheeks turning bright red. Before she could respond, a rush of doctors flooded the room. Half of them went to aid Magda, while the others raced for Dagmara. A sudden fear surged through Dagmara as her best friend was pulled away, but her heart quickly settled as Claude appeared out of the chaos.

The pain was unbearable as the doctors mended and wrapped her injured wrist. She could still feel her pulse through her fingers, and tears pricked her eyes. By the time they had finished tending to her injuries, she had no energy left. Magda had been taken away by the royal doctors, and Ravi had accompanied her. Teos had gone to speak with Bernadette about the battle.

Dagmara was upright on the table, her arm in a sling, with Claude a few paces away. He leaned against the wall, surveying the remaining doctors as they vacated. As soon as the last one scampered from the room, he shifted his gaze to meet hers. Blood splattered his clothes from the battle, and sweat dampened his brow, but he had never been more attractive.

A long silence filled the space, both of them staring at one another. Finally, Dagmara opened her lips. "Yes?" she prompted.

"I have walked straight into battle," he said, "I became a king as a child and was asked to save a dying kingdom. I even fought the First Prince." He pushed off the wall, approaching her steadily. "But I have never felt fear as overwhelming as when you were dying." He stopped before her, his eyes roaming every inch of her face, as if making sure she was there. "I beg you, don't do that to me again."

She gave him a soft smile. "I will do my best." Reaching out with her good hand, she interlaced her fingers with his. "It's all over now."

He nodded, before grabbing her thighs and pulling her to the edge of the table. Her legs opened to either side of his body, allowing him to step closer. She was forced to tilt her head back in order to meet his gaze. His fingers traced her exposed neck, before his palm settled against her cheek.

"Because I don't say it enough," he paused, leaning closer until his forehead met hers. "I love you."

It was only a whisper, but the words rushed through Dagmara, sending warmth through her body. She let her eyes close, feeling safe in his arms. "And I love you," she replied.

He exhaled a shaky breath before pulling her into his embrace. He whispered, "Let's go home."

She hesitated, before asking, "Will they accept me?"

He stilled. "Why wouldn't they?"

Pulling away, she met his concerned gaze. "I have Void magic. The people must think that with Eligor dead, the Void magic died too. To them, the Void is part of what made him so evil."

He shook his head. "The Void doesn't make someone evil." He placed his forehead against hers. "You could never be like the First Prince."

She swallowed the lump in her throat. "You're right..." she muttered, yet she couldn't shake the unease. How would they ever accept a Void guardian as the Queen of Ilusauri? Was there a way to lock the Void back in the tomb and get rid of the branch of magic once more? Did she even want that for herself?

She closed her eyes, sinking back into Claude's arms once more. Ilusauri aside, she had to decide. She could keep her magic a secret, try to return it to the tomb, or embrace it—risking whatever the unknown branch of magic entailed.

And there was only one way she could make her decision.

CHAPTER 81
Magdalena

The sun was setting, and Magda made her way back to the courtyard to survey the damage. Teos had given her an extra one of his crutches, and she hobbled over to the servants and knights, giving them orders on how to clean-up the fortress and attend to the wounded.

Claude remained with Dagmara inside the apothecary, while Ravi and Teos found the royal doctors once more, helping them administer medical aid.

Magda went to the balcony that overlooked the cliff edge and the Sea of Scarlet, leaning her crutch against the railing. Then she stared out at the decrepit and ruined lands, knowing her mission was not over. She straightened the crown on her head, feeling its power surge through her once more. She still had to choose a Spirit Guardian, and she still had to activate the emblems underneath Dreadmarrow.

A soft bark sounded beside her as her pet padded over.

"Odie!" Magda exclaimed. Odie's tongue slobbered all over Magda's leg, and she slightly winced, fighting back the pain. She stroked his fur. "Odie, you did it. You saved the day, good boy!"

"Magda," a familiar voice called, and Magda turned to see Ishani approaching, both her axes at her hips. Her sweaty hair was falling out of the bun, and her tight, leather armor and corset was splattered with blood.

Ishani gave a soft smile, "You did it. You killed Eligor."

"Yes," Magda breathed, a sigh of relief escaping her lips.

"Well, after all this, I need a long trip out to sea," Ishani let out a huff, leaning over the railing beside Magda, "but you kind of appointed me as the new ruler."

"I didn't take my decision lightly," Magda joked. "We were kind of about to be killed by a pack of hounds."

"I know," Ishani raised her eyebrows, and a glimmer of yellow sparks could be seen in her eyes. "To be honest, there were a few times in that last battle where I thought we were going to die, but you pulled your weight nicely. I only had to save your ass a few times, and it will be much easier now with the magic."

"Hey! Parting with the Soul magic will be the hardest of all," said Magda. "I was quite fond of it."

"It's extraordinary." Ishani sighed. Then Ishani slid her hand over to Magda's, grasping it sincerely. "Thank you for making me a guardian again. I was so focused on ensuring Kiran was happy and safe that maybe I couldn't admit that somewhere, deep down, I missed being one myself."

"Thank you," Magda replied, squeezing Ishani's hand in response. "I couldn't have done this without you. Any of it."

Ishani smiled. "Maybe there's an opportunity to do something different in Flaustra now. To have more representation from the people."

"Kiran would be proud," said Magda.

Ishani nodded. "I know," she spoke. Then her body shifted towards Magda's, giving her a soft nudge with her shoulder. "Promise you'll come to Flaustra? I for one don't think I'll be able to stay away."

"Only if you promise to escort me on your ship," Magda teased.

"I think we can make an arrangement," said Ishani with a twinkle in her eye. "We can do guardian stuff."

"Which is?" Magda raised her eyebrows.

"You'll see," Ishani said. "The palace, city, and sea will be ours. You'll like that." Then her tone grew more serious. "But I'm guessing you're first going to ask me to escort you back to Dreadmarrow?"

"Yes," Magda admitted. Then she acknowledged Eligor's crown, which was still on her head. "We should all head there and reset the magic. And then I'll have an opportunity to actually help the miners and the townspeople. The sickness should cease too once I can better coordinate the medicine distribution."

"A lot of the prison crumbled when the tomb opened," Ishani said.

Magda nodded. "I'm not worried about getting back into Dreadmarrow—but there may be a lot of escaped prisoners on the island."

Ishani shrugged. "Nothing we can't handle." She paused, before meeting Magda's gaze. "You're going to make your brother proud too."

"I always thought he would win the trials," Magda stated. "I wonder if I would have earned the magic if things were different."

"You can't live in 'what if,'" Ishani said. "Besides, the trials aren't all they're made out to be."

"I don't know." Magda shrugged. "Maybe if I had won the magic, it would have been easier to feel as if I deserve this gift."

Ishani said, "You do deserve it. And you'll never have to compete in the trials because you're the last Life Guardian."

Magda smiled, looking back at her kingdom. She liked the sound of it. Life Guardian. Not a Master Guardian. She echoed Ishani's words under her breath, letting the weight of it settle in the air. "I'm the last Life Guardian."

CHAPTER 82
Sabien

The first thought that crossed his mind was of Dagger.

The second was that he was still alive.

A cough erupted from his chest as his eyes flew open. He jerked upright and instantly heaved onto the ground. Choking, he continued to spit up blood, his entire body fighting him. Until suddenly, a hand gripped his shoulder like iron. He was propelled flat against the cot, his head slamming against the mattress abruptly. A figure towered over him, her red hair glistening in the dim light of the room.

"You were not supposed to try and kill her," the woman growled.

He parted his lips to reply, but only choked. He broke into another bout of coughs, and the woman relinquished him. She stepped back, letting him catch his breath. But every ragged inhale tasted foul, the remnants of blood and rotting flesh in the air.

"You stupid, stupid boy," the woman said, crossing into the shadows.

Once Sabien caught his breath, he placed a hand against his chest. His shirt was torn to pieces, barely covering his muscular body. He gazed across the small room, lit by a candle, and saw Viette leaning against the far wall.

"I thought you were dead," he said, barely audible.

She glanced down at her body, then her hands, before meeting his gaze. "Hmm no, not dead. I'm a Mind Guardian, it's called an illusion. Lucky for you."

He slowly pulled himself upright on the cot, every ounce of his body screaming in pain. "How did you save me?"

She shrugged. "Some eroxis," she stated before tossing a vial in Sabien's direction. He hastily caught it, fumbling the small potion in his grasp. Flipping it over in his hands, he examined the churning blue liquid. An antidote. But it was impossible. He was dead—

"I diluted her smierc with calthyne," Viette announced.

His head snapped up. "And when did you have time for that?"

"When you were wasting your time doing Eligor's bidding," she fired back. "You should thank me. If I hadn't messed with her poisons, I doubt the eroxis would have worked. She had you." A proud smile creased Viette's face.

Sabien's jaw shifted, and his fingers folded around the eroxis, pocketing it. There was enough left for another dose, and he planned to hold onto it.

But it was true. His Dagger would have killed him if the smierc was fully concentrated. It was as if she wanted him dead.

He would find her again, of that he was certain. And he couldn't wait to see her expression when she realized he was still alive. Maybe she would smile. Maybe her lips would curl into that vicious smirk he had seen time and time again—the one that both incited anger and desire.

Once more, his Dagger was preoccupying his thoughts. A magnanimous woman, with equal parts lethal and seductive. Now she was a guardian, as if she had the capacity to hold more power over him. And even when she had poisoned him—even when his blood was burning him inside out—she looked divine on the ground at his feet.

Shaking his head, he forced his mind to focus. He hardened his voice. "She *almost* had me," he corrected. "But I'm alive."

"Yes, you are." An eyebrow raised on Viette's head, and then a smile creased on her pristine face. "So, are you joining me?" she asked. "Or should I dispose of you?"

"Joining you?" Sabien let out a bark of laughter. "We work for Eligor."

"The man who tried to kill you?" Viette replied.

Holding his tongue, Sabien was silent. The memory was palpable at the front of his mind. Sabien's jaw clenched, resentment simmering in his stomach.

Viette watched the emotions play out on Sabien's face, intrigue lighting her eyes. She continued, "Besides, I don't work for dead men."

"He's..."

"Dead, yes."

Sabien leaned forward on the cot, wincing as his body fought him. "I don't believe you saved me out of the goodness in your heart." He gripped the edge of the mattress, his fingers digging into the fabric to steady himself.

Matching his movement, Viette leaned toward him, planting her hands on the front of her knees as she met him at eye level. "You're welcome."

"Tell me why," he demanded.

She dropped her voice to a whisper, but each word was crisp with venom. "I couldn't risk him regaining Life magic."

A weight settled in Sabien's chest. He narrowed his eyes. "What game are you playing?"

Straightened, Viette flipped her hair behind her shoulder. "The First Prince isn't the only thing that came out of that tomb."

The dormant branch of magic.

"You never cared about the First Prince," Sabien followed.

"Now you're catching on." She clasped her hands in front of her.

"You only care about the Void."

She nodded.

He couldn't separate the Void from Dagger. She was a Guardian of the Void—the thought of it annihilating. The woman he memorized. Tormented. Tasted.

A new thought ignited, and his gaze narrowed on the Mind Guardian in the shadows. "How did you know she would use smierc? How do you even know about poisons—the antidote?" He paused, his brow furrowing, his voice deepening. "Who are you really?"

A full smile curled on Viette's face. She stepped out of the darkness, revealing herself in the dim candlelight. As though he were dreaming, he watched her transform before his eyes. Her red hair faded, her porcelain skin creased to reveal her true age, and her features transformed to—

"By the guardians," he exhaled, unable to tear his eyes away. Every muscle in his body had frozen. All thoughts ceased to exist as he stared at *her*.

"Hello," she said, her voice transformed to a new accent.

Then, she tore the dream from his grasp. Her illusion flickered back into place, her body transforming back to the Viette he had come to know.

"The return of the Void not only returned the magic to the lineage," she stated, unfazed by his dumbfounded expression, "but also the option to revive the Mystic South. The land that was dead for a millennia can now be restored." She let the statement hang in the air between them before she took another step forward. "So, I'll ask again. Are you joining me?"

Rising from the cot, the pain lacing through every ounce of his body, Sabien straightened before Viette—if that even was this woman's name. This twist of fate would be the death of him. The agony pulsing through his bloodstream strengthened him to ask, "What's in the Mystic South?"

CHAPTER 83
Dagmara

The Void glistened, darkness swirling around Dagmara's boots. She stood in the center of the Void citadel, before the throne. The Mystic South was an undiscovered region, long forgotten. And yet, it was home to the Void lineage—this was where they had ruled a millennia ago. There was so much to discover and so little the world knew about the locked branch.

With the rest of the group planning on returning to Dreadmarrow to activate the emblems, Dagmara knew that there were still so many uncertainties about the Void. Before, the reigning guardians had chosen to seal away the powers because of who Eligor was. Now, the magic belonged to Dagmara. Destroying an entire branch of magic because of the sins of one individual seemed flawed. She knew all too well the injustices that could emerge when one judged too quickly.

A faint ticking sounded, the alert of claws on the ballroom floor. A hound approached her, reaching her side and grazing his head against her hand. The feel of his scale and fur was foreign to Dagmara, but not for long. More hounds surrounded her, flanking her on all sides. What were they exactly? And how did they end up here?

She stepped away from them, walking up to the throne. Her hand traced the chair, her fingertips gliding across the structure.

The citadel belonged to her ancestors, and now it belonged to her. This land, though forgotten, in theory should be restored to its full glory once the emblem was reactivated. Though she used the rift in the Sea of Scarlet to get there, the Mystic South was reachable on land. People were able to return—if others hadn't taken the area for themselves by now. What did this forgotten kingdom hold?

It was up to her to find out.

She sat down on her throne. One hound laid down at her feet, resting his head on its massive paws. The other creatures followed suit, all of them falling asleep—relaxed in her presence. They knew that she was their master.

It was time to discover what secrets awaited her in the vast unknown beyond.

CHAPTER 84
Ravi

Ravi rounded the streets of Gorzhelm, taking in the breeze and admiring the cloudy sky. He found his own rhythm as he carried a box of potions in his hands. It was the first new mixture that the Azuremi doctors had concocted to combat the sicknesses across Azurem.

He exhaled, knowing that Laila would be proud her research was being put to good use. For a moment, his thoughts drifted to his family, finding comfort, before focusing on his task once more. He scaled across debris heading to the center of town, appreciating that the world had come to a soft pianissimo after the battle against Eligor. Gorzhelm was significantly smaller than Eloquas, and there was a stillness in the air that brought Ravi peace, unlike the loud dynamics of Flaustra.

He scoured his knowledge of Azuremi music, his thoughts tumbling over themselves like a fugue. He wondered if the culture was open to learning new styles, instruments, and techniques. Music was a source of comfort back home, and maybe, to help the citizens of Azurem heal, he could also use his musical talents.

Quickly, he ran through a list of songs he had memorized and wondered where he could find a violin at this hour. He pictured his hand completing the familiar scales, envisioning an Azuremi Mazurka in his mind.

One, two, three.

One, two, three.

He beamed, knowing how much Magda would like the score.

The tempo of Ravi's footsteps picked up against the ground as he turned onto a side street, contrasting the triple meter of the song he was composing.

One, two, three, four.

One, two, three, four.

The sounds coming from the center of town crescendoed as he grew closer.

"Can you help me?" a high-pitched voice called.

The tune in his head fell flat as he turned to greet the voice.

He stood before a middle-aged woman with a long, violet cloak.

Ravi gave a warm smile. "How can I help?" he asked.

Suddenly, her appearance changed as frosted silver magic fell from her body, revealing a woman with red hair and striking features.

Ravi was instantly on the defensive, but he didn't look away in time.

Viette's voice peaked in intonation as her eyes turned silver:

"I need you to do something for me."

Acknowledgments

A huge thank you to everyone that has been on this wonderful journey with us as we wrote the sequel to *The Mad King and the False Queen*. *The First Prince and the Last Heir* was incredibly exciting to write, and we are so happy to finally be able to share the next chapter of Dagmara and Magdalena's stories.

Thank you to our friends and family, including Mom, Emily, Kirill, and Dan. You have been there since the very beginning, and thank you for all of your love and support.

Thank you to our incredibly talented cover designer, Stefanie Saw, who has brought the vision for this series to life.

Thank you to our colleagues who have supported us in every aspect of writing this book.

Thank you to our amazing beta readers, arc readers, and friends who gave us such incredible feedback and input. We couldn't have done it without you!

And thank you to our readers who have joined us on our journey as indie authors! We can't wait to share more with you.

As indie authors, the best way you can show your support is via a review on Goodreads or amazon!

We are excited to announce that there will be another installment in the series, following all of the characters—and Odie too! Follow us to stay up to date on the announcement of the next book release. We are also in the midst of another exciting project and can't wait to share more details.

Thank you!

From the Abrom sisters, a completed high-stakes fantasy trilogy!

Keep reading for a sneak peek!

Prologue

A crisp wind blew the bedroom curtains. They danced in the breeze, extending inwards to a ghostly, stone room located on the high floors of Sun Castle. The beacon at Sun Spire cast a glowing aura through the open window, creating an orange outline on the bedroom floor. The wind was sharper than usual for the dry moorland, signaling that something was rushing in from the horizon.

The distant crying of an infant rang throughout the room. Despite the exhaustion that ate away at every limb, Landon's eyes shot open. He fixated on the ornate canopy that concealed the bed. He jostled himself awake and sat up, stealing a glance at his wife beside him.

Anastasia shifted, hearing the call of her child from the nursery.

Landon placed his hand on her shoulder. "Stay here."

Anastasia gave him a tired smile before pulling the blankets higher.

Landon stood up from the bed. Through the windowpane, the lights surrounding Sun Castle sparkled against the night sky. Another sharp gust of wind blew, rattling the wooden frame that held the curtains.

PROLOGUE

He crossed to the nursery door, guided by the light from the outside. When he reached the door, his daughter's crying ceased.

Landon entered the nursery, remaining quiet. He slid into the room before shutting the door behind him, letting his wife remain asleep.

The nursery was spacious. Ornaments hung from the ceiling, dangling above the cribs on one side, and a large window was on the opposite wall.

The silhouette of a man was at the window, his back to Landon. The figure was shrouded in a veil of fog as if he was made of smoke.

The sight poisoned Landon with fear, his heart dropping in his chest.

"Who are–"

"Shhh..." the man said as he turned around, revealing himself to Landon. He held Landon's daughter in his arms, bouncing her gently. She was wrapped tightly in a pale, pink blanket and was only a few months old.

The man was young and muscular, with a sharp jawline and pale skin. The fog continued to ripple down his legs, pooling at his boots. His bottomless eyes pierced through Landon like arrows. If it weren't for the sledgehammer strapped to the intruder's back, the man's resemblance to Landon was uncanny.

His brother.

"Mortimer?" Landon finally spoke.

"I did it," Mortimer said. "I found the Shadow of Eclipse."

Landon stiffened. "What?"

Mortimer's eyes glistened with darkness. His lips curled upwards. "The royals lied to us. The magic was never a myth – it was a man."

Landon's eyes widened. "A man?"

"Yes," Mortimer said, "and I killed him."

Fear surged through Landon's body. His palms began to sweat, and his heart beat faster.

PROLOGUE

Landon extended his arms out toward his brother, gesturing to the child. "Let me hold her."

"Don't you understand?" Mortimer ignored Landon's request. "They kept the truth of our ancestors from us, hoping that we would never find out. Well, it's time that the royals die for their heinous atrocities, including the lies that put them on the throne."

"What lies?"

"That we...that I...am supposed to protect Morbaeda." The fog swirled around his figure as though it were alive, increasing in speed to match its master's emotions.

Landon shook his head. "I won't let you kill the royal family."

"You will help me, or else." Mortimer lifted his hand to touch the baby's cheek, the lifelike darkness extending from his fingers like talons.

Landon's voice escaped him. He could sense the power devouring his brother's body, ensnaring Mortimer in its grasp and transforming him into an other-worldly being. He couldn't allow Mortimer to overthrow the royals.

Landon took a step forward. "Please, don't hurt my child," he pleaded.

"I'm going to make you a deal," Mortimer said as he bounced the baby. The smoke followed him, remaining transfixed around his body. "Since the king has the Teardrop, I can't get close enough to him to take the key," Mortimer explained, "but you can."

"I'm not making a deal with you," Landon said.

"You will," Mortimer responded, certain. "If you get me the key...," he paused to look down at the baby in his arms, "I will give you the child."

"Don't do this. Please, give her to me!"

Landon raced forward, hoping to save his child from the dark fog surrounding her. With a raise of his chin, Mortimer summoned a telekinetic force. An invisible wave threw Landon back, and he landed a few paces away. His breath was knocked out of him, and he clutched his chest as he lay flat on his back, his mind trying to process the magic that had occurred.

"I don't need you!" Mortimer shouted. "I can make anyone else get me what I need, but I'm giving you a chance."

Landon struggled to regain his breath. He remained on the floor and shook his head. "I'm going to kill you."

Mortimer laughed. "No, you won't," he said. "Now, is it a deal?"

Landon was silent. He stared at his child in Mortimer's hands. Tears started to burn his eyes, but he bit his tongue, holding them back.

Mortimer noticed the elongated pause. "It's a deal," he answered his own question. "Until we meet again, brother."

The black smoke swirled around Mortimer. The wind blew the curtains and ruffled Landon's hair, forcing Landon to squint against the sharp air.

"Stop!" Landon found the strength to get to his feet. He rushed forward, extending his arms outwards to hold his child, but Mortimer's telekinetic force pummeled into Landon's chest once more. He was thrust backward again.

"Oh, one more thing." Mortimer called out over the howling of the wind. "If you don't do what I ask, I will kill the child, and you will never see her again."

The smoke thickened and began swallowing Mortimer, consuming Landon's child.

The door burst open, and Anastasia stood there, her eyes wide.

The fog had entirely devoured Mortimer. He evaporated into black smoke along with the baby. The black mass swirled harshly before traveling out the window and vanishing into the night.

"No!" Anastasia screamed, running to the window. She watched the cloud as it traveled across the moor, disappearing into the darkness.

Landon pulled himself to his knees, feeling his rib cage pulsing in pain.

PROLOGUE

Another baby began crying. It screamed from its crib, flailing its arms aimlessly. But the baby's twin sister was gone.

Anastasia whipped around and went straight for the crib with the crying child before picking it up, trying to soothe it. Tears streamed down her cheeks, but her full attention was on the child in her arms.

Landon struggled to stand, clutching his side in pain. "I need to warn the king."

Anastasia froze. "You need to get our child back."

Landon searched for words, his mind racing. There was no doubt the Shadow army would go for the royals, even if Mortimer couldn't get close himself. Landon needed to warn them – he needed to protect the newborn prince.

He needed to protect the key.

"You're helpless," Anastasia said. She took a step forward, extending the child toward Landon. He was forced to scoop the baby out of her arms and cradle it.

Anastasia's eyes narrowed. "I'm going to save my daughter."

She whipped to the door and stormed out of the nursery.

"Anastasia!" Landon called, but she was gone.

She couldn't face Mortimer by herself.

The baby continued to cry, the wailing piercing Landon's ears. He looked down at the child.

Landon crossed to the crib and set the baby down, disregarding the cries. Then he turned his back on his child and left.

Also by the Abrom Sisters

Designated Protector Series:
Book 1 Designated Protector
Book 2 Parallel Voyagers
Book 3 Forbidden Sorcerer

About the Author

Amanda Abrom and Hope Abrom are sisters and co-authors originally from Lancaster, Pennsylvania. Currently, they live on two opposite sides of the US. Amanda lives in NYC with her husband and works in education while Hope works in LA at a post-production house as an editor. They first started pursuing creative projects together when they wrote the book and lyrics for an original musical, Royal Shadows, also a fantasy romance. *The First Prince and the Last Heir* is the sixth book that they have co-authored, and they have plans for many more! In their spare time, they both enjoy seeing musicals, reading, traveling, and writing the next book!

Made in the USA
Las Vegas, NV
22 April 2025